SABBATH'S THEATER

SABBATH'S THEATER

· · ·

Philip Roth

JONATHAN CAPE
LONDON

First published 1995

1 3 5 7 9 10 8 6 4 2

The author is grateful for permission to quote "Meru" and lines from "For
Anne Gregory", from *The Poems of W. B. Yeats: A New Edition*, edited by
Richard J. Finneran. Copyright 1934 by Macmillan Publishing Company,
renewed 1962 by Bertha Georgie Yeats. "The Sheik of Araby" by Harry
B. Smith, Ted Snyder and Francis Wheeler. All rights reserved. Made in
U.S.A. Used by permission of Warner Bros. Publications Inc., Miami,
Florida 33014. The quotation on page 88 is from *Western Attitudes Toward
Death from the Middle Ages to the Present* by Philippe Ariés, Johns
Hopkins University Press, 1974. The quotation on page 280 is from "A
proposal to classify *happiness* as a psychiatric disorder", by R. P. Bentall,
Journal of Medical Ethics, June 1992.

First published in the United Kingdom in 1995 by
Jonathan Cape
Random House, 20 Vauxhall Bridge Road,
London SW1V 2SA

Random House Australia (Pty) Limited
20 Alfred Street, Milsons Point, Sydney,
New South Wales 2061, Australia

Random House New Zealand Limited
18 Poland Road, Glenfield,
Auckland 10, New Zealand

Random House South Africa (Pty) Limited
PO Box 337, Bergvlei, 2012 South Africa

Random House UK Limited Reg. No.954009

A CIP catalogue record for this book
is available from the British Library

Papers used by Random House UK Limited are natural,
recyclable products made from wood grown in sustainable forests.The
manufacturing processes conform to the
environmental regulations of the country of origin

ISBN 0 224 04157 6

Book design by Robert Overholtzer

Printed and bound in Great Britain by
Mackays of Chatham PLC

FOR TWO FRIENDS

———

JANET HOBHOUSE
1948–1991

MELVIN TUMIN
1919–1994

PROSPERO:

Every third thought shall be my grave.

— *The Tempest,* act v, scene 1

1

THERE'S NOTHING THAT KEEPS ITS PROMISE

· · ·

IE ITHER FORSWEAR fucking others or the affair is over.

This was the ultimatum, the maddeningly improbable, wholly unforeseen ultimatum, that the mistress of fifty-two delivered in tears to her lover of sixty-four on the anniversary of an attachment that had persisted with an amazing licentiousness—and that, no less amazingly, had stayed their secret—for thirteen years. But now with hormonal infusions ebbing, with the prostate enlarging, with probably no more than another few years of semi-dependable potency still his—with perhaps not that much more life remaining—here at the approach of the end of everything, he was being charged, on pain of losing her, to turn himself inside out.

She was Drenka Balich, the innkeeper's popular partner in business and marriage, esteemed for the attention she showered on all her guests, for her warmhearted, mothering tenderness not only with visiting children and the old folks but with the local girls who cleaned the rooms and served the meals, and he was the forgotten puppeteer Mickey Sabbath, a short, heavyset, white-bearded man with unnerving green eyes and painfully arthritic fingers who, had he said yes to Jim Henson some thirty-odd years earlier, before *Sesame Street* started up, when Henson had taken him to lunch on the Upper East Side and asked him to join his clique of four or five people, could have been inside Big Bird all these years. Instead of Caroll Spinney, it would have been Sabbath who was the fellow inside Big Bird, Sabbath who had got himself a star on the Hollywood Walk of Fame, Sabbath who had been to China with Bob Hope—or so his wife, Roseanna, delighted in reminding him back when she was still drinking herself to death for her two unchallengeable reasons: because of all that had not happened and because of all that had. But as Sabbath wouldn't have been any happier inside Big Bird than he was inside Roseanna, he was not much bruised by the heckling. In 1989, when Sabbath had been publicly disgraced for the gross sexual harassment of a girl forty years his junior, Roseanna had had to be interned for a month in a psychiatric institution because of the alcoholic breakdown brought on by the humiliation of the scandal.

"One monogamous mate isn't enough for you?" he asked Drenka. "You like monogamy so much with him you want it with me too? Is there no connection you can see between your husband's enviable fidelity and the fact that he physically repels you?" Pompously he continued, "We who have never stopped exciting each other impose on each other no vows, no oaths, no restrictions, whereas with him the fucking is sickening even for the two minutes a month he bends you over the dinner table and does it from behind. And why is that? Matija is big, powerful, virile, a head of black hair like a porcupine. His hairs are *quills*. Every old dame in the county is in love with him, and not just for his Slavic charm. His looks turn them on. Your little waitresses are all nuts about the cleft in his chin. I've watched him back in the kitchen when it's a hundred degrees in August and they're waiting ten deep on the terrace for tables. I've seen him churning out the dinners, grilling those kebabs in his sopping T-shirt. All agleam with grease, he turns *me* on. Only his wife he repels. Why? The ostentatiously monogamous nature, that is why."

Drenka dragged herself mournfully beside him, up the steep wooded hillside to the heights where their bathing brook bubbled forth, clear water rippling down a staircase of granite boulders brokenly spiraling between the storm-slanted, silvery-green birches that overhung the banks. During the early months of the affair, on a solitary hiking expedition in search of just such a love nest, she had discovered, within a clump of ancient fir trees not far from the brook, three boulders, each the size and the shade of a small elephant, that enclosed the triangular clearing they would have instead of a home. Because of mud, snow, or drunken hunters out shooting up the woods, the crest of the hill was not accessible in all seasons, but from May through early October, except when it rained, it was here they retreated to renovate their lives. Years back a helicopter had once appeared out of nowhere to hover momentarily a hundred feet overhead while they were naked on the tarpaulin below, but otherwise, though the Grotto, as they'd come to call the hideaway, was fifteen minutes by foot from the only paved road connecting Madamaska Falls to the valley, no human presence had ever threatened their secret encampment.

Drenka was a dark, Italian-looking Croat from the Dalmatian coast, on the short side like Sabbath, a full, firmly made woman at the provocative edge of being just overweight, her shape, at her heaviest, reminiscent of those clay figurines molded circa 2000 B.C., fat little dolls with big breasts and big thighs unearthed all the way from Europe down to Asia Minor and worshiped under a dozen different names as the great mother of the gods. She was pretty in a rather efficient, businesslike way, except for her nose, a surprisingly bridgeless prizefighter's nose that created a sort of blur at the heart of her face, a nose slightly out of plumb with the full mouth and the large dark eyes, and the telltale sign, as Sabbath came to view it, of everything malleable and indeterminate in her seemingly well-deployed nature. She looked as though she had once been mauled, in earliest childhood damaged by a crushing blow, when in fact she was the daughter of kindly parents, both of them high school teachers religiously devoted to the tyrannical platitudes of Tito's Communist party. Their only child, she had been abundantly loved by these nice, dreary people.

The blow in the family had been delivered by Drenka. At twenty-two, an assistant bookkeeper with the national railway, she married Matija Balić, a handsome young waiter with aspirations whom she had met when she went for her vacation to the hotel that belonged to the railroad syndicate workers on the island of Brač, just off Split. The two went to Trieste for their honeymoon and never returned home. They ran away not merely to become rich in the West but because Matija's grandfather had been imprisoned in 1948, when Tito broke with the Soviet Union and the grandfather, a local party bureaucrat, a Communist since 1923 and an idealist about big Mother Russia, had dared to discuss the matter openly. "My both parents," Drenka had explained to Sabbath, "were convinced Communists and they loved Comrade Tito, who is there with his smile like a smiling monster, and so I figured out early how to love Tito more than any other child in Yugoslavia. We were all Pioneers, little boys and girls who would go out and sing wearing a red scarf. We would sing songs about Tito and how he is this flower, this violet flower, and how all the youth loves him. But with Matija it was different. He was a little boy who loved his grandfather. And somebody told on his grandfather—is that the word? Reported. He was reported. As an enemy of the regime. And the enemies of the regime were all sent to this horrible prison. It was the most horrible time when they were like cattle thrown into the ships. Taken by ships from the mainland to the island. And who survives survives and who doesn't doesn't. It was a place where the stone was the only element. All they had to do, they had to work those stones, cut them, without a reason. Many families had someone who went to this Goli Otok that means Naked Island. People report on others for whatever reason—to advance, for hatred, for whatever. There was a big threat always hanging in the air about being proper, and proper is to support the regime. On this island they didn't feed them, they didn't give them water even. An island just off the coast, a little bit north of Split—from the coast you can see the island in the distance. His grandfather got hepatitis there and he died just before Matija graduated from high school. Died of cirrhosis. He suffered all those years. The prisoners would send cards home, and they had to claim in the cards that they were reformed. His mother told Matija that her father was not good and that he did not listen to Comrade Tito and that's why he has to go to prison. Matija was nine. She knew what she was telling him when she was telling that. So at school he would not be provoked to say something else. His grandfather said he would be good and love *Drug* Tito, so he was only in jail for ten months. But he got hepatitis there. When he came back, Matija's mother makes a big party. He came back, he was forty kilos. That's ninety pounds or so. And he was, like Maté, a big man. Totally destroyed physically. There was a guy that told on him and that was that. And this is why Matija wished to run away after we married."

"And why did *you* wish to run away?"

"Me? I didn't care about politics. I was like my parents. During the old Yugoslavia, the king and all that stuff, before Communism, they loved the king. Then Communism came and they loved Communism. I didn't care, so I said yes, yes to the smiling monster. What I loved was the adventure. America seemed so grand and so glamorous and so enormously different. America! Hollywood! Money! Why did I go? I was a girl. Wherever would be the most fun."

Drenka shamed her parents by fleeing to this imperialist country, broke their hearts, and they too died, both of cancer, not long after her defection. However, she so loved money and so loved "fun" that she probably had the tender attentions of these convinced Communists to thank for whatever impeded the full, youthful body with the tantalizingly thuggish face from doing with itself something even more capricious than becoming enslaved to capitalism.

The only man she would ever admit to having charged for the night was the puppeteer Sabbath, and over the thirteen years this had occurred only once, when he had presented the offering of Christa, the runaway German au pair working at the gourmet food shop, whom he had scouted and patiently recruited for their joint delectation. "Cash," Drenka had informed him, though for months now, ever since Sabbath had first come upon Christa hitchhiking into town, Drenka had anticipated the adventure with no less excitement than Sabbath and needed no urging to conspire. "Crisp bills," she said, prankishly narrowing her eyes but meaning it all the same. "Stiff and new." Adapting without hesitation to the role she'd so swiftly devised for him, he asked, "How many?" Tartly she answered, "Ten." "Can't afford ten." "Forget it then. Leave me out." "You're a hard woman." "Yes. Hard," she replied with relish. "I have a sense of my worth." "It's taken some doing to arrange this, you know. It's not been a snap setting this up. Christa may be a wayward child but she still requires a lot of attention. It's I who ought to be paid by you." "I don't want to be treated like a fake whore. I want to be treated like a real whore. A thousand dollars or I stay home." "You're asking the impossible." "Never mind then." "Five hundred." "Seven fifty." "Five hundred. The best I can do." "Then I must be paid before we get there. I want to walk in with the money in my purse knowing that I've got a job to do. I want to feel like a real whore." "I doubt," suggested Sabbath, "that, to feel like a real whore, money alone will suffice." "It will for me." "Lucky you." "Lucky *you*," said Drenka defiantly—"okay, five hundred. But before. I have to have all of it the night before."

The terms of the deal were negotiated while they manipulated each other manually on the tarpaulin up at the Grotto.

Now, Sabbath had no interest in money. But since arthritis had finished him off as a performing puppeteer at the international festivals, and his Puppet Workshop was no longer welcome in the curriculum of the four-college program because of his unmasking there as a degenerate, he was dependent for support on his wife, with the result that it was not painless for him to peel off five of the two hundred and twenty hundred-dollar bills earned annually by Roseanna at the regional high school and hand them over to a woman whose family-run inn netted $150,000 a year.

He could have told her to fuck off, of course, especially as Drenka would have participated as ardently in the threesome without the money as with, but to agree for a night to act as her john seemed to do as much for him as it did for her to pretend to be his prostitute. Sabbath, moreover, had no right *not* to yield—her licentious abandon owed its full flowering to him. Her systematic efficiency as hostess-manager of the inn—just the sheer pleasure, year after year, of banking all that dough—might long ago have mummified her lower life had not Sabbath suspected from the flatness of the nose, from the roundness of the limbs— from nothing more than that to begin with—that Drenka Balich's perfectionism on the job was not her only immoderate inclination. It was Sabbath who, a step at a time, the most patient of instructors, had assisted her in becoming estranged from her orderly life and in discovering the indecency to supplement the deficiencies of her regular diet.

Indecency? Who knows? Do as you like, Sabbath said, and she did and liked it and liked telling him about how much she had liked it no less than he liked hearing about it. Husbands, after weekending at the inn with their wives and children, phoned Drenka secretly from their offices to tell her they had to see her. The excavator, the carpenter, the electrician, the painter, all the laborers assisting around the inn invariably maneuvered to eat their lunches close to the office where she did the bookkeeping. Men wherever she went sensed the intangible aura of invitation. Once Sabbath had sanctioned for her the force that wants more and more—a force to whose urging she was never wholly averse even before Sabbath had come along—men began to understand that this shortish, less than startling-looking middle-aged woman corseted by all her smiling courtesy was powered by a carnality much like their own. Inside this woman was someone who thought like a man. And the man she thought like was Sabbath. She was, as she put it, his sidekicker.

How could he, in good conscience, say no to the five hundred bucks? No was not a part of the deal. To be what she had learned to want to be (to be what he needed her to be), what she needed from Sabbath was yes. Never mind that she used the money to buy power tools for her son's basement workshop. Matthew was married and a state trooper with the barracks down in the valley; Drenka adored him and, once he became a cop, worried about him all the time. He was not big and handsome with porcupinish black hair and a deep cleft in his chin like the father whose anglicized name he bore but much more patently Drenka's offspring, short in stature—only five feet eight and 135 pounds, he'd been the smallest guy in his class at the police academy as well as the youngest—and at the center of his face a bit of a blur, the noseless nose a replica of hers. He had been groomed to one day be proprietor of the inn and had left his father desolated by quitting hotel management school after just a year to become a muscular, crew-cutted trooper with the big hat, the badge, and lots of power, the kid cop whose first assignment running radar with the traffic squad, driving the chase car up and down the main highways, was the greatest job in the world. You meet so many people, every car you stop is different, a different person, different circumstances, a different speed. . . . Drenka repeated to Sabbath everything Matthew Junior told her about life as a trooper, from the day he had entered the academy seven years earlier and the instructors there began to yell at them and he swore to his mother, "I'm not going to let this beat me," until the day he graduated and, little as he was, they awarded him an excellence pin in physical fitness and told him and the classmates who had survived the twenty-four-week course, "You're not God but you're the next closest thing to him." She described to Sabbath the virtues of Matthew's fifteen-shot nine-millimeter pistol and how he carried it in his boot or at the back in his belt when he was off duty and how that terrified her. She was constantly afraid that he was going to be killed, especially when he was transferred from the traffic squad to the barracks and had to work the midnight shift every few weeks. Matthew himself came to love cruising in his car as much as he'd loved running radar. "Once you're gone on your shift, you're your own boss out there. Once you get into that car, you can do what you want out there. Freedom, Ma. Lots of freedom. Unless something happens, all you do is ride. Alone in the car, cruising, just driving the roads until they call you for something." He'd grown up in what the state police called the North Patrol. Knew the area, all the roads, the woods, knew the businesses in the towns and found an enormous manly satisfaction in driving by at night and checking them out, checking out the banks, checking out the bars, watching the people leaving the bars to see how bad off they were. Matthew had a front seat, he told his mother, at the greatest show on earth—accidents, burglaries, domestic disputes, suicides. Most people never see a suicide victim, but a girl whom Matthew had gone to school with had blown her head off in the woods, sat under an oak tree and blew out her brains, and Matthew, in his first year out of the academy, was the cop on the scene to call the medical examiner and wait for him to come. In that first year, Matthew told his mother, he was so pumped up, felt so invincible, he believed he could stop bullets with his teeth. Matthew walks in on a domestic dispute where both of the people are drunk and screaming at each other and hating each other and throwing punches and he, her son, talks to them and calms them down so that by the time he leaves everything is okay and neither of them has to be pinched for breach of peace. And sometimes they're so bad he does pinch 'em, handcuffs the woman and handcuffs the man, and then waits for another trooper to come, and they take the couple in before they kill each other. When a kid was showing a gun in a pizza place on 63, flashing it around before leaving, it was Matthew who found the car the kid was driving and, without any backup, knowing the kid had a gun, told him over the loud-speaker to come out with his hands in the air and had his own gun drawn right on the guy . . . and these stories, establishing for his mother that Matthew was a good cop who wanted to do a good job, to do it as he'd been taught to do it, frightened her so that she bought a scanner, a little box with an antenna and a crystal that monitored the police signals on Matthew's frequency, and some-times when he was on the midnight shift and she couldn't sleep, she would turn on the scanner and listen to it all night long. The scanner would pick up the signal every time Matthew was called, so that Drenka knew more or less where he was and where he was going and that he was still alive. When she heard his number—415B—boom, she was awake. But so was Matthew's father—and enraged to be reminded yet again that the son he had been training every summer in the kitchen, the heir to the business he had built from nothing as a penniless immigrant, was now an expert in karate and judo instead, out at three in the morning stupidly trailing an old pickup truck that was going suspiciously slowly crossing Battle Mountain. The bitterness between father and son had grown so bad that it was only with Sabbath that Drenka could share her fears about Matthew's safety and recount her pride in the amount of motor vehicle activity he was able to produce in a week: "It's out there," he told her. "There's always something—speeding, stop signs, taillights out, all kind of violations. . . ." To Sabbath, then, it came as no surprise when Drenka admitted that with the five hundred dollars he had paid her to complete the trio with Christa and himself she had bought, for Matthew's birthday, a portable Makita table saw and a nice set of dado blades.

All in all, things couldn't have worked out better for everyone. Drenka had found the means by which to be her husband's dearest friend. The one-time puppet master of the Indecent Theater of Manhattan made more than merely tolerable for her the routines of marriage that previously had almost killed her—now she cherished those deadly routines for the counterweight they provided her recklessness. Far from seething with disgust for her unimaginative husband, she had never been more appreciative of Matija's stolidity.

Five hundred was *cheap* for all that everyone was getting in the way of solace and satisfaction, and so, however much it disturbed him to fork over those stiff, new banknotes, Sabbath displayed toward Drenka the same sangfroid that she affected as, lightly enjoying the movie cliché, she folded the bills in half and deposited them into her bra, down between the breasts whose soft fullness had never ceased to captivate him. It was supposed to be otherwise, with the musculature everywhere losing its firmness, but even where her skin had gone papery at the low point of her neckline, even that palm-size diamond of minutely crosshatched flesh intensified not merely her enduring allure but his tender feeling for her as well. He was now six short years from seventy:

what had him grasping at the broadening buttocks as though the tattooist Time had ornamented neither of them with its comical festoonery was his knowing inescapably that the game was just about over.

Lately, when Sabbath suckled at Drenka's uberous breasts— uberous, the root word of *exuberant,* which is itself *ex* plus *uber- are,* to be fruitful, to overflow like Juno lying prone in Tintoretto's painting where the Milky Way is coming out of her tit—suckled with an unrelenting frenzy that caused Drenka to roll her head ecstatically back and to groan (as Juno herself may have once groaned), "I feel it deep down in my cunt," he was pierced by the sharpest of longings for his late little mother. Her primacy was nearly as absolute as it had been in their first incomparable decade together. Sabbath felt something close to veneration for that natural sense of a destiny she'd enjoyed and, too—in a woman with as physical a life as a horse's—for the soul embedded in all that vibrating energy, a soul as unmistakably present as the odorous cakes baking in the oven after school. Emotions were stirred up in him that he had not felt since he was eight and nine years old and she had found the delight of delights in mothering her two boys. Yes, it had been the apex of her life, raising Morty and Mickey. How her memory, her *meaning,* expanded in Sabbath when he recalled the alacrity with which she had prepared each spring for Passover, all the work of packing away the year-round dishes, two sets of them, and then lugging in their cartons, from the garage, the glass Passover dishes, washing them, shelving them—in less than a day, between the time he and Morty left for school in the morning and they returned in midafternoon, she'd emptied the pantry of *chumitz* and cleansed and scoured the kitchen in accordance with every last holiday prescription. Hard to determine from the way she tackled her tasks whether it was she who was serving necessity or necessity that was serving her. A slight woman with a large nose and curly dark hair, she hopped and darted to and fro like a bird in a berry bush, trilling and twittering a series of notes as liquidly bright as a cardinal's song, a tune she exuded no less naturally than she dusted, ironed,

mended, polished, and sewed. Folding things, straightening
things, arranging things, stacking things, packing things, sorting
things, opening things, separating things, bundling things—her
agile fingers never stopped nor did the whistling ever cease, all
throughout his childhood. That was how content she was, immersed in everything that had to be done to keep her husband's
accounts in order, to live peaceably alongside her elderly mother-
in-law, to manage the daily needs of the two boys, to see to
it, during even the worst of the Depression, that however little
money the butter-and-egg business yielded, the budget she devised did not impinge on their happy development and that, for
instance, everything handed down from Morty to Mickey, which
was nearly everything Mickey wore, was impeccably patched,
freshly aired, spotlessly clean. Her husband proudly proclaimed
to his customers that his wife had eyes in the back of her head and
two pairs of hands.

Then Morty went off to the war and it all changed. Always
they had done everything as a family. They had never been separated. They were never so poor that they would rent out the house
in the summer and, like half the neighbors living as close to the
beach as the Sabbaths did, move in back to a shitty little apartment over the garage, but they were still a poor family by American standards and none of them had ever gone anywhere. But
then Morty was gone and for the first time in his life Mickey slept
alone in their room. Once they went up to see Morty when he was
training in Oswego, New York. For six months he trained in
Atlantic City and they drove to see him there on Sundays. And
when he was in pilot school in North Carolina, they took the
drive all the way down south, even though his father had to turn
the truck over to a neighbor he paid to run deliveries the days they
were gone. Morty had bad skin and wasn't particularly handsome, he wasn't great in school—a B-C student in everything but
shop and gym—he had never had much success with girls, and yet
everybody knew that with his physical strength and his strong
character he would be able to take care of himself, whatever
difficulties life presented. He played clarinet in a dance band in

high school. He was a track star. A terrific swimmer. He helped his
father with the business. He helped his mother in the house. He
was great with his hands, but then, they all were: the delicacy
of his powerful father candling the eggs, the fastidious dexterity
of his mother ordering the house—the Sabbath digital artful-
ness that Mickey, too, would one day exhibit to the world. All
their freedom was in their hands. Morty could repair plumbing,
electrical appliances, anything. Give it to Morty, his mother used
to say, Morty'll fix it. And she did not exaggerate when she said
that he was the kindest older brother in the world. He enlisted
in the Army Air Corps at eighteen, a kid just out of Asbury
High, rather than wait to be drafted. He went in at eighteen and
he was dead at twenty. Shot down over the Philippines December 12, 1944.

For nearly a year Sabbath's mother wouldn't get out of bed.
Couldn't. Never again was she spoken of as a woman with eyes in
the back of her head. She acted at times as though she didn't even
have eyes in the front of her head, and, as far as the surviving son
could still recall while panting and gulping as though to drain
Drenka dry, she was never again heard to whistle her signature
song. Now the seaside cottage was silent when he walked up the
sandy alleyway after school, and he could not tell till he got inside
if she was even in the house. No honey cake, no date and nut
bread, no cupcakes, nothing ever again baking in the oven after
school. When the weather turned nice, she sat on the boardwalk
bench overlooking the beach to which she used to rush out with
the boys at dawn to buy flounder off the fishing boats at half what
it cost in the store. After the war, when everybody came home, she
went there to talk to Mort. As the decades passed, she talked to
him more rather than less, until in the nursing home in Long
Branch where Sabbath had to put her at ninety she talked to
Morty alone. She had no idea who Sabbath was when he drove
the four and a half hours to visit her during the last two years of
her life. The living son she ceased to recognize. But that had
begun as long ago as 1944.

And now Sabbath talked to *her*. And this he had not expected.

To his father, who had never deserted Mickey however much Morty's death had broken him too, who primitively stood by Mickey no matter how incomprehensible to him his boy's life became when he went to sea after high school or began to perform with puppets on the streets of New York, to his late father, a simple, uneducated man, who, unlike his wife had been born on the other side and had come to America all on his own at thirteen and who, within seven years, had earned enough money to send for his parents and his two younger brothers, Sabbath had never uttered a word since the retired butter-and-egg man died in his sleep, at the age of eighty-one, fourteen years earlier. Never had he felt the shadow of his father's presence hovering nearby. This was not only because his father had always been the least talkative one in the family but because no evidence had ever been offered Sabbath to persuade him that the dead were anything other than dead. To talk to them, admittedly, was to indulge in the most defensible of irrational human activities, but to Sabbath it was alien just the same. Sabbath was a realist, ferociously a realist, so that by sixty-four he had all but given up on making contact with the living, let alone discussing his problems with the dead.

Yet precisely this he now did daily. His mother was there every day and he was talking to her and she was communing with him. Exactly how present *are* you, Ma? Are you only here or are you everywhere? Would you look like yourself if I had the means to see you? The picture I have keeps shifting. Do you know only what you knew when you were living, or do you now know everything, or is "knowing" no longer an issue? What's the story? Are you still so miserably sad? That would be the best news of all—that you are your whistling old self again because Morty's with you. Is he? Is Dad? And if there's you three, why not God too? Or is an incorporeal existence just like everything else, in the nature of things, and God no more necessary there than he is here? Or don't you inquire any further about being dead than you did about being alive? Is being dead just something you do the way you ran the house?

Eerie, incomprehensible, ridiculous, the visitation was nonetheless real: no matter how he explained it to himself he could not make his mother go away. He knew she was there in the same way he knew when he was in the sun or in the shade. There was something too natural about his perceiving her for the perception to evaporate before his mocking resistance. She didn't just show up when he was in despair, it didn't happen only in the middle of the night when he awoke in dire need of a substitute for every-thing disappearing—his mother was up in the woods, up at the Grotto with him and Drenka, hovering above their half-clad bod-ies like that helicopter. Maybe the helicopter had *been* his mother. His dead mother was with him, watching him, everywhere encir-cling him. His mother had been loosed on him. She had returned to take him to his death.

♦   ♦   ♦

Fuck others and the affair is over.

He asked her why.

"Because I want you to."

"That won't do."

"Won't it?" said Drenka tearfully. "It would if you loved me."

"Yes, love is slavery?"

"You are the man of my life! Not Matija—you! Either I am your woman, your *only* woman, or this all *has* to be over!"

It was the week before Memorial Day, a luminous May af-ternoon, and up in the woods a high wind was blowing sprigs of new leaves off the great trees and the sweet scent of everything flowering and sprouting and shooting up reminded him of Scia-rappa's Barber Shop in Bradley, where Morty took him for his haircuts when he was a small kid and where they brought their clothes to be fixed by Sciarappa's wife. Nothing was merely itself any longer; it all reminded him of something long gone or of everything that was going. Mentally he addressed his mother. "Smell the smells, can you? Does the out-of-doors register in any way? Is being dead even worse than heading there? Or is it Mrs. Balich that's the awfulness? Or don't the trivialities bother you now one way or the other?"

Either he was sitting in his dead mother's lap or she was sitting in his. Perhaps she was snaking in through his nose along with the scent of the mountain in bloom, wafting through him as oxygen. Encircling him and embodied within him.

"And just when did you decide this? What has happened to bring this on? You are not yourself, Drenka."

"I am. *This is myself.* Tell me you will be faithful to me. Please tell me that that's what you will do!"

"First tell me why."

"I'm *suffering.*"

She was. He'd seen her suffer and this was what it looked like. The blurriness broadened out from the middle of her face rather like an eraser crossing a blackboard and leaving in its wake a wide streak of negated meaning. You didn't see a face any longer but a bowl of stupefaction. Whenever the rift between her husband and their son erupted in a screaming fight she invariably wound up looking just this awful when she ran to Sabbath, numb and incoherent with fear, her sprightly cunning having evaporated before their improbable capacity for rage and its vile rhetoric. Sabbath assured her—largely without conviction—that they would not kill each other. But more than once he had himself contemplated with a shudder what might be roiling away beneath the lid of the relentlessly genial good manners that made the Balich men so impenetrably dull. Why *had* the boy become a cop? Why did he want to be out risking his life looking for criminals with a revolver and handcuffs and a lethal little club when there was a small fortune to be made pleasing the happy guests at the inn? And, after seven years, why couldn't the amiable father forgive him? Why did he wind up charging his son with wrecking his life every single time they met? Granted that each had his own hidden reality, that like everyone else they were not without duality, granted that they were not entirely rational people and that they lacked wit or irony of any kind—nonetheless, where *was* the bottom in these Matthews? Sabbath privately conceded that Drenka had good reason to be as agitated as she was by the tremendous force of their antagonism (especially as one of them was armed), but since she was never remotely their target, he advised her neither to take a side nor to intercede—in time the heat would have to die down, et cetera, et cetera. And eventually, when her terror had begun to lift and the liveliness that was Drenka repossessed her features, she told him that she loved him, that she couldn't possibly live without him, that, as she so spartanly put it, "I couldn't carry out my responsibilities without you." Without what they got up to together, she could never be so good! Licking those sizable breasts, whose breastish reality seemed no less tantalizingly outlandish than it would have when he was fourteen, Sabbath told her that he felt the same about her, allowed it while looking up at her with that smile of his that did not make entirely clear who or what precisely he had it in mind to deride—confessed it certainly with nothing like her declamatory ardor, said it almost as though deliberately to make it appear perfunctory, and yet, stripped of all its derisive trappings, his "Feel the same way about you" happened to be true. Life was as unthinkable for Sabbath without the successful innkeeper's promiscuous wife as it was for her without the remorseless puppeteer. No one to conspire with, no one on earth with whom to give free rein to his most vital need!

"And you?" he asked. "Will you be faithful to me? Is that what you are suggesting?"

"I don't *want* anyone else."

"Since when? Drenka, I see you suffering, I don't want you to suffer, but I cannot take seriously what you are asking of me. How do you justify wishing to impose on me restrictions that you have never imposed on yourself? You are asking for fidelity of a kind that you've never bothered to bestow on your own husband and that, were I to do what you request, you would still be denying him because of *me*. You want monogamy outside marriage and adultery inside marriage. Maybe you're right and that's the only way to do it. But for that you will have to find a more rectitudinous old man." Elaborate. Formal. Perfectly overprecise.

"Your answer is no."

"Could it possibly be yes?"

"And so now you will get rid of me? Overnight? Like that? After thirteen years?"

"I am confused by you. I can't follow you. What exactly is happening here today? It's not I but you who proposed this ultimatum out of the fucking blue. It's you who presented *me* with the either/or. It's you who is getting rid of *me* overnight . . . unless, of course, I consent to become overnight a sexual creature of the kind I am not and never have been. Follow me, please. I must become a sexual creature of the kind that you have yourself never dreamed of being. In order to preserve what we have remarkably sustained by forthrightly pursuing together our sexual desires— are you with me?—*my* sexual desires must be deformed, since it is unarguable that, like you—you until today, that is—I am not by nature, inclination, practice, or belief a monogamous being. Period. You wish to impose a condition that either deforms me or turns me into a dishonest man with you. But like all other living creatures I suffer when I am deformed. And it shocks me, I might add, to think that the forthrightness that has sustained and excited us both, that provides such a healthy contrast to the routine deceitfulness that is the hallmark of a hundred million marriages, including yours and mine, is now less to your taste than the solace of conventional lies and repressive puritanism. As a self-imposed challenge, repressive puritanism is fine with me, but it is Titoism, Drenka, *inhuman Titoism,* when it seeks to impose its norms on others by self-righteously suppressing the satanic side of sex."

"You *sound* like stupid Tito when you lecture me like this! Please stop it!"

They hadn't spread their tarpaulin or removed a single item of their clothing but had remained in their sweatshirts and jeans, and Sabbath in his knitted seaman's cap, sitting backed against a rock. Drenka meanwhile paced in rapid circles the high ring of elephantine boulders, her hands fluttering anxiously through her hair or reaching out to feel against her fingertips the cool familiar surface of their hideaway's rough walls—and could not but remind him of Nikki in the last act of *The Cherry Orchard.* Nikki, his first wife, the fragile, volatile Greek American girl whose pervasive sense of crisis he'd mistaken for a deep spirit and whom he had Chekhovianly nicknamed "A-Crisis-a-Day" until a day came when the crisis of being herself simply swept Nikki away.

The Cherry Orchard was one of the first plays he'd directed in New York after the two years of puppet school on the GI Bill in Rome. Nikki had played Madame Ranyevskaya as a ruined flapper, for someone so absurdly young in that role, counterbalancing delicately the satire and the pathos. In the last act, when everything has been packed and the distraught family is preparing to abandon forever the ancestral home, Sabbath had asked Nikki to go silently around the empty room brushing all the walls with the tips of her fingers. No tears, please. Just circle the room touching the bare walls and then leave—that'll do it. And everything she was asked to do, Nikki did exquisitely . . . and it was for him rendered not quite satisfactory by the fact that whatever she played, however well, she was still also Nikki. This "also" in actors drove him eventually back to puppets, who had never to pretend, who never acted. That he generated their movement and gave each a voice never compromised their reality for Sabbath in the way that Nikki, fresh and eager and with all that talent, seemed always less than convincing to him because of being a real person. With puppets you never had to banish the actor from the role. There was nothing false or artificial about puppets, nor were they "metaphors" for human beings. They were what they were, and no one had to worry that a puppet would disappear, as Nikki had, right off the face of the earth.

"Why," Drenka cried, "are you making fun of me? Of *course* you outsmart me, you outsmart everyone, *outtalk* every—"

"Yes, yes," he replied. "Luxurious unseriousness was what the outsmarter often felt the greater the seriousness with which he conversed. Detailed, scrupulous, loquacious rationality was generally to be suspected when Morris Sabbath was the speaker. Though not even he could always be certain whether the nonsense so articulated was wholly nonsensical. No, there was nothing simple about being as misleading—"

"Stop it! Stop it, please, being a maniac!"

"Only if *you* stop it being an idiot! Why on this issue are you suddenly so stupid? Exactly what am I to do, Drenka? Take an oath? Are you going to administer an oath? What are the words to the oath? Please list all the things that I am not allowed to do. Penetration. Is that it, is that all? What about a kiss? What about a phone call? And will you take the oath too? And how will I know if you've upheld it? You never have before."

And just when Silvija is coming back, Sabbath was thinking. Is that what's provoked all this, her fear of what she might be impelled to do for Sabbath in the excitement of the excitement? The summer before, Silvija, Matija's niece, had lived with the Baliches up at the house while working as a waitress in the inn's dining room. Silvija was an eighteen-year-old college student in Split and had taken her vacation in America to improve her English. Having shed any and all qualms in twenty-four hours, Drenka had brought to Sabbath, sometimes stuffed in her pocket, sometimes hidden in her purse, Silvija's soiled underthings. She wore them for him and pretended to be Silvija. She passed them up and down the length of his long white beard and pressed them to his parted lips. She bandaged his erection in the straps and cups, stroked him enwrapped in the silky fabric of Silvija's tiny bra. She drew his feet through the legs of Silvija's bikini under-pants and worked them up as far as she could along his heavy thighs. "Say the things," he told her, "say everything," and she did. "Yes, you have my permission, you dirty man, yes," she said, "you can have her, I give her to you, you can have her tight young pussy, you dirty, filthy man. . . ." Silvija was a slight, seraphic thing with very white skin and reddish ringlets who wore small round glasses with metal frames that made her look like a stu-dious child. "Photographs," Sabbath instructed Drenka, "find photographs. There must be photographs, they all take photo-graphs." No, no way. Not meek little Silvija. Impossible, said Drenka, but the next day, going through Silvija's dresser, Drenka uncovered from beneath her cotton nighties a stack of Polaroids that Silvija had brought from Split to keep from becoming home-sick. They were mainly pictures of her mother and father, her older sister, her boyfriend, her dog, but one photograph was of Silvija and another girl her age wearing only pantyhose and posing sideways in the doorway between two rooms of an apartment. The other girl was much larger than Silvija, a robust, bulky, big-breasted girl with a pumpkinish face who was hugging Silvija from behind while Silvija bent forward, her minute buttocks thrust into the other one's groin. Silvija had her head thrown back and her mouth wide open, feigning ecstasy or perhaps just laughing heartily at the silliness of what they were up to. On the reverse side of the photograph, in the half inch at the top where she carefully identified the people in each of the pictures, Silvija had written, in Serbo-Croatian, "Nera odpozadi"—Nera from the rear. The "odpozadi" was no less inflammatory than the picture, and he looked from one side of the photograph to the other all the while that Drenka improvised for him with Silvija's toylike brassiere. One Monday, when the kitchen at the inn was closed and Matija had taken Silvija off for the day to see historic Boston, Drenka squeezed into the folk dirndl with the full black skirt and the tight, embroidered bodice in which Silvija, like the other waitresses, served the Baliches' customers and, in the guest room where Silvija was spending the summer, laid herself fully clothed across the bed. There was she "seduced," "Silvija" protesting all the while that "Mr. Sabbath" must promise never to tell her aunt and her uncle what she had agreed to do for money. "I never had a man before. I only had my boyfriend, and he comes so soon. I never had a man like you." "Can I come inside you, Silvija?" "Yes, yes, I always wanted a man to come inside me. Just don't tell my aunt and my uncle!" "I fuck your aunt. I fuck Drenka." "Oh, do you? My aunt? Do you? Is she a better fuck than me?" "No, never, no." "Is her pussy tight like me?" "Oh, Silvija—your aunt is standing at the door. She's watching us!" "Oh, my God—!" "She wants to fuck with us, too." "Oh, my God, I never tried that before—"

Little was left undone that first afternoon, and Sabbath was still safely out of Silvija's room hours before the girl returned with her uncle. They couldn't have enjoyed themselves more—so said

Silvija, Matija, Drenka, Sabbath. Everybody was happy that summer, including even Sabbath's wife, to whom he was more kindly disposed than he had been for years—there were times now over breakfast when he not only pretended to inquire about her AA meeting but pretended to listen to her answer. And Matija, who on his Mondays off drove Silvija into Vermont and New Hampshire and, on one occasion, to the very end of Cape Cod, seemed to have rediscovered in the role of uncle to his brother's daughter something akin to the satisfaction he had once derived from, all too successfully, making a real American out of his son. The summer had been an idyll for everyone, and when she left for home after Labor Day Silvija was speaking endearingly unidiomatic English and carried a letter from Drenka to her parents—*not* the one devilishly composed in English by Sabbath—reiterating the invitation for the youngster to return to work in the restaurant and live with them again the next summer.

To Sabbath's question—whether, if she herself were to swear to an oath of fidelity, she would have the strength to uphold it—Drenka replied of course she would, yes, she *loved* him.

"You love your husband, too. You love Matija."

"That is not the same."

"But what about six months from now? For years you were angry at him and hated him. Felt so imprisoned by him you even thought of poisoning him. That's how crazy one man was making you. Then you began to love another man and discovered in time that you could now love Matija as well. If you didn't have to pretend to desire him, you could be a good and happy wife to him. Because of you I'm not entirely horrible to Roseanna. I admire Roseanna, she's a real soldier, trooping off to AA every night—those meetings are for her what this is for us, a whole other life to make home endurable. But now you want to change all that, not just for us, but for Roseanna and Matija. Yet why you want to do this you won't tell me."

"Because I want you to say, after thirteen years, 'Drenka, I love you, and you are the only woman I want.' The time has come to *tell* me that!"

"Why has it come? Have I missed something?"

She was crying again when she said, "I sometimes think you miss everything."

"I don't. No. I disagree. I actually don't think I miss anything. I haven't missed the fact that you were frightened to leave Matija even when things were at their worst, because if you left you'd be high and dry, without your share of the inn. You were afraid to leave Matija because he speaks your language and ties you to your past. You were afraid to leave Matija because he is, without doubt, a kind, strong, responsible man. But mostly Matija means money. Despite all this love you have for me, you never once suggested that we leave our mates and run off together, for the simple reason that I am penniless and he is rich. You don't want to be a pauper's wife, though it is all right to be a pauper's girlfriend, especially when you are able, with the pauper's encouragement, to fuck everybody else on the side."

This made Drenka smile—even in her misery the cunning smile that few aside from Sabbath had ever got to admire. "Yes? And if I had announced I was leaving Matija, you would have run away with me? As stupid as I am? Yes? As bad an accent as I have? Without all the life that I am bound by? Of course it's you that makes marriage to Matija possible—but it's Matija that makes it work for *you*."

"So you stay with Matija to make me happy."

"As much as anything—yes!"

"And that explains the other men as well."

"But it does!"

"And Christa?"

"Of course it was for you. You know it was for you. To please you, to excite you, to give you what you wanted, to give you the woman you never had! I love you, Mickey. I love being dirty for you, doing everything for you. I would give you anything, but I can no longer endure you to have other women. It hurts too much. The pain is just too great!"

As it happened, since picking up Christa several years back Sabbath had not really been the adventurous libertine Drenka claimed she could no longer endure, and consequently she already had the monogamous man she wanted, even if she didn't know it. To women other than her, Sabbath was by now quite unalluring, not just because he was absurdly bearded and obstinately peculiar and overweight and aging in every obvious way but because, in the aftermath of the scandal four years earlier with Kathy Goolsbee, he'd become more dedicated than ever to marshaling the antipathy of just about everyone as though he were, in fact, battling for his rights. What he continued to tell Drenka, and what Drenka continued to believe, were lies, and yet deluding her about his seductive powers was so simple that it amazed him, and if he failed to stop himself it was not to delude himself as well, or to preen himself in her eyes, but because the situation was irresistible: gullible Drenka hotly pleading, "What happened? Tell me everything. Don't leave anything out," even while he eased into her the way Nera pretended in the Polaroid to be penetrating Silvija. Drenka remembered the smallest detail of his exciting stories long after he had forgotten even the broad outline, but then he was as naively transfixed by her stories, the difference being that hers were about people who were real. He knew they were real because, after each new liaison had got under way, he would listen on the extension while, beside him on the bed, holding the portable phone in one hand and his erection in the other, she drove the latest lover crazy with the words that never failed to do the trick. And afterward, each of these sated fellows said to her exactly the same thing: the ponytailed electrician with whom she took baths in his apartment, the uptight psychiatrist whom she saw alternate Thursdays in a motel across the state line, the young musician who played jazz piano one summer at the inn, the nameless middle-aged stranger with the JFK smile whom she met in the elevator of the Ritz-Carlton . . . each one of them said, once he had recovered his breath—and Sabbath heard them saying it, craved their saying it, exulted in their saying it, knew it himself to be one of the few wonderfully indisputable, unequivocal truths a man could live by—each one conceded to Drenka, "There's no one like you."

And now she was telling him that she no longer wished to be this woman unanimously acknowledged as unlike all others. At fifty-two, stimulating enough still to make even conventional men reckless, she wanted to change and become somebody else—but did she know why? The secret realm of thrills and concealment, this was the poetry of her existence. Her crudeness was the most distinguishing force in her life, lent her life its distinction. What was she otherwise? What was *he* otherwise? She was his last link with another world, she and her great taste for the impermissible. As a teacher of estrangement from the ordinary, he had never trained a more gifted pupil; instead of being joined by the contractual they were interconnected by the instinctual and together could eroticize anything (except their spouses). Each of their marriages cried out for a countermarriage in which the adulterers attack their feelings of captivity. Didn't she know a marvel when she saw one?

He was badgering her so relentlessly because he was fighting for his life.

She not merely sounded as though she were fighting for hers but she looked it, looked as though she and not his mother were the ghost. During the last six months or so Drenka had been suffering with abdominal pains and nausea, and he wondered now if they were not symptoms of the anxiety that had been mounting in her as she approached the day in May that she had chosen to present this crazy ultimatum. Until today he had tended to account for her cramps and the occasional bouts of vomiting as the result of the pressures at the inn. Having been at the job for over twenty-three years, she was herself not surprised by the toll the work was now taking on her health. "You have to know food," she lamented wearily, "you have to know the law, you have to know every aspect of life there is. This happens in this business, Mickey, when you have to serve the public all the time— you become a burnt-out case. And Matija still cannot be flexible. This rule, that rule—but the smarter thing is to accommodate the people where you can instead of to say always no. If I could just get a break from the bookkeeping part of it. If I could get away from the staff part of it. Our older staff, they are people full of problems all their lives. The people who are married, the house-keepers, the dishwashers, you can know from the way they be-have something is going on that has nothing to do with us. They bring in what's going on outside. And they never go to Matija to tell him what's wrong. They go to me, because I'm the easier one. Every summer he is going, going, going, and I'll say, 'So-and-so did this, did that,' and Matija says to me, 'Why do you always bring me these problems? Why don't you tell me something pleas-ant!' Well, because I'm upset by what's going on. To have these kids on the staff. I can't take any more kids. They don't know shit from Adams. So I wind up doing their job on the floor, like I'm the kid. Trays all over the place. I clean up. Carrying trays. A busgirl. It builds up, Mickey. If we had our son with us. But Matthew thinks the business is stupid. And sometimes I don't blame him. We have a million dollars' worth of liability insurance. Now I have to get *another* million dollars. We are advised to do this. The dock in the water at the inn's beach that everybody enjoys? The insurance company says, 'Don't do that anymore. Somebody's going to hurt themselves.' So the good things you would like to provide to the American public, they will just get you in trouble. And now—computers!"

The big thing was to get computers in before the summer, an expensive system that had to be wired all over the place. Every-body had to learn to use the new system, and Drenka had to teach them after she had learned herself at a two-month course at Mount Kendall Community College (a course taken also by Sab-bath so that once a week they could meet afterward, just down from Mount Kendall, at the Bo-Peep Motel). For Drenka, with her bookkeeping skills, the computer course had been a snap, though teaching the staff was not. "You have to think like that computer thinks," she told Sabbath, "and most of my staff don't even think like a human being yet." "Then why do you keep working so hard? You keep getting sick—you don't enjoy any-thing any longer." "I do. The money. I still enjoy that. And mine is not the hard job anyway. In the kitchen is the harder job. I don't care how hard for me my job is, how big an emotional strain it is. The physical stamina that you need in the kitchen—you have to be a horse to do that. Matija is a gentleman, thank God, and he doesn't resent that he has the horse's job. Yes, I enjoy the profit. I enjoy that the business is running. Only this year for the first time in twenty-three years we will not go forward financially. That's something else to get sick about. We will go backward. I keep the books, I see week by week how much our restaurant has been declining since Reagan. In the eighties the people from Boston were coming. They didn't mind eating dinner at nine-thirty on a Saturday night, so we'd get the turnover. But the people from around here don't want to do that. There was all the money around then, there was not the competition then. . . ."

No wonder she had cramps . . . the hard work, the worry, profits down, new computers in, and all her men besides. And me—the work with me! Talk about the horse's job. "I can't do everything," she complained to Sabbath when the pain was at its worst. "I can only be who I *am*." Which, Sabbath still believed, was someone who *could* do everything.

◆   ◆   ◆

When, while he was fucking Drenka up at the Grotto, his mother hovering just above his shoulder, over him like the home plate umpire peering in from behind the catcher's back, he would wonder if she had somehow popped out of Drenka's cunt the moment before he entered it, if that was where his mother's spirit lay curled up, patiently awaiting his appearance. Where else should ghosts come from? Unlike Drenka, who seemed for no reason to have been seized by the taboos, his tiny dynamo of a mother was now beyond all taboos—she could be on the lookout for him anywhere, and wherever she was he could detect her as though there were something supernatural about him as well, as though he transmitted a beam of filial waves that bounced off his invisible mother's presence and gave him her exact location. Either that, or he was going crazy. One way or another, he knew she was about a foot to the right of Drenka's blood-drained face. Perhaps she was not only listening to his every word from there, perhaps every provocative word he spoke she had a puppeteer's power to *make* him speak. It might even be she who was leading him to the disaster of losing the only solace he had. Suddenly his mother's focus had changed and, for the first time since 1944, the living son was more real to her than the dead one.

The final kink, thought Sabbath, searching the dilemma for a solution—the final kink is for the libertines to be faithful. Why not tell Drenka, "Yes, dear, I'll do it"?

Drenka had dropped in exhaustion onto the large granite outcropping near the center of the enclosure where they sometimes sat on beautiful days like this one eating the sandwiches she'd brought in her knapsack. There was a wilted bouquet at her feet, the first wildflowers of the spring, there from when she'd plucked them the week before while tramping up through the woods to meet him. Each year she taught him the names of the flowers, in her language and in his, and from one year to the next he could not remember even the English. For nearly thirty years Sabbath had been exiled in these mountains, and still he could name hardly anything. They didn't have this stuff where he came from. All these things growing were beside the point there. He was from the shore. There was sand and ocean, horizon and sky, daytime and nighttime—the light, the dark, the tide, the stars, the boats, the sun, the mists, the gulls. There were the jetties, the piers, the boardwalk, the booming, silent, limitless sea. Where he grew up they had the Atlantic. You could touch with your toes where America began. They lived in a stucco bungalow two short streets from the edge of America. The house. The porch. The screens. The icebox. The tub. The linoleum. The broom. The pantry. The ants. The sofa. The radio. The garage. The outside shower with the slatted wooden floor Morty had built and the drain that always clogged. In summer, the salty sea breeze and the dazzling light; in September, the hurricanes; in January, the storms. They had January, February, March, April, May, June, July, August, September, October, November, December. And then January. And then again January, no end to the stockpile of Januaries, of

Mays, of Marches. August, December, April—name a month, and they had it in spades. They'd had endlessness. He'd grown up on endlessness and his mother—in the beginning they were the same thing. His mother, his mother, his mother, his mother, his mother . . . and then there was his mother, his father, Grandma, Morty, and the Atlantic at the end of the street. The ocean, the beach, the first two streets in America, then the house, and in the house a mother who never stopped whistling until December 1944.

If Morty had come home alive, if the endlessness had ended naturally instead of with the telegram, if after the war Morty had started doing electrical work and plumbing for people, had become a builder at the shore, gone into the construction business just as the boom in Monmouth County was beginning . . . Didn't matter. Take your pick. Get betrayed by the fantasy of endlessness or by the fact of finitude. No, Sabbath could only have wound up Sabbath, begging for what he was begging, bound to what he was bound, saying what he did not wish to stop himself from saying.

"I'll tell you what"—his milk-of-human-kindness intonation— "I'll make a deal. I'll make the sacrifice you want. I will give up every woman but you. I'll say, 'Drenka, I love only you and want only you and will take whatever oath you wish to administer itemizing everything that I am forbidden to do.' But in return you must make a sacrifice."

"I will!" Excitedly she rose to her feet. "I want to! Never another man! Only you! To the end!"

"No," he said, approaching with his arms extended to her, "no, no, I don't mean that. That, you tell me, constitutes *no* sacrifice. No, I'm asking for something to test your stoicism and to test your truthfulness as you will be testing mine, a task just as repugnant to you as breaking the sacrament of infidelity is to me."

His arms were around her now, grasping her plump buttocks through her jeans. *You like when I turn around on you and you can see my ass. All men like that. But only you stick it in there, only you, Mickey, can fuck me there!* Not true, but a nice sentiment.

"I will give up all other women. In return," he told her, "you must suck off your husband twice a week."

"Aacch!"

"Aacch, yes. Aacch, exactly. You're gagging already. 'Aacch, I could never do that!' Can't I find something kinder? No."

Sobbing, she pulled herself free of him and pleaded, "Be serious—this is serious!"

"I am being serious. How odious can it be? It's merely monogamy at its most inhumane. Pretend it's someone else. That's what all good women do. Pretend it's the electrician. Pretend it's the credit-card magnate. Matija comes in two seconds anyway. You'll be getting everything you want and surprising a husband in the bargain, and it'll take only four seconds a week. And think of how it will excite *me*. The most promiscuous thing you have ever done. Sucking off your husband to please your lover. You want to feel like a real whore? That ought to do it."

"Stop!" she cried out, throwing her hands over his mouth. "I have cancer, Mickey! Stop! The pain has been because of cancer! I can't believe it! I *don't!* I can *die!*"

Just then the oddest thing happened. For the second time in a year a helicopter flew over the woods and then circled back and hovered directly above them. This time it had to be his mother.

"Oh, my God," said Drenka and, with her arms around him, squeezed so tightly that the full weight of her clinging caused his knees to buckle—or perhaps they were about to buckle anyway.

Mother, he thought, this can't be so. First Morty, then you, then Nikki, now Drenka. There's nothing on earth that keeps its promise.

"Oh, I wanted, oh," cried Drenka as the helicopter's energy roared above them, a dynamic force to magnify the monstrous loneliness, a wall of noise tumbling down on them, their whole carnal edifice caving in. "I wanted you to say it without *knowing*, I wanted you to do it on your *own*," and here she wailed the wail that authenticates the final act of a classical tragedy. "I can die! If they can't stop it, darling, I will be dead in a year!"

Mercifully she was dead in six months, killed by a pulmonary embolus before there was time for the cancer, which had spread omnivorously from her ovaries throughout her system, to torture Drenka beyond even the tough capacity of her own ruthless strength.

UNABLE TO SLEEP, Sabbath lay beside Roseanna overcome by a stupendous, deforming emotion of which he had never before had firsthand knowledge. He was jealous now of the very men about whom, when Drenka was living, he could never hear enough. He thought about the men she had met in elevators, airports, parking lots, department stores, at hotel association conferences and food conventions, men she had to have because their looks appealed to her, men she slept with just once or had prolonged flings with, men who five and six years after she'd last been to bed with them would unexpectedly phone the inn to extol her, to praise her, often without sparing the graphic obscenities to tell her how she was the least inhibited woman they had ever known. He remembered her explaining to him—because he had asked her to—what exactly made her choose one man in a room over another, and now he felt like the most foolishly innocent of husbands who uncovers the true history of an unfaithful wife— he felt as stupid as the holy simpleton Dr. Charles Bovary. The diabolical pleasure this had once afforded him! The happiness! When she was alive, nothing excited or entertained him more than hearing, detail by detail, the stories of her second life. Her *third* life—*he* was the second. "It's a very physical feeling that I get. It's the appearance, it's something chemical, I almost would like to say. There's an energy that I sense. It makes me very aroused and I feel it then, I become sexualized, and I feel it in my nipples. I feel it inside, in my body. If he is physical, if he is strong, the way he walks, the way he sits, the way he's himself, if he's juicy. Guys with small dry lips, they turn me off, or if they smell bookish—you know, this dry pencil smell of men. I often look at their hands to see if they have strong, expressive hands. Then I imagine that they have a big dick. If there is any truth to this I don't know, but I do it anyway as a little research. Some kind of confidence in the way they move. It isn't that they have to look elegant—it is rather an animalistic appearance under the elegance. So it's a very intuitive thing. And I know it right away and I have always known it. And so I say, 'Okay, I go and fuck him.' Well, I have to open the channels for him. So I look at him and I flirt with him. I just start laughing or show my legs and sort of show him that it's all right. Sometimes I make a real bold gesture. 'I wouldn't mind having an affair with you.' Yeah," she said, laughing at the extent of her own impulsiveness, "I could say something like that. That guy I had in Aspen, I felt his interest. But he was in his fifties and there I always question how hard can they get. With a younger guy you know it's an easier thing. With an older one you don't know. But I felt this kind of vibration and I was really turned on. And, you know, you move your arm closer or he moves his arm closer and you know you're in this aura of sexual feeling together and everybody else in the room is excluded. I think with that man I actually openly stated that it was okay, that I was interested."

The boldness with which she went after them! The ardor and skill with which she aroused them! The delight she found in watching them jerk off! And the pleasure she then took in telling all she'd learned about lust and what it is for men . . . and the torment all this was to him now. He'd not had the faintest idea that he could feel such distress. "What I enjoyed was to see how they were by themselves. That I could be the observer there, and to see how they played with their dick and how it was formed, the shape of it, and when it became hard, and also the way they held their hand—it turned me on. Everybody jerks their dick differently. And when they abandon themselves into it, when they allow themselves to abandon themselves, this is very exciting. And to see them come that way. This Lewis guy, he was in his sixties and he'd never jerked off, he said, in front of a woman. And he was sort of holding his hand this way"—she turned her wrist so that the little finger was at the top of her fist and the second knuckle of her thumb at the bottom—"well, to see that particularity of it and, as I say, to see when they get so hot they can't stop themselves in spite of being shy, that's very exciting. That's what I like best—watching them lose control." The shy ones she would softly suck for a few minutes and then place their hands for them on themselves and help them along until they were safely into it and on their own. Then, beginning lightly to finger herself, she would lean back and look on. When she next saw Sabbath she would demonstrate on him the peculiar "particularity" of each man's technique. He was tremendously stirred by this . . . and now it made him jealous, maddeningly jealous—now that she was dead he wanted to shake her and shout at her and tell her to stop. "Only me! Fuck your husband when you have to, but otherwise, no one but me!"

In fact, he didn't want her to fuck Matija either. Him least of all. On the rare occasions when she used to report those details to Sabbath, too, they had hardly engrossed him, provoked not the slightest erotic interest. Yet now there was barely a night when he was free of the mortifying memory of Drenka allowing her husband to take her like a wife. "Checking Matija in bed, I saw his erection. I was certain he would not act on it without my taking first initiative, so quickly I undressed. I could not get aroused even if I had strong, tender feelings for my husband. Seeing his hard cock, smaller than yours, Mickey, and with a foreskin, which when the skin is pulled down is much redder than yours . . . thinking about the way we had just fucked . . . well, longing for your big, hard dick, it was almost painful. How could I abandon myself to this man who loves me? When he penetrated me, lying on top of me, Matija was moaning louder than I ever recollect. It was almost as if he was crying. Since it never takes him long to come, the whole thing was over soon. After sleeping one or two hours I woke up sick to my stomach. I had to throw up and take some Mylanta."

How dare he! What *chutzpah!* Sabbath wanted to murder Matija. And why didn't I? Why didn't *we?* Uncircumcised dog! Smite him *thus!*

. . . One brilliantly sunny day back in February, Sabbath had come upon Drenka's widowed husband up at the Stop & Shop in Cumberland. For the first time that winter it hadn't snowed in four consecutive days and so, after donning an old knit seaman's cap in which to swab down the bathroom and kitchen floors and give the house a vacuuming, Sabbath had driven up to Cumberland—blinded much of the way by the light off the gargantuan drifts banked at the side of the road—to do the grocery shopping, one of his weekly household chores. And there was Matija, almost unrecognizable since he'd seen him silent and stone-faced at the funeral. His black hair had gone white, completely white in just the three months. He looked so weak, so slight, his face emaciated—and all of this in just three months! He could have passed for a senior citizen, older even than Sabbath, and he was only in his mid-fifties. The inn was closed every year from New Year's Day to April 1, and so Matija was out shopping for the few things he needed living alone in the Baliches' big new house up from the lake and the inn.

Balich was directly behind him in the checkout line and, though he nodded when Sabbath looked his way, registered no recognition.

"Mr. Balich, my name is Mickey Sabbath."

"Yes? How do you do?"

"Does 'Mickey Sabbath' mean anything to you?"

"Yes," said Balich kindly after feigning a moment's thought, "I believe you have been a patron of mine. I recognize you from the inn."

"No," said Sabbath, "I live in Madamaska Falls but we don't eat out much."

"I see," replied Balich and, after smiling for a few seconds more, somberly returned to his thoughts.

"I'll tell you how we know each other," said Sabbath.

"Yes?"

"My wife was your son's art teacher at the high school. Rose-anna Sabbath. She and your Matthew became great friends."

"Ahhh." Again he smiled courteously.

Sabbath had never realized before how much there was in Drenka's husband of the subdued and courtly European gentle-man. Maybe it was the white hair, the grief, the accent, but he had about him the magisterial air of a senior diplomat from a small country. No, Sabbath hadn't known this about him, the dignified composure came as a surprise, but then the other guy is often just a blur. Even if he's your best friend or the fellow across the street who more than once has jump-started your car, he *becomes* a blur. He becomes *the husband,* and sympathetic imagination dwindles away, right along with conscience.

The only time Sabbath ever before had occasion to observe Matija in public was the April preceding the Kathy Goolsbee scandal, when he went over to the inn on the third Tuesday of the month—with the thirty or so Rotarians who gathered there for their luncheon meeting the third Tuesday of every month—as a guest of Gus Kroll, the service station owner, who never failed to pass on to Sabbath the jokes he heard from the truckers who stopped to gas up and use the facilities. Gus had a great audience in Sabbath, because even when the jokes were not uniformly of the first rank, the fact that Gus rarely bothered to wear his den-tures while he was telling them furnished Sabbath with sufficient delight. Gus's impassioned commitment to repeating the jokes had long ago led the puppeteer to understand that they were what gave unity to Gus's vision of life, that they alone answered the need of his spiritual being for a clarifying narrative with which to face day after day at the pump. With every joke that poured forth from Gus's toothless mouth, Sabbath was reassured that not even a simple guy like Gus was free of the human need to find a strand of significance that will hold together everything that isn't on TV.

Sabbath had asked Gus if he would be kind enough to invite him to the meeting to hear Matija Balich address the Rotary Club on the topic "Innkeeping Today." By then Sabbath already knew that Matija had been agonizingly preparing the speech for weeks—Sabbath had even read the speech, or the first short version of it, when Drenka had brought it to him to look at. She had typed the six pages for her husband, done her best to catch the errors, but she wanted Sabbath to double-check the English and amiably he agreed to help. "It's fascinating," he said after twice reading it through. "It is?" "It moves along the track like a goddamn train. Really, it's wonderful. Two problems, however. It's too short. He's not thorough enough. It's got to be three times as long. And this expression, this idiom here, is wrong. It isn't 'nuts and bolts.' You don't say in English, 'If you watch the nuts and bolts. . . .'" "No?" "Who told him it was 'nuts and bolts,' Drenka?" "Stupid Drenka did," she replied. "Nuts and *bulbs*," said Sabbath. "Nuts and bulbs," she repeated and wrote on the back of the last page. "And write down there that he stops too soon," said Sabbath. "Three times as long, at least. They'll listen," he told her. "This is stuff nobody knows."

Gus came by Brick Furnace Road to pick up Sabbath in the tow truck, and no sooner were they off than Gus started in entertaining him with what he knew to be taboo for what Gus called the "churchy guys" in town.

"Can you take a joke that's not too appreciative of women?" Gus asked him.

"The only kind I *can* take."

"Well, this truck driver, whenever he goes away, his wife, she gets cold and lonely. So when he comes back from a trip he brings her a skunk, a big, furry live skunk, and he tells her that next time he goes away she should take it to bed with her and when she goes to sleep she should put it between her legs. So she says to him, 'What about the smell?' And he says, 'He'll get used to it. I did.'"

"Well, if you like that one," said Gus when he heard Sabbath's laughter, "I got another one along the same lines," and so in no time they arrived for the meeting.

The Rotarians were already milling around in the rustic barroom with the exposed beams across the low ceiling and the cheerful white tile hearth, all of them packed closely together in the one smallish room, perhaps because of the cozy fire burning there on a cold, gusty spring day or perhaps because of the platters, on the bar, of *ćevapčići*, a Yugoslav national specialty that was also a specialty of the inn. "I have to feed you with *ćevapčići*," Drenka had told Sabbath when they were still newly lovers, playing post-coital pranks in bed. "Feed me anything you want." "Three types of meat," she told him, "one is beef, one is pork, then is lamb. All is ground. Then some onions are added to it and some pepper. It is like a meatball but a different shape. Very small. It is obligatory to eat *ćevapčići* with onion. An onion cut into small pieces. You can have little peppers, too. Red. Very hot." "It doesn't sound bad at all," said Sabbath, full of pleasure with her, smiling away. "Yes, I am going to feed you *ćevapčići*," she said adoringly. "And I, in turn, will fuck your brains out." "Oh, my American boyfriend—that means you will fuck me seriously?" "Quite seriously." "It means hard?" "Very hard." "And it means what else? I have learned to do it in Croatian, to say all the words and not be shy, but never anyone has taught me to do it in American. Tell me! Teach me! Teach me what all the things mean in American!" "It means every which way." And then, as conscientiously as she had explained to him how to make *ćevapčići*, he went ahead to teach her what every which way meant.

. . . Or perhaps they were in the barroom because, tending bar, Drenka was wearing a black crepe blouse that buttoned up to a V-neck and that did her plumpness full justice whenever she ducked down to fill a glass with ice. Sabbath stood back by the door for close to half an hour watching her flirting with the chiropractor, a strong young fellow with a loud bark of a laugh who didn't do at all well hiding his sexual orientation, and then with the former state representative who was owner of the three branches of Cumberland BanCorp, and finally even with Gus, who, fully fitted out now in his uppers and lowers and for the occasion wearing a string tie at the neck of his coveralls, was just the man he'd like to see her fuck to be assured that she was as wonderful as he thought she was. Oh, she was jolly, all right—the only woman amid all these men, the blissful stimulus serving their blissful stimulant, plainly ecstatic just to be living on earth.

When Sabbath pushed through the hubbub up to the bar and asked for a beer, she registered her surprise at his presence by instantly turning white. "What kind do you like, Mr. Sabbath?" "Do you have Pussy from Yugoslavia?" "From the tap or a bottle?" "Which do you recommend?" "More foam from the tap," she said, smiling at him, now that she had recovered her wits, with a smile that he would have taken for a startlingly open proclamation of their secret had he not seen the same smile bestowed earlier on Gus. "Draw me one, will ya?" he said with a wink. "I like the foam."

When the meal ended—big pork chops with apple rings in a Calvados sauce, chocolate ice cream sundaes, cigars, and for those who wanted an after-luncheon drink, Prošek, a sweetish white Dalmatian wine that Drenka, as their charming Old World hostess, ordinarily served to paying guests compliments of the house—Matija was introduced by the Rotary president as "Matt Balik." The innkeeper was wearing a red cashmere turtleneck, a blazer with gold buttons, new cavalry-twill trousers, and unworn, unmarked Bally boots polished to a high gloss. Snappily decked out like that, he looked more impressively brawny even than when he was working in a T-shirt and worn jeans. The allure of a heavily muscled male figure conventionally clothed for social intercourse. *An animalistic appearance under the elegance.* Sabbath had had it himself once, or so Nikki used to tell him when she urged him to buy a dark blue suit with a vest so the world could appreciate how gorgeous he was. Gorgeous Sabbath. Those were the fifties.

Matija's passion was to rebuild the stone walls falling to pieces in the fifty acres of fields adjacent to the house and the inn. On the island of Brač, where he had relatives and where he had been working as a waiter when he met Drenka, there was a tradition of masonry, and while he was on the island he would spend his days off helping a cousin who was building himself a house of stone.

And, of course, Matija had never forgotten the grandfather cutting stone in the quarries, an aging man imprisoned on Goli Otok as an enemy of the regime . . . which made lugging the big stones and setting them in place something almost of a commemorative rite for Matija. That was how he spent his breaks from the kitchen: outside half an hour moving rocks and he was ready for another three, four, five hours on his feet in a temperature of a hundred degrees. He spent much of each winter moving those rocks. "His only friends," reported Drenka, sadly, "are the walls and me."

"Some people," Matija began, "think this business is fun. It is not fun. It is a business. Read the industry magazines. People say, 'I want to get away from corporate life. An inn, this is my dream.' But I am dedicated to this inn as though I am *going* every day to a corporate structure."

The pace at which Matija read made it possible for his audience to follow without trouble, despite his heavy accent. At the end of every sentence he allowed them a long moment to consider all the implications of what he had just said. Sabbath enjoyed the pauses no less than the monotony of the uninflected sentences they separated, sentences that caused him to remember for the first time in many years a lonely archipelago of uninhabitable islands that the merchant ships passed leaving Veracruz for the south. Sabbath enjoyed the pauses because he was responsible for them. He had told Drenka to instruct Matija to be sure to take his time. Amateur speakers always rush. Don't rush, he told her to tell him. There's a lot for an audience to digest. The slower the better.

"For instance, we have been audited twice," Matija told them.

From the large bay windows at the head of the rectangular dining room, Sabbath and the guests on his side of the table could see clear down to where the wind was whipping up Lake Madamaska. Their eyes could have traveled from one end to the other of that long washboard of a lake before Matija appeared to conclude that the impact of the two audits had been fully absorbed.

"There is nothing wrong," he then continued. "My wife keeps our books straight and we go to an accountant for advices. So we run it as a business and it is our livelihood. If you watch the nuts and bulbs, the business works for you. If you don't watch, and go out and talk with the guests all the time, you are losing money.

"Years ago we did not serve all the time through the afternoon on Saturday. We still don't. But we make food available to the people. The smart thing is to give people what they want rather than say no, I have this rule, I have that rule. I am pretty strict about the way I think about things. But the public teaches me to be not so strict.

"We have fifty in staff, including part-time. Serving staff is thirty-five—waitresses, bus staff, dining room supervisors. We have twelve rooms plus the annex. We can take twenty-eight people and are full most weekends, though not during the week.

"In the restaurant we can seat one hundred and thirty inside and one hundred on the terrace. But we never seat two hundred and thirty people altogether. The cooking line can't handle it. What we look for is turnover.

"The other serious problem comes with the staff. . . ."

This went on for an hour. There was a fire blazing in the main dining room, as well as the smaller one burning in the bar, and because of the cold winds blowing outside, the windows were all shut tight. The fireplace was only some six feet behind Matija, but the heat of it did not seem to affect him the way it did the Scotch drinkers at the table. They were the first to pass out. The beer drinkers were able to hold on longer.

"We are not absentee owners. I am the main fellow. If everybody else leaves, I am still standing here. My wife can do everything except two cooking-line jobs. She can't work on the broiler, because she has no idea how to cook. And she can't do the sauté, where you are basically frying in pans. But all other jobs she can do: the bartender, the dishwasher, serving, bookkeeping, working the floor. . . ."

Gus, on the wagon these days, drank Tab, but Sabbath saw that Gus was out. Just from Tab. And now the beer drinkers were losing their grip and beginning to look enfeebled—the owner of the bank, the chiropractor, the big mustached guy who ran the gardening center. . . .

Drenka was listening from the bar. When the puppeteer turned in his seat to smile at her, he saw that, leaning over the bar on her elbows, her face balanced on her fists, she was crying, and this was with half the Rotarians still clinging to consciousness.

"It is not always nice for us that our staff doesn't like us. I think some of our staff likes us a lot. A lot of them don't care for us at all. In some places the bar is open to the staff after hours. We don't have that kind of thing here. Those are the places that go bankrupt and where the staff is in terrible auto accidents on the way home. Not here. Here it is not party time with the owners. Here it is not fun. My wife and I are not fun at all. We are work. We are a business. All Yugoslavs when they go abroad, they are very hardworking. Something in our history pushes them for survival. Thank you."

There were no questions, but then there were barely a handful at the long table still capable of asking one. The Rotary president said, "Well, thanks, Matt, thanks a million. That took us through the process pretty thoroughly." Soon people began to wake up to go back to work.

On Friday of that same week, Drenka went to Boston and fucked her dermatologist, the credit-card magnate, the university dean, and then, back at home, just before midnight—making a total of four for the day—she was fucked, holding her breath for the few minutes it lasted, by the orator she was married to.

◆　◆　◆

Now, down in the abandoned center of Cumberland, where the movie theater was long gone and the stores mostly vacant, there was an impoverished wreck of a grocery where Sabbath liked to get a container of coffee and drink it standing up right there after he'd done the weekly shopping. The place, Flo 'n Bert's, was dark, with dirty, worn wooden floors, undusted shelves largely empty of goods, and the most wretched potatoes and bananas Sabbath had ever seen for sale anywhere. But Flo 'n Bert's, grisly mortuary

though it was, smelled exactly like the old grocery in the basement of the LaReine Arms, a block away from their house, where
Sabbath used to go first thing every morning to get two fresh rolls
for his mother so she could make Morty sandwiches to take to his
high school for lunch—cream cheese and olive, peanut butter and
jelly, but mainly canned tuna, the sandwiches double-wrapped
with wax paper and stuffed in the paper bag from the LaReine
Arms. Each week, after Stop & Shop, Sabbath walked around Flo
'n Bert's with his coffee container in his hand, trying to figure out
what the ingredients were that went into that smell, which was
also like something he smelled up at the Grotto in late autumn,
after the fallen leaves and the dying underbrush had been damp-
ened down by the rains and begun to rot. Maybe it was that:
damp rot. He loved it. The coffee that he had to drink there
was undrinkable but he could never resist the pleasure of that
smell.

Sabbath stationed himself outside the door to Stop & Shop
and, when Balich emerged carrying a plastic bag in either hand,
he said, "Mr. Balich, how about a hot cup of coffee?"

"Thank you, sir, no."

"Come on," said Sabbath good-naturedly, "why not? It's ten
degrees out here." Should he convert that into Celsius for him, as
he would for Drenka when she telephoned, before going up to the
Grotto, to ask what it *really* was outside? "There's a place down
the hill. Follow me. The Chevy. A cup of coffee to warm you up."

Leading Balich's car between the one-story-high snowbanks
and across the railroad tracks agleam from the frost, Sabbath had
to admit that he had no idea what he was planning to do. All he
could think of was this guy daring to lie across his Drenka, moaning with pleasure as though he were crying, penetrating her with a
dog-red cock that afterward made her throw up.

Yes, it was time that he and Balich met—to go through life
without meeting him face-to-face would be making life too easy
for himself. He would long ago have died of boredom without his
extensive difficulties.

The putrid coffee was poured from the Silex by a sullen, stupid girl in her late teens who had been a sullen, stupid girl in her late teens ever since Sabbath had begun dropping in to smell Flo 'n Bert's some fifteen years back. Maybe they were all from the same family, daughters of Flo and Bert who successively grew into the job, or maybe, more likely, there was an inexhaustible supply of these girls turned out by the Cumberland school system. On-the-prowl, insinuating, unselective Sabbath had never been able to get anything more than a grunt out of any of them.

Involuntarily Balich made a face when he tasted the coffee—which turned out to be about as cold as the day—but politely said, "Oh no, very good, but one is enough," when Sabbath asked if he'd like a second cup.

"It has not been easy for you without your wife," Sabbath said. "You look very thin."

"These have been dark days," Balich replied.

"Still?"

He nodded sadly. "It's awful still. I'm right at the bottom. After thirty-one years, I'm in my third month of a new regime. Somehow in some ways every day it gets worse."

That it does. "And your son?"

"He's in a bit of a state of shock too. He misses her terribly. But he's young, he's strong. Sometimes, his wife tells me, in the dark hours of the night . . . but he seems to be coping."

"That's good," Sabbath said. "That is about the strongest bond in the world, the mother and the little boy. There couldn't be anything stronger."

"Yes, yes," said Balich, his soft gray eyes growing teary from talking to somebody so understanding. "Yes, and when I looked at her dead, with my son at the hospital in the middle of the night . . . she was lying there with all the tubes and when I looked at her and I saw that it was broken, that bond with our son, I could not believe that this strongest thing in the world that you say was no longer in existence. There she was, all her beauty lying there, and that strongest thing wasn't anymore. She was gone. So I kissed her good-bye, my son did and I did, and they took all the tubes out. And this piece of human sunlight was there, but dead."

"How old was she?"

"Fifty-two. It's the most cruel thing that could have happened."

"Of all the people in the world who would have died in their fifties like that," said Sabbath, "I would never have imagined your wife on the list. The few times I ever saw her in town, as you say, she lit up everything. And your son works with you at the inn?"

"Innkeeping is not on my mind at all. Whether that comes back ever, I don't know. I do have a staff of good workers, but innkeeping is not on my mind. Our whole marriage was tied up with the inn. I am thinking of leasing the business. If some Japanese corporation wanted to come along and buy it . . . Every time I go into her office to try to deal with her things, it's awful, it makes me sick. I don't want to be there and I go."

Sabbath had not been mistaken, he thought, to have never written Drenka a single letter or to have insisted that it should be he, and not she, who filed away for safekeeping the Polaroids he'd taken of her at the Bo-Peep.

"The letters," Balich said, looking imploringly toward Sabbath, as though to make an appeal. "Two hundred and fifty-six letters."

"Of consolation?" asked Sabbath, who, of course, had not himself received a single one. When Nikki disappeared, however, he'd got mail about her, care of the theater. Though by now he'd forgotten how much—maybe fifty letters in all—at the time he'd been stupefied enough to keep a careful count, too.

"Of sympathy, yes. Two hundred and fifty-six. I shouldn't have been amazed at how she lit up everyone's life. I'm getting letters still. And from people I can't even remember. Some came to the inn when we first opened at the other end of the lake. Letters from all kinds of people about her and about how she affected their life. And I believe them. They are true. I got a long two-page letter, a handwritten letter, from the ex-mayor of Worcester."

"Really?"

"He remembers our barbecues for the guests and how she made everyone happy. How she came into the dining room at breakfast and talked to everybody. She just touched everybody. I am strict, I have a rule for everything. But she knew how to treat the guests. Everything was always possible for the guests. For her to be pleasant it was never an effort. One owner is strict, the other is flexible and pleasant. We were a perfect pair to make a successful inn. It's amazing what she did. A thousand different things. She did it all gracefully and always with great pleasure. I can't stop dwelling on it. There is nothing that can take away even a little of this misery. It's impossible to believe. One minute here, the next minute not."

The ex-mayor of Worcester? Well, she had secrets from both of us, Matija.

"And what is your son's occupation?"

"A state trooper."

"Married?"

"His wife is pregnant. The baby will be Drenka if it is a girl."

"Drenka?"

"My wife's name," said Balich. "Drenka, Drenka," he muttered. "There will never be another Drenka."

"Do you see him much, your son?"

"Yes," he lied, unless since Drenka's death there had been a rapprochement.

Balich suddenly had no more to say. Sabbath used the break to smell the moribund market's smell. Either Balich did not want to talk about his grief over Drenka with a stranger any longer or he did not want to talk about his grief over his state trooper son who thought innkeeping was a stupid business.

"How come your son isn't a partner in the inn? Why doesn't he take over with you, now that your wife is gone?"

"I see," said Balich after carefully setting his half-full cup on the counter beside the register, "that you have arthritic fingers. This is a painful disorder. My brother has arthritic fingers."

"Really? Silvija's father?" asked Sabbath.

Openly surprised, Balich said, "You know my little niece?"

"My wife met her. My wife told me about her. She said she was a very, very pretty and charming child."

"Silvija loved her aunt very much. She worshiped her aunt. Silvija became our daughter, too." In his quiet voice there was little intonation now other than the unmistakable intonation of sorrow.

"Is Silvija at the inn in the summertime? My wife said she was working there to learn English."

"Silvija comes every summer while she is in university."

"What are you doing—training *her* to take over your wife's job?"

"No, no," said Balich, and Sabbath was surprised by how disappointed he was to hear this. "She will be a computer programmer."

"That's too bad," said Sabbath.

"That's what she wants to be," said Balich flatly.

"But if she could help you run the inn, if she could light up the place the way your wife did . . ."

Balich reached into his pocket for money. Sabbath said, "Please—" but Balich was not listening any longer. Doesn't like me, Sabbath thought. Didn't take to me. Must have said the wrong thing.

"My coffee?" Balich asked the sullen girl at the register.

She answered with as few sounded consonants as possible. Other things on her mind.

"What?" Balich asked her.

Sabbath translated. "Half a dollar."

Balich paid and, nodding formally at Sabbath, concluded his initial encounter with someone he clearly did not wish to meet ever again. It was Silvija that had done it, Sabbath's modifying "very" with "very." But that was as close as the puppeteer had come to telling Balich in their first five minutes together that the woman who had vomited after having had to fuck him had had every reason to vomit, because all the while she had been as good as someone else's wife. Of course he understood Balich's feelings—for him, too, the shock of her death was only getting worse by the day—but that didn't mean that Sabbath could forgive him.

• • •

Five months after her death, a damp, warm April night with a full moon canonizing itself above the tree line, effortlessly floating—luminously blessed—toward the throne of God, Sabbath stretched out on the ground that covered her coffin and said, "You filthy, wonderful Drenka cunt! Marry me! Marry me!" And with his white beard down in the dirt—the plot was still grassless and without a stone—he envisioned his Drenka: it was bright inside the box and she looked just like herself before the cancer stripped her of all that appealing roundness—ripe, full, ready for contact. Tonight she was wearing Silvija's dirndl. And she was laughing at him.

"So now you want me all to yourself. Now," she said, "when you don't have to have only me and live only with me and be bored only by me, now I am good enough to be your wife."

"Marry me!"

Smiling invitingly, she replied, "First you'll have to die," and raised Silvija's dress to reveal that she was without underpants—dark stockings and a garter belt but no underpants. Even dead, Drenka gave him a hard-on; alive *or* dead, Drenka made him twenty again. Even with temperatures below zero, he would grow hard whenever, from her coffin, she enticed him like this. He had learned to stand with his back to the north so that the icy wind did not blow directly on his dick but still he had to remove one of his gloves to jerk off successfully, and sometimes the gloveless hand would get so cold that he would have to put that glove back on and switch to the other hand. He came on her grave many nights.

The old cemetery was six miles out of town on a little-used road that curved up into the woods and then zigzagged down the western side of the mountain, where it emptied into a superannuated truck route to Albany. The cemetery was set into an open hillside that rolled gently up to an ancient stand of hemlock and white pine. It was beautiful, still, aesthetically charming, melancholy perhaps, but not a cemetery that made you downhearted when you entered it—it was so charming that it sometimes looked as though it had nothing to do with death. It was old, very old, though there were some even older in the nearby hills, their eroded tombstones, fallen aslant, dating back to the earliest years of colonial America. The first burial here—of a certain John Driscoll—had been in 1745; the last burial had been of Drenka, on the last day of November 1993.

Because of the seventeen snowstorms that winter it was often impossible for him to make his way up to the cemetery, even on nights when Roseanna had hurried off to an AA meeting in her four-wheel drive and he was all alone. But when the roads were plowed, the weather was good, the sun down, and Roseanna gone, he drove his Chevy up to the top of Battle Mountain and parked at the cleared entrance to a hiking path about a quarter mile east of the cemetery and made his way along the highway to the graveyard and then, using a flashlight as sparingly as he could, across the treacherous glaze of the drifted snow to her grave. He never drove out during the day, however much he needed to, for fear of running into one of her Matthews or, for that matter, anyone who could take to wondering why, at the coldest spot in the state's "icebox" county, in the midst of the worst winter in local history, the disgraced puppeteer was paying his respects to the remains of the innkeeper's peppy wife. At night he could do what he wished to do, unseen by anyone but his mother's ghost.

"What do you want? If you want to say something . . ." But his mother never did communicate with him, and just because she didn't he came dangerously close to believing that she was not a hallucination—if he was hallucinating, then easily enough he could hallucinate speech for her, enlarge her reality with a voice of the kind with which he used to enliven his puppets. These visitations had been going on too regularly to be a mental aberration . . . unless he was mentally aberrant and the unreality was going to worsen as life became even more unendurable. Without Drenka it *was* unendurable—he didn't have a life, except at the cemetery.

The first April after her death, on this early spring night, Sabbath lay spread-eagled atop her grave, reminiscing with her about Christa. "Never forget you coming," he whispered into the dirt,

"never forget you begging her, 'More, more. . . .'" Invoking
Christa did not exacerbate his jealousy, remembering Drenka lying back in his arms while Christa maintained the steady pressure
of the point of her tongue on Drenka's clitoris (for close to an
hour—he'd timed them) only intensified the loss, even though,
shortly after the three had first got together, Christa began taking
Drenka to a bar in Spottsfield to dance. She went so far as to make
Drenka the gift of a gold chain that she'd lifted from her former
employer's jewelry drawer on the morning she'd decided she'd
had enough of looking after a kid so hyperactive that he was
about to be enrolled in a special school for the "gifted." She told
Drenka that the value of *everything* she'd walked off with (including a pair of diamond stud earrings and a slithery little bracelet of
diamonds) didn't come to half of what she was entitled to for
having been stuck, sight unseen, with that kid.

Christa lived in an attic room on Town Street, overlooking
the green, just above the gourmet food shop where she worked.
Her rent was free, lunches were free, and in addition she was
paid twenty-five dollars a week. For two months, on Wednesday
nights, Drenka and Sabbath would go, in separate cars, to lie with
Christa in the attic. Nothing was open on Town Street after dark,
and they could get up unobserved to Christa's by an outside back
staircase. Three times Drenka had been by herself to see Christa
there but, fearful that Sabbath would be angry with her if he
knew, she did not tell him until a year after Christa had turned
against the two of them and moved out to the countryside, into
the rented farmhouse of a history instructor on the Athena faculty, a woman of thirty with whom Christa had begun a love
affair even before she had undertaken her little caprice with the
elderly. Abruptly she stopped answering Sabbath's phone calls,
and when he ran into her one day—while he pretended to be
studying the window display of the gourmet shop, a display
which hadn't changed since Tip-Top Grocery Company had
evolved in the late sixties into Tip-Top Gourmet Company to accommodate the ardor of the times—she said to him angrily, her
mouth so minute it looked like something omitted from her face,

"I don't want to talk to you anymore." "Why? What happened?" "You two exploited me." "I don't think that's true, Christa. To exploit someone means to use someone selfishly for one's own ends or to utilize them for profit. I don't think either of us exploited you any more than you exploited either of us." "You're an old man! I am twenty years old! I do not want to talk to you!" "Won't you at least talk to Drenka?" "Leave me alone! You're nothing but a fat old man!" "So was Falstaff, kiddo. So was that huge hill of flesh Sir John Paunch, sweet creator of bombast! 'That villainous abominable misleader of youth, Falstaff, that old white-bearded Satan'!—" but she was by this time already into the shop, leaving Sabbath to sadly contemplate—along with a Christaless future—two jars of Mi-Kee Chinese Duck Sauce, two jars of Krinos Grape Leaves in Brine, two cans of La Victoria Refried Beans, and two cans of Baxter's Cream of Smoked Trout Soup, all of them encircling a bottle fancily wrapped in a sun-faded whitish paper shroud and positioned on a pedestal at the center of the window as if it were the answer to all our cravings, a bottle of Lea & Perrins Worcestershire Sauce. Yes, a relic much like Sabbath himself of what was considered oh-so-spicy in a bygone era less . . . in a bygone era more . . . in a bygone era when . . . in a bygone era whose . . . Idiot! The mistake was never to have given her money. The mistake was to have given Drenka the money instead. All he'd slipped Christa—and this only to get a foot in the door the first time—was thirty-five dollars for a quilt she'd made. He should have been slipping her that much per week. To have imagined that Christa was in it for the fun of making Drenka crazy, that Drenka's coming was for her remuneration enough—idiot! idiot!

Sabbath and Christa had met one night in 1989 when he'd given her a lift home. He saw her out on the shoulder of 144, wearing a tuxedo, and he circled back. If she had a knife, she had a knife—did it matter living a few years more or less? It was impossible to leave standing all alone on the side of the road with her thumb lifted a young blond girl in a tuxedo who looked like a young blond boy in a tuxedo.

She explained her outfit by saying she had been to a dance down in Athena, at the college, where you were to come wearing "something crazy." She was petite but hardly childlike—more a miniaturized woman, with a very crisp, self-confident air about her and a tightly held little mouth. The German accent was gentle but inflammatory (for Sabbath, any attractive woman's accent was inflammatory), the haircut was short as a Marine recruit's, and the tuxedo suggested that she was not without the inclination to play a provocative role in life. Otherwise the kid was all business: no sentiment, no longings, no illusions, no follies, and, he'd bet his life on it—he had—no taboos to speak of. Sabbath liked the cruel toughness, the shrewdness of the calculating, mistrustful little German mouth and saw the possibilities right off. Remote, but there. Admiringly he thought, Unbesmirched by selflessness, a budding beast of prey.

As he drove along he had been listening to a tape of Benny Goodman's *Live at Carnegie Hall*. He and Drenka had just parted for the night at the Bo-Peep, some twenty miles south on 144.

"Are they black?" the German girl asked.

"No. A few are black but mainly, Miss, they are white. White jazz musicians. Carnegie Hall in New York. The night of January 16, 1938."

"You were there?" she asked.

"Yes. I took my children, my little children. So they would be present at a musical milestone. Wanted them beside me the night that America changed forever."

Together they listened to "Honeysuckle Rose," Goodman's boys jamming with half a dozen members of the Basie band. "This is jumpin'," Sabbath told her. "This is what's called a foot mover. Keeps your feet movin'. . . . Hear that guitar back there? Notice how that rhythm section is driving them on? . . . Basie. Very lean piano playing. . . . Hear that guitar there? Carryin' this thing. . . . *That's* black music. You're hearin' black music now. . . . Now you're going to hear a riff. That's James. . . . Underneath all this is that steady rhythm section carrying this whole thing. . . . Freddie Green on guitar. . . . James. Always have the feeling he's tearing that instrument apart—you can hear it tear. . . . This figure they're just dreaming up—watch them build it now. . . . They're workin' their way into the ride-out. Here it comes. They're all tuned into each other. . . . They're off. They're *off*. . . . Well, what do you make of that?" Sabbath asked her.

"It's like the music in cartoons. You know, the cartoons for kids on TV?"

"Yes?" said Sabbath. "And it was thought to be hot stuff at the time. The innocent old ways of life—everywhere you look, except in our sleepy village here," he said, stroking his beard, "the world's at war against them. And you, what brings you to Madamaska Falls?" asked Father Time jovially. There is no other way to play it.

She told him about the tedium of her au pair job in New York, how by the second year she couldn't stand the child anymore, and so she had just picked up one day and run off. She had found Madamaska Falls by closing her eyes and putting her finger down on a map of the Northeast. Madamaska Falls wasn't even on the map, but she had got a ride as far as the traffic light by the green, stopped for a coffee at the gourmet shop, and, when she asked if there was any work around, a job materialized right there. For five months now the gentleman's sleepy village had been her home.

"You were escaping your job in New York with the kid."

"I was going crazy."

"What else are you escaping?" he asked, but lightly, lightly, probing not at all.

"Me? I'm not escaping anything. Just to get a taste of life. In Germany there is no adventure for me. I know everything and how it works. Here a lot of things happen to me that would never have happened to me back home."

"You don't get lonely?" asked the nice, concerned man.

"Sure. I get lonely. It's hard to make friendships with Americans."

"Is it?"

"In New York it is. Sure. They want to use you. In any possible way. That's the first idea that comes to their mind."

"I'm surprised to hear this. People in New York are worse than people in Germany? History would seem to some to tell a different story."

"Oh no, definitely. And cynical. In New York they keep their true motives to themselves and announce to you other motives."

"Young people?"

"No, mostly older than me. In their twenties."

"Did you get hurt?"

"Yeah. Yeah. But then they're very friendly—'Hi, how are you doing? It's very lovely to see you.'" She enjoyed her imitation of an American dope and he laughed appreciatively, too. "And you don't even *know* this person. Germany is very different," she told him. "Here there's all this friendliness—and it's fake. 'Hey, hi, how are you?' You have to. The American way. I was very naive when I came here. I was eighteen. I run into lots of people, strangers I don't know. I go out for coffee. You have to be naive when you come as a stranger. Of course you learn. You learn all right."

The trio—Benny, Krupa, Teddy Wilson's piano. "Body and Soul." Very dreamy, very danceable, just lovely, right down to the Krupa three-thump finale. Though Morty thought that Krupa's pyrotechnics were always ruining the damn thing. "Just let it *swing*," Morty would say. "Krupa is the worst thing that ever happened to Goodman. Too obtrusive," and Mickey would repeat this as his own opinion at school. Morty would say, "Benny's never shy about taking up half the piece," and Mickey would repeat that. "A beautiful clarinet player, nobody near him," and that, too, he repeated. . . . He wondered if it might not soften up this German girl, the late-night languor-inducing beat and that tactful, torchy something in Goodman's playing, and so for three minutes he said nothing to her and, to the seductive coherence of "Body and Soul," the two drove on through the dark of the wooded hills. Nobody else abroad. Also seductive. He could take her anywhere. He could turn at Shear Shop Corner and take her up to Battle Mountain and strangle her to death in her tuxedo. Painting by Otto Dix. Maybe not in congenial Germany but in cynical, exploitative America she was running a risk out on the road in that tuxedo. Or would have been, had she been picked up by one of those Americans rather more American than I.

"The Man I Love." Wilson playing Gershwin like Gershwin was Shostakovich. Uncanny eeriness of Hamp on the vibes. January 1938. I am almost nine, Morty is soon to be fourteen. Winter. McCabe Avenue beach. He is teaching me to throw the discus on the empty beach after school. Endless.

"May I ask how you got hurt?" said Sabbath.

"They're there for you if you're pretty and outgoing and smiling, but if you have any trouble, 'Come back when you're better.' I had very few true friends in New York. Most of them were just crap."

"Where did you meet these people?"

"Clubs. At night I go to clubs. To get away from the job. To get my mind on something else. Being with a kid all day . . . brrrr. I couldn't stand it, but it got me to New York. I would just go to clubs where people I know come."

"Clubs? I'm out of my element. What are clubs?"

"Well, I have one club I go to. I get in free. I get drinks, tickets. I don't have to worry about that, I just show up. I was going there for over a year. The same people come all the time. People you don't even know their names. They have club names. You never know what they're doing in the daytime."

"And they come to the club to do what?"

"To have a good time."

"Do they?"

"Sure. Where I go there are five different floors. The basement is reggae, and black people come there. The next floor is dance music, disco. Yuppies stay on the floor with the disco, people like that. And then there is techno, and then there is more techno—music made by a machine. It's a sound that just makes you dance. The lights can make you crazy. But that's because you get to feel the music very good. You dance. You dance for three, four hours."

"Whom do you dance with?"

"People just stand and dance by themselves. It's a meditation kind of thing. The big main scene is a mix of everybody, standing and dancing by themselves."

"Well, you can't dance by yourself to 'Sugarfoot Stomp.' Hear that?" said Sabbath, good-natured and grinning. "To 'Sugarfoot Stomp' you've got to dance the lindy and you've got to dance the lindy with somebody else. To this you must jitterbug, my dear."

"Yes," she said politely, "it's very beautiful." Respect for the aged. This callous girl has a sweet side after all.

"What about drugs—at the clubs?"

"Drugs? Yeah, it exists."

He'd fucked up with "Sugarfoot Stomp." Alienated her completely, managed even to arouse her repugnance by overplaying how unmenacing, unfrightening an old fuddy-duddy he was. And deprived her of the spotlight. But then this was a situation in which there was never really a right thing to do, except to remember to be tirelessly patient. If it takes a year, it takes a year. You've just got to bank on living one more year. This is the contact. Delight in that. Get her back to drugs, get her onto herself and the significance of her life in the clubs.

He turned off the tape. All she had to hear was Elman's klezmer trumpet oleaginizing "Bei Mir Bist Du Sheyn" and she'd leap from the moving car, even out in the middle of nowhere.

"What drugs? Which drugs?"

"Marijuana," she said. "Cocaine. They have this drug, heroin and cocaine mixed together, and they call it Special K. It's what the drag queens take to go really nuts. It's a lot of fun. They dance. They're fascinating. It's a gay scene, definitely. A lot of Hispanic. Puerto Rican guys. Lots of black men. A lot of them are young boys, nineteen, twenty. They lip-synch to some old song and they're all dressed up like Marilyn Monroe. You laugh a lot."

"How did *you* dress up?"

"I wore a black dress. Tight long dress. Low neck. A ring in my nose. Long jumbo eyelashes. Big platform shoes. Everybody's hugging each other and kissing each other and all you do is party and dance all night long. Go there at midnight. Stay till three.

That's the New York I knew. The America. That's all. I thought I should see more. So here I come."

"Because you were exploited. People exploited you."

"I don't want to talk about that. There was a whole thing that just broke down. Comes down to money. I thought I had a friend but I had a friend who was using me."

"Really? How terrible. Using you how?"

"Oh, I was working with her and she gave me half of the money I was supposed to have. And I'd been working for her a lot. I thought this was a girlfriend of mine. I said, 'You cheated me out of my money. How could you do this to me?' 'Oh, you found out?' she says. 'I'm not able to pay you back.' So I'll never talk to her again. But what can you expect? The American way. Next time I have to be ready."

"I'll say. How did you meet this person?"

"Through the club scene."

"Was it painful?"

"I felt so stupid."

"What were you doing? What was the work?"

"I was dancing in a club. My past."

"You're young to have a past."

"Oh yeah," she said, laughing loudly at her unmaidenly precocity, "I do have a past."

"A girl of twenty with a past. What's your name?"

"Christa."

"Mine is Mickey, but up here the boys call me Country."

"Hi, Country."

"Most girls of twenty," he said, "haven't begun to live."

"That's the American girls. I never made an American girl-friend. Guys, yeah."

"Is meeting women what the adventure is about?"

"Yes, I would like to meet girlfriends. But mostly it's older women. You know, mother kind of types. Which is okay with me. But girls my own age? Just doesn't work out. They're kids."

"So it's mother types for Christa."

"I guess," she said, laughing again.

At Shear Shop Corner he took the turn up to Battle Mountain. The voice counseling patience was having trouble being heard. *Mother kind of types.* He could not let her get away. He could never in his life let a new discovery get away. The core of seduction is persistence. Persistence, the Jesuit ideal. Eighty percent of women will yield under tremendous pressure if the pressure is *persistent.* You must devote yourself to fucking the way a monk devotes himself to God. Most men have to fit fucking in around the edges of what they define as more pressing concerns: the pursuit of money, power, politics, fashion, Christ knows what it might be—skiing. But Sabbath had simplified his life and fit the other concerns in around fucking. Nikki had run away from him, Roseanna was fed up with him, but all in all, for a man of his stature, he had been improbably successful. Ascetic Mickey Sabbath, at it still into his sixties. The Monk of Fucking. The Evangelist of Fornication. *Ad majorem Dei gloriam.*

"What was dancing in the club like?"

"It's like—what can you say? I liked it. It was something I had to do for my own curiosity. I don't know. I just have to do everything in life."

"How long did you do that?"

"Oh, I don't want to talk about it. I listen to advice from everybody, then I go out and do my own thing."

He stopped talking and on they drove. In that silence, in that darkness, every breath assumed its importance as that which kept you alive. His aims were clear. His dick was hard. He was on automatic pilot, excited, exultant, following behind his own headlights as though in a torch-led procession to the nocturnal moisture of the starry mountaintop, where celebrants were convening already for the wild worship of the stiff prick. Dress optional.

"Hey, are we lost?" she asked.

"No."

By the time they had ascended halfway up the mountain she could take her own silence no longer. Yep, played it perfectly. "I entertained more at private parties, if you want to know. Bachelor parties. For about a year. With my girlfriend. But then you go shopping together and spend all the money anyway. These girls who do this are very lonesome. They have a bitchy mouth because they've been through a lot. And I just look at them, and I say, 'Oh, my God, I'm too young, I gotta get out of this.' Because it was because of money that I did it. And I got cheated. But that's New York. Anyway, I needed a change. I want to spend my time doing something else, a job dealing with people. And I missed the nature. In Germany I was a child in a village till my parents got divorced. I miss the nature and all that's peaceful. There are more things in life than money. So I came to live here."

"And how is it here?"

"It's great. People turn out to be very friendly. Very nice. I don't feel a stranger here. Which is nice. In New York everywhere I go people try to pick me up. It happens all the time. That's what New Yorkers love to do. I tell them go away and they go away. I'm pretty good at handling the situation. The thing is, don't show fear. I'm not afraid of you. People in New York can get a little strange. But not here. I feel at home here. I like America now. I even do patchwork," she said, with a giggle. "*Me*. I'm a real American. I make quilts."

"How did you learn?"

"I read about it in books."

"Well, I love quilts. I collect quilts," said Sabbath. "I'd like to see yours someday. Would you sell me one?"

"Sell?" she said, laughing heartily now, laughing huskily, like a boozer twice her age. "Why not? Sure, I'll sell it, Country. It's your money."

And he erupted in laughter, too. "By God, we *are* lost!"—and he made a sharp U-turn and got her back to her place over the gourmet shop in fifteen minutes. All the way there they talked animatedly about their common interest. Unimaginable as it seemed, the gap was bridged—antipathy evaporates, affinity is established, a date is made. Quilts. The American way.

"Thank you," Drenka had said to Christa when it was time for the old couple to get up and get dressed and go home, "thank you," she said, her voice faintly tremulous, "thank you thank you thank you. . . ." She took Christa back into her arms and rocked her there like a baby. "Thank you thank you." Christa gently kissed each of Drenka's breasts. Her little mouth broke out in a warm, youthful smile when she cuddled closer to Drenka and, making big eyes, girlishly said, "A lot of straight women like it."

Though Sabbath had masterminded the evening and given Drenka the money she had demanded to participate, he'd found himself more or less superfluous from the moment Drenka knocked on the door and he let her into the attic room where he'd arrived early himself, thinking that it might be necessary, even after a month of delicate diplomacy, to continue negotiations right down to the wire. There was nothing small about this endeavor, and he was still not sure how reliable a person Christa was—she had not entirely cleansed herself in Madamaska Falls of her European suspicions, nor had Sabbath observed in her, as he hoped to, a single encouraging sign of the development of a more selfless point of view. "Drenka," he said when he opened the door to let her in, "this is my friend Christa," and though previously Drenka had seen Christa only through the window of the gourmet shop—strolled by a few times at Sabbath's suggestion—she walked directly across to where Christa was sitting on the second-hand couch in tight torn jeans and a sequined velvet jacket a shade of violet matching her eyes. Sinking to her knees on the bare floorboards, Drenka grabbed Christa's close-cropped head between her two hands and kissed her strongly on the mouth. The speed with which Drenka unbuttoned Christa's jacket and with which Christa undid Drenka's silk blouse and cleared aside her push-up bra astonished Sabbath. But Drenka's boldness always astonished him. He had imagined a warm-up would be required—talking and joking overseen by him, a heart-to-heart talk, maybe even a sympathetic look through Christa's boring quilts to put the two of them at their ease—when, in fact, the five hundred dollars in Drenka's purse had emboldened her, in her words, "to just go in like a whore and do it."

Afterward Drenka couldn't say enough wonderful things about

Christa. While Sabbath drove Drenka to where she'd parked behind Town Street, she snuggled adoringly into his side, kissing his
beard, licking his neck—she, the woman of forty-eight, as excited
as a child just home from the circus. "With a lesbian, there is
a sense of *love* that I received from her. Such great experience
she had in how to touch a woman's body. And the kissing! Her
knowledge of the female body, how to caress it, how to kiss it,
how to touch my skin and to make my nipples hard and to suck
my nipples, and that loving, giving, very sexual way, very like a
man, that kind of erotic vibration that she would deliver to me
made me so very hot. To know exactly how to touch my body in a
way almost *more* superior than sometimes men can know how to
do it. To find on my cunt the little button, and to hold it there
exactly the amount of time that was needed to make me come.
And when she started kissing me—you know, going down and
sucking me—the skill of the tongue pressure right on the right
place . . . oh, that was very exciting."

Up on the bed, only inches away, following every movement
like a medical student observing his first surgical procedure, he'd
had a good time too and once even been able to be of assistance
when Christa, her muscular tongue anchored between Drenka's
thighs, went groping around the sheets searching blindly for a vi-
brator. Earlier on, she had removed three of them from the bedside table—ivory-colored vibrators ranging in length from three
to six inches—and Sabbath was able to locate one for her, the
longest of them, and to place it, correctly oriented, into her out-
stretched hand. "So, you didn't need me at all," he said. "Oh, no.
I find it very wonderful and exciting to have another woman,
but," said Drenka, lying, as it would later turn out, "I wouldn't
want to have to do it alone with her. It couldn't turn me on. I have
to have the male penis there, the male excitement to urge me on.
But I do find very erotic a young woman's body, the beauty of it,
the round curves, the small breasts, the way she is shaped, and the
smell of it, and the softness of it, and then as I come down myself
to the cunt, I find the cunt actually quite beautiful. I never would
have thought that looking in the mirror. You come with your

shame to look at yourself and you look at your sexual organs and they are not acceptable from the aesthetic perspective. But in this setting, I can see the whole thing, and although it is a mystique that I am a part of, it's a mystery to me, a total mystery."

• • •

Drenka's grave was near the base of the hill about forty feet from a pre-Revolutionary stone wall and a row of enormous maples fencing off the cemetery from the blacktop that meandered over the mountaintop. In all these months, the headlights of maybe half a dozen rattling vehicles—pickup trucks from the sound of them—had flickered by while Sabbath grieved there over his loss. He had only to drop to his knees to be as invisible from the road as any of those buried around him, and often he was on his knees already. There had not yet been a single nighttime visitor to the cemetery other than himself—a remote rural graveyard eighteen hundred feet above sea level did not strike people, even in spring-time, as a place to come to roam around in after dark. Noises from beyond the cemetery—deer abounded on Battle Moun-tain—had seriously agitated Sabbath during his first months visit-ing the grave, and he was often quite sure that at the edge of his vision there was something darting among the tombstones, some-thing he believed was his mother.

In the beginning he hadn't known that he was to become a regular visitor. But then he hadn't imagined that, looking down at the plot, he would see through to Drenka, see her inside the coffin raising her dress to the stimulating latitude at which the tops of her stockings were joined to the suspenders of her garter belt, once again see that flesh of hers that reminded him always of the layer of cream at the top of the milk bottle when he was a child and Borden delivered. It was stupid not to have figured on car-nal thoughts. "Go down on me," she said to Sabbath. "Eat me, Country, the way Christa did," and Sabbath threw himself onto the grave, sobbing as he could not sob at the funeral.

Now that she was gone for good, it was incredible to Sabbath that not even when he was very much the crazy, cuntstruck lover, before Drenka became just an absorbing diversion there to have fun with, to fuck with, to plot and to scheme with, that not even back then had he thought to exchange the excruciating boredom of a drunk, de-eroticized Roseanna for marriage to someone whose affinity to him was unlike any woman's he had known outside a whorehouse. A conventional woman who would do anything. A respectable woman who was enough of a warrior to challenge his audacity with hers. There couldn't be a hundred such women in the entire country. Couldn't be fifty in all of America. And he'd had no idea. Never in thirteen years had he tired of looking down her blouse or looking up her skirt, and still he'd had no idea!

But now the thought undid him—no one would believe the scandalous town polluter, swinish Sabbath, to be susceptible to such a flood of straightforward feeling. He let go with a convulsive ardor that exceeded even her husband's on the icy November morning of the funeral. Young Matthew, wearing his trooper's uniform, betrayed no emotion other than hard-bitten rage mutely contained, the most violent of urges masterfully organized by a cop with a conscience. It was as though his mother had died not of a terrible disease but from an act of violence perpetrated by a psychopath he would go out and find and quietly take in, once the ceremony was over. Drenka had always wished that he could show the same admirable restraint as a son with his father that he did out on the road, where, to hear her tell it, he never got upset or lost control, whatever the provocation. Drenka ingenuously repeated to Sabbath, in Matthew's words, whatever Matthew boasted to her about himself. Her reveling in the boy's achievements was, to Sabbath, perhaps not the most beguiling thing about her, but it was far and away the most innocent. You wouldn't have thought—if you were yourself a guileless ingenue—that such extreme polarity in any one person was possible, but Sabbath, a great fan of human inconsistency, was often transfixed by how worshipful his taboo-free, thrill-seeking Drenka could be of the son who saw the impeccable enforcement of the law as the most serious thing in life, who no longer had any friends but cops—who, he explained to her, had become totally mistrustful of people who *weren't* cops. When he was still fresh out of the academy, Matthew used to tell his mother, "You know something, I have more power than the president. You know why? I can take people's rights away. Their rights of freedom. 'You're under arrest. You're pinched. Your freedom is gone.'" And it was a sense of responsibility to all this power that caused Matthew so assiduously to toe the line. "He never gets upset," his mother told Sabbath. "If there's another cop who is mouthing off, calling the suspect a this or a that, Matthew tells him, 'It's not worth it. You're going to get yourself in trouble. We're doing what we're supposed to do.' Last week they brought a guy in, he was kicking the cruiser and everything, and Matthew said, 'Let him do what he's going to do, he's pinched. What are we going to prove by screaming at him and swearing at him? This is all stuff he can bring up in court. It's just another reason for this guy to get out of what he's done wrong.' Matthew says they can swear, they can do whatever they want—they've got handcuffs on, he's in control of the situation, not them. Matthew says, 'He's trying to get me to lose control. There are cops who do lose control. They start screaming at them—and why, Ma? For what?' Matthew is just quiet and takes them in."

For Madamaska Falls, the crowd at the funeral had been huge. Aside from friends from town and the many past and present employees of the inn, there were, up from New York, in from Providence and Portsmouth and Boston, dozens of guests to whom Drenka had been the gracious, energetic hostess over the years—and among the guests were a number of men she had fucked. In the face of each the haggard look of loss and sorrow was clearly visible to Sabbath, who chose to observe them from the rear of the crowd. Which was Edward? Which was Thomas? Which was Patrick? That very tall guy must be Scott. And not far from where Sabbath was standing, also back as far from the coffin as he could get, was Barrett, the new young electrician from Blackwall, the shabby town just to the north that was home to five tough taverns and a state mental hospital. Sabbath had happened to pull in behind Barrett's pickup down in the crowded cemetery lot—across the truck's tailgate were painted the words "Barrett Electric Co. 'We'll fix your shorts.'"

Barrett, who wore his hair in a ponytail and sported a Mexican mustache, stood beside his pregnant wife. She was holding a bundle that was their tiny baby and weeping openly. Two mornings a week, when Mrs. Barrett drove down to the valley to her secretarial job with the insurance company, Drenka would drive up past the reservoir to Blackwall and take baths with Mrs. Barrett's husband. He didn't look at all well that day, maybe because his suit was tight or maybe because without a coat to wear he was freezing to death. He shifted from one long leg to the other constantly as though at the conclusion of the service he was in danger of being lynched. Barrett was Drenka's latest catch from among the workers making repairs around the inn. Last catch. A year younger than her son. He rarely spoke except when the bath was over, and then, with his hick enthusiasm, he would delight Drenka by telling her, "You are somethin', you are really somethin' else." Aside from the youth and the youthful body, what excited Drenka was that he was "a physical man." "He is not unhandsome," she told Sabbath. "He has this animal thing that I like. He is like I have a twenty-four-hour fucking service if I want it. His muscles are strong and his stomach is completely flat, and then he has this big dick, and he sweats a lot, there is all this sweat coming out of him, he is all red in his face, and he is like you, he is also, 'I don't want to come yet, Drenka, I don't want to come yet.' And then he says, 'Oh my God, I'm coming, I'm coming,' and then 'Ohhh. Ohhh,' those big sounds he makes. And the relief, it's like they collapse almost. And that he lives in a working-class environment and that I go there—all that adds to the excitement. A little apartment building with horrible horses on the walls. They have two rooms, and the taste is horrible. The other people there are attendants from the insane asylum. The bathroom has one of those old bathtubs that stand on the floor. And I say to him, 'Turn the bathtub on so I can take a bath.' I remember one time I came there at noon and I was very hungry and we were going to have a pizza. I undressed right away and I run to the bathtub. Yes, I think we get very hot in the bathtub, jerking him a little, you know. You can fuck in the bathtub, and we did, but then the water runs over. What I like is the *way* we are fucking, which is specific to him. He will sort of sit up and, because his prick is big, we sort of sit and fuck that way. We work very hard and there is a lot of sweating, a lot of physical movement, much more than I can think of with anyone else. I love to take baths *and* showers. Part of the excitement is the lathering. The soap. You start at the face and then the chest and the stomach and then you come down to the dick, and that gets big, or it is big already. And then you start to fuck. If you're standing in the shower, you stand up and fuck. Sometimes he will lift my legs up and he carries me like that in the shower. If it's in the bathtub, then I will tend to sit on top of him and fuck that way. Or I can bend over and he will fuck me. I love the bathtub, to fuck my stupid electrician there. I love it."

Her mistake was to take to Barrett the bad news. "You told me," he said, "you promised me—you weren't going to complicate everything, and here you go. I've got a baby to support, I've got a pregnant wife to look after. I got a new business to worry about, and one thing I don't need right now, from you, me, or anybody, is cancer."

Drenka phoned Sabbath and drove immediately to meet him at the Grotto. "You should never have told him," Sabbath said, seated on the granite outcropping and rocking her in his lap. "But," she said, crying pitifully, "we're lovers—I wanted him to know. I didn't know he was this *shit*." "Well, if you'd looked at it from the point of view of the pregnant wife, that might have occurred to you. You knew he was stupid. You liked that he was stupid. 'My stupid electrician.' It turned you on that he had this animal thing, lived in a horrible place, was stupid." "But I was talking to him about *cancer*. Even a *stupid* person—" "Shhh. Shhh. Not one, apparently, as stupid as Barrett."

Sabbath was completing his mourning—by scattering his seed across Drenka's oblong patch of Mother Earth—when the head-

lights of a car turned off the blacktop and into the wide gravel
drive where the hearses ordinarily entered the cemetery. The
headlights advanced waveringly and then they were out and the
quiet engine went dead. Zipping up his trousers, Sabbath scur-
ried, bent over, toward the nearest maple tree. There, on his
knees, he hid his white beard between the massive tree trunk and
the old stone wall. He could discern from the silhouette of the
car—more or less the shape and the size of a hearse—that it was a
limousine. And a figure was marching steadily up in the direction
of Drenka's grave, tall, in a large overcoat, and wearing what
looked to be high boots. He was guiding himself by the beam of a
flashlight that he kept switching on and off. In the hazy half-dark
of the moonlit cemetery he looked gigantic bounding forward
on those boots. He must have been expecting cold weather up
here. He must be from—it was the credit-card magnate! It was
Scott!

Six feet five inches tall. Scott Lewis. Five-foot two-inch Drenka
had smiled up at him in an elevator in Boston and asked if he
knew the correct time. It took only that. She used to sit on his dick
in the backseat of the limo while the driver took a slow tour of the
suburbs, driving sometimes past Lewis's own house. Scott Lewis
was one of those men who told Drenka that there was no other
woman like her in the world. Sabbath had heard him say it from
the telephone of the limousine.

"He is very interested in my body," she reported promptly to
Sabbath. "He wants to take photographs and he wants to look at
me and he wants to kiss me all the time. He is a big cunt licker—
and very tender." Yet, tender fellow that he was, the second evening she rendezvoused with him at a Boston hotel, a call girl
Lewis had ordered came knocking at their door only ten minutes
after Drenka's arrival. "What I didn't like about it," Drenka told
Sabbath on the phone the next morning, "was that I didn't have a
say in it, that it was just put upon me." "So what did you do
about it?" "I just had to make the best of it, Mickey. She comes to
the hotel room dressed like an upper-class whore. She pulls open
her bag and she has all these things in there. Do you want a little

maid's uniform? Do you want it Indian style? And then she takes out her dildos and she says, 'Do you like this or that?' And then, okay, now you start. But how do you get aroused by that? That was kind of hard even for me. Anyway, I guess we sort of got started. The idea was that the guy was more the voyeur. Interested in seeing how two women do it. He asked her mostly to go down on me. It all seemed to me so technical and cold, but I decided, okay, I'm going to be game for it. So eventually I did some work and I was able to get excited by it. But finally I fucked more Lewis—we two were fucking while she was just sort of in the picture somewhere. After he came, I started kissing her pussy, but it was very dry, though after a while she started moving a little bit and that then became sort of my mission. Could I make a whore hot? I think maybe I did to some extent, but it was hard to know if she wasn't just playing it. You know what she said to me? To *me?* She says, when we're all getting dressed, 'You're very hard to make come!' She was *angry*. 'The husbands want me to do this all the time'—she thought we were husband and wife—'but you took unusually hard work.' Husbands and wives are very common, Mickey. The whore said that's what she does all the time." "That's difficult for you to believe?" he asked. "You mean," she replied, laughing happily, "everybody is crazy like us?" "Crazier," Sabbath assured her, "much, much crazier."

Drenka called Lewis's erection "the rainbow" because, as she liked to explain, "His dick is rather long and sort of curved. And there is a little bend to it, to one side." On Sabbath's instruction she had traced its outline on a piece of paper—Sabbath still had the drawing somewhere, probably in among those dirty pictures of her that he had not been able to look at since her death. Lewis was the only one of her men other than Sabbath whom she had allowed to fuck her in the ass. He was that special. When Lewis had wanted to do it to the whore as well, the whore said sorry, that was where she drew the line.

Oh yes, the jolly time Drenka had with this guy's crooked dick! Infuriating! And yet, back when it was happening, Sabbath frequently had to slow her down while she was telling him her stories, had to remind her that nothing was too trivial to recount, no detail too minute to bring to his attention. He used to solicit this kind of talk from her, and she obeyed. Exciting to them both. His genital mate. His greatest pupil.

It had, however, taken him years to make Drenka a decent narrator of her adventures, since her inclination, in English at least, was to pile truncated sentences one on the other until he couldn't understand what she was talking about. But gradually, as she listened to him and talked to him, there was an ever-increasing correlation between all she was thinking and what she said. She certainly became syntactically more urbane than nine-tenths of the locals up on their mountain, even though her accent remained to the end remarkably juicy: *chave* for *have*, *cheart* for *heart*; at the conclusion of *stranger* and *danger*, a strong rolling *r*; and her *l*'s almost like a Russian's, emerging from a long way back in the mouth. The effect was of a delightful shadow cast on her words, making just a little mysterious the least mysterious utterance— phonetic seduction enthralling Sabbath all the more.

She was weakest at retaining idiomatic English but managed, right up to her death, to display a knack for turning the clichéd phrase, proverb, or platitude into an objet trouvé so entirely her own that Sabbath wouldn't have dreamed of intervening—indeed, some (such as "it takes two to tangle") he wound up adopting. Remembering the confidence with which she believed herself to be smoothly idiomatic, lovingly recalling from over all the years as many as he could of Drenka's malapropisms stripped him now of every defense, and once again he descended to the very pit of his sorrow: bear and grin it . . . his days are counted . . . a roof under my head . . . when the shithouse hit the fan . . . you can't compare apples and apples . . . the boy who cried "Woof!" . . . easy as a log . . . alive and cooking . . . you're pulling my leg out . . . I've got to get quacking . . . talk for yourself, Johnny . . . a closed and shut case . . . don't keep me in suspension . . . beating a dead whore . . . a little salt goes a long way . . . he thinks I'm a bottomless piss . . . let him eat his own medicine . . . the early bird is never late . . . his bark is worse than your cry . . . it took me for a loop . . . it's like bringing coals to the fireplace . . . I feel as though I've been run over by a ringer . . . I have a bone to grind with you . . . crime doesn't pay off . . . you can't teach an old dog to sit. . . . When she wanted Matija's dog to stop and wait at her side, instead of saying "Heel!" Drenka called out, "Foot!" And once when Drenka came up to Brick Furnace Road to spend an afternoon in the Sabbaths' bedroom—Roseanna was visiting her sister in Cambridge—though it was raining only lightly when she arrived, by the time they had eaten the sandwiches Sabbath had prepared and had smoked a joint and gotten into bed, the day had all but turned into a moonless night. An eerie black hour of silence passed and then the storm broke over their mountain—on the radio Sabbath later learned that a tornado had torn apart a trailer park only fifteen miles west of Madamaska Falls. When the turbulence overhead was most noisily dramatic, hammering down like artillery that had found its target in Sabbath's property, Drenka, clinging to him beneath the sheet, said to Sabbath in a woozy voice, "I hope there is a thunder catcher on this house." "I am the thunder catcher on this house," he assured her.

When Sabbath saw Lewis bending over the grave to place a bouquet on the plot, he thought, But she's mine! She belongs to me!

What Lewis did next was such an abomination that Sabbath reached crazily about in the dark for a rock or a stick with which to rush forth and beat the son of a bitch over the head. Lewis unzipped his fly and from his shorts extracted the erection whose outlined drawing Sabbath had retained in his files, he now remembered, under "Misc." He was a long time rocking back and forth, rocking and moaning, until at last he turned his face upward to the starry sky and a full, fervent basso profundo echoed across the hills. "Suck it, Drenka, suck me dry!"

Though it was not phosphorescent, enabling Sabbath visually to chart its course, though it was not sufficiently clotted or dense for him to hear it splatter to the ground even in that mountaintop silence, simply from the stillness of Lewis's silhouette and from the fact that his breathing was audible thirty feet away, Sabbath knew that the tall lover had just commingled his wad with the short one's. In the next moment Lewis had fallen to his knees and, before her grave, in a low tearful voice he was lovingly reciting, ". . . tits . . . tits . . . tits . . . tits. . . ."

Sabbath could endure only so much. A rock he'd kicked out from between the large, protuberant roots of the maple, a rock as big around as a bar of soap, he picked up and hurled in the direction of Drenka's grave. It clanged against a tombstone nearby, causing Lewis to leap to his feet and look frantically about. Then he ran down the hill to the waiting limo, whose engine immediately started up. The car backed out of the drive and into the road, and only then did the headlights come on and the limousine whiz away.

When he rushed across to Drenka's grave, Sabbath saw that Lewis's bouquet was huge, containing perhaps as many as four dozen flowers. The only ones he could recognize, with the aid of his flashlight, were the roses and the carnations. He didn't know any of the others by name, despite all those summers of Drenka's tutoring. Kneeling down, he gathered up the bouquet by its bulky bundle of stems and clutched it to his chest as he started along the dirt path toward the highway and his car. At first he imagined that the bouquet was wet from the shop, where the flowers would have been kept fresh in vases of water, but then the texture made him understand what, of course, the wet substance was. The flowers were drenched with it. His hands were covered with it. So was the chest of the dirty old hunting jacket with the enormous pockets in which he used to carry puppets down to the college before the scandal with Kathy Goolsbee.

Drenka had once told Sabbath that after her marriage, when, within their first year as émigrés, Matija grew depressed and lost all interest in fucking her, she was so desolated that she went to a doctor in Toronto, where they lived briefly after fleeing Yugoslavia, and asked him how many times a husband was supposed to do it with a wife. The doctor asked her what she thought a reasonable expectation might be. Without even stopping to think, the young bride replied, "Oh, about four times a day." The doctor asked where a working couple was to find the time that would take, other perhaps than on the weekend. She explained, her fingers doing the calculating, "You do it once about three in the morning when sometimes you hardly know you do it. You do it at seven when you wake up. You do it when you come home from work and before you sleep. You can even do it two times before you go to sleep."

Why this story had come to him as he cautiously descended the dark cemetery hill—the bespattered flowers still clutched in his hands—was because of that triumphant Friday, only seventy-two hours after Matija's Rotary speech, when she had ended the day—not the week, the day—awash with the sperm of four men. "Nobody can accuse you, Drenka, of being timid in the face of your fantasies. Four," he said. "Well, I'd be honored to be numbered among them should there ever be a next time." He found, on hearing this story, not merely his desire inflamed but his veneration, too—there *was* something great about it: something heroic. This shortish woman a little on the plump side, darkly pretty but with an oddly damaged-looking nose, this refugee who knew hardly anything of the world beyond her schoolgirl Split (pop. 99,462) and the picturesque New England village of Mada-maska Falls (pop. 1,109), seemed to Sabbath *a woman of serious importance.*

"It was the time I went to Boston," she told him, "to see my dermatologist. That was very exciting. You sit in the doctor's office and you know you're his mistress and he's turned on and he shows you he has a big hard-on right in the examination room, and he takes it out and he fucked me right there. During the appointment. I used to go years ago to fuck him in his office on Saturdays. And he was a good fuck. And anyway from there I went to the credit-card magnate, the Lewis guy. And it was excit-ing that another man was waiting, that I could turn another guy on. Maybe I felt strong about that, to be able to seduce more than one man. Lewis fucked me and came inside me. That made me feel good. Nobody knows it but I. I am a woman walking around who has this sperm from two guys. The third guy was the dean, that college guy who stayed at the inn with his wife. His wife was in Europe so I was having dinner with him. I didn't know him—that was the first time. You want me to be really blunt about the whole thing? I discovered that I had got my period. I'd met him when we have our cocktail party for the guests. He stood next to me and he had pushed his arms onto my nipples. And he told me that he had a big hard-on, and I could almost see it. A dean at a college—this is the way we were talking at the cocktail party. Those kind of settings are what turn me on, when you do it in public, but secretly in public. So he had prepared this elaborate dinner. We were both very passionate but very shy at the same time or nervous about it. We ate in their dining room and I was answering his questions about my childhood under Communism and eventually we went upstairs, and he was sort of a strong guy and he held me and he really almost crushed my ribs. He had unbelievable manners. Maybe he was shy and frightened. He said, 'Well, we don't have to do anything if you don't want to.' I was a little hesitant because by now I had my period but I wanted to fuck him, so I went into the bathroom and took out my tampon. We started undressing and it was all very hot and very exciting. A tall guy, very strong, and he said many beautiful words. I was very excited and wanted to know the size his dick was. So when we finally undressed I was disappointed that he seemed to have a very small dick. I don't know if he was frightened of me so he couldn't really get it up. Then I said, 'Well, I have my period,' and he said, 'That doesn't matter.' I said, 'Let me go and get a towel.' So we put a towel down on the bed and we really went into it. He was doing everything with me. He couldn't really get a very good hard-on. I worked hard on getting him to have a hard-on but I think he was scared. He was frightened about me, that I was so free. That's what I sensed—that he was a bit overwhelmed. Though he did actually come three times." "Without a hard-on. *And* overwhelmed. Quite a feat," noted Sabbath. "It was a small hard-on," she explained. "How did he come? You sucked him?" "No, no, he came inside me, actually. And he sucked me even though I was bleeding all over the place. So that was a big mess, a lot of fucking and a lot of blood coming out. The fact that there was the blood—there was an added drama to it. A lot of juice and grease—it's not grease; how do I describe it? It's thick liquid, body fluids that were mixed in together. And after it's all finished and we get up—you get up, and what do you do, you don't know this person, and you're a little embarrassed, and we're stuck with this towel." "Describe the towel." "It was a white towel. And it was not completely red. The size of a bath towel. There were enormous spots. If I would wring it, it would come out, blood from it. It was like juice, a juicy liquid. But it wasn't that the whole thing was completely red, by any means. There were big, big spots on it, and it was very heavy. It's a definite—not an alibi; how do you say it in English? The opposite of that?" "Evidence?" "Yes, it's evidence of the crime. So we were discussing it and he said, 'Well, what can I do with this?' And he stood there, this tall man, this strong man, holding this towel like a child. A little embarrassed, but not wanting to show that to me. And I didn't want to be crimelike, I didn't want to pretend, 'Oh, this is a bad thing.' This was natural to me to do it, so I wanted to be cool about it. He said, 'I can't let the maid wash it and I can't throw it in the hamper. I guess I have to throw it out. But where can I throw it?' and I said, 'I'll take it.' And the relief on his face was enormous. And I put it in a plastic bag and I took it with me, this wet bundle, in a shopping bag. So he was very happy and then I drove home, and I put it into the washing. And it came out clean. And then of course he called me the next day and he said, 'Dear Drenka, this was certainly very dramatic,' and I said, 'Well, I have the towel and it's clean. Do you want it back?' and he said, 'No, thank you.' He didn't want the towel back and I guess his wife never found out about it." "And so who is the fourth you fucked that day?" "Well, I came home and I went down to the basement and threw the towel into the machine and then I came upstairs and Matija wants me to perform my marital duty at midnight. He sees me going naked into the shower and it excites him. This is something I have to do, so I do it. Thank God it's not often." "And so how does it feel after four men?" "Well, Matija fell asleep. I guess I felt very chaotic, if you really want to know. I think it is very taxing to do that. I had done three before, a number of times, but never four. Sexually it was very—very defiant and somehow exciting, even if the fourth was Maté. And maybe slightly perverse in a way. Part of me enormously enjoyed that. But in terms of what I really felt—I couldn't sleep, Mickey; it made me feel unsettled, restless, and it made me feel I did not know to whom I belong. I kept thinking of you, and that helped, but that was a high price to pay for it, all that confusion. If I could take the confusion away, how do you say—extrapolate it?—and make it just a sexual thing, I think that it's an exciting thing to do." "The most exciting ever, Donna Giovanna?" "Oh, my God," she said, laughing heartily, "I don't know about that. Let me think." "Yes, think. Il catalogo." "Oh, in the past, maybe thirty years ago, maybe more, I would go on a train, for example, through Europe, and do it with the train conductor. You know, it was pre-AIDS time. Yes, the Italian train conductor." "Where do you do it with a train conductor?" She shrugged. "You find a compartment that isn't busy." "Is that true?" Laughing again, she said, "Yes. True." "Were you married?" "No, no, this is when I worked a year in Zagreb. I guess he would come in the train car, a little good-looking Italian guy who speaks Italian, and you know, they're sexy, and maybe my friends, we're having a party or something like that—I can't remember who initiates what. No, I did it. I sold him cigarettes. It was expensive to travel in Italy and so you take with you something to sell. You buy it cheaply in Yugoslavia. Cigarettes were inexpensive. And Italians would buy out these cigarettes. They had the names of rivers, the Yugoslav cigarettes. Drina. Morava. Ibar. Yes, they were then all words of rivers. You make twice as much, maybe three times as much as you paid, so I sold him cigarettes. That's how it started. When I was working in Zagreb that year after high school, I loved to be fucked. It made me feel very, very good to have my cunt full of sperm, of come, it was a wonderful, maybe a powerful feeling. Whoever was the boyfriend, you would go to work that next day knowing you had been well fucked and you're all wet and the pants were wet and you walked around wet—I enjoyed that. And I remember I knew this older guy. He was a retired gynecologist and somehow we were talking about this and he thought it was very healthy to keep the come in the cunt after you had fucked, and I agreed with him. This turned him on. But it was no use. He was too old. I was curious to do it with a very old man, but he was already seventy and it was a closed and shut case."

When Sabbath reached his car, he walked beyond it some twenty feet along the hiking trail into the woods and there he hurled the bouquet into the dark mass of the trees. Then he did something strange, strange even for a strange man like him, who believed himself inured to the limitless contradictions that enshroud us in life. Because of his strangeness most people couldn't stand him. Imagine then if someone had happened upon him that night, in the woods a quarter mile down from the cemetery, licking from his fingers Lewis's sperm and, beneath the full moon, chanting aloud, "I am Drenka! I am Drenka!"

Something horrible is happening to Sabbath.

BUT HORRIBLE THINGS are happening to people all the time. The next morning Sabbath learned about Lincoln Gelman's suicide. Linc had been the producer of Sabbath's Indecent Theater (and the Bowery Basement Players) during those few years in the fifties and early sixties when Sabbath had amassed his little audience on the Lower East Side. After Nikki's disappearance, he had stayed a week with the Gelmans in their big Bronxville house.

Norman Cowan, Linc's partner, called with the news. Norman was the subdued member of the duo, if not the office's imaginative spearhead then its levelheaded guardian against Linc's overreaching. He was Linc's equilibrium. In any discussion, even of the location of the men's room down the hall, he could come to the point in about one-twentieth of the time that Linc liked to take to explain things to people. The educated son of a venal Jersey City jukebox distributor, Norman had shaped himself into a precise and canny businessman exuding the aura of quiet strength that lean, tall, prematurely balding men often appear to possess, particularly when they come, as Norman did, scrupulously attired in gray pinstripes.

"His death," Norman confided, "was a relief to many. Most of the people we're lining up to speak at the funeral haven't seen him in five years."

Sabbath hadn't seen him in thirty.

"These are all current business associates, close Manhattan

friends. But they couldn't see him. Linc was impossible to be with—depressed, obsessive, trembling, frightened."

"How long was he like that?"

"Seven years ago he fell into a depression. He never again had a painless day. A painless *hour*. We carried him in the office for five years. He'd just float around with a contract in his hand, saying, 'Are we sure this is all right? Are we sure this isn't illegal?' The last two years he's been at home. A year and a half ago, Enid couldn't take it any longer and they found an apartment for Linc around the corner and Enid furnished it and he lived there. A housekeeper came every day to feed him and to clean up. I would try to get over once a week, but I had to force myself. It was awful. He would sit and listen to you and then sigh and shake his head and say, 'You don't know, you don't know. . . .' For years now that's all I heard him say."

"You don't know what?"

"The dread. The anguish. Unceasing. No medication helped. His bedroom looked like a pharmacy, but not a single drug worked. They all made him sick. He hallucinated on the Prozac. He hallucinated on the Wellbutrin. Then they started giving him amphetamines—Dexedrine. For two days it looked as though something was happening. Then the vomiting began. All he ever got were the side effects. Hospitalization didn't work, either. He was hospitalized three months, and when they sent him home they said he was no longer suicidal."

His drive, his gusto, his pep, his speediness, his effectiveness, his diligence, his loquacious joking, someone—Sabbath remembered—wholly at one with his time and place, a highly adapted New Yorker tailor-made for that frenetic reality and oozing with the passion to live, to succeed, to have fun. His sentiments transported tears to his eyes too easily for Sabbath's taste, he talked rapidly in a flood of words that revealed how strong the compulsions were that fueled his hyperdynamism, but his life *was* a solid achievement, full of aim and purpose and the delight of being the energizer of others. *And then life took a turn and never righted itself. Everything vanished. The irrational overturned everything.* "Something specific set it off?" Sabbath asked.

"People come apart. And aging doesn't help. I know a number of men our age, right here in Manhattan, clients, friends, who've been going through crises like this. Some shock just undoes them around sixty—the plates shift and the earth starts shaking and all the pictures fall off the wall. I had my bout last summer."

"You? Hard to believe about you."

"I'm still on Prozac. I had the whole thing—fortunately the abridged version. Ask why and I couldn't tell you. I just stopped sleeping at some point and then, a couple of weeks later, the depression descended—the fear, the trembling, the suicide thoughts. I was going to buy a gun and blow the top of my head off. Six weeks until the Prozac kicked in. On top of that, it happens not to be a dick-friendly drug, at least for me. I'm on it eight months. I don't remember what a hard-on feels like. But at this age it's an up-and-down affair anyway. I got out alive. Linc didn't. He got worse and worse."

"Could it have been something other than just depression?"

"Just depression's enough."

But Sabbath knew as much. His mother had never gone ahead to take her life, but then, for fifty years after losing Morty, she had no life to take. In 1946, at seventeen, when, instead of waiting a year to be drafted, Sabbath went to sea only weeks after graduating high school, he was motivated as much by his need to escape his mother's tyrannical gloom—and his father's pathetic brokenness—as by an unsatisfied longing that had been gathering force in him since masturbation had all but taken charge of his life, a dream that overflowed in scenarios of perversity and excess but that he now, in a seaman's suit, was to encounter thigh-to-thigh, mouth-to-mouth, face-to-face: the worldwide world of whoredom, the tens of thousands of whores who worked the docks and the portside saloons wherever ships made anchor, flesh of every pigmentation to furnish every conceivable pleasure, whores who in their substandard Portuguese, French, and Spanish spoke the scatological vernacular of the gutter.

"They wanted to give Linc electric shock treatment but he was too frightened and he refused. It might have helped, but whenever it was suggested, he curled up in a corner and cried. Whenever he saw Enid he broke down. Called her, 'Mommy, Mommy, Mommy.' Sure, Linc was one of the great Jewish criers—they play the national anthem out at Shea and he cries, he sees the Lincoln Memorial and he cries, we take our boys up to Cooperstown and there's Babe Ruth's mitt and Linc starts crying. But this was something else. This was not crying, this was bursting. This was bursting under the pressure of unspeakable pain. And in that bursting there wasn't anything of the man I knew or you knew. By the time he died, the Linc we'd known had been dead for seven years."

"The funeral?"

"Riverside Chapel, tomorrow. Two P.M. Amsterdam and 76th. You'll see some old faces."

"Won't see Linc's."

"Can, actually, if you want to. Somebody has to identify the body before the cremation. The law in New York. I'm doing it. Come along when they open the coffin. You'll see what happened to our friend. He looked a hundred years old. His hair completely white and his face just a terrified, tiny thing. One of those skulls the savages shrink."

"I don't know," Sabbath replied, "that I can make it tomorrow."

"If you can't, you can't. I thought you should know before you read about it in the papers. In the papers the cause of death will be a heart attack—that's the cause the family prefers. Enid wouldn't have an autopsy. Linc was dead some thirteen or fourteen hours before he was found. Dead in his bed, the story goes. But the housekeeper tells a different story. I think by now Enid has come to believe her own. All along she honestly expected him to get better. She was sure of it down to the end, even though he had already slashed his wrists ten months ago."

"Look, thanks for remembering me—thanks for calling."

"People remember you, Mickey. A lot of people remember you with great admiration. One of the people Linc got teary about was you. I mean back when he was still himself. He never thought it was a great idea to take a talent like yours out to the boondocks. He loved your theater—he thought you were a magician. 'Why did Mickey do it?' He thought you never should have left to live up there. He talked about that often."

"Well, that's all long ago."

"You should know that Linc never for a moment considered you responsible in any way for Nikki's disappearance. I certainly didn't—and don't. The fucking well poisoners—"

"Well, the well poisoners were right and you boys were wrong."

"Standard Sabbath perversity. You can't believe that. Nikki was doomed. Tremendously gifted, extremely pretty, but so frail, so needy, so neurotic and fucked-up. No *way* that girl would ever hold together, none."

"Sorry, can't make it tomorrow," and Sabbath hung up.

◆ ◆ ◆

Roseanna's uniform these days was a Levi's jacket and washed-out jeans as narrow as her cranelike legs, and recently Hal in Athena had cut her hair so short that at breakfast that morning Sabbath intermittently kept imagining his be-denimed wife as one of Hal's pretty young homosexual friends from the college. But then, even with shoulder-length hair she'd emanated the tomboy-ish aura; ever since adolescence she'd had it—flat-chested and tall, with a striding gait and a way of cocking her chin when she spoke that had its appeal for Sabbath well before the disappearance of his fragile Ophelia. Roseanna looked to belong to another group of Shakespearean heroines entirely—to the saucy, robust, realistic circle of girls like Miranda and Rosalind. And she wore no more makeup than Rosalind did attired like a boy in the Forest of Arden. Her hair was still its engaging golden brown and, even clipped short, had a soft, feathery sheen that invited touching. The face was an oval, a wide oval, and there was a carved configu-ration to her small upturned nose and her wide, full, unboyishly seductive mouth, a hammered-and-chiseled look that, when she was younger, gave the fairy-tale illusion of a puppet infused with life. Now that she was no longer drinking, Sabbath saw traces in the modeling of Roseanna's face of the lovely child she must have been before her mother left and the father all but destroyed her. She was not only thinner by far than her husband but a head taller, and what with daily jogging and the hormone replacement therapy, she looked—on those rare occasions when the two of them were out together—less a fifty-six-year-old wife than an anorexic daughter.

What did Roseanna hate most about Sabbath? What did Sabbath hate most about her? Well, the provocations changed with the years. For a long time she hated him for refusing even to consider having a child, and he hated her for incessantly yammering on the phone to her sister, Ella, about her "biological clock." Finally he had grabbed the phone away from her to communicate directly to Ella the degree to which he found their conversation offensive. "Surely," he told her, "Yahweh did not go to the trouble of giving me this big dick to assuage a concern as petty as your sister's!" Once her childbearing years were behind her, Roseanna was able better to pinpoint her hatred and to despise him for the simple fact that he existed, more or less in the same way that he despised *her* for existing. In addition was the predictable bread-and-butter stuff: she hated the unthinking way he brushed the crumbs onto the floor after cleaning the kitchen table, and he hated her unamusing goy humor. She hated the conglomeration of army-navy surplus he had been wearing for clothing ever since high school, and he hated that, for as long as he'd known her, she would never, even during the adulterous phase of glorious abandon, graciously swallow his come. She hated that he hadn't touched her in bed for ten years and he hated the unruffled monotone in which she spoke to her local friends on the phone—and he hated the friends, do-gooders gaga over the environment or ex-drunks in AA. Each winter the town road crew went around cutting down 150-year-old maple trees that lined the dirt roads, and each year the maple-tree lovers of Madamaska Falls lodged a petition of protest with the first selectman, and then the next year the road crew, claiming the maples were dead or diseased, would clear another sylvan lane of ancient trees and thereby pick up enough dough—by selling the logs for firewood—to keep themselves in cigarettes, porn videos, and booze. She despised his inexhaustible bitterness about his career the way he had despised her drinking—how she would be drunk and argumentative in public places and, whether at home or out, speak in an aggressively loud and insulting voice. And now that she was sober he hated her AA slogans and the way of talking she had picked up from AA meetings or from her abused women's group, where poor Roseanna was the only one who'd never been battered by a husband. Sometimes when they argued and she felt swamped Roseanna claimed Sabbath was "verbally" abusing her, but that didn't count for much with her group of predominantly uneducated rural women, who'd had their teeth knocked out or chairs broken over their heads or cigarettes held to their buttocks and breasts. And those words she used! "And afterward there was a discussion and we shared about that particular step. . . ." "I haven't shared that many times yet. . . ." "Many people shared last night. . . ." What he loathed the way good people loathe *fuck* was *sharing*. He didn't own a gun, even out on the lonely hill where they lived, because he didn't want a gun in a house with a wife who spoke daily of "sharing." She hated that he was always bolting out the door without explanation, always leaving at all hours of the day and night, and he hated that artificial laugh of hers that hid both so much and so little, that laugh that was sometimes a bray, sometimes a howl, sometimes a cackle but that never rang with genuine pleasure. She hated his self-absorption and the outbursts about the arthritic joints that had ruined his career, and she hated him, of course, for the Kathy Goolsbee scandal, though had it not been for the breakdown brought on by the disgrace of it she would never have been hospitalized and begun her recovery. And she hated that, because of the arthritis, because of the scandal, because of his being the superior, impossible failure that he was, he earned not a penny and she alone was the breadwinner, but then Sabbath hated that too—that was one of their few points of agreement. They each found it repellent to catch even a glimpse of the other unclothed: she hated his increasing girth, his drooping scrotum, his apish hairy shoulders, his white, stupid biblical beard, and he hated the jogger's skinny titlessness—ribs, pelvis, sternum, everything that in Drenka was so softly upholstered, skeletonized as on a famine victim. They had remained in the house together all these years because she was so busy drinking that she didn't know what was going on and because he had found Drenka. That had made for a very solid union.

Driving home from her job at the high school, Roseanna used to think about nothing but the first glass of chardonnay when she hit the kitchen, a second and third glass while she prepared dinner, a fourth with him when he came in from the studio, a fifth with dinner, a sixth when he went back to his studio with his dessert, and then, the rest of the evening, another bottle all for herself. As often as not, she woke up in the morning as her father used to—still dressed—and in the living room, where the night before she had stretched out on the sofa, glass in hand, the bottle beside her on the floor, to watch the flames in the fireplace. In the mornings, dreadfully hung over, feeling bloated, sweating, full of shame and self-loathing, she never exchanged a word with him, and rarely did they have their coffee together. He took his to the studio and they did not see each other again until dinnertime, when the ritual began anew. At night, though, everybody was happy, Roseanna with her chardonnay and Sabbath off in the car somewhere, going down on Drenka.

Since her "coming into recovery," all had changed. Now seven nights a week, directly after dinner, she drove off to an AA meeting from which she returned around ten with her clothes stinking of cigarette smoke and her mood decisively serene. Monday evenings there was an open discussion meeting in Athena. Tuesday evenings there was a step meeting in Cumberland, her home group, where she had recently celebrated the fourth anniversary of her sobriety. Wednesday evenings there was a step meeting in Blackwall. She didn't like that meeting much—tough-guy workers and mental hospital attendants from Blackwall who were so aggressive, angry, and obscene that it made Roseanna, who'd lived until she was thirteen in academic Cambridge, very nervous;

but, despite all the angry guys screaming at one another, she went because it was the only Wednesday meeting within fifty miles of Madamaska Falls. Thursdays she went to a closed speaker meeting in Cumberland. Fridays to another step meeting, this one in Mount Kendall. And Saturdays and Sundays there were meetings in both the afternoon—in Athena—and the evening—in Cumberland—and she went to all four. Generally an alcoholic would tell his or her story and then they would choose a discussion topic such as "Honesty" or "Humility" or "Sobriety." "Part of the recovery principle," she told him, whether he wished to listen or not, "is that you try to become honest with yourself. We talked a lot about that tonight. To find out what feels comfortable within yourself." He also didn't own a gun because of the word *comfortable*. "Isn't it tedious feeling so 'comfortable'? Don't you miss all the discomforts of home?" "I haven't found it so yet. Sure, there are drunkalogs where you fall asleep when you listen to them. But what happens with the story format," she went on, oblivious not merely to his sarcasm but to the look in his eyes of someone who had taken too many sedative pills, "is that you can identify. 'I can identify with that.' I can identify with the woman who didn't drink in bars but sat secretly drinking at home at night and had similar sorts of suffering, and that's a very comfortable sort of feeling for me. I'm not unique, and somebody else can understand where I'm coming from. People that have long sobriety, that have this aura of inner peace and spirituality—that makes them appealing. Just to sit with them is something. They seem to be at peace with life. That's inspiring. You can get hope from that." "Sorry," mumbled Sabbath, hoping himself to deal her soberalog a deathblow, "can't identify." "That we know," said Roseanna, undaunted, and continued speaking her mind now that she was no longer his drunk. "You hear people at meetings say over and over that their family is what exacerbates everything. At AA you have a more neutral family that is, paradoxically, more loving, more understanding, less judgmental than your own family. And we don't interrupt each other, which is also different from at home. We call that cross-talk. We don't use cross-talk. *And* we don't tune out. One person talks and everybody listens until he or she is finished. We have to learn not just about our problems but how to listen and to be attentive." "And is the only way to get off the booze to learn to talk like a second grader?" "As an active alcoholic I compromised myself so horribly hiding alcohol, hiding the disease, hiding the behavior. You *have* to start all over, yes. If I sound like a second grader, that's fine with me. You're as sick as your secrets." It was not for the first time that he was hearing this pointless, shallow, idiotic maxim. "Wrong," he told her—as if it really mattered to him what she said or he said or anyone said, as if with their mouthings any of them approached even the borderline of truth—"you're as adventurous as your secrets, as abhorrent as your secrets, as lonely as your secrets, as alluring as your secrets, as courageous as your secrets, as vacuous as your secrets, as lost as your secrets; you are as human as—" "No. You're as unhuman, inhuman, and sick. It's the secrets that prevent you from sitting right with your internal being. You can't have secrets," she told Sabbath firmly, "and achieve internal peace." "Well, since manufacturing secrets is mankind's leading industry, that takes care of internal peace." No longer so serene as she would have liked to be, glaring at her beast with the old engulfing hatred, she went off to immerse herself in one of her AA pamphlets while he returned to his studio to read yet another book about death. That's all he did there now, read book after book about death, graves, burial, cremation, funerals, funerary architecture, funeral inscriptions, about attitudes toward death over the centuries, and how-to books dating back to Marcus Aurelius about the art of dying. That very evening he read about *la mort de toi,* something with which he had already a share of familiarity and with which he was destined to have more. "Thus far," he read, "we have illustrated two attitudes toward death. The first, the oldest, the longest held, and the most common one, is the familiar resignation to the collective destiny of the species and can be summarized by the phrase, *Et moriemur,* and we shall all die. The second, which appeared in the twelfth century, reveals the importance given throughout the entire modern period to the self, to one's own existence, and can be expressed by another phrase, *la mort de soi,* one's own death. Beginning with the eighteenth century, man in western societies tended to give death a new meaning. He exalted it, dramatized it, and thought of it as disquieting and greedy. But he already was less concerned with his own death than with *la mort de toi,* the death of the other person. . . ."

If they ever happened to be together on a weekend, walking along the half mile of Town Street, Roseanna had a hello for just about everybody passing or driving by—old ladies, delivery boys, farmers, *everyone.* One day she even waved to Christa, of all people, who was standing in the window of the gourmet shop sipping a cup of coffee. Drenka and his Christa! The same happened when they went to see a doctor or the dentist down in the valley—she knew everybody there, too, from the meetings. "Was the whole county drunk?" Sabbath asked. "Whole country's more like it," Roseanna replied. One day in Cumberland she confided that the elderly man who'd just nodded at her when he passed by had been a deputy secretary of state under Reagan—he always came early to meetings so as to make the coffee and put out the cookies for the snack. And whenever she went up to Cambridge to visit Ella overnight—great days, those, for Sabbath and Drenka—she'd return ecstatic about the meeting there, a women's meeting. "They fascinate me. I'm amazed how competent they seem to be, how accomplished, how self-assured, how well they look. Adjusted. They're really an inspiration. I go in there and I don't know anybody and they ask, 'Anybody from outside?' and I raise my hand and I say, 'I'm Roseanna from Madamaska Falls.' Everybody claps and then if I have a chance to talk, I talk about whatever is on my mind. I tell them about my childhood in Cambridge. About my mother and father and what happened. And they listen. These terrific women listen. The sense of love that I experience, the sense of understanding of my suffering, the sense of great sympathy and empathy. And *accepting.*" "*I* understand your suffering. *I* have sympathy. *I* have empathy. *I'm* accepting." "Oh, yeah, sometimes you ask how did your meeting go, that's true. I can't talk to *you,* Mickey. You wouldn't understand—you *couldn't* understand. You can't begin to understand it innately, and so it becomes boring and silly to you. Something more to satirize." "My satire is my sickness." "I think you liked it better when I was an active drunk," she said. "You enjoyed the superiority. As if you're not superior enough, you could look down on me for that, too. I could be responsible for all your disappointments. Your life had been ruined by this fucking disgusting falling-down drunk. One guy the other night was talking about how degraded he became as an alcoholic. He was living then in Troy, New York. On the streets. They, the other drunks, just stuck him in a garbage pail and he couldn't get out of the garbage pail. He sat there for hours and people would walk by on the streets and wouldn't care about this human being who was sitting there with his legs scrunched up, in a garbage pail, and who couldn't get out. And that's what I was for you when I was drinking. In a garbage pail." "I can identify with that," Sabbath said.

Now that she was four years out of the garbage pail, why did she go on with him? Sabbath was surprised by how long it was taking Barbara, the therapist in the valley, to get Roseanna to find the strength to strike out on her own like the competent, accomplished, self-assured women in Cambridge who showered her with so much sympathy for her suffering. But then her problem with Sabbath, the "enslavement," stemmed, according to Barbara, from her disastrous history with an emotionally irresponsible mother and a violent alcoholic father for *both* of whom Sabbath was the sadistic doppelgänger. Her father, Cavanaugh, a geology professor at Harvard, had raised Roseanna and Ella after their mother could stand his drinking and his bullying no longer and, in terror of him, abandoned the family to run off to Paris with a visiting professor of Romance languages to whom she remained quite miserably bandaged for five long years before returning alone to Boston, her own birthplace, when Roseanna was thirteen and Ella eleven. She wanted the girls to come live on Bay State Road with her, and shortly after they decided that they would and left their father—of whom they, too, were terrified—and his new second wife, who couldn't stand Roseanna, he hanged himself in the attic of their Cambridge house. And this explained to Roseanna what she was doing all these years with Sabbath, to whose "domineering narcissism" she had been no less addicted than to alcohol.

These connections—between the mother, the father, and him—were far clearer to Barbara than they were to Sabbath; if there was, as she liked to put it, a "pattern" in it all, the pattern eluded him.

"And the pattern in *your* life," Roseanna asked, angrily, "that eludes you, too? Deny till you're red in the face, but it's there, it's *there*."

"Deny *it*. The verb is transitive, or used to be before the eloquence of the blockheads was loosed upon the land. As for the 'pattern' governing a life, tell Barbara it's commonly called chaos."

"Nikki was a helpless child you could dominate and I was a drunk looking for a savior, who thrived on degradation. Is that not a pattern?"

"A pattern is what is printed on a piece of cloth. We are not cloth."

"But I *was* looking for a savior, and I *did* thrive on degradation. I thought I had it coming to me. Everything in my life was frenzy and noise and mess. Three girls from Bennington living together in New York, with black underwear hanging up and drying everywhere. Boyfriends calling everybody all the time. Men calling. Older men. Some married poet naked in somebody's room. The place a mess. Never any meals. A perpetual soap opera of angry lovers and outraged parents. And then one day in the street I saw your screwy finger show and we met and you invited me to your workshop for a drink. Avenue B and 9th Street, just by the park. Five flights up and this perfectly still, tiny white room with everything in place and dormer windows. I thought I was in Europe. All the puppets in a row. Your workbench—every tool hanging in place, everything tidy, clean, orderly, in place. Your file cabinet. I couldn't believe it. How calm and rational and steady-seeming, and yet on the street, performing, it could have been a madman behind that screen. Your sobriety. You didn't even offer me a drink."

"Jews never do."

"I didn't know. All I knew was that you had your crazy art and that all that mattered to you in the world was your crazy art, that why I had come to New York was for *my* art, to try to paint and to sculpt, and instead all I had was a crazy *life*. You were so *focused*. So *intense*. The green eyes. You were very handsome."

"In his thirties, everyone is handsome. What are you doing with me now, Roseanna?"

"Why did you stay with me when I was a drunk?"

Had the moment come to tell her about Drenka? *Some* moment had come. Some moment had been coming for months now, since the morning he learned that Drenka was dead. For years he had been drifting without any sense of anything being imminent and now not only was the moment galloping toward him but he was rushing into the moment and away from all he'd lived through.

"Why?" Roseanna repeated.

They'd just had dinner and she was off to a meeting, and he was off, after she'd gone, to the cemetery. She was already in her denim jacket, but because she no longer feared the "confrontations" she formerly evaded via the chardonnay, she was not leaving the house until she had forced him, this once, to take *seriously* their miserable history.

"I am sick of the humorous superiority. I am sick of the sarcasm and the perpetual joke. Answer me. Why did you stay with me?"

"Your paycheck. I stayed," he said, "to be supported."

She seemed about to cry, and bit her lip rather than try to speak.

"Come off it, Rosie. Barbara didn't break the news today."

"It's just hard to believe."

"Doubt Barbara? Next thing you know you'll be doubting God. How many people are there left in the world, let alone here in Madamaska Falls, with a full understanding of what is going on? It has always been a premise of my life that there are no such people left, and that I am their leader. But to find someone, like

Barbara, with a full grasp of what is happening, to discover, out in the sticks, someone with a fairly complete idea of everything, a human being in the largest sense of the word, whose judgment is grounded in the knowledge of life she acquired at college studying psychology . . . what other dark mystery has Barbara helped you to penetrate?"

"Oh, not such a mystery."

"Tell me anyway."

"That there may have been real pleasure for you in watching me destroy myself. As you watched Nikki destroy *her*self. That could have been another inducement to stay."

"*Two* wives whose destruction I have had the pleasure of watching. The pattern! But doesn't the pattern now call for me to enjoy your disappearance as much as I enjoyed Nikki's? Doesn't the pattern now call for you to disappear, too?"

"It does; it did. It's precisely where I was headed four years ago. I was as close to death as I could come. I couldn't wait for winter. I wanted only to be under the ice of the pond. You were hoping Kathy Goolsbee would put me there. Instead she saved me. Your masochistic student-slut saved my life."

"And why do I so much enjoy the misery of my wives? I'll bet it's because I hate them."

"You hate all women."

"Can't hide a thing from Barbara."

"Your *mother*, Mickey, *your mother.*"

"To blame? My little mother, who went to her death half out of her mind?"

"She's not 'to blame.' She was what she was. She was the *first* to disappear. When your brother was killed, she disappeared from your life. She deserted you."

"And that, if I follow Barbara's logic, that is why I find you so fucking boring?"

"Sooner or later you'd find any woman boring."

Not Drenka. Never Drenka.

"So when is Barbara planning to have you throw me out?"

This was further along in the confrontation than Roseanna had planned to go just yet. He knew this because she looked suddenly as she had the previous April on Patriots' Day, when she'd taken her first crack at the Boston Marathon and fainted just beyond the finish line. Yes, the subject of getting rid of Sabbath wasn't to have come up until she was just a little better prepared to be on her own.

"So for when," he repeated, "is the date set to throw me out?"

Sabbath watched her come to the decision to abandon the old schedule and tell him "Now." This necessitated her sitting down and putting her face in her hands, the keys to the car still dangling from one finger. When she looked up again there were tears running down her face—and only that morning he had overheard her telling someone on the phone, maybe even Barbara herself, "I want to live. I'll do anything it takes to get well, anything. I'm feeling strong and able to give everything to my work. I go off to work and I love every *minute* of it." And now she was in tears. "This isn't the way I wanted it to happen," she said.

"When is Barbara planning for you to throw me out?"

"Please. *Please.* You're talking about thirty-two years of my life! This is not easy at all."

"Suppose I make it easy. Throw me out tonight," Sabbath said. "Let's see if you have the sobriety for it. Throw me out, Roseanna. Tell me to go and never come back."

"This is not fair of you," she said, weeping more hysterically than he had seen her weep in years. "After my father, after all that, *please* don't say 'throw me out.' I cannot *hear* that."

"Tell me that if I don't go you're calling the cops. They're probably all pals from AA. Call the state trooper, the innkeeper's kid, the Balich boy; tell him that you have a family at AA that is more loving, more understanding, less judgmental than your husband and you want him to be thrown *out.* Who wrote the Twelve Steps? Thomas Jefferson? Well, call *him,* share with *him,* tell him that your husband hates women and must be thrown *outtt!* Call Barbara, my Barbara. *I'll* call her. I want to ask her how long you two blameless women have been planning my eviction. You're as sick as your secrets? Well, for just how long has off-loading Morris been your little secret, dear?"

"I cannot take this! I don't deserve this! You have no anxiety about relapse—you live in a *permanent* relapse!—but I do! With great effort and enormous suffering I have reclaimed myself, Mickey. Reclaimed myself from a horrendously devastating and potentially deadly disease. And don't make a face! If I didn't tell you my difficulties, you would never know. I say this without self-pity or sentimentality. To get well has taken all my energy and commitment. But I am *still* in a great state of change. It is still often painful and frightening. And this shouting I cannot stand. I will not stand! Stop it! You are shouting at me like my *father.*"

"The fuck that's who I'm shouting at you like! I'm shouting at you like *myself!*"

"Shouting is *irrational,*" she cried despairingly. "You cannot think straight if you're shouting! Nor can I!"

"Wrong! It's only when I'm shouting that I *begin* to think straight! It's my rationality that *makes* me shout! Shouting is how a Jew *thinks things through!*"

"What does 'Jew' have to do with it? You're saying 'Jew' deliberately to intimidate me!"

"I do *everything* deliberately to intimidate you, Rosie!"

"But where will you *go,* if you g   You are *not* thinking. How can you *live?* You're sixty-four years old. You don't have a penny. You cannot go away," she wailed, "to kill yourself!"

It did not pain him to say "No, you couldn't endure that, could you?"

And that's how it happened. Five months after Drenka's death, that was all it took for *him* to disappear, to leave Roseanna, to pick up finally and leave their home, such as it was—to get into his car and drive to New York to see what Linc Gelman looked like.

•   •   •

Sabbath took the long way to Amsterdam and 76th. He had eighteen hours for a three-and-a-half-hour trip, so instead of driving east for twelve miles to hook up with the turnpike, he decided to cross over Battle Mountain to 92 and then take the back roads and catch the turnpike some forty miles south. That way he could

pay a last visit to Drenka. He had no idea where he was going or
what he was doing and he did not know if he would visit that
cemetery ever again.

And what the hell *was* he doing? Get off her ass about AA. Ask
her about the kids at school. Give her a hug. Take her on a trip.
Eat her pussy. It's no big deal and might turn things around. When
she was a rangy aspiring artist fresh out of college living in
that flat full of sex-crazed girls, you did it all the time, couldn't
get enough of those long bones of hers encircling your ears.
Spirited, open, independent—someone he'd thought not in need
of round-the-clock protection, the wonderful new antithesis of
Nikki. . . .

She'd been his puppet partner for years. When they met she
had sculpted nude figures for six months and painted abstractions
for six months and then started doing ceramics and making necklaces, and then, even though people liked them and began buying
them, after a year she'd lost interest in the necklaces and begun
doing photography. Then through Sabbath she discovered puppets and a use for all her skills, for drawing, sculpting, painting,
tinkering, even for collecting bits and pieces of things, squirreling
all sorts of things away, which she had always done before but to
no purpose. Her first puppet was a bird, a hand puppet with
feathers and sequins, nothing like Sabbath's idea of a puppet. He
explained that puppets were not for children; puppets did not say,
"I am innocent and good." They said the opposite. "I will play
with you," they said, "however I like." She stood corrected, but
that didn't mean that, as a puppetmaker, she ever really stopped
looking for the happiness that she'd known at seven, when she
still had a Mom and a Dad and a childhood. Soon she was sculpting puppets' heads for Sabbath, sculpting them out of wood like
the old European puppets. Sculpted them, sanded them, painted
them beautifully in oil paint, taught herself how to make the eyes
blink and the mouths move, sculpted the hands. In her excitement
at the beginning she naively told people, "I start with one thing
and something else happens. A good puppet makes itself. I just go
with it." Then she went out and bought a machine, the cheapest

Singer, read the instructions, and started to design and sew the costumes. Her mother had sewed and Roseanna hadn't had the slightest interest. Now she was at the machine half the day. All the things people discarded, Roseanna collected. "Whatever you don't want," she began telling her friends, "give to me." Old clothes, stuff off the street, the stuff people cleaned out of closets, it was amazing how she could use everything—Roseanna, recycler of the world. She designed the sets on a big pad, made them, painted them—sets that rolled up, sets that turned like pages— and always fastidiously, for ten and twelve hours a day the most fastidious worker. For her a puppet was a little work of art, but even more, it was a charm, magical in the way it could get people to give themselves to it, even at Sabbath's theater, where the atmosphere was insinuatingly anti-moral, vaguely menacing, and at the same time, rascally fun. Sabbath's hands, she said, gave her puppets life. "Your hand is right where the puppet's heart is. I am the carpenter and you are the soul." Though she was softly romantic about "art," high-flown and a bit superficial where he was remorselessly mischievous, they were a team nonetheless, and if never quite aglow with happiness and unity, a team that worked for a long time. A fatherless daughter, she encountered her man so soon, at a time when she was not yet fully exposed to the spikes of the world, that she was never fully exposed to her own mind, and for years and years she did not know what to think without Sabbath to tell her. There was something exotic to her about the amount of life to which he had opened himself while still so young, and that included the loss of Nikki. If she was sometimes the victim of his withering presence, she was too enamored of the withering presence to dare to be a young woman without it. He had been an avid pupil early of the hard lessons, and she innocently saw, no less in his seafaring than in his cleverness and cynicism, a crash course in survival. True, she was always in danger around him, on edge, afraid of the satire, but it was even worse if she wasn't around him. It wasn't until she went down in a vomiting stupor in her early fifties and got to AA that she located there, in that language they spoke, in those words she embraced without a shadow of irony, criticism, or even, perhaps, full understanding, a wisdom for herself that wasn't Sabbath's skepticism and sardonic wit.

Drenka. One of them is driven to drink and one of them is driven to Drenka. But then, ever since he'd been seventeen he couldn't resist an enticing whore. He should have married that one in the Yucatán when he was eighteen years old. Instead of becoming a puppet artist he should have become a pimp. At least pimps have a public and make a living and don't have to go crazy every time they turn on TV and catch sight of the Muppets' fucking mouths. Nobody thinks of whores as entertainment for kiddies—like puppetry that means anything, whores are meant to delight adults.

Delightful whores. When Sabbath and his best friend, Ron Metzner, hitchhiked up to New York a month after high school graduation and someone in New York told them they could get out of the country without a passport by going down to the Norwegian Seamen's Center in Brooklyn, young Sabbath had no idea that at the other end there was all that pussy. His sexual experience till then had been feeling up the Italian girls from Asbury and, at every opportunity, masturbating. The way he remembered it now, as a ship approached harbor in Latin America, you got this unbelievable smell of cheap perfume, coffee, and pussy. Whether it was Rio, or Santos, or Bahia, or any of the other South American ports, there was that delicious smell.

The motive, to begin with, was simply to run away to sea. He'd been looking at the Atlantic every morning of his life and thinking, "One day, one day. . . ." It was very insistent, that feeling, and he did not then wholly attach it to a desire to escape his mother's gloom. He had been looking at the sea and fishing in the sea and swimming in the sea all his life. It seemed to him—if not to his bereft parents a mere nineteen months after Morty's death— only natural that he should go to sea to get a real education now that obligatory schooling had taught him to read and write. He learned about the pussy the moment he got aboard the Norwegian tramp steamer to Havana and he saw that everybody was

talking about it. To the old hands on board the fact that when
you got off the ship you would head for the whores was in no
way extraordinary, but to Sabbath, at seventeen—well, you can
imagine.

As if it weren't sufficiently exciting to slip by moonlight past
the Morro Castle in Havana harbor, as memorable an entrance to
a port as any in the world, once they'd tied up he was off the ship
and heading straight for the one thing he had never done before.
This was in Batista's Cuba, which was one big American whorehouse and gambling casino. In thirteen years, Castro was going to
come down out of the hills and put an end to all the fun, but
ordinary seaman Sabbath was lucky enough to get his licks in just
in the nick of time.

When he got his merchant mariner documents and joined the
union, he could choose his ships. He hung around the union hall
and—since he had tasted paradise—waited for the "Romance
Run": Santos, Monte, Rio, and B.A. There were guys who spent
their whole lives doing the Romance Run. And the reason, for
them as for Sabbath, was whores. Whores, brothels, every kind of
sex known to man.

Driving slowly up toward the cemetery, he calculated that he
had seventeen dollars in his pocket and three hundred in the joint
checking account. At a New York bank he'd have to write a check
first thing in the morning. Get the dough out before Rosie did.
Had to. She was pulling down a salary check twice a month and it
would be a year before he qualified for Social Security and Medi-
care. His only talent was this idiotic talent with his hands, and his
hands were no damn good anymore. Where could he live, how
would he eat, suppose he got sick? . . . If she divorced him for
desertion, what would he do for medical insurance, where would
he get money for his anti-inflammatory pills and for the pills he
took to keep the anti-inflammatory pills from burning out his
stomach, and if he couldn't afford the pills, if his hands were in
pain all the time, if there was never again to be any relief . . .

He had caused his heart to begin palpitating. The car was
nosed into the usual hideaway, a quarter of a mile from Drenka's

grave. All he had to do was to calm down and back out and head home. He wouldn't have to explain himself. He never did. He could sleep on the sofa and tomorrow resume reveling in his old nonexistence. Roseanna could never throw him out—her father's suicide wouldn't permit it, no matter what rewards Barbara promised in the way of inner peace and comfort. As for himself, however hateful life was, it was hateful in a home and not in the gutter. Many Americans hated their homes. The number of home- . less in America couldn't touch the number of Americans who had homes and families and hated the whole thing. Eat her pussy. At night, when she gets in from the meeting. It'll astonish her. *You* become the whore. Not as good as having married one, but you're six years from seventy so do it—eat her for money.

By this time, Sabbath was out of the car and prowling with his flashlight along the road to the cemetery. He had to find out if there was somebody there.

No limousine. Tonight a pickup truck. He was afraid to cross over to look at the plates, in case somebody was at the wheel. Could be just the local boys holding a moonlight circle-jerk up on the hill or sitting around on the tombstones smoking grass. Mostly he'd run into them over in Cumberland, on the checkout line at the supermarket, each with two or three little kids and a little underage wife—who already looks as though life has passed her by—with poor coloring and a pregnant belly pushing a cart piled with popcorn, cheese bugles, sausage rolls, dog food, potato chips, baby wipes, and twelve-inch-round pepperoni pizzas stacked up like money in a dream. Could tell them by the bumper stickers. Some had bumper stickers that read, "Our God Reigns," some had bumper stickers that read, "If You Don't Like The Way I Drive Dial 1-800-EAT-SHIT," some had both. A psychiatrist from the state hospital in Blackwall who ran a private practice a couple of days a week once told Sabbath, who'd asked what it was he treated people for up here in the mountains, "Incest, wife beating, drunkenness—in that order." And this was where Sabbath had lived for thirty years. Linc had it right: he should never have left after Nikki's disappearance. Norman Cowan had it right: nobody could blame him for her disappearance. Who remembered it, other than him? Maybe he was headed for New York to confirm, after all this time, that he had no more destroyed Nikki than he had killed Morty.

Nikki—all talent, enchanting talent, and absolutely nothing else. She couldn't tell her left from her right, let alone add, subtract, multiply, or divide. She could not tell north from south or east from west, even in New York, where she had lived much of her life. She couldn't bear the sight of ugly people or old people or disabled people. She was afraid of insects. She was afraid to be alone in the dark. If something made her nervous—a yellow-jacket, a Parkinson's victim, a drooling child in a wheelchair—she'd pop a Miltown, and the Miltown made her a madwoman with a wide, vacant stare and trembling hands. She jumped and cried out whenever a car backfired or someone nearby slammed a door. She knew best how to yield. When she tried to be defiant it was only minutes before she was in tears and saying, "I'll do anything you want—just don't *go* at me like this!" She did not know what reason was; either she was childishly obstinate or childishly submissive. She would startle him by wrapping herself in a towel when she came out of the shower and, if he was in her path, rushing past him for the bedroom. "Why do you do that?" "Do what?" "What you did—hide your body from me." "I didn't do any such thing." "You did, under the towel." "I was keeping warm." "Why did you run, as though you didn't want me to see?" "You're mad, Mickey, you're making this up. Why do you have to *go* at me all the time?" "Why do you act as though your body is ugly?" "I don't *like* my body. I hate my body! I hate my breasts! Women shouldn't have to have breasts!" Yet she could not walk by any kind of reflecting surface without taking a quick look to see if she was as fresh and lovely as in the photos displayed outside the theater. And once she was on the stage the million phobias vanished, all the peculiarities simply ceased to exist. The things that frightened her most about life she could pretend to face in a play with no difficulty at all. She did not know which was stronger, her love of Sabbath or her hatred of him—all she knew for sure was that she could not have survived without his protection. He was her armature, her coat of mail.

In her early twenties, Nikki was already as malleable an actress as a willful director like Sabbath could want. On stage, even just in rehearsal, even standing around and waiting to be given notes, there was not a sign of her jitteriness, all that fidgeting with her ring, the tracing of the fingers around the collar, the tapping on a table with whatever was at hand. She was calm, attentive, tireless, uncomplaining, clear-minded, intelligent. Whatever Sabbath asked of her, minutely pedantic or over the top, she could reproduce on the spot, exactly as he'd imagined it for himself. She was patient with the bad actors and inspired with the good ones. At work she was never discourteous toward anyone, whereas at a department store Sabbath had seen her display a snobbish superiority toward the salesgirl that made him want to slap her face. "Who do you think you are?" he asked her once they were back out on the street. "Why are you going for me *now?*" "Why treat that girl like shit?" "Oh, she was just a little tramp." "And who the fuck are you? Your father owned a lumberyard in Cleveland. Mine sold butter and eggs from a truck." "Why do you dwell on my father? I hated my father. How can you dare bring up my father!" Another of the women in Sabbath's life who reckoned her father a flop. Drenka's was a stupid party member whom she scorned for his gullible fidelity. "I can understand if you're an opportunist—but to be a *believer.*" Rosie's was an alcoholic suicide who terrified her, and Nikki's was a bullying, vulgar businessman to whom cards, taverns, and girls meant rather more than his responsibility to a wife and child. Her father had met her mother when he was in Greece with his parents for the funeral of his grandmother and afterward went traveling around the country by himself, primarily to see what the pussy was like. There he courted his wife-to-be, a bourgeois girl from Salonika, and a few months later he brought her back to Cleveland, where his own father, an even more bullying and vulgar businessman, owned the lumberyard. The old man's people had been country people, and when he spoke in Greek it was with a terrible village dialect. And

the cursing over the phone! "Gamóto! Gamó ti mána sou! Gamó
ti panaghía sou!" Fuck it! Fuck your mother! Fuck your Holy
Mother! . . . And pinching her behind, his own daughter-in-law!
Nikki's mother fancied herself a poetic young woman, and her
philandering husband, the coarse in-laws, provincial Cleveland,
the bouzouki music these people loved—all of it drove her mad.
She couldn't have made a bigger mistake than marrying Kantarakis and his horrible family, but at nineteen she was of course
in flight from a domineering, old-fashioned father *she* loathed,
and the high-spirited American who made her blush so easily—
and, for the first time in her life, come so easily—seemed to her at
the time a man called to great things.

Her salvation was the beautiful little Nikoleta. She doted on
her. She took her everywhere. They were inseparable. She began
to teach Nikki, who was musical, to sing in Greek and English.
She read to her aloud and taught her to recite. But still the mother
wept every night, and finally she moved with Nikki to New York.
To support them, she worked in a laundry, then as a mailroom
sorter, and eventually for Saks, first selling hats and, a few years
later, as head of the millinery department. Nikki went to the High
School of Performing Arts—it was she and her mother against the
world until, in 1959, an obscure blood disease abruptly ended her
mother's struggle. . . .

Sabbath made his way parallel to the cemetery's long stone
wall, low to the ground and moving as quietly as he could over
the soft earth at the margin of the road. There was somebody in
the cemetery. At Drenka's grave! In jeans—lanky, pigeon-toed, his
hair in a ponytail. . . . It was the *electrician's* pickup. It was Barrett, whom she'd loved to fuck in the bathtub and lather in the
shower. *You start at the face and then the chest and the stomach
and then you come down to the dick, and that gets big, or it is big
already.* Yes, it was Barrett's night to pay his respects to the dead,
and he was indeed big already. *Sometimes he will lift my legs up
and he carries me like that in the shower.* Once again Sabbath was
searching for a rock. Since he was a good fifteen feet farther from
Barrett than he'd been from Lewis, he looked for a light rock that

he might have a chance of pitching somewhere near the strike zone. It took time in the dark to locate something the right weight and size, and all the while Barrett stood at the foot of her grave silently beating off. To bean him one right on the cock just as he started to come. Sabbath was trying to gauge the advent of the orgasm by the speed of Barrett's stroke when he saw a second figure in the cemetery, slowly ascending the hill. In a uniform. The sexton? The uniformed figure moved stealthily, unnoticed and unseen, until he was just about three feet behind Barrett, who was oblivious by now to everything except the impending surge.

Deliberately, almost languidly, the uniformed figure raised his right arm, degree by degree. In the hand he was holding a long object that culminated in a bulge. A flashlight. A drone arose from Barrett, a steady monotonous drone that suddenly terminated in a fanfare of incoherent babble. Sabbath held his fire, but the ecstatic climax turned out to be the cue as well for the man with the flashlight, who brought it down like an ax on Barrett's skull. There was a muted thud when Barrett hit the ground, then two swift thumps—the young electrician . . . *you are somethin',* *you are really somethin' else* . . . getting it twice in the balls.

Only when the assailant hopped into his own car—he had slipped it in just behind the pickup—and turned on the engine did Sabbath realize who it was. Out of arrogant, open defiance or plain unquenchable rage, the state trooper's cruiser pulled away, all lights flashing.

THAT NIGHT, on the drive to New York for Linc's funeral, he thought only of Nikki. All he could talk about with his mother, who was gliding about inside the car, drifting and plunging like debris in the tide, was what had led to Nikki's disappearance. During his four years of marriage, his mother had seen Nikki only five or six times and said little or nothing to her when she did, could hardly comprehend who Nikki was or why she was there, however earnestly, with the brokenhearted naiveté of a bright, kindly child, Nikki tried to make conversation with her. What with her terror of the aged and the deformed and the ill, Nikki was scarcely up to the ordeal of Sabbath's suffering mother and she invariably got stomach cramps driving to Bradley. Once, when Mrs. Sabbath was looking particularly gaunt and unkempt as they came upon her dozing in a kitchen chair with her teeth beside her on the table's oilcloth covering, Nikki couldn't help herself and ran out the back door. From then on, Sabbath would go alone to see his mother. He took her for lunch to a Belmar seafood restaurant that served Parker House rolls, once a favorite of hers, and back in Bradley, at his insistence, he held her by the arm and they strolled on the boards for ten minutes. Much to her relief, he then took her home. He did not press her to say anything, and over the years there were visits when he said only, "How are you, Ma?" and "So long, Ma." That and two kisses, one coming, one going. Whenever he brought a box of chocolate-covered cherries he would find it the next time unopened and exactly where she'd put it down after taking it from his hand. He never considered staying the night in Morty and his old room.

But now that she was fluttering invisibly about in his dark car, shed of affliction, drained of grief, now that his little mother was purely spirit, purely mind, an imperishable being, he reckoned she could endure to hear the full story of the catastrophe in which the first marriage had perished. No doubt she had been present earlier to observe the ending of the second marriage. And wasn't she there whenever he awoke at four A.M. and couldn't fall back asleep? Hadn't he asked her in the bathroom that very morning, while he trimmed the fringe of his beard, if his was not a replica of the flowing beard worn by her own father, the rabbi for whom he was named and whom he had apparently resembled from the moment of birth? Wasn't she regularly at his side, in his mouth, ringing his skull, reminding him to extinguish his nonsensical life?

Nothing but death, death and the dead, for three and a half hours, nothing but Nikki, her unaccountability, her strangeness, her appearance, the hair and the eyes primordial in their blackness, the skin ethereal, maidenly, an angelic, powdery white . . . Nikki and her talent to embody everything in the soul that is contradictory and unfathomable, even the monstrousness that paralyzed her with fear.

When Nikki was awarded a full scholarship to the Royal Academy of Dramatic Art in London, she moved there with her mother. At first they relied on the generosity of a first cousin of Nikki's mother who was married to an English physician and lived comfortably in Kensington. Her mother found work in an expensive hat shop on South Audley Street, and the gracious owners, Bill and Ned, having fallen for timorous Nikki's eloquent delicacy, allowed them to rent the two small rooms above the store for virtually nothing. They even supplied furniture from the attic of their country house, including a small bed on which Nikki slept in the minute "extra" room and the couch in the "parlor" where her insomniac mother, with the help of a novel, chain-smoked herself through each night. The toilet was downstairs, at the back of the shop. The place was so small that Nikki could as well have been a kangaroo in her mother's pouch. She wouldn't really have minded if it had been smaller still, with but one bed for the two of them.

After graduating from the drama school, Nikki returned to New York, but her mother, who could never get over her memories of Cleveland and who found Americans, altogether, loud and barbarous—certainly by comparison with her customers at the up-market hat shop, who were as kind and thoughtful as they could be to the widowed (that was the story) milliner (of aristocratic Cretan lineage, according to Bill and Ned)—her mother stayed in London. The time had come for Nikki to strike out on her own while her mother remained safely among the many good friends she had made through the "boys," as everyone referred to her bosses—she and Nikki were frequently invited away to somebody's country house for a holiday weekend, and not a few wealthy customers looked on Mrs. Kantarakis as a confidante. And then there was the security furnished by cousin Rena and the doctor, who had been extraordinarily generous, especially to Nikki. Everyone was generous to Nikki. She was an enchantress, though one who, upon her departure for America, had as yet no sexual experience with men. For that matter, since fleeing her father's house in her mother's arms at the age of seven, she'd had hardly any familiarity with men who were not homosexual. It remained to be seen just how much she would enchant them.

"Her mother," Sabbath told his own mother, "died early one morning. Nikki had flown there to be with her during the last stages of the illness. Her ticket was paid for by Bill and Ned. There was nothing more to be done for her in the hospital, so the mother came back to the rooms over the hat shop to die. As the end approached, Nikki sat beside her mother, holding her hand and making her comfortable for nearly four days. Then the fourth morning she went down behind the shop to use the toilet and when she came back upstairs her mother had stopped breathing. 'My mother died just now,' she told me on the phone, 'and I wasn't there. I wasn't there for her. I wasn't there for her, Mickey!

She died alone!' Compliments of Bill and Ned, I flew to London
on the evening plane. I arrived around breakfast time the next
day and made straight for South Audley Street. What I found
was Nikki looking calm and unruffled in a chair beside her
mother. It was the next day and the corpse was still in her nightgown—and there. And remained there for seventy-two hours
more. When I could no longer stand the spectacle of it, I shouted
at Nikki, 'You are not a Sicilian peasant! Enough is enough! It is
time for your mother to go!' 'No. No. *No!*' and when she started
flailing at me with her fists, I backed away, retreated down the
stairs, and wandered around London for hours. What I was trying to tell her was that the vigil she had initiated over the body
had exceeded my sense not of what was seemly but of what
was sane. I was trying to tell her that her unconstrained intimacy
with her mother's corpse, the chatty monologue with which she
was entertaining the dead woman as she sat beside her through
each day, knitting at her mother's unfinished knitting and wel-
coming the friends of the boys, the fondling of the dead woman's
hands, the kissing of her face, the stroking of her hair—all this
obliviousness to the raw physical fact—was rendering her taboo
to me."

Was Sabbath's mother following this story? He somehow
sensed that her interest lay elsewhere. He was down into Con-
necticut now, driving along a beautiful, creepy stretch of river,
and he thought his mother might be thinking, "It wouldn't be
hard out in that river." But not before I see Linc, Ma. . . . He had
to see what it looked like before he did it himself.

And this was the first time that he realized or admitted what he
had to do. The problem that was his life was never to be solved.
His wasn't the kind of life where there are aims that are clear and
means that are clear and where it is possible to say, "This is
essential and that is not essential, this I will not do because I
cannot endure it, and that I will do because I can endure it."
There was no unsnarling an existence whose waywardness constituted its only authority and provided its primary amusement.
He wanted his mother to understand that he wasn't blaming

the futility on Morty's death, or on her collapse, or on Nikki's disappearance, or on his stupid profession, or on his arthritic hands—he was merely recounting to her what had happened before this had happened. That's all you could know, though if what you think happened happens to not ever match up with what somebody else thinks happened, how could you say you know even that? Everybody got everything wrong. What he was telling his mother was wrong. If it were Nikki listening instead of his mother, she would be shouting, "It wasn't like that! *I* wasn't like that! You misunderstand! You always misunderstood! You're always going at me for no reason at all!"

Homeless, wifeless, mistressless, penniless . . . jump in the cold river and drown. Climb up into the woods and go to sleep, and tomorrow morning, should you even awaken, keep climbing until you are lost. Check into a motel, borrow the night clerk's razor to shave, and slit your throat from ear to ear. It could be done. Lincoln Gelman did it. Roseanna's father did it. Probably Nikki herself had done it, and with a razor, a straight razor very like the one with which she had exited each night to kill herself in *Miss Julie*. About a week after her disappearance, it had occurred to Sabbath to go to the prop room and look for the razor that the valet, Jean, hands to Julie after she sleeps with him, feels herself polluted by him, and finally asks of him, "If you were in my place, what would you do?" "Go, now while it's light—out to the barn, . . ." replies Jean, and hands her his razor. "There's no other way to end. . . . Go!" he says. The play's last word: go! So Julie takes the razor and goes—and embattled Nikki ineluctably follows. The razor had turned up in the drawer in the prop shop just where it was supposed to be, but there were times, nonetheless, when Sabbath could still believe that the horror was autohypnosis, that their catastrophe stemmed from the selfless, ruthless sympathy with which Nikki almost criminally embraced the sufferings of the unreal. Eagerly she surrendered her large imagination not to the overbearing beastliness of Sabbath's imagination but to the overbearing beastliness of Strindberg's. Strindberg had done it for him. Who better?

"I remember thinking by the third day, 'If this goes on any longer, I'll never fuck this woman again—I won't be able to lie with her in the same bed.' It wasn't because these rites she was concocting were strange to me and at cross-purposes with rituals I was accustomed to witnessing among Jews. Had she been a Catholic, a Hindu, a Muslim, guided by the mourning practices of this religion or that; had she been an Egyptian under the reign of the great Amenhotep, observing every last detail of the ceremonial rigmarole decreed by the death god Osiris, I believe I would have done nothing more than watch in respectful silence. My chagrin was over Nikki out there *all on her own*—she and her mother against the world, apart from the world, alone together and cut off from the world, with no church, no clan to help her through, not even a simple folk formality around which her response to a dear one's death could mercifully cohere. Two days into her vigil we happened to see a priest walking by, down on South Audley Street. 'Those are the real ghouls,' Nikki said. 'I hate them all. Priests, rabbis, clergymen with their stupid fairy tale!' I had wanted to say to her, 'Then get a shovel and do it yourself. I'm no fan of the clergy myself. Get a shovel and bury her in Ned's garden.'

"Her mother was laid out on the couch, under an eiderdown. She looked—before the embalmer showed up and, in Nikki's words, 'pickled her'—she looked as though she were merely sleeping out the day in our presence, her chin, just as she carried it in life, angled slightly to one side. Beyond the windows it was a fresh spring morning. The sparrows she fed every day were flitting about on the flowering trees and bathing in the gravel on top of the garden shed in the yard, and through the open rear windows you could see down to the sheen on the tulips. A bowl of half-eaten dog food lay beside the door but her mother's lapdog was gone by then, taken in by Rena. It was from Rena that I later learned what had happened on the morning of the death. Nikki had told me that an ambulance had been sent for by the doctor who had come to view the body and to write up the death certificate but that she had decided to keep her mother at home until the funeral and sent the ambulance away. Rena, who had rushed over to be with Nikki at the time, told me that the ambulance the doctor called had not been 'sent away.' When the driver had come through the door and started up the narrow staircase, Nikki had told him, 'No, no!'; when he insisted he was only doing his job, Nikki struck him across the face so hard that he ran off and her wrist was sore for days. I had seen her rubbing the wrist on and off during the vigil but didn't know what it meant until Rena told me."

And just who did he think he was talking to? A self-induced hallucination, a betrayal of reason, something with which to magnify the inconsequentiality of a meaningless mess—*that's* what his mother was, another of his puppets, his last puppet, an invisible marionette flying around on strings, cast in the role not of guardian angel but of the departed spirit making ready to ferry him to his next abode. To a life that had come to nothing, a crude theatrical instinct was lending a garish, pathetic touch of last-minute drama.

The drive was interminable. Had he missed a turn or was this itself the next abode: a coffin that you endlessly steer through the placeless darkness, recounting and recounting the uncontrollable events that induced you to become someone unforeseen. And so fast! So quickly! Everything runs away, beginning with who you are, and at some indefinable point you come to half understand that the ruthless antagonist is yourself.

His mother had by now draped her spirit around him, she had enwrapped him within herself, her way of assuring him that she did indeed exist unmastered and independent of his imagination.

"I asked Nikki, 'When will the funeral be?' But she didn't answer. 'It's quite unacceptable,' she said, 'it's quite unacceptably sad.' She was seated on the edge of the couch where her mother was laid out. I was holding one of Nikki's hands and with the other she reached over and touched her mother's face. 'Manoúlamou, manoulítsamou.' Greek diminutives for 'my dear little mother.' 'It's unbearable. It's dreadful,' Nikki said. 'I'm going to stay with her. I'll sleep here. I don't want her to be alone.' And as

I didn't want Nikki to be alone, I sat with her and her mother until, late in the afternoon, a funeral director from a large London firm contacted by Rena's doctor husband came to discuss the funeral arrangements. I was a Jew accustomed to the dead's being buried when possible within twenty-four hours, but Nikki was nothing, nothing but her mother's child, and when I reminded her, while we were waiting for the funeral director, of what Jewish custom was, she said, 'To put them in the ground the next *day?* How cruel of the Jews!' 'Well, that's one way of looking at it.' 'It *is,*' she said, 'it's cruel! It's horrible!' I said no more. She had confirmed that she didn't want a funeral ever.

"The funeral director arrived in striped trousers and a black cutaway at around four. He was extremely polite and deferential and explained that he had rushed over from his third funeral of the day and hadn't had a chance to change. Nikki announced that her mother was not to be moved but was to stay right where she was. He responded at a very high level of euphemism, one to which he adhered, but for a single lapse, throughout the consultation. He affected an upper-class accent. 'As you wish, Miss Kantarakis. We won't want to give offense, however. If mother remains with you, then one of our people will have to come and give her an injection.' I took him to mean that she would have to be cleaned out and embalmed. 'Don't worry,' he assured us crisply, 'our man is the best in England.' He smiled proudly. 'He does the royal family. A very witty fellow, in fact. You have to be in this business. We couldn't be a morbid lot.'

"A fly meanwhile had alighted on the corpse's face and I was hoping that Nikki wouldn't see it and it would go away. But she did see and jumped up, and for the first time since I arrived, there was a hysterical outburst. 'Let her,' the funeral director said to me. I, too, had jumped up to shoo the fly away. 'Let it come out,' he said sagely.

"After she had been calmed down, Nikki laid a tissue across her mother's face to keep the fly from returning. Later in the day, at her request, I went out to buy some bug repellant and came back to spray the room—careful not to spray in the corpse's direction—and Nikki took the tissue and put it in her sweater pocket. Unknowingly—or not unknowingly—around dusk she used the tissue to blow her nose . . . and that seemed to me altogether crazy. 'At the risk of being indelicate,' the funeral director asked, 'how tall was Mother? My associates will be asking when I ring.'

"He called his office some minutes later and asked what was available at the crematorium on Tuesday. It was still only Friday, and given Nikki's condition, Tuesday seemed a long way off. But as she would as soon have had no funeral and kept her mother there for good, I'd decided on Tuesday as better than never.

"The funeral director waited while they checked the crematorium schedule. Then he looked up from the phone and said to me, 'My associates say there's a one o'clock slot.' 'Oh, no,' Nikki whimpered, but I nodded okay. 'Grab it,' he snapped into the phone, and revealed at last that he was able to speak as though the world were a real place and we were real people. 'And the service?' he asked Nikki after he'd hung up. 'I don't care who does it,' she said vaguely, 'as long as they don't go on about God.' 'Nondenominational,' he said, and wrote that down in his book, along with her mother's height and the grade of coffin that Nikki had chosen to have incinerated with her. He then set about to describe, delicately, the cremation procedure and to lay out the options available. 'You can leave before the coffin disappears or you can wait until it disappears.' Nikki was too stunned by the thought to answer and so I said, 'We'll wait.' 'And the ashes?' he asked. 'In her will,' I said, 'she just asked that they be scattered.' Nikki, looking at the motionless tissue over her mother's nostrils and lips, said to no one in particular, 'I suppose we'll take them back to New York. She hated America. But I suppose they should come with us.' 'You can take them,' the funeral director replied, 'you certainly can, Miss Kantarakis. According to the law of 1902, you can do anything you wish with them.'

"The embalmer didn't arrive until seven-thirty. The funeral director had described him to me—with a trace of Dickensian enjoyment such as you might not be likely to hear from a funeral director anywhere other than in the British Isles—as 'tall, with thick spectacles, and quite witty.' But he wasn't merely tall when he appeared in the dusk at the downstairs door; he was huge, a giant strongman out of the circus, wearing the thick spectacles and completely bald but for two sprigs of black hair that stuck up at either side of his enormous head. He stood in the doorway in a black suit, bearing two large black boxes, each sizable enough to hold a child. 'You're Mr. Cummins?' I asked him. 'I'm from Ridgely's, sir.' He might as well have said he was from Satan's. I would have believed him, Cockney accent and all. He didn't look witty to me.

"I led him up to where the corpse was tucked in under her eiderdown. He removed his hat and bowed slightly to Nikki, as respectful as he might have been were we the royals themselves. 'We'll leave you alone,' I said. 'We'll take a walk and be back in about an hour.' 'Give me an hour and a half, sir,' he said. 'Fine.' 'May I ask a few questions, sir?'

"As Nikki was sufficiently astonished by his hugeness—by his hugeness on top of everything else—I didn't think she'd need to hear his questions, which could not be anything but macabre. As it was, she couldn't lift her gaze from the large black boxes, which he'd now set down. 'You go outside a moment,' I told her. 'Go downstairs and get some air while I finish up with this guy.' Silently she obeyed. She was leaving her mother for the first time since she'd gone to the toilet the day before and returned to find her dead. But anything rather than to be with that man and those boxes.

"Back inside, the embalmer asked me how the corpse should be dressed. I didn't know, but instead of rushing out to question Nikki, I told him to leave her in her nightgown. Then I realized that if he was preparing her for the funeral and the cremation, her jewelry should be removed. I asked if he would do that for us. 'Let's see what she has on, sir,' he said and beckoned for me to examine the body with him.

"I hadn't been expecting that, but as it seemed to be a matter of professional ethics for him not to remove valuables without a witness present, I stood beside him while he pulled back the eider-down to reveal the corpse's bluish stiffened fingers and, where the nightgown had hiked up, the pipe-thin legs. He removed her ring and gave it to me and then he lifted her head to unscrew her earrings. But he couldn't manage by himself, and so I held her head while he worked the earrings. 'The pearls, too,' I said, and he slid them around on her neck so that the catch was turned to the front. Only the catch wouldn't come undone. He struggled in vain with his inordinately large circus-strongman fingers while I continued to hold the weight of her head in one hand. She and I were never physically cozy together and this was by far the most intimate we had been. The head seemed to weigh so much dead. She is so dead, I thought—and this is becoming insufferable. Eventually I took a crack at opening the catch myself and after a few minutes of fiddling, when I couldn't do it either, we gave up and drew the pearl necklace, which was a very tight fit, over her head and her hair as best we could.

"I was careful not to trip as I stepped back between his black boxes. 'All right, then,' I told him, 'I'll return in an hour and a half.' 'You'd better phone before, sir.' 'And you'll leave her ex-actly as she is now?' 'Yes, sir.' But then he looked at the windows that faced onto Ned's garden and the rear windows of the houses on the street opposite and he asked, 'Can they see in from over there, sir?' I was suddenly alarmed about leaving this attractive forty-five-year-old woman alone with him, dead though she was. But what I was thinking was unthinkable—I thought—and I said, 'You better pull the curtains to be safe.' The curtains were new, a birthday gift from Nikki bought the year before and hung only during the last week of her mother's illness. Her mother had insisted that she didn't need new curtains, refused even to unwrap them, and had only accepted them when, at her bedside, Nikki, lying, said to the dying woman that they had cost her less than ten pounds.

"At Rena's, where we were staying, Rena and I tried to get Nikki to bathe and to eat. She would do neither. She would not even wash her hands when I asked her to after a day of fondling her dead mother. She waited silently in a chair until it was time to go back. After an hour passed, I phoned to see how far the embalmer had got.

"'I'm finished, sir,' he said. 'Is everything as it was?' 'Yes, sir. Flowers beside her on the pillow.' They hadn't been when we left; he must have taken the flowers that Ned had picked earlier in the day and moved them. 'Had to straighten her head,' he told me. 'Best for the coffin.' 'All right. When you go, just pull the downstairs door shut behind you. We'll be right over. Can you leave a lamp on?' 'I have, sir. The little lamp by her head.' He had arranged a tableau.

"The first thing I saw—"

It was *Sabbath* he had meant to smash on the head. Of course! It was Sabbath he had set out to catch desecrating his mother's grave! For weeks, maybe even for months now, Matthew, on night patrol, must have been observing him from the cruiser. Ever since Sabbath's monstrous exploitation of Kathy Goolsbee, Matthew, like so many others in the affronted community, had come to lose his respect for Sabbath, and this he made clear, whenever his car happened to pass Sabbath's on the road, by failing to acknowledge that he recognized the driver. As he drove around, Matthew ordinarily loved to throw a salute to the folks he'd known as a kid in Madamaska Falls, and he was still well known in town for being lenient with townsfolk about their infractions. He had been ingratiatingly lenient once with Sabbath himself, when he was just a few months out of the academy, not very wily yet, and driving a chase car with the traffic squad. He'd gone after Sabbath—who was moving along well over the speed limit after a joyous afternoon up at the Grotto—and forced him, with his siren, to the side of the road. But when Matthew strode up to the driver's window and looked inside and saw who it was, he blushed and said, "Ooops." He and Roseanna had become pals during his last year at the high school, and more than once (drunk she said everything more than once) she'd remarked that Matthew Balich was among the most sensitive boys she'd ever had in a class at Cumberland. "What did I do wrong, Officer Balich?"

inquired Sabbath, seriously, as every citizen is entitled to do. "Jesus, you know you were *flying, sir.*" "Uh-oh," replied Sabbath. "Look, don't worry," Matthew told him, "when it comes to folks I know, I'm not your typical gung-ho trooper. You don't have to go telling people, but it just isn't in me to be that way toward somebody I know. I drove fast before I was a trooper. I'm not going to be a hypocrite." "Well, that's more than kind. What should I do?" "Well," said Matthew, grinning broadly with that noseless face—exactly as his mother had earlier in the afternoon, coming for the third or fourth time—"you could slow down, for one thing. And then you could just get out of here. Go away! See ya, Mr. Sabbath! Say hi to Roseanna!"

So that was the end of that. He could not dare visit Drenka's grave ever again. He could never return to Madamaska Falls. In flight not just from home and marriage but now from the law at its most lawless.

"The first thing I saw when we got back was that the vacuum cleaner was out of the closet and in a corner of the larger room. Had he used it to clean up? Clean what up? Then I smelled the awful chemicals.

"The woman under the eiderdown was no longer the woman we had been with all day. 'It's not her,' Nikki said and broke into tears. 'It looks like me! It's me!'

"I understood what she meant, insane as her words first sounded. Nikki possessed a severe, spectacular variant of her mother's refined good looks, and so whatever resemblance there had been before the embalming was now even chillingly stronger. She walked back to the body and stared at it. 'Her head is straight.' 'He straightened it,' I told her. 'But she always carried her head on the side.' 'She doesn't anymore.' 'Oh, you're looking awfully stern, manoulítsa,' Nikki said to the corpse.

"Stern. Sculpted. Statuelike. Very officially very dead. But Nikki nonetheless sat back down in her chair and set about resuming the vigil. The curtains were closed and only the little light was glowing and the flowers were on the pillow beside the embalmed head. I had to suppress an impulse to grab them and throw them into the wastebasket and put a stop to the whole thing. All her fluid self is gone, I thought, suctioned into those black cases and then—what? Down the toilet bowl at the back of the shop? I could just see that giant in his black suit tossing about the naked body once it was the two of them alone in the room with the curtains drawn and there was no longer any need to be as dainty as he'd been with the jewelry. Evacuating the bowels, emptying the bladder, draining the blood, injecting the formaldehyde, if formaldehyde was what I smelled.

"I should never have allowed this, I thought. We should have buried her in the garden ourselves. I was right to begin with. 'What are you going to do?' I asked. 'I'll stay here tonight,' she said. 'You can't,' I said. 'I don't want her to be alone.' 'I don't want *you* to be alone. You can't be alone. And I'm not going to sleep here. You're coming back to Rena's. You can return in the morning.' 'I can't leave her.' 'You have to come with me, Nikki.' 'When?' 'Now. Say good-bye to her now and come.' She got out of the chair and knelt beside the couch. Touching her mother's cheeks, her hair, her lips, she said, 'I did love you, manoulítsa. Oh, manoulítsamou.'

"I opened a window to air the place out. I began to clean the refrigerator at the kitchen end of the parlor. I poured the milk that was in an open carton down the drain. I found a paper bag and put the contents of the refrigerator into the bag. But when I came back to Nikki, she was still talking to her. 'It's time to go for tonight,' I said.

"Without resisting me, Nikki got up from the floor when I offered to help her. But standing in the doorway to the stairwell, she turned back to look at her mother. 'Why can't she just stay like that?' she asked.

"I led her down the stairs to the side door, carrying the garbage out with us. But again Nikki turned around and I followed her back up into the parlor with my bag of garbage. Again she went up to the body to touch it. I waited. Ma, I waited and I waited and I thought, Help her, help her out of this, but I didn't know what to do to help her, whether to tell her to stay or to force her to go. She pointed to the corpse. 'That's my mother,' she said. 'You have to come with me,' I said. Eventually, I don't know how much later, she did.

"But the next day it was worse—Nikki was better. In the morning she couldn't wait to get to her mother's and when, after dropping her off there, I phoned an hour later and asked, 'How is it?' she said, 'Oh, very peaceful. Sitting here knitting. And we had a little chat.' And so I found her at the end of the afternoon when I came to take her back to Rena's. 'We had such a nice little chat,' she said. 'I was just telling Momma . . .'

"On Sunday morning—finally, finally, finally—in a heavy rainstorm, I went around to open the door for the hearse that had come to take her away. 'It's another twenty-five pounds,' the funeral director warned me, 'to get the staff out on Sunday, sir—funerals are expensive enough already.' But I said to him, 'Just get 'em.' If Rena wouldn't pay, I would—and I had then, as now, not a dollar to spare. I didn't want Nikki to come with me, and only when she insisted that she had to did I raise my voice and say, 'Look, start thinking. It's pissing rain. It's miserable. You're not going to like it at all when they carry your mother out of that room and into this storm in a box.' 'But I must go to see her this afternoon.' 'You can, you can. I'm sure you can.' 'You must ask them if I can come this afternoon!' 'Whenever they have her ready, I'm sure you can go there. But the scene this morning you can skip. Do you want to watch her leave South Audley Street?' 'Maybe you're right,' she said, and, of course, I was wondering if I was and if watching her mother leave South Audley Street might be just what she needed for reality to begin to seep in. But what if keeping reality at bay was all that was keeping her from coming completely apart? I didn't know. No one knows. That's why the religions have the rituals that Nikki hated.

"But at three she was back with her mother at the funeral home, which happened to be not far from the flat of an English friend I had arranged to visit. I had given her the address and the phone number and told her to come to his house when she was finished. Instead she called me to say that she would stay until my visit was over and that I should then come to pick her up at the funeral home. It wasn't what I'd had in mind. She's stuck, I thought, I cannot unstick her.

"I had lingering hopes that she would show up at my friend's anyway, but when it got to be five o'clock, I walked over and, at the front door, asked the on-duty officer, who appeared to be alone on a Sunday, to call her. He said that Nikki had left a message for me to be brought to where she was 'visiting' her mother. He led me along the corridors and down a long stairway and into another corridor, lined with doors, which I imagined issued onto cubicles where bodies were laid out to be seen by relatives. Nikki was in one of those tiny rooms with her mother. She was seated in a chair drawn up beside the open coffin, working at her mother's knitting again. When she saw me she laughed lightly and said, 'We had a wonderful chat. We laughed about the room. It's just about the size of the one in Cleveland the time we ran away. Look,' she said to me, 'look at her sweet little hands.' She turned back the lace coverlet to show me her mother's intertwined fingers. 'Manoulítsamou,' she said, kissing and kissing them.

"I think even the on-duty officer, who had remained in the open doorway to accompany us upstairs, was shaken by what he'd just seen. 'We have to go,' I said flatly. She began to cry. 'A few more minutes.' 'You've been here for over two hours.' 'I love I love I love I love—' 'I know, but we have to go now.' She got up and began kissing and stroking her mother's forehead, repeating, 'I love I love I love I love—' Only gradually was I able to pull her out of the room.

"At the door she thanked the officer. 'You've all been so kind,' she said, looking a bit dazed, and then, as we came outside, she asked if the next morning I would mind if she just stopped by first thing with some fresh flowers for her mother's room. I thought, We are dealing here with *death,* fuck the flowers! but I did not really cut loose until we were back in the room at Rena's. We walked silently through Holland Park on a beautiful May Sunday, past the peacocks and the formal gardens, then down through

Kensington Gardens, where the chestnut trees were blossoming, and finally we got to Rena's. 'Look,' I said to her, closing the door to our room, 'I can't stand by and watch it anymore. You are not living with the dead, you are living with the living. It's as simple as that. You are alive and your mother is dead, very sadly dead at forty-five, but this has all become too much for me. Your mother is not a doll to play with. She is not laughing with you about anything. She is dead. Nobody is laughing. This must stop.'

"But she did not seem yet to understand. She replied, 'I've seen her pass through each stage.' 'There are no stages. She is dead. That is the only stage. Do you hear me? That is the only stage, and you are not *on* the stage. This is no act. This is all becoming very offensive.' There followed a befuddled moment and then she opened her purse and took out a prescription bottle. 'I should never have taken these.' 'What are they?' 'Pills. I asked the doctor. When he came for Momma, I asked him to give me something to get through the funeral.' 'How many of these have you been taking?' 'I had to' was all she answered. And then she wept all evening and I threw the pills down the toilet.

"The next morning, after coming out of the bathroom, where she'd been brushing her teeth, she looked at me—looked at me exactly like herself—and said, 'That's over. My mother's not there anymore,' and she never went back to the funeral home, or kissed her mother's face again, or laughed with her, or bought her curtains, or anything else. And she missed her every single day thereafter—missed her, cried over her, talked to her—until she herself disappeared. And that's when I took on the job and began a life with the dead that has, by now, put those antics of Nikki's to shame. To think how repelled I was by her—as though it were Nikki and not Death who had overstepped the limits."

◆ ◆ ◆

In 1953—nearly ten years before the notoriously histrionic decade when jugglers, magicians, musicians, folksingers, violinists, trapeze artists, agitprop acting troupes, and youngsters in odd costumes with little to go on other than what they were high on

began to exhibit themselves all over Manhattan—Sabbath,
twenty-four and recently returned from studying in Rome, set up
his screen on the east side of Broadway and 116th, just outside
the gates to Columbia University, and became a street performer.
Back then his street specialty, his trademark, was to perform with
his fingers. Fingers, after all, are made to move, and though their
range is not enormous, when each is moving purposefully and has
a distinctive voice, their power to produce their own reality can
astonish people. Sometimes, just drawing the length of a woman's
sheer stocking over one hand, Sabbath was able to create all sorts
of lascivious illusions. Sometimes, by piercing a hole in a tennis
ball and inserting a fingertip, Sabbath gave one or more of the
fingers a head, a head with a brain, and the brain provided with
schemes, manias, phobias, the works; sometimes a finger would
invite a spectator close to the screen to punch the little hole and
then to assist further by affixing the brainy ball over the fingernail. In one of his earliest programs Sabbath liked to conclude the
show by putting the middle finger of his left hand on trial. When
the court had tried the finger and found it guilty—of obscenity—a
small meat grinder was rolled out and the middle finger was
tugged and pulled by the police (the right hand) until its tip was
forced into the oval mouth at the top of the meat grinder. As the
police turned the crank, the middle finger—passionately crying
out that it was innocent of all charges, having done only what
comes naturally to a middle finger—disappeared into the meat
grinder and spaghetti strands of raw hamburger meat began to
emerge from the grinder's nether spout.

In the fingers uncovered, or even suggestively clad, there is
always a reference to the penis, and there were skits Sabbath
developed in his first years on the street where the reference
wasn't that veiled.

In one skit his hands appeared in a close-fitting pair of black
kid gloves, each with a fastener at the wrist. It took ten minutes
for him to slip the gloves off, finger by finger—a long time, ten
minutes, and when finally the fingers had all been exposed, each
by the others—and some not at all willingly—more than a few

young men in the audience could have been found to be tumescent. The effect on the young women was more difficult to discern, but they stayed, they watched, they were not embarrassed, even in 1953, to drop some coins into Sabbath's Italian peaked cap when he emerged from behind the screen at the conclusion of the twenty-five-minute show, smiling most wickedly above his close-clipped black chin beard, a small, ferocious, green-eyed buccaneer, from his years at sea as massive through the chest as a bison. He had one of those chests you don't want to get in the way of, a squat man, a sturdy physical plant, obviously very sexed-up and lawless, who didn't give a damn what anybody thought. He appeared rapidly babbling bubbly Italian and broadly gesturing his gratitude, giving no indication that holding your hands up uninterruptedly for twenty-five minutes is hard work requiring endurance and frequently painful, even for someone as strong as he was in his twenties. Of course, all the voices in the show had spoken English—Sabbath spoke Italian only afterward, and simply for the fun of it. The very reason he had established the Indecent Theater of Manhattan. The very reason he'd signed on six times for the Romance Run. The very reason he'd done just about everything since leaving home seven years earlier. He wanted to do what he wanted to do. This was his cause and it led to his arrest and trial and conviction, and for precisely the crime he'd foreseen in the meat-grinder skit.

Even from behind the screen, it was possible from certain angles for Sabbath to catch a glimpse of the audience, and whenever he spotted an attractive girl among the twenty or so students who had stopped to watch, he would break off the drama in progress or wind it down, and the fingers would start in whispering together. Then the boldest finger—a middle finger—would edge nonchalantly forward, lean graciously out over the screen, and beckon her to approach. And girls did come forward, some laughing or grinning like good sports, others serious, poker-faced, as though already mildly hypnotized. After an exchange of polite chitchat, the finger would begin a serious interrogation, asking if the girl had ever dated a finger, if her family approved of fingers, if she herself could find a finger desirable, if she could imagine living happily with only a finger . . . and the other hand, meanwhile, stealthily began to unbutton or unzip her outer garment. Usually the hand went no further than that; Sabbath knew enough not to press on and the interlude ended as a harmless farce. But sometimes, when Sabbath gauged from her answers that his consort was more playful than most or uncommonly spellbound, the interrogation would abruptly turn wanton and the fingers proceed to undo her blouse. Only twice did the fingers undo a brassiere catch and only once did they endeavor to caress the nipples exposed. And it was then that Sabbath was arrested.

How could they resist each other? Nikki was just back from RADA and answering audition calls. She lived in a room near the Columbia campus and, several days running, was among the pretty young women beckoned toward the screen by that sly, salacious middle finger. For the first time in her life she was without mother and therefore petrified on the subway, frightened on the street, fiercely lonely in her room but scared stiff about going out. She was also beginning to despair as audition after audition led nowhere, and was probably less than a week from returning across the Atlantic to the kangaroo pouch when that middle finger fingered her to join the fun. It could not have done otherwise. He was five feet five and she was nearly six feet tall, black as black can be where she was black and white as white can be where she was white. She smiled that smile that was never insignificant, the actress's smile that aroused the irrational desire to worship her even in sensible people, the smile whose message, oddly enough, was never melancholy but that said, "There are absolutely no difficulties in life"—however, she would not move an inch from where she was rooted at the far edge of the crowd. But after the show, when Sabbath burst forth with that beard and those eyes, spinning Italian sentences, Nikki had not left and did not look as though she intended to. When he approached her, begging, "Bella signorina, per favore, io non sono niente, non sono nessuno, un modest'uomo che vive solo d'aria—i soldi servono ai miei sei piccini affamati e alla mia moglie tisica—" she placed the dollar bill that was in her hand—and that represented one one-hundredth of what she had to live on per month—into his cap. This was how the couple met, how Nikki became the leading lady of the Bowery Basement Players, and how Sabbath got his chance not only to play with his fingers and his puppets but to manipulate living creatures as well.

He'd never before been a director but he was afraid of nothing, even when—especially when—he emerged guilty, with a suspended sentence and a fine, from the obscenity trial. Norman Cowan and Lincoln Gelman put up production money for the ninety-nine-seat theater on Avenue C, as poor a street as there was then in lower Manhattan. Indecent Theater finger and puppet shows were presented from six to seven three nights a week and then at eight the Bowery Basement productions, in repertory, with a company all about Sabbath's age or younger and working virtually for nothing. No one over twenty-eight or -nine was ever on stage, even in his disastrous *King Lear*, with Nikki as Cordelia and none other than the rookie director as Lear. Disastrous, but so what? The main thing is to do what you want. His cockiness, his self-exalted egoism, the menacing charm of a potentially villainous artist were insufferable to a lot of people and he made enemies easily, including a number of theater professionals who believed that his was an unseemly, brilliantly disgusting talent that had yet to discover a suitably seemly means of "disciplined" expression. Sabbath Antagonistes, busted for obscenity as far back as 1956. Sabbath Absconditus, whatever happened to him? His life was one long flight from what?

• • •

At just past 12:30 A.M. Sabbath arrived in New York and found a spot for the car a few blocks from Norman Cowan's Central Park West apartment. He hadn't been back to the city in nearly thirty years, yet upper Broadway in the dark of night looked much as he remembered it when he used to set up his screen outside the 72nd Street subway station and put on a rush-hour finger show. The side streets seemed to him unchanged, except for the bodies bundled up in rags, in blankets, under cardboard cartons, bodies encased in torn and shapeless clothing, lying up against the masonry of the apartment buildings and along the railings of the brownstones. April, yet they were sleeping out-of-doors. Sabbath knew about them only what he'd overheard Roseanna saying on the phone to the do-gooding friends. For years he had not read a paper or listened to the news if he could avoid it. The news told him nothing. The news was for people to talk about, and Sabbath, indifferent to the untransgressive run of normalized pursuits, did not wish to talk to people. He didn't care who was at war with whom or where a plane had crashed or what had befallen Bangladesh. He did not even want to know who the president was of the United States. He'd rather fuck Drenka, he'd rather fuck *anyone*, than watch Tom Brokaw. His range of pleasures was narrow and never did extend to the evening news. Sabbath was reduced the way a sauce is reduced, boiled down by his burners, the better to concentrate his essence and be defiantly himself.

But mostly he did not follow the news because of Nikki. He couldn't leaf through a paper, any paper anywhere, without searching still for some clue about Nikki. It was years before he was able to answer the ringing phone without thinking that it would be either Nikki or someone who knew about her. Crank phone calls were the worst. When Roseanna picked up the phone and it was an obscene caller or a breather, he would think, Was it somebody who knew my wife, somebody who is trying to tell me something? Could the breather have been Nikki herself? But did Nikki know where he'd moved to; had she ever even heard of Madamaska Falls? Did she know he had married Roseanna? Had she run away that night, leaving no hint of why she was going or where, because earlier in the evening she had seen him with Roseanna, the two of them crossing Tompkins Square Park and headed for his workshop?

In New York her disappearance was all he could think about— out on the streets it was obsessional, it had no end—and this was why he'd never returned. Back when he was still in their apart-

ment on St. Marks Place, he never went out that he did not think
he would pass her in the street, and so he looked at everybody and
started following people. If a woman was tall and had the right
hair—not that Nikki couldn't have dyed hers or taken to wearing
a wig—he would follow her until he caught up and then he would
measure himself against the person and, if she was about right,
would step around to look directly at her face—Let me see if this
is Nikki! It never was, though he made the acquaintance of some
of these women anyway, took them for coffee, took them for a
walk, tried to fuck them; half the time did. But he did not find
Nikki, nor did the police or the FBI or the famous detective whom
he went to hire with the help of Norman and Linc.

Back in those days—the forties, the fifties, the early sixties—
people didn't disappear the way they do today. Today if somebody disappears you're pretty sure, you immediately know, what
happened: they were murdered, they're dead. But in 1964 nobody
thought first thing of foul play. If there was no certification of
their death, you had to believe they were alive. People didn't just
drop off the edge of the earth with anything like the frequency
they do now. And so Sabbath had to think she was alive somewhere. If there wasn't a body to bury physically, he could not bury
her mentally. Although since moving to Madamaska Falls he'd
never told anybody, even Drenka, about the wife who disappeared, the fact was that Nikki wouldn't die until he did. He had
moved to Madamaska Falls when he felt himself beginning to go
crazy looking for her on the New York streets. A person could
still walk everywhere in the city in those days, and that's what he
did—walked everywhere, looked everywhere, found nothing.

The police had distributed circulars to police departments all
around the country and in Canada. Sabbath had himself sent
out hundreds of circulars, to colleges, to convents, to hospitals,
to newspaper reporters, to columnists, to Greek restaurants in
Greektowns all over America. The "missing" circular had been
assembled and printed by the police: Nikki's photo, age, height,
weight, and hair color, even what she was wearing. They knew
what clothes she'd had on because Sabbath had spent a weekend

going through her dresser and her closet until he was able to recall the items no longer there. She appeared to have left with only the clothes on her back. And how much money could she have had? Ten dollars? Twenty? Nothing had been drawn from their small bank account and not even the pile of change on the kitchen table had been disturbed. She had not taken even that.

A description of what she'd been wearing and her photo were all he could offer the detective. She had left no note, and, according to the detective, most people did. "Voluntary disappearances," he called these. The detective took down from the shelf behind his desk whole loose-leaf notebooks, as many as ten of them, with pictures and descriptions of people who had disappeared and still not been located. "Usually," he said, "they leave *something*—a note, a ring. . . ." Sabbath told him that Nikki was obsessed with the dead mother she had loved and the living father she hated. Maybe she had been seized by an impulse—God knew she was a creature of impulse—and had flown out to Cleveland to forgive the crass vulgarian she had not seen since she was seven— or to murder him. Or perhaps, despite the fact that her passport was still in a drawer in their apartment, she had somehow made her way back to London and to the spot alongside the Serpentine in Kensington Gardens where on a Sunday morning, with all the children floating their boats and flying kites, he had watched her scatter the ashes over the water.

But she could be anywhere, everywhere—where was the detective to begin? No, he wouldn't take the case, and so Sabbath went back to sending out more circulars, always with a handwritten letter from him that read, "This is my wife. She disappeared. Do you know or have you seen this person?" He sent the circulars to wherever his imagination could take him. He even thought of whorehouses. Nikki was beautiful, submissive, and certainly eye-catching in America, with her long, long body and her long-nosed black and white Greek looks—maybe she'd wound up in a whorehouse like the college girl in *Sanctuary*. He could remember once, though only once, coming upon a young woman of great refinement in a whorehouse, in Buenos Aires.

Two things, the American girl next door (that was Roseanna) and the exotic (Nikki, the romance of port life, brothel life), came together for him in New York when he started to go to whorehouses looking for his wife. There were places on upper Third Avenue where you *met* the girl next door. You walked up the stairs into a kind of salon and sometimes they tried to make it look like an old-fashioned salon out of Lautrec or some fake version of that. And there were young women lounging around, and there one found the girl next door but never, never Nikki. He became a customer at three or four of these places and showed Nikki's picture to the madams. He asked if they'd ever seen her around. The madams all gave the same answer: "I wish I had."

Then there were the fifty or so letters addressed to him at the theater, from people who had seen Nikki perform and who wanted to communicate their sympathy. He had stored the letters for her return in her dresser drawer, with the jewelry she had inherited from her mother, among them the pieces he and the embalmer had removed from the corpse—she had not taken any of that either. If he could forward her these letters—no, better if he could send the writers, transport them to wherever she was hiding out and seat her in a chair in the middle of the room, ask her to be still and to let them pass before her one at a time and take as long as they liked to tell her what she had meant to them in Strindberg, Chekhov, Shakespeare. Long before they'd all stepped up to deliver to her their emotional tributes, she would be weeping uncontrollably, not for her mother but for herself now and for the gift she had abandoned. And only after her last admirer had spoken would Sabbath enter the room. And here she would stand and put on her coat—the black form-fitting coat that was missing from the closet, the one they'd bought together at Altman's—and, without any resistance, allow him to lead her back to where she could feel coherent, of a piece, and strong, where she could think of herself as controlling events, if only for two hours—back to the stage, the only place on earth where she wasn't acting and her demons ceased to be. Being on stage was what held her together—what held *them* together. The intensification she gave everything by stepping out under the lights!

The unending mourning for her mother had made her unendurable to him; it was the actress he had to save.

As with millions upon millions of young couples, in the beginning was the sexual excitement. However baffling a mixture, Nikki's narcissism, pure as a gushing geyser, and her stupendous talent for self-abnegation seemed faultlessly wedded in her when she lay nude on the bed imploringly looking up to see what he would do with her first. And the soulfulness was there, that was always there, the romantic, ethereal side of her, her ineffectual protest against everything ugly. The taut concavity that was her belly, the alabaster apple that was her cleft behind, the pale, maidenly nipples of a fifteen-year-old, the breasts so small that you could cup them in your hand the way you hold a ladybug to prevent its flying away, the impenetrability of the eyes that drew you in and in and told you nothing, yet told you nothing so eloquently—the excitement of the yielding of all that fragility! Merely looking down at her he felt that his prick was about to burst.

"You're a vulture standing there," she said. "Does that horrify you?" "Yes," she replied. They were both surprised by what they were doing together when he first struck her backside with his belt. Nikki, who was tyrannized by nearly everyone, displayed no true fear of being whipped a little. "Not too hard," but the leather grazing her, at first lightly, then not so lightly, as she lay obligingly on her stomach, put her into an exalted state. "It's, it's . . ." "Tell me!" "It's tenderness— going wild!" It was impossible to tell who was imposing whose will on whom—was it merely Nikki once again submitting or was this the meat of her desire?

There was a nonsensical side too, of course, and more than once, disengaged from the drama by its comic dimension, Sabbath would leap up on the bed to portray that. "Oh, don't take it to heart," said Nikki, laughing; "other things hurt more than that." "For example?" "Getting up in the morning." "I like your base qualities so much, Nikoleta." "I only wish I had more for you." "You will." Smiling and frowning at once, she said sadly, "I don't think so." "You'll see," said the triumphant puppeteer, standing statuelike above her, erection in one hand and the silky sash to tie her to the bedstead in the other.

It was Nikki who turned out to be right. In time, item after item disappeared from the night table—the belt, the sash, the gag, the blindfold, the baby oil heated a little in a saucepan on the stove; after a while he could enjoy fucking her only when they'd smoked a joint, and then it needn't have been Nikki who was there, or any human thing at all.

Even the orgasms that so enthralled him began to bore him after a while. Climaxes overtook her seemingly from without, breaking upon her like a caprice, a hailstorm freakishly exploding in the middle of an August day. All that had been going on before the orgasm was for her some sort of attack that she did nothing to repel but that, however arduous, she could endlessly absorb and easily survive; yet the frenzy of her climax, the thrashing, the whimpering, the loud groaning, the opaque eyes staring fixedly upward, the fingernails digging into his scalp—that seemed a barely tolerable experience from which she might never recover. Nikki's orgasm was like a convulsion, the body bolting its skin.

Roseanna's, on the other hand, had to be galloped after like the fox in the hunt, with herself in the role of bloodthirsty foxhuntress. Roseanna's orgasm required a great deal of her, an urging onward that was breathtaking to watch (until he grew bored watching *that*). Roseanna had to fight against something resisting her and committed to another cause entirely—orgasm was not a natural development but an oddity so rare that it had to be laboriously hauled into existence. There was a suspenseful, heroic dimension to her achieving a climax. You never knew until the final moment whether or not she was going to make it or whether you yourself could stand fast without an infarction. He began to wonder if there wasn't an exaggerated and false side to her struggle, as there is when an adult plays checkers with a child and pretends to be stymied by the child's every move. *Something* was wrong, seriously wrong. But then, when you'd about given up hope, she made it, she did it, in at the kill, riding atop him, her entire being compressed in her cunt. He eventually came to feel that he needn't have been there. He could have been one of those antique marionettes with a long wooden dick. He needn't have been there—so he wasn't.

With Drenka, it was like tossing a pebble into a pond. You entered and the rippling uncoiled sinuously from the center point outward until the entire pond was undulating and aquiver with light. Whenever they had to call it quits for the day or the night, it was because Sabbath was not just at the end of his endurance but dangerously beyond it for a fatso over fifty. "Coming is an industry with you," he told her; "you're a factory." "Old-timer," she said—a word he'd taught her—while he struggled to recover his breath, "you know what I want next time you get a hard-on?" "I don't know what month that will be. Tell me now and I'll never remember." "Well, I want you to stick it all the way up." "And then what?" "Then turn me inside out over your cock. Like somebody peels off a glove."

◆ ◆ ◆

After the first year he began to fear that he might go mad looking for Nikki. And it didn't help any to leave town. Out of New York, he searched for her name in the local telephone directory. She could have changed it, of course, or shortened it, as Greek Americans frequently shortened their names for convenience' sake. The short version of Kantarakis was generally Katris—at one point Nikki had been thinking of taking Katris for a stage name, or that was the reason she gave, perhaps not even herself understanding that a new name was not going to lessen in any way her loathing for the father who had made a decent life impossible for her mother.

One winter day Sabbath was flying back from a performance at a puppet festival in Atlanta when the weather in New York became stormy and his plane was diverted to Baltimore. In the waiting room he went to a phone booth and looked up Kantarakis *and* Katris. There it was: N. Katris. He dialed the num-

ber but got no answer, and so he ran out of the airport and had a
taxi take him to the address. The house was a brown wooden
bungalow, not much more than a large shack, on a street of little
wooden bungalows. A BEWARE DOG sign was stuck into the
ground in the middle of the untended front yard. He climbed the
broken steps and knocked on the door. He wandered all around
the house trying to look in the windows, even going so far as to
climb almost to the top of the six-foot-high wire-mesh fence surrounding the front yard. One of the neighbors must have called
the police, because two officers drove up and arrested Sabbath.
Only at the station house, when he was able to phone Linc and
tell him what had happened and get him to explain to the police
that Mr. Sabbath had indeed had a wife who had disappeared
a year ago, were the charges dropped. Outside the station, despite
the police's warning him against going back and prowling, he
hailed another taxi to return him to the shack belonging to N.
Katris. It was evening now but there were no lights on. This time
in response to his knock he got the barking of what sounded like
a very large dog. Sabbath shouted, "Nikki, it's me. It's Mickey.
Nikki, you are in there! I know you are in there! Nikki, Nikki,
please open the door!" The only answer came from the dog.
Nikki would not open the door, because she never wanted to see
the son of a bitch again or because she was not there, because she
was dead, because she had killed herself or been raped and murdered and cut into pieces and thrown overboard in a weighted
sack a couple of miles out to sea from Sheepshead Bay.

To escape the increasing wrath of the dog he ran to the next
bungalow and knocked on that door. A black woman's voice
called from within, "Who is that?" "I'm looking for your neighbor—Nikki!" "For what?" "I'm looking for my wife, Nikki Katris." "Nope" was all he got back from her. "Next door. Number
583, your neighbor, N. Katris. Please, I have to find my wife. She
disappeared!" The door was opened by an alarmingly thin and
wrinkled elderly black woman, holding herself upright with a
cane and wearing dark glasses. She spoke with tender amusement.
"You beat her, now you want her back to beat again." "I did not

beat her." "How come she disappear? You beat a woman, she got half a brain, she run away." "Please, who lives next door? Answer me!" "Your wife, she got herself a new boyfriend by now. And know what? *He* gonna beat her. Some women is like that." With this observation she shut the door.

He got a flight to New York later that evening. It had taken that blind old black woman to get him to understand that he had been jilted, discarded, abandoned! She had spurned him, left a year ago with somebody else and he was still out looking for her and grieving for her and wondering where she was! It wasn't him fucking Roseanna that had caused her to flee! It was Nikki fucking somebody new!

At home he began to fall apart for the first time since she had disappeared, and, up with the Gelmans in Bronxville, he had cried in his room every night for two weeks. Roseanna was living with him in the apartment now, making her ceramic necklaces again and selling them to a shop in the Village so they had some money to survive on. Sabbath's drama company had very nearly dissolved and the audience had deserted him, largely because there was no one in the company—maybe no one her age in New York—with anything like Nikki's magic. Over the months the acting had become worse and worse because of Sabbath's inattention—he would watch a rehearsal and see not a thing. And he rarely went out in the streets with his finger act, because all he did out on the street was begin to look for Nikki. Look at women and follow women. Sometimes he screwed them. Might as well.

Roseanna had been hysterical when he reached home that night. "Why didn't you phone me! Where were you? Your plane landed without you! What was I to think? What do you *think* I thought?"

In the bathroom, Sabbath got down on his knees on the tile floor and said to himself, "You can't do this anymore or you *will* go crazy. Roseanna will go crazy. You will be insane for the rest of your life. I cannot cry about it ever again. Oh, God, just don't let me do this ever again!"

Not for the first time he thought of his mother sitting on the boardwalk waiting for Morty to come back from the war. She never believed he was dead, either. The one thing you can't think is that they're dead. They have another life. You give yourself all sorts of reasons why they haven't come home. You get into the rumor business. Somebody would swear he had seen Nikki performing under another name in a summer theater in Virginia. The police would report that somebody had spotted a crazy woman who resembled her description on the Canadian border. Only Linc, when they were alone, had the courage to say to him, "Mick, don't you really know she's dead?" And the answer was always the same: "Where is the body?" No, the wound never closes, the wound remains fresh, as it had till the very end for his mother. She had been stopped when Morty was killed, stopped from going forward, and all the logic went out of her life. She wanted life, as all people do, to be logical and linear, as orderly as she made the house and her kitchen and the boys' bureau drawers. She had worked so hard to be in control of a household's destiny. All her life she waited not only for Morty but for the explanation from Morty: why? The question haunted Sabbath. Why? Why? If only someone will explain to us *why*, maybe we could accept it. Why did you die? Where did you go? However much you may have hated me, why don't you come back so we can continue with our linear, logical life like all the other couples who hate each other?

Nikki had had a performance of *Miss Julie* that night, Nikki, who never once failed to show up to work, even reeling with a fever. Sabbath, as usual, was spending the evening with Roseanna and so had not found out what happened until he got home half an hour before Nikki was due back from the theater. That was what was wonderful about having an actress for a wife—at night you always knew her whereabouts and how long she would be gone. At first he thought that maybe she had gone out looking for him; maybe because she had her suspicions, she had taken a circuitous route to the theater and come upon Sabbath crossing the park with his hand on Roseanna's ass. She might well have seen them going through the front door of the brownstone where he had his tiny workshop room at the rear of the top floor. Nikki was explosive, crazily emotional, and could do and say bizarre things and not even remember them afterward, or remember but fail to see why they were bizarre.

Sabbath had been complaining to Roseanna that night about his wife's incapacity to separate fantasy from reality or to understand the connection between cause and effect. Early on in life either she or her mother, or both conspiring together, had cast little Nikki as the blameless victim, and consequently she could never see where she was responsible for anything. Only on the stage did she shed this pathological innocence and take over, herself determining how things were going to come out, and, with exquisite tact, turn something imagined into something real. He told Roseanna the story of her slapping the face of the ambulance driver in London and then talking to her mother's corpse for three days, about how, even down to a few days before her disappearance, Nikki was repeating how glad she was she'd "said good-bye to Momma" as she had, how satisfying that remained. She even made a crack, as she did each time she recalled the three days of fondling the corpse, about how cruel it was of the Jews to "dump" their dead as soon as they could, a remark that Sabbath decided once more not to call her on. Why correct that idiocy rather than all the other idiocies? In *Miss Julie* she was everything she couldn't be outside *Miss Julie:* cunning, knowing, radiant, imperious—everything *but* shrinking from the reality. The reality of the play. It was only the reality of reality by which she was benumbed. Nikki's aversions, her fears, her hysteria—he was full of grievance, yet another spouse absolutely steeped in it, didn't know, he told Roseanna, how much more he could take.

And he and Roseanna fucked and she left and he went to St. Marks Place, and there were Norman and Linc sitting on the steps of his building. Sabbath had hurried home to shower away Rosie's smell before Nikki got in. One night when Nikki believed Sabbath was asleep, she had begun to sniff under the blankets and he realized only then that he had forgotten Rosie's visit at lunchtime and had gone to bed having washed his face and nothing more. And that was just a week earlier.

Norman told him what had happened, while Linc sat there with his head in his hands. Nikki had no understudy and so, even though the house was sold out, as it had been since the opening, the performance had to be canceled, the money refunded, and everybody sent home. And nobody could find Sabbath to tell him. His producers had been waiting on the steps for over an hour. Linc, woefully wracked by all this, pleadingly asked Sabbath if he knew where she was. Sabbath assured him that as soon as she had calmed down and had begun to get over whatever it was that had upset her, she'd call and come back. He wasn't worried. Nikki could behave oddly, very oddly; they didn't *know* how oddly. "This," said Sabbath, "is just one of her strange things."

But upstairs in the apartment his two young producers made Sabbath call the police.

◆ ◆ ◆

He was in New York less than five minutes when he began to be haunted all over again by "Why?" He had to restrain himself from using the tip of his muddied old boots (muddied from the treks out to the graveyard) to awaken, one by one, those bodies buried under their rags, to see if perhaps a white woman was among them who had once been his wife. Withdrawn, mannerly, intense, tremulous, unearthly, moody, mesmeric Nikki, a difficult personality impossible ever to grasp, whose mark on him was indelible, who could more confidently imitate someone than be someone, who'd clung to her emotional virginity until the day she'd disappeared, whose fears, even without danger or misfortune at hand, were streaming through her all the time, whom he had married out of sheer fascination with her gift, at only twenty-two, for unartificial self-transformation, for duplicating realities she knew virtually nothing about, who unfailingly imparted to everything anyone ever said an inward, idiosyncratic, insulting significance, who was never really at home outside the fairy tale, a juvenile whose theatrical specialty was the most mature roles . . . into whom had she been changed by an existence free of him? What had become of her? And why?

As of April 12, 1994, there was still no certification of her death, and though our need to bury our dead is strong, we have first to be sure the person *is* dead. *Had* she returned to Cleveland? To London? To Salonika to pretend there to be her mother? But she'd had neither a passport nor money. Had she run away from him or from everything, or had she run away from being an actress just when it had become overwhelmingly apparent that she could not avoid an extraordinary career? That had already begun to terrify her, the demands of that kind of success. She would be fifty-seven in May. He never failed to remember her birthday or the date she'd disappeared. What did Nikki look like now? Her mother before the formaldehyde or after? She had already outlived her mother by twelve years—if she had lived beyond November 7, 1964.

What would Morty look like now if he had walked away from his downed plane in 1944? What did Drenka look like now? If they dug her up, could you still tell she'd been a woman, the most womanly of women? Could he have fucked her after she was dead? Why not?

Yes, fleeing for New York that evening he'd believed he was running off to see Linc's corpse, but it was the body of his first wife he could never stop thinking about, *her* body, alive, that he might at last be shepherded to. It did not matter that the idea made no sense. Sabbath's sixty-four years of life had long ago released him from the falsity of sense. You would think this would make him deal better with loss than he did. Which only goes to show what everyone learns sooner or later about loss: the absence of a presence can crush the strongest people.

"But why bring it up?" he snarled at his mother. "Why Nikki, Nikki, Nikki when I'm close to death myself!" And she finally spoke out, his little mother, gave it to him on the corner of Central Park West and West 74th Street as she never dared to in life once he was twelve and already muscular and belligerently grown-up. "That's the thing you know best," she told him, "have thought about most, *and you don't know anything.*"

S TRANGE," Norman said, reflecting on Sabbath's tribulations.
Sabbath waited to let sympathy work the man over just a little
more before he quietly corrected him. "Extremely," said Sabbath.
"Yes," Norman shot back, "I think it's fair to say extremely."
They were at the kitchen table, a beautiful table, large glazed
ivory-colored Italian tiles bordered by bright hand-painted tiles of
vegetables and fruit. Michelle, Norman's wife, was asleep in their
bedroom, and the two old friends, seated across from each other,
were speaking softly of the night when Nikki failed to turn up at
the theater and nobody knew where she was. Norman wasn't at
all as at ease with Sabbath as he'd been on the phone the night
before; the scope of Sabbath's transfiguration seemed to astonish
him, in part perhaps because of his own mammoth treasure of
satisfied dreams, apparent everywhere Sabbath looked, including into Norman's bright, brown, benevolent eyes. Tanned from
a tennis vacation in the sun and as thin and athletically flexible as
he'd been as a young man, he showed no sign that Sabbath could
see of his recent depression. Since he was already bald by the time
he left college, *nothing* about him seemed changed.

Norman was no fool, had read books and traveled widely, but
to comprehend, in the flesh, a failure like Sabbath's appeared to
be as difficult as coming to terms with Linc's suicide, and maybe
more so. Linc's condition he had observed worsening each year,
while the Sabbath who had forsaken New York in 1965 had

virtually no affinity to the man sighing over a sandwich at the kitchen table in 1994. Sabbath had washed his hands, face, and beard in the bathroom, and still, he realized, he unnerved Norman no less than if he had been a tramp whom Norman had foolishly invited home to spend the night. Perhaps over the years Norman had come to inflate Sabbath's departure to a high artistic drama—a search for independence in the sticks, for spiritual purity and tranquil meditation; if Norman thought of him at all, he would, as a spontaneously good-hearted person, have tried to remember what he admired about him. And why did that annoy Sabbath? He was irritated not nearly so much by the perfect kitchen and the perfect living room and the perfect everything in all the rooms that opened off the book-lined corridor as by the charity. That he, Sabbath, could inspire such feelings of course entertained him. Of course it was fun to see himself through Norman's eyes. But it was hideous as well.

Norman was asking if Sabbath had ever come close to picking up Nikki's trail after she had disappeared. "I left New York in order to stop trying," Sabbath replied. "It bothered me sometimes to realize that she didn't know where I lived. What if she wanted to find me? But if she did, she'd find Roseanna, too. Once I was up in the mountains I never allowed myself the pleasure of keeping Nikki in my life. I didn't imagine her with a husband and children. I was going to find her, she was going to turn up—I stopped all that. The only way for me to understand it was not to think about it. You have to take this bizarre thing and put it away in order to proceed with your life. What was the point of thinking about it?"

"And is that what the mountain represents? A place not to think about Nikki?"

Norman was trying to ask only intelligent questions, and they *were* intelligent, and they missed entirely the point of Sabbath's descent.

Sabbath went on exchanging sentences with Norman that could as well have been true as not. It was a matter of indifference to him. "My life was changed. I just couldn't go forward with that

amount of speed anymore. I couldn't go forward at all. The idea
of controlling anything went completely out of my head. The
thing with Nikki left me," he said, smiling with what he hoped
would be a wan expression, "in a somewhat awkward position."

"I would think."

If I had appeared at the door without having called from the
road, if I had got by the doorman unnoticed and taken the elevator to the eighteenth floor and knocked on the Cowans' door,
Norman would never have recognized the man in the foyer as me.
With the oversize hunting jacket atop the rube's flannel shirt and
these big muddy boots on my feet, I look like a visitor from
Dogpatch, either like a bearded character in a comic strip or
somebody at your doorstep in 1900, a wastrel uncle from the
Russian pale who is to sleep in the cellar next to the coal bin for
the rest of his American life. Through the lens of unforewarned
Norman, Sabbath saw what he looked like, had come to look
like, didn't care that he looked like, deliberately looked like—and
it pleased him. He'd never lost the simple pleasure, which went
way back, of making people uncomfortable, comfortable people
especially.

Yet there was something thrilling in seeing Norman. Sabbath
felt much as poor parents do when they visit their kids in the
suburbs who've made it big—humbled, mystified, out of their
element, but proud. He was proud of Norman. Norman had lived
in the theatrical shit-world for a lifetime and had not himself
become a stupid shit. Could he be so considerate on the job, so
goodnatured and decent and thoughtful? They would tear him to
pieces. And still to Sabbath it seemed that Norman's humane
disposition had only enlarged with age and success. There wasn't
enough he could do to make Sabbath feel at home. Maybe it
wasn't repulsion at all that he felt but something like awe at the
sight of white-bearded Sabbath, come down from his mountaintop like some holy man who has renounced ambition and worldly
possessions. Can it be that there *is* something religious about me?
Has what I've done—i.e., failed to do—been saintly? I'll have to
phone Rosie and tell her.

Whatever lay behind it, Norman couldn't have been more so-
licitous. But then, he and Linc, sons of prosperous fathers and
Jersey City friends since childhood, could not have been kinder
from the moment they set up their partnership fresh out of Columbia and paid the expenses arising from Sabbath's obscenity
trial. They had extended to Sabbath that respect edged with reverence which was associated in Sabbath's mind less with the way
you deal with an entertainer (the most he'd ever been—Nikki was
the artist) than with the manner in which you approach an elderly
clergyman. There was something exciting for these two privileged
Jewish boys in having, as they liked to say then, "discovered Mick
Sabbath." It kindled their youthful idealism to learn that Sabbath
was the son of a poor butter-and-egg man from a tiny working-
class Jersey shore town, that instead of attending college he had
shipped out as a merchant seaman at seventeen, that he'd lived
two years in Rome on the GI Bill after coming out of the Army,
that married only a year he was already on the prowl, that the
spookily beautiful young wife whom he bossed around off the
stage as well as on—an oddball herself but obviously much better
born than he and probably, as an actress, a genius, too—couldn't
seem to survive half an hour without him. There was an excitement about the way he affronted people without caring. He was
not just a newcomer with a potentially huge theatrical talent but a
young adventurer robustly colliding with life, already in his twenties a real-lifer, urged on to excess by a temperament more ele-
mental than either of their own. Back in the fifties there was
something thrillingly alien about "Mick."

Sitting safely in the Manhattan kitchen sipping the last of the
beer Norman had poured him, Sabbath was by now certain
whose head Officer Balich had meant to split open. Either something incriminating had turned up in Drenka's belongings or Sabbath had been observed at the cemetery at night. Wifeless, mistressless, penniless, vocationless, homeless . . . and now, to top
things off, on the run. If he weren't too old to go back to sea, if his
fingers weren't crippled, if Morty had lived and Nikki hadn't been
insane, or he hadn't been—if there weren't war, lunacy, perversity,

sickness, imbecility, suicide, and death, chances were he'd be in a lot better shape. He'd paid the full price for art, only he hadn't made any. He'd suffered all the old-fashioned artistic sufferings—isolation, poverty, despair, mental and physical obstruction—and nobody knew or cared. And though nobody knowing or caring was another form of artistic suffering, in his case it had no artistic meaning. He was just someone who had grown ugly, old, and embittered, one of billions.

Obeying the laws of disappointment, disobedient Sabbath began to cry, and not even he could tell whether the crying was an act or the measure of his misery. And then his mother spoke up for the second time that evening—in the kitchen now, and trying to comfort her only living son. "This is human life. There is a great hurt that everyone has to endure."

Sabbath (who liked to think that distrusting the sincerity of everyone armed him a little against betrayal by everything): I've even fooled a ghost. But while he thought this—his head a lumpish, sobbing sandbag on the table—he also thought, And yet how I crave to cry!

Crave? Please. No, Sabbath didn't believe a word he said and hadn't for years; the closer he tried to get to describing how he arrived at becoming this failure rather than another, the further he seemed from the truth. True lives belonged to others, or so others believed.

Norman had reached across the table to take one of Sabbath's hands in his.

Good. They'd let him stay for at least a week.

"You," he said to Norman, "you understand what matters."

"Yeah, I'm a master of the art of living. That's why I'm eight months on Prozac."

"All I know how to do is antagonize."

"Well, that and a few other things."

"A really trivial, really shitty life."

"The beers went to your head. When someone is exhausted and down like you, everything gets exaggerated. Linc's suicide has a lot to do with it. We've *all* been through it."

"Repugnant to everyone."

"Come *on,*" Norman replied, increasing the firmness of his hold on Sabbath's hand . . . but when was he going to tell him, "I think you had better move in with us"? Because Sabbath could not go back. Roseanna wouldn't have him in the house, and Matthew Balich had found him out and was furious enough to kill him. He had nowhere to go and nothing to do. Unless Norman said, "Move in," he was finished.

Suddenly Sabbath raised his head from the table and said, "My mother was in a catatonic depression from the time I was fifteen."

"You never told me that."

"My brother was killed in the war."

"I didn't know that either."

"We were one of those families with a gold star in the window. It meant that not only was my brother dead, my mother was dead. All day at school I thought, 'If only when I get home, he's there; if only when the war is over, he's there.' What a frightening thing that gold star was to see when I came home from school. Some days I'd actually manage to forget about him, but then I'd walk home and see the gold star. Maybe that's why I went to sea, to get the fuck away from the gold star. The gold star said, 'People have suffered something terrible in this house.' The house with the gold star was a blighted house."

"Then you get married and your wife disappears."

"Yes, but that left me all the wiser. I could never again think about the future. What did the future hold for me? I never think in terms of expectations. My expectation is how to deal with bad news."

Trying to talk sensibly and reasonably about his life seemed even more false to him than the tears—every word, every *syllable,* another moth nibbling a hole in the truth.

"And it still throws you to think about Nikki?"

"No," said Sabbath, "not at all. Thirty years later all I think is, 'What the fuck was that?' It becomes more unreal the older I get. Because the things I told myself when I was young—maybe she went here, maybe she went there—those things don't apply any longer. She was struggling always for something only her mother seemed able to give—maybe she's out there looking for it still. That's what I thought then. At this distance, it's just, 'Did all that really happen?'"

"And the ramifications?" Norman asked. He was relieved to see Sabbath back under control but continued nonetheless to hold on to him. And Sabbath allowed him to, however annoying that had become. "Its effect on you. How did it injure you?"

Sabbath took time to think—and this is more or less what he was thinking: These questions are futile to answer. Behind the answer there is another answer, and an answer behind that answer, and on and on. And all Sabbath is doing, to satisfy Norman, is to pretend to be someone who does not understand this.

"I seem injured?"

They laughed together, and Norman only then let go of his hand. Another sentimental Jew. You could fry the sentimental Jews in their own grease. Something was always *moving* them. Sabbath could never really stand either of these morally earnest, supercoddled successes, Cowan *or* Gelman.

"That's like asking how much did it injure me to be born. How can I know? What can I know about it? I can only tell you that the idea of controlling anything is out of my mind. And that's how I choose to move along in life."

"Pain, pain, so much pain," said Norman. "How can you possibly get over minding it?"

"What difference would it make if I minded? It wouldn't change anything. Do I mind? It never occurs to me to mind. Okay, I got overemotional. But *minding*? What's the point of minding? What was the point of trying to find reason or meaning in any of these things? By the time I was twenty-five I already knew there wasn't any."

"And isn't there any?"

"Ask Linc tomorrow, when they open the coffin. He'll tell you. He was antic and funny and full of energy. I remember Lincoln very well. He didn't want to know anything ugly. He wanted it to be nice. He loved his parents. I remember when his old man came backstage. A carbonated-drink manufacturer. A tycoon in seltzer if I remember correctly."

"No. Quench."

"Quench. That was the stuff."

"Quench Wild Cherry sent Linc to Taft. Linc called it Kvetch."

"A suntanned little endurer with steel-gray hair, the old man. Started out with just the crap he bottled and a truck he drove himself. In his undershirt. Crude. Ungrammatical. Built like something that had been baled. Linc was sitting on a chair in Nikki's dressing room and just took his father and pulled him onto his lap and held him there while we were all talking after the show, and neither of them thought anything of it. He adored his old man. He adored his wife. He adored his kids. At least when I knew him he did."

"He always did."

"So where's the meaning?"

"I have some ideas."

"You don't know anything, Norman—you don't know anything about anyone. Did I know Nikki? Nikki had another life. Everybody has another life. I knew she was eccentric. But so was I. I understood I wasn't living with Doris Day. A little irrational, out of touch, prone to crazy outbursts, but irrational enough and crazy enough for what happened to happen? Did I know my mother? Sure. She went around whistling all day long. Nothing was too much for her. Look what became of her. Did I know my brother? The discus, the swimming team, the clarinet. Killed at twenty."

"Disappear. Even the word is strange."

"Stranger is the word *reappear*."

"How is Roseanna?"

Sabbath looked at his watch, a round stainless steel watch half a century old this year. Black face, white luminous dial and hands. Morty's Army Benrus, with twelve- and twenty-four-hour numbers and a second hand you could stop by pulling on the crown. For synchronization when you flew a mission. A lot of good the synchronization did Morty. Once a year Sabbath sent the watch to a place in Boston where they cleaned and oiled it and replaced worn-out parts. He had been winding the watch every morning since it became his in 1945. His grandfathers had laid tefillin every morning and thought of God; he wound Morty's watch every morning and thought of Morty. The watch had been returned by the government with Morty's things in 1945. The body came back two years later.

"Well," said Sabbath, "Roseanna . . . Just about seven hours ago, Roseanna and I split up. Now *she's* disappeared. That's what it comes down to, Mort: folks disappearin' left and right."

"Where is she? Do you know?"

"Oh, at home."

"Then it's you who have disappeared."

"Trying," said Sabbath, and again, suddenly, a great onslaught of tears, anguish so engulfing that in the first moment he could no longer even ask himself whether or not this second collapse of the evening was any more or less honestly manufactured than the first. He was drained of skepticism, cynicism, sarcasm, bitterness, mockery, self-mockery, and such lucidity, coherence, and objectivity as he possessed—had run out of everything that marked him as Sabbath except desperation; of that he had a superabundance. He had called Norman Mort. He was crying now the way anyone cries who has had it. There was passion in his crying—terror, great sadness, and defeat.

Or was there? Despite the arthritis that disfigured his fingers, in his heart he was the puppeteer still, a lover and master of guile, artifice, and the unreal—this he hadn't yet torn out of himself. When that went, he *would* be dead.

"Are you all right, Mick?" Norman had come around the table to place his hands on Sabbath's shoulders. "*Did* you leave your wife?"

Sabbath reached up to cover Norman's hands with his own. "I have amnesia suddenly about the circumstances, but . . . yes, it appears that way. She's no longer enslaved by alcohol or me. Both demons driven out by AA. What it probably comes down to is she wants to keep the paycheck for herself."

"She was supporting you."

"I had to live."

"Where will you go after the funeral?"

He looked at Norman, smiling broadly. "Why not with Linc?"

"What are you telling me? You're going to kill yourself? I want to know if that's what you're thinking. Are you thinking about suicide?"

"No, no, I'll go on to the end."

"Is that the truth?"

"I'm inclined to think so. I'm a suicide like I'm everything: a pseudosuicide."

"Look, this is serious business," Norman told him. "We're now in this together."

"Norman, I haven't seen you in a hundred years. We're not in anything together."

"We are in *this* together! If you're going to kill yourself, you're going to do it in front of me. When you're ready you have to wait for me to get there and then do it in front of me."

Sabbath did not reply.

"You have to see a doctor," Norman told him. "You have to see a doctor tomorrow. Do you need money?"

From his wallet, full of illegible notes and telephone numbers scribbled on paper scraps and matchbook covers—fat with everything but credit cards and cash—Sabbath fished out a blank check for his and Roseanna's account. He made it out for three hundred dollars. When he realized that Norman, watching him write, saw printed on the check the names of husband and wife both, Sabbath explained, "I'm cleaning it out. If she's beaten me to it and it bounces, I'll send you back the cash."

"Forget that. Where's three hundred dollars going to get you? You're in a bad way, boy."

"I have no expectations."

"You tried that on me. Why don't you sleep here tomorrow night too? Stay as long as you need us. All the children are gone. The baby, Deborah, is away at Brown. The house is empty. You can't rush off after the funeral not knowing where you're going, and feeling the way you do. You have got to see a doctor."

"No," said Sabbath, "no. I can't stay here."

"Then you have to be hospitalized."

And this brought forth Sabbath's third round of tears. He had cried like this only once before in his life, over Nikki's disappearance. And when Morty died he had watched his mother cry worse than this.

Hospitalized. Until that word was spoken he had believed that all this crying could easily be spurious, and so it was a considerable disappointment to discover that it did not seem within his power to switch it off.

While Norman coaxed him up out of the kitchen chair and walked him across the dining room, through the living room, and down the corridor to Deborah's bedroom, then steered him onto the bed, untied the caked laces of his Dogpatch boots and pulled them off his feet, Sabbath shook. If he was not coming apart but only simulating, then this was the greatest performance of his life. Even as his teeth chattered, even as he could feel his jowls tremble beneath his ridiculous beard Sabbath thought, So, something new. And more to come. And perhaps less of it to be chalked up to guile than to the fact that the inner reason for his being— whatever the hell that might be, perhaps guile itself—had ceased to exist.

He managed only three words Norman could fully understand. "Where is everybody?"

"They're here," Norman said, to soothe him. "They're all here."

"No," replied Sabbath once he was alone. "They all escaped."

•   •   •

While Sabbath ran a bath in the girlishly pretty pink and white bathroom just off Deborah's room, he interested himself in the contents, all jumbled together, of the two drawers beneath the sink—the lotions, the ointments, the pills, the powders, the Body Shop jars, the contact lens cleaner, the tampons, the nail polish, the polish remover. . . . Working through the clutter to the bottom of each drawer, he found not a single photograph—let alone a stash—of the kind Drenka had unearthed from among Silvija's things during the next-to-last summer of her life. The one item at all beguiling, aside from the tampons, was a tube of vaginal lubricating cream twisted back on itself and nearly empty. He removed the cap to squeeze a speck of the amber grease into the palm of his hand and rubbed it between his thumb and his middle finger, remembering things as he smeared the stuff over his fingertips, all sorts of things about Drenka. He screwed the cap back on and set the tube out on the tiled counter for experimentation later.

After undressing in Deborah's room, he had looked at all the photographs in their transparent plastic frames on her bureau and desk. He would get to the drawers and closets in time. She was a dark-haired girl with a demure, pleasing smile, an intelligent smile. He couldn't tell much else because her figure was hidden from view by the other young people in the pictures; yet of all the faces hers alone had about it at least a touch of the enigmatic. Despite the juvenile innocence she so abundantly offered the camera, she looked to have something of a mind, even some wit, and lips whose protuberance was her greatest treasure, a hungry, seductive mouth set in the most undepraved face you could imagine. Or that's how Sabbath read it at close to two A.M. He had been hoping for a girl more tantalizing, but the mouth and the youth would have to do. Before getting into the bath, he trundled in the nude back to her bedroom and took from the desk the largest picture of her he could find, a photograph in which Deborah was nestled up against the muscular shoulder of a burly redhead of about her age. He was beside her in virtually every photograph. The deadly boyfriend.

All Sabbath did for the moment was lie in the wonderful warm bath in the pink-and-white-tiled bathroom and scrutinize the picture, as though in his gaze lay the power to transport Deborah home to her tub. Reaching out with one arm, Sabbath was able to raise the lid to expose the seat of Deborah's pink toilet. He rubbed his hand round and round the satiny seat and was just beginning to harden when there was a light rap on the bathroom door. "You all right in there?" Norman asked and pushed the door open a ways to be sure Sabbath wasn't drowning himself.

"Fine," said Sabbath. It had taken no time to retract his hand from the toilet seat, but the photograph was in the other hand and the twisted tube of vaginal cream was up on the counter. He held out the picture so that Norman could see which one it was. "Deborah," Sabbath said.

"Yes. That is Deborah."

"Sweet," said Sabbath.

"Why do you have the photograph in the bathtub?"

"To look at it."

The silence was indecipherable—what it meant or foretold Sabbath could not imagine. All he knew for sure was that Norman was more frightened of him than he was of Norman. Being nude also seemed to bestow an advantage with a conscience as developed as Norman's, the advantage of seeming defenselessness. Sabbath's talent for this sort of scene Norman could not hope to equal: the talent of a ruined man for recklessness, of a saboteur for subversion, even the talent of a lunatic—or a simulated lunatic—to overawe and horrify ordinary people. Sabbath had the power, and he knew it, of being no one with anything much to lose.

Norman hadn't seemed to notice the vaginal cream tube.

Which of us is lonelier at this moment, Sabbath wondered. And what is he thinking? "Enter our terrorist. *I* should drown him." But Norman needed admiration in the ways that Sabbath never had, and more than likely he wouldn't do it.

"It would be a shame," Norman finally said, "if it got wet."

Sabbath didn't believe he had an erection, but an ambiguity in Norman's words caused him to wonder. He didn't look to see but instead asked a perfectly innocent question. "Who's the lucky boy?"

"Freshman-year sweetheart. Robert." Norman spoke with his hand extended toward the photograph. "Only recently replaced by Will." Sabbath leaned forward in the tub and handed the photograph over, noting, alas, as he moved, his dick angled upward in the water.

"You're feeling like yourself again," Norman said, staring Sabbath in the eyes.

"I am, thank you. Much better."

"It's never been easy to say what you really are, Mickey."

"Oh, failure will do."

"But at what?"

"Failure at failing, for one."

"You always fought being a human being, right from the beginning."

"To the contrary," said Sabbath. "To being a human being I've always said, 'Let it come.'"

Here Norman picked up the vaginal cream from the tile counter, opened the bottom drawer beneath the sink, and tossed in the tube. He seemed to have surprised himself more than Sabbath by the force with which he slammed the drawer shut.

"I've left a glass of milk on the nightstand," Norman said. "You may need it. Warm milk sometimes helps sedate me."

"Great," Sabbath said. "Good night. Sleep tight."

As Norman was about to leave, he took a look over at the toilet. He would never guess why the cover was up. And yet the final glance he turned on Sabbath suggested otherwise.

After Norman's departure, Sabbath lifted himself out of the tub and, dripping water as he moved, went to get the photograph from where Norman had returned it to Deborah's desk.

In the bathroom again, Sabbath opened the drawer, withdrew the vaginal cream, and held the tube to his lips. He squirted a pea-size gob on his tongue and rolled it across his palate and up against his teeth. A vaguely Vaseline-like aftertaste. That was all. But then, what was he hoping for? The tang of Deborah herself?

Back in the tub with the photograph, he resumed at the point where he had been interrupted.

• • •

Up not once to use the john. First time in years. The father's milk pacifying the prostate, or was it the daughter's bed? First he'd removed the fresh pillowcase and, scavenging with his nose, hunted down the odor of her hair clinging to the pillow itself. Then, by a process of trial and error, he'd detected a barely perceptible furrow just to the right of the mattress's vertical midpoint, a minuscule groove cast by the mold of her body, and between her sheets, on her caseless pillow, in that groove, he had *slept*. In this Laura Ashley'd room of pink and yellow, a computer comatose on the desk, a Dalton School decal decorating the mirror, teddy bears tumbled together in a wicker basket, Metropolitan Museum posters up on the walls, K. Chopin, T. Morrison, A. Tan, V. Woolf in the bookcase, along with childhood favorites—*The Yearling*, Andersen's *Fairy Tales*—and on the desk and the dresser framed photos in abundance of the gang, wearing swimsuits, skiing gear, formal attire . . . in this candy-striped room with the flowery border, where she'd first fallen upon her clitoral entitlements, Sabbath was himself seventeen again, aboard a tramp steamer full of drunken Norwegians docking at one of the great Brazilian ports—Bahia, at the entrance of Todos os Santos Bay, the Amazon, the great Amazon, unwinding not far away. There was that smell. Unbelievable. Cheap perfume, coffee, and pussy. His head wrapped round with Deborah's pillow, a full body press on her groove, he was remembering Bahia, where there was a church and a whorehouse for every day of the year. So said the Norwegian seamen, and at seventeen he had no reason not to believe them. Be nice to go back and check it out. If she were mine, I'd send Deborah there for her junior year. Free play for the imagination in Bahia. With the American sailors alone she'd have the time of her life—Hispanic, black, even Finns, Finnish Americans, every type of redneck, old men, young boys. . . . Learn more about creative writing in one month in Bahia than in four years at Brown. Let her do something unreasonable, Norman. Look what it did for me.

Whores. Played a leading role in my life. Always felt at home with whores. Particularly fond of whores. The stewlike stink of those oniony parts. What has ever meant more to me? Real reasons for existence then. But now, preposterously, the morning hard-on was gone. The things one has to put up with in life. The morning hard-on—like a crowbar in your hand, like something growing out of an ogre. Does any other species wake up with a hard-on? Do whales? Do bats? Evolution's daily reminder to male *Homo sapiens* in case, overnight, they forget why they're here. If a woman didn't know what it was, it might well scare her to death. Couldn't piss in the bowl because of that thing. Had to force it downward with your hand—had to train it as you would a dog to the leash—so that the stream struck the water and not the upturned seat. When you sat to shit, there it was, loyally looking up at its master. There eagerly waiting while you brush your teeth—"What are we going to do today?" Nothing more faithful in all of life than the lurid cravings of the morning hard-on. No deceit in it. No simulation. No insincerity. All hail to that driving force! Human living with a capital *L!* It takes a lifetime to determine what matters, and by then it's not there anymore. Well, one must learn to adapt. How is the only problem.

He tried to think of a reason to get up, let alone to go on living. Deborah's toilet seat? A glimpse of Linc's corpse? Her *things*— and remembering delving into *the things,* he was out of the bed and across to the dresser beside the Bang & Olufsen music system.

Brimming! A treasure trove! Brilliant hues of silk and satin. Childish cotton underpants with red circus stripes. String bikinis with satin behinds. Stretch satin thong bikinis. Floss your teeth with those thongs. Garter belts in purple, black, and white. Renoir's palette! Rose. Pale pink. Navy. White. Purple. Gold. Red. Peach. Underwired black embroidered bras. Lace push-up bras with little bows. Scalloped lace half-bras. Satin half-bras. C cup. A vipers' nest of multicolored pantyhose. In white, black, and a chocolatey brown, sheer silk-lace *panty* pantyhose of the kind that Drenka wore to drive him nuts. A delicious butter-scotch-color silk camisole. Leopard-print panties with matching bra. Lace body stockings, *three,* and all black. A strapless black satin bodysuit with padded push-up cups, edged with lace and hooks and straps. Straps. Bra straps, garter straps, Victorian cor-set straps. Who in his right mind doesn't adore straps, all the abracadabra of holding and lifting? And what about strap*less?* A strapless bra. Christ, everything works. That thing they call a teddy (Roosevelt? Kennedy? Herzl?), all in one a chemise up top and, down below, loose-fitting panties with leg holes that you slip right into without removing a thing. Silk floral bikini underpants. Half-slips. Loved the outmoded half-slip. A woman in a half-slip and a bra standing and ironing a shirt while seriously smoking a cigarette. Sentimental old Sabbath.

He sniffed the pantyhose to find a pair that hadn't been washed, then headed with it for the bathroom. Sat to piss the way D. did. D.'s seat. D.'s pantyhose. But the morning hard-on was of the past. . . . Drenka! It *was* a crowbar with you! Fifty-two years old, a source of life to a hundred men, and dead! It isn't fair! The urge, the urge! You've seen it over and over again, done it over and over again, and five minutes later it fascinates you *again.* What every man knows: the urge to indulge *again.* I should never have given it up, thought Sabbath—the life of the sensual port like Bahia, even of the shitty little ports around the Amazon, literally jungle ports, where one could mix with the crews of all kinds of ships, sailors of as many colors as Debby's underthings, from all kinds of countries, and they were all going to the same place, all ended up in the whorehouse. Everywhere, as in a lurid dream, sailors and women, women and sailors, and I was learning my trade. The eight-to-twelve watch and then working all day as a seaman on deck, chipping and painting, chipping and paint-ing, and then the watch, the sea watch in the bow of the ship. And sometimes it was gorgeous. I had been reading O'Neill. I was reading Conrad. A guy on board had given me books. I was reading all that stuff and jerking myself off over it. Dos-toyevsky—everybody going around with grudges and immense fury, rage like it was all put to music, rage like it was two hundred pounds to lose. Rascal Knockoff. I thought: Dostoyevsky fell in love with him. Yes, I would stand in the bow on those starry nights in the tropical sea and promise myself that I would stick at it and go through all the shit and become a ship's officer. I would urge myself to do all those exams and become a ship's officer and

live like that for the rest of my life. Seventeen, a strong young kid
... and like a kid I didn't do it.

Drawing open the curtains, he discovered that Deborah's was
a corner room whose windows looked out across Central Park to
the apartment buildings on the East Side. The daffodils and the
leafing of the trees still had three weeks to work their way to
Madamaska Falls, but Central Park could have been Savannah.
The panorama Debby had teethed on, but he'd still take the shore
any day. What had he been doing in a forest on a mountaintop? When he'd fled Nikki's disappearance, he and Roseanna
should have gone to Jersey to live by the sea. Should have become
a commercial fisherman. Should have dumped Roseanna and
gone *back* to sea. Puppets. Of all the fucking callings. Between
puppets and whores, he chooses puppets. For that alone he de-
serves to die.

Only now did he see the assorted pieces of Deborah's underwear strewn about at the foot of the bureau, as though she had
just hurriedly undressed—or been undressed—and run from the
room. Pleasant to imagine. He could only guess that he had already been into the underwear during the night—he had no recollection. He must have got up in his sleep to look at her things and
spilled some onto the floor. Deep into self-caricature now. I am
more of a menace than I realize. This is serious. Premature senil-
ity. Senilitia, dementia, hell-bent-for-disaster erotomania.

And what of it? A natural human occurrence. The word's *reju-
venation*. Drenka is dead but Deborah lives and, round the clock
at the sex factory, the furnaces are burning away.

As he dressed in what he wore wherever he went, day in and
day out—frayed flannel shirt over an old khaki T-shirt, baggy
bottom-heavy corduroys—he listened to hear if anyone was
home. Only eight-fifteen but already emptied out. He could not at
first choose, from what lay on the floor, between a black under-
wire bra and a pair of silk floral bikini underpants, but thinking that the bra, because of the wiring, might prove bulky and
draw attention, he took the panties, shoved them into his trouser
pocket, and dropped the rest into the piled-up drawer. He could

play there again tonight. And in the other drawers. And in the closet.

He noticed now two sachets in that top drawer, one of mauve velvet that was lavender-scented and one of red gingham giving off the crisp odor of pine needles. Neither was the smell he was looking for. Funny—modern kid, Dalton graduate, already a connoisseur of the Metropolitan's Manets and Cézannes, yet didn't appear to have the slightest understanding that what men pay good money to sniff is not the needles of the pine. Well, Miss Cowan will find out, one way or another, once she starts wearing this underwear to something other than class.

Old salt that he was, he made up her bed square and tight.

Her bed.

Two simple words, each a syllable as old as English, and their power over Sabbath was nothing short of tyrannical. How tenaciously he clings to life! To youth! To pleasure! To hard-ons! To Deborah's underthings! And yet all the while he had been looking down from the eighteenth floor across the green tinge of the park and thinking that the time had come to jump. Mishima. Rothko. Hemingway. Berryman. Koestler. Pavese. Kosinski. Arshile Gorky. Primo Levi. Hart Crane. Walter Benjamin. Peerless bunch. Nothing dishonorable signing on there. Faulkner as good as killed himself with booze. As did (said Roseanna, authority now on the distinguished dead who might be alive had they "shared" at AA) Ava Gardner. Blessed Ava. Wasn't much about men could astonish Ava. Elegance and filth, immaculately intertwined. Dead at sixty-two, two years younger than me. Ava, Yvonne de Carlo— *those* are role models! Fuck the laudable ideologies. Shallow, shallow, shallow! Enough reading and rereading of *A Room of One's Own*—get yourself *The Collected Works of Ava Gardner*. A tweaking and fingering lesbian virgin, V. Woolf, erotic life one part prurience, nine parts fear—an overbred English parody of a borzoi, effortlessly superior, as only the English can be, to all her inferiors, who never took her clothes off in her life. But a suicide, remember. The list grows more inspiring by the year. I'd be the first puppeteer.

The law of living: fluctuation. For every thought a counter-thought, for every urge a counterurge. No wonder you either go crazy and die or decide to disappear. Too many urges, and that's not even a tenth of the story. Mistressless, wifeless, vocationless, homeless, penniless, he steals the bikini panties of a nineteen-year-old nothing and, riding a swell of adrenaline, stuffs them for safekeeping in his pocket—these panties are just what he needs. Does no one else's brain work in quite this way? I don't believe that. This is aging, pure and simple, the self-destroying hilarity of the last roller coaster. Sabbath meets his match: life. The puppet is *you*. The grotesque buffoon is *you*. *You're* Punch, schmuck, the puppet who toys with taboos!

In the large kitchen with the terra-cotta floor, a kitchen ablaze with sunshine on polished copperware, robust as a greenhouse with gleaming potted plants, Sabbath found a place set for him at the table, facing the view. Surrounding his dishes and cutlery were boxes of four brands of cereals, three differently shaped, differently shaded loaves of hearty-looking bread, a tub of margarine, a dish of butter, and eight jars of preserves, more or less the band of colors you get by passing sunlight through a prism: Black Cherry, Strawberry, Little Scarlet . . . all the way to Greengage Plum and Lemon Marmalade, a spectral yellow. There was half a honeydew as well as half a grapefruit (segmented) under a taut sheet of Saran Wrap, a small basket of nippled oranges of a suggestive variety he'd not come across before, and an assortment of tea bags in a dish beside his place setting. The breakfast crockery was that heavy yellow French stuff decorated with childlike renderings of peasants and windmills. Quimper. Beyond quimper.

Now why do I alone in America think this is shit? Why didn't *I* want to live like this? To be sure, producers characteristically provide for themselves more like pashas than transgressive puppeteers do, but this *is* awfully nice to wake up to. Pocket full of panties and jar upon jar of Tiptree Preserves. Affixed to its lid, the Little Scarlet sported a price tag reading "$8.95." What have I achieved that could possibly quimper? It's hard not to be dis-

gusted with yourself when you see a spread like this. There is so
much and I have so little of it.

There was the park again, out the kitchen window, and, to the
south, the spectacle of metropolitan spectacles, midtown Manhattan. In his absence, while up on a northern mountain Sabbath
futzed away the years with puppets and his prick, Norman had
grown rich and remained an exemplary person, Linc had gone
nuts, and Nikki had, for all he knew, become a bag lady shitting
on the floor of a 42nd Street subway station, fifty-seven years old,
gaga, obese—"*Why?*" he would cry, "*Why?*" and she wouldn't
even know who he was. But then, she could as easily be living in a
Manhattan apartment as large and luxurious as Norman's, with a
Norman of her own. She could have disappeared for as ordinary
a reason as that. . . . It's the shock of seeing New York still here
that's reminded me of Nikki. I will not think about it. I cannot.
That is the perennial time bomb.

Strange. The one thing you never think is that she's dead. That
even goes *for* the dead. Me up here in the light and the warmth
and, fucked-over as I am, with five senses, a mind, and eight
kinds of preserves—and the dead dead. Immediate reality is outside that window; so big it is, so much of it, everything entangled
in everything else. . . . What large thought was Sabbath struggling to express? Is he asking, "Whatever did happen to my own
true life?" Was it taking place elsewhere? But how then can looking out of this window be so gigantically real? Well, that is the
difference between the true and the real. We don't get to live in
the truth. That's why Nikki ran away. She was an idealist, an
innocent, touching, talented illusionist who wanted to live *in the
truth*. Well, if you found it, kid, you're the first. In my experience
the direction of life is toward incoherence—precisely what you
would never confront. Maybe that was the only coherent thing
you could think to do: die to deny incoherence.

"Right, Ma? You had incoherence in spades. The death of
Morty still defies belief. You were right to shut up after that."

"You think like a failure," Sabbath's mother replied.

"I am a failure. I was saying that to Norm only last night. I am at the very pinnacle of failure. How else should I think?"

"All you ever wanted were whorehouses and whores. You have the ideology of a pimp. You should have been one."

Ideology, no less. How knowing she had become in the after-life. They must give courses.

"It's too late, Ma. The black guys have got the market cornered. Try again."

"You should have led a normal and productive life. You should have had a family. You should have had a profession. You shouldn't have run away from life. Puppets!"

"It seemed a good idea at the time, Mother. I even studied in Italy."

"You studied whores in Italy. You deliberately set out to live on the wrong side of existence. You should have had *my* worries."

"But I do. I do . . ." Crying again. "I do. I have your worries exactly."

"Then why do you go around with an *alte kocker*'s beard and wearing your playground clothes—and with whores!"

"Quarrel, if you like, with the clothes and the whores, but the beard is essential if I don't want to look at my face."

"You look like a beast."

"And what should I look like? A Norman?"

"Norman was always a lovely boy."

"And I?"

"You always got your excitement in other ways. Always. Even as a tiny child you were a little stranger in the house."

"Is that true? I didn't know that. I was so happy."

"But always a little stranger, making everything into a farce."

"Everything?"

"You? Of course. Look now. Making death itself into a farce. Is there anything more serious than dying? No. But you want to make it into a farce. Even killing yourself you won't do with dignity."

"That's asking a lot. I don't think anyone who kills himself kills himself 'with dignity.' I don't believe that's possible."

"Then you be the first. Make us proud."

"But *how*, Mother?"

Beside his place setting was a longish note beginning GOOD MORNING. In caps. The note was from Norman, computer-generated.

> GOOD MORNING
>
> We're off to work. Linc's service begins at two. Riverside at 76th. See you there—will save seat with us. Cleaning woman (Rosa) comes at nine. If you want her to wash or iron anything, just ask her to. Need anything, ask Rosa. I'm at office all morning (994-6932). I hope sleep restored you some. You're under tremendous stress. I wish you would talk to a psychiatrist while you're here. Mine's no genius but smart enough. Dr. Eugene Graves (surname unfortunate but gets the job done). I phoned him and he said you should call if you want to (562-1186). He has cancellation late this afternoon. Please consider it seriously. He got me out of my summer mess. You could be helped with medication—and by talking to him. You're in bad shape and you need help. ACCEPT IT. Please call Gene. Michelle sends her regards. She'll be at the service. We expect you to have dinner at home with us tonight. Quiet, the three of us. Until you're back on your feet, we expect you to stay. The bed is yours. The place is yours. You and I are old friends. There aren't that many left.
>
> Norman

Paper-clipped to the note there was a plain white envelope. Fifty-dollar bills. Not just the six that would have covered the check from the joint account that Sabbath had made payable to Norman the evening before but four more in addition. Mickey Sabbath had five hundred bucks. Enough to pay Drenka to fuck in a threesome if Drenka . . . Well, she wasn't, and since chances were Norman had no intention of cashing Sabbath's check—probably already had torn it up to ensure Roseanna wouldn't get screwed out of her share of the dough—Sabbath had only to hurry, find one of those check-cashing places that take ten percent for commission, and write out a new check for three hundred on the joint account. That would give him seven seventy altogether. Suddenly he had thirty to fifty percent less reason to die.

"First you make a farce of suicide, now again you make a farce of life."

"I don't know any other way to do it, Mother. Leave me be. Shut up. You don't exist. There are no ghosts."

"Wrong. There are only ghosts."

Sabbath proceeded then to enjoy an enormous breakfast. He hadn't eaten with such pleasure since before Drenka had taken ill. It made him feel magnanimous. Let Roseanna *have* the three hundred. Deborah's furrow was now his furrow. Michelle, Norman, and Dr. Coffin were going to put him back on his feet.

Graves.

After packing himself full as a suitcase so stuffed with clothing you can't zipper it shut, he rollingly strolled around the apartment with his old sailor's gait, inspecting all the rooms, the baths, the library, the sauna; opened all the closets and examined the hats, the coats, the boots, the shoes, the stacks of sheets, the differently colored piles of soft towels; wandered down the hallway lined with mahogany bookcases holding only the world's best books; admired the rugs on the floors, the watercolors on the walls; scrutinized the Cowans' quietly elegant everything—lamps, fixtures, doorknobs, even the toilet bowl cleaners appeared to have been designed by Brancusi—all the while devouring the hard heel of the seeded pumpernickel plastered thick with Little Scarlet at $8.95 a jar and pretending that the place was his.

If only things had been different, everything would be otherwise.

His fingers still sticky with the sweet jam, Sabbath ended up back in Deborah's room sifting through the drawers of her desk. Even Silvija had them. They all had them. Just a matter of finding where they stash them away. Not even Yahweh, Jesus, and Allah have been able to stamp out the fun you can have with a Polaroid.

Gloria Steinem herself can't do it. In the contest between Yahweh, Jesus, Allah, and Gloria on the one side and on the other the innermost itch that gives life its tingle, I'll give you the three boys and Gloria and eighteen points.

Now where have you hidden them, Deborah? Am I hot or am I cold? The desk was a big oak antique with polished brass handles, originating probably in the office of some nineteenth-century lawyer. Unusual. Most kids like the plastic crap. Or is this what's called camp? He began removing the contents of the long top drawer. Two large leatherbound scrapbooks with dried leaves and flowers pressed between each pair of pages. Botanically beguiling, delicately done . . . but you ain't foolin' anyone. Scissors. Paper clips. Glue. Ruler. Smallish address books with floral-design covers and no addresses as yet entered in. Two gray boxes about five by six inches. Eureka! But within, only her personalized stationery, mauve like the lavender sachet. In one box, some handwritten sheets folded in two that looked promising momentarily but were only the drafts of a poem on love unrequited. "I opened my arms but no one saw . . . I opened my mouth and no one heard. . . ." You have not been reading your Ava Gardner, dear. Next drawer, please. Dalton yearbooks from 1989 to 1992. More teddy bears. Six here plus eight in the wicker basket. Camouflage. Clever. Next. Diaries! The jackpot! A stack of them, bound in cardboard with colorful flowery designs very like those on the underpants in his pocket. He took them out to quimper. Yep, matching underpants, diaries, and address books. The kid's got everything. Except. Except! Where are the pictures hidden, Debby? "Dear Di, I find myself becoming more and more drawn to him, trying to work out my feelings. Why, why are relationships so *hard*?" Why not write about fucking him? Hasn't anybody at Brown taught you what writing is for? Page after page of crap quite unworthy of her until he came upon an entry beginning as the others did—"Dear Di"—but divided by a ruled pen stroke into two columns, one labeled MY STRENGTHS and the other MY WEAKNESSES. Something here? He'd take anything by now.

MY STRENGTHS	MY WEAKNESSES
Self-discipline	Low self-esteem
My backhand	My serve
Hopefulness	Infatuations
Amy	Mother
Sarah L.	~~Low self-esteem~~
Robert (?)	Robert!!!!
Nonsmoker	Too emotional
Nondrinker	Impatience with Mom
	Thoughtlessness with Mom
	My legs
	Butting in
	Not always listening
	Eating

Whew, this is work. A thin three-ring notebook with a college decal on the front and beneath it a white label on which was typed "Yeats, Eliot, Pound. Tues. Thurs. 10:30. Solomon 002. Prof. Kransdorf." In the notebook were her class notes, along with photocopies of poems that Kransdorf must have distributed to the class. The very first was by Yeats. Called "Meru." Sabbath slowly read it . . . the first poem he'd read by Yeats—and one of the last he'd read by anyone—since leading the life of a seaman.

> Civilisation is hooped together, brought
> Under a rule, under the semblance of peace
> By manifold illusion; but man's life is thought,
> And he, despite his terror, cannot cease
> Ravening through century after century,
> Ravening, raging, and uprooting that he may come
> Into the desolation of reality:
> Egypt and Greece good-bye, and good-bye, Rome!
> Hermits upon Mount Meru or Everest,
> Caverned in night under the drifted snow,
> Or where that snow and winter's dreadful blast
> Beat down upon their naked bodies, know
> That day brings round the night, that before dawn
> His glory and his monuments are gone.

1934

Debby's notes were written on the sheet, directly below the poem's date of composition.

> Meru. Mountain in Tibet. In 1934, WBY (Irish poet) wrote introduction to Hindu friend's translation of a holy man's ascent into renouncing the world.
>
> K: "Yeats was at the verge beyond which all art is vain."
>
> The theme of the poem is that man is never satisfied unless he destroys all that he has created, e.g. the civilizations of Egypt and Rome.
>
> K: "The poem's emphasis is on man's obligation to strip away all illusion in spite of the terror of nothingness with which he will be left."
>
> Yeats comments in a letter to a friend: "We free ourselves from obsession that we may be nothing. The last kiss is given to the void."
>
> man=human
>
> Class criticized poem for its lack of a woman's perspective. Note unconscious gender privileging—*his* terror, *his* glory, *his* (phallic) monuments.

He ransacked the remaining drawers. Letters to Deborah Cowan dating back to grade school. Perfect place to hide Polaroids. Patiently he went through the envelopes. Nothing. A handful of acorns. Postcards, blank on one side, reproductions on the other. The Prado, the National Gallery, the Uffizi . . . Box of staples, which he opened, curious to see if this nineteen-year-old girl who pretended to love flowers and teddy bears best of all might be using the staple box to secrete half a dozen joints. But only staples were secreted in the staple box. What's wrong with this kid?

Bottom drawer. Two ornamentally carved wooden boxes. Nope. Nothing. Doodads. Tiny beaded bracelets and necklaces. Braided hairpieces. Headbands. A hair clip with a black velvet bow. Smelling of nobody's hair. Smelling of lavender. This child is perverted, but the wrong way.

The closets packed. Pleated skirts with floral prints. Loose silk pants. Black velvet jackets. Jogging suits. Tons of paisley kerchiefs on the overhead shelf. Big baggy things that looked like maternity dresses. Short linen dresses. (With her legs?) Size 10. What size was Drenka? He could no longer remember! Loads of pants. Corduroy. Blue jeans galore. Now why does she leave at home all her underwear and all her clothes, jeans included, when she goes to school? Does she have even more stuff there—are they that ostentatiously rich?—or is this what privileged girls do, leave it all behind rather the way certain animals, to mark their terrain, leave behind them a trail of pee?

He went through the pockets of all the jackets and all the pants. He searched among the heaps of kerchiefs. By now he was getting good and angry. Where the fuck are they, Deborah?

The drawers. Calm down. There are still three drawers to go. Since he'd been in the top, the underwear drawer, more than once already, and since he was beginning to feel the pressure of time—his plan was to get downtown before the funeral to visit the site of his first and only theater—he skipped to the second drawer. It was hard to pull the drawer open, so stuffed was it with T-shirts, sweatshirts, baseball caps, and socks of every variety, some with slots of different colors for each of the toes. How cute. He plunged right through to the bottom. Nothing. He worked his hands in among the T-shirts. Nothing. He pulled open the drawer below. Bathing suits, all kinds, a delight to touch, but he'd have to examine them more exhaustively later. Also cotton flannel pajamas with nice things like hearts printed all over them, and nightgowns with ruffled hems and lace trim. Pink and white. Back to them, too. Time, time, *time* . . . and there were not only T-shirts on the carpet by the dresser but skirts and pants on the floor in the closet, kerchiefs all the way over on the bed, the desk a mess, drawers all open and her diaries scattered across the top. Everything to be put back with fingers that were now killing him.

The bottom drawer. Last chance. Camping equipment. Vuarnet sunglasses, three pairs without cases. She had three, six, ten of everything. Except! Except! And there it was.

There it was. The gold. His gold. At the bottom of the bottom drawer, where he should have begun in the first place, in among a jumble of old schoolbooks and more teddy bears, a simple Scotties box, design of white, lilac, and pale green flowers on a lemony-white background. "Each box of Scotties offers the softness and strength you want for your family. . . ." You're no fool, D. Handwritten label on the box read, "Recipes." You cunning girl. I love you. Recipes. I'll give you teddy bears up the gazoo!

Inside the Scotties box were her recipes—"Deborah's Sponge Cake," "Deborah's Brownies," "Deborah's Chocolate Chip Cookies," "Deborah's Divine Lemon Cake"—neatly written in blue ink in her hand. A fountain pen. The last kid in America to write with a fountain pen. You won't last five minutes in Bahia.

A short, very stout woman was standing in the doorway of Deborah's bedroom screaming. Only her mouth was she able to move; the rest of her appeared to be paralyzed with the terror. She was wearing tan stretch pants stretched to their limit and a gray sweatshirt bearing the name and logo of Deborah's university. In a large, broad face excavated by irregular patches of pockmarks, only her lips were prominent, elongated and sharply etched, the lips of the indigenous, as Sabbath knew, south of the border down Mexico way. The eyes were the eyes of Yvonne de Carlo. Nearly everybody has at least one good feature, and in mammals it's usually the eyes. His own were thought by Nikki to be his arresting feature. She made much of them back when he weighed seventy pounds less. Green like Merlin's, Nikki said back when it was all still play, when she was Nikita and he was *agápe mou, Mihalákimou, Mihalió.*

"Don't shoot. No shoot me. Four childs. One here." She pointed to her belly, a belly as pierceable as a small balloon. "No shoot. Money. I find money. No money here. I show money. No shoot me, Mister. Cleaning woman."

"I don't want to shoot you," said he, from where he was seated on the carpet, the recipes in his lap. "Don't scream. Don't cry. It's okay."

Gesturing jerkily, hysterically—toward him, toward herself—she told him, "I show money. You take. I stay. You go. No police. All money you." She motioned now for him to follow her out of Deborah's defiled room and down the book-lined corridor. In the master bedroom, the big bed was as yet unmade, books and nightclothes flung to either side of it, books strewn about the bed like alphabet blocks in a baby's playroom. He stopped to examine the book jackets. How does the educated rich Jew put himself to sleep these days? Still Eldridge Cleaver? *John Kennedy: Profile of Power. Having Our Say: The Delany Sisters' First One Hundred Years. The Warburgs . . .*

Why *don't* I live like this? The bedsheets weren't worn and antiseptic white like those that he and Roseanna slept at either edge of but glowed warmly, a pale golden pattern that reminded him of the radiant glory of the October day up at the Grotto when Drenka had run roughshod over her own record and come thirteen times. "More," she begged, "more," but in the end he fell back with a terrible headache and told her he couldn't continue risking his life. He seated himself heavily on his haunches, pale, perspiring, breathless, while on her own Drenka took over the quest. This was like nothing he had ever seen before. He thought, It's as though she is wrestling with Destiny, or God, or Death; it's as though, if only she can break through to yet one more, nothing and no one will stop her again. She looked to be in some transitional state between woman and goddess—he had the queer feeling of watching someone leaving this world. She was about to ascend, to ascend and ascend, trembling eternally in the ultimate, delirious thrill, but instead something stopped her and a year later she died.

Why does one woman love you madly when she swallows it and another hate your guts if you suggest she even try it? Why is the woman who swallows it with rapacity the dead mistress, while the one who holds you to the side, so you squirt your heart out into the air, is the living wife? Is this luck only mine, or is it everyone's? Was it Kennedy's? The Warburgs'? The Delany sisters'? In my forty-seven-year experiment with women, which I hereby declare officially concluded . . . And yet the colossal balloon that was Rosa's behind piqued his curiosity no less than the pregnant belly did. When she bent to open one of the master bedroom's bureau drawers he remembered back to his initiation in Havana, the classic old brothel where you go into a salon and the girls are marched in for the clients. The young women came in from wherever they were lounging around, wearing nothing resembling those baggy garments in Deborah's closet but all in skintight dresses. What was amazing was that while he chose Yvonne de Carlo, his friend Ron—he'd never forgotten this—chose a pregnant one. Sabbath couldn't figure out why. Then when he grew more knowledgeable, the opportunity, strangely enough, had never come his way.

Till now.

She thinks I've got a gun. Let's see where this leads us. Last time he had anything like as much fun was watching Matthew split Barrett's skull open instead of his own.

"Here," she pleaded. "Take. Go. No shoot me. Husband. Four childs."

She had opened a drawer stacked about a foot high with lingerie, not the hot stuff that the kid had ordered from some mail-order catalog but smooth, lustrous, and perfectly piled. Collector's items. And Sabbath was a collector, had been all his life. I can't tell a pansy from a marigold, but underwear? If I can't identify it, nobody can.

Rosa gingerly lifted from the drawer a generous helping of nightgowns and laid them lightly at the foot of the bed. The nightgowns had been hiding two nine-by-twelve manila envelopes. She handed him one and he opened it. One hundred hundred-dollar bills, paper-clipped together in wads of ten each.

"Whose is this? This money belongs to—?" He was pointing to the bed, to one side, then the other.

"La señora. Secret money." Rosa was looking down at her belly, her hands—chubby and astonishingly tiny—crossed there like the hands of a child being rebuked.

"Always this much? Siempre diez mil?" Virtually all his whorehouse Spanish was gone, yet he could still remember the numbers, the prices, the levy imposed, the fact that you could go out and buy it like a papaya or pomegranate or a watch or a book, like anything that you wanted enough to part with your hard-earned dough to get it. "Cuánto? Cuántos pesos?" "Para qué cosa?" Et cetera.

Rosa made the gesture to indicate sometimes more, sometimes less. If he could just calm her down long enough to break through to the base instincts . . .

"Where does she get the money?" he asked.

"No comprendo."

"Is this money she earns at work? In italiano, lavoro."

"No comprendo."

Trabajo! God, it was coming back. *Trabajo.* How he'd loved his *trabajo.* Painting, chipping, painting, chipping, and then fucking himself silly on shore. It was just as natural as getting off the ship and going into a bar and having a drink. In no way was it extraordinary. But to me and Ron it was the most extraordinary thing in the world. You got off the ship and you headed straight for the one thing you had never done before. And never would want to stop doing again.

"How does Missus make her living? Qué trabajo?"

"Odontología. Ella es una dentista."

"A dentist? La señora?" He tapped a front tooth with his fingernail.

"Sí."

Men in and out of the office all day long. Gives 'em gas. That nitrous oxide. "The other envelope," he said. "El otro, el otro, por favor."

"No money," she replied flatly. There was opposition in her now. Suddenly she looked a little like General Noriega. "No money. En el otro sobre no hay nada."

"Nothing at all? An empty envelope hidden under fifteen nightgowns at the bottom of her bottom drawer? Gimme a break, Rosa."

The woman was astonished when he concluded with "Rosa,"

but she appeared not to know whether to be more frightened of him or less. Spoken inadvertently enough, her name turned out to be just the thing to resuscitate her uncertainty as to what kind of madman she was dealing with.

"Absolutamente nada," she said bravely. "Está vacío, señor! Umpty!" Here she gave way and began to cry.

"I'm not going to shoot you. I told you that. You know that. What are you afraid of? No peligro." What the whores used to tell him when he inquired about their health.

"Is umpty!" declared Rosa, sobbing like a child into the crook of her arm. "Es verdad!"

He didn't know whether to follow his inclination and put a hand out to comfort her or to appear more ruthless by reaching for the pocket where she thought the pistol was. The main thing was to keep her from screaming again and running for help. His remaining so calm while in a state of tremendous excitement he could not account for—he might not look it, he might never have looked it, but he was really a high-strung fellow. Delicate feelings. To be callous quite like this was not in his nature (except with a perpetual drunk). Sabbath did not care to make people suffer beyond the point that he wanted them to suffer; he certainly didn't want to make them suffer any more than made him happy. Nor was he ever dishonest more than was pleasant. In this regard, at least, he was much like others.

Or was Rosa having him on? He'd bet Rosa was a lot less high-strung than he was. Four childs. Cleaning woman. No English. Never enough money. On her knees, crossing herself, praying—all an act to prove what? Why drag in Jesus, who has his own troubles? A nail through either palm you sympathize with when you suffer osteoarthritis in both hands. He had roared with laughter recently (first time since Drenka's death) when Gus told him over the gas pump that his brother-in-law and sister had been in Japan at Christmas, and when they went to shop at the biggest department store in some big city there, first thing they saw up above the entrance was a gigantic Santa Claus hanging from a cross. "Japs don't get it," Gus said. Why should they? Who does?

But in Madamaska Falls Sabbath kept his retort to himself. He had got into difficulty enough explaining to one of Roseanna's fellow teachers that he could take no interest in her specialty, Native American literature, because Native Americans ate *treyf.* She had to consult a Jewish American friend to find out what that meant, but when she did she let him have it. He hated them all, except Gus.

He watched Rosa *dovening. That's* what was bringing out the Jew in him: a Catholic down on the floor. Always did. *You finished? Get off!* Whores can fool you. Cleaning women can fool you. *Anybody* can fool you. Your *mother* can fool you. Oh, Sabbath so wanted to live! He thrived on this stuff. Why die? Had his father gone off at dawn to peddle butter and eggs so that *both* boys should die before their time? Had his impoverished grandparents crossed from Europe in steerage so that a grandson of theirs who had escaped the Jewish miseries should throw away a single fun-filled moment of American life? Why die when these envelopes are hidden away by women beneath their Bergdorf lingerie? There alone was a reason to live to a hundred.

He still had the ten thousand bucks in his hands. Why is Michelle Cowan hiding this money? Whose is it? How did she earn it? With the money he'd had to pay Drenka that first time with Christa, she bought the power tools for Matthew; with the hundreds that Lewis, the credit-card magnate, slipped into her purse, she bought *tchotchkees* for the house—ornamental plates, carved napkin rings, antique silver candelabra. To Barrett, the electrician, she *gave* money, liked to stuff a twenty down into his jeans as he was pinching her nipples in their last embrace. He hoped Barrett had saved that money. He might not be fixing shorts for a while.

Norman's first wife had been Betty, the high school sweetheart, whom Sabbath no longer remembered. What Michelle looked like he now discovered from the contents of the second envelope. He had once again directed Rosa to take it from the drawer, and hurriedly she obliged when he began to edge his hand toward the pocket in which there was no gun.

He'd been looking for pictures in the wrong room. Virtual
replicas of his pictures of Drenka someone had taken of Michelle. Norman? After thirty years and three kids, unlikely. Besides, if Norman had taken them, why hide them? From Deborah? Best thing for Deborah would be to give her a good look at
them.

Michelle was an extremely slender woman—narrow shoulders,
fleshless arms, and straight, polelike legs. Rather longish legs,
like Nikki's, like Roseanna's, like the legs that, before Drenka, he
used to like best to climb. The breasts were a pleasant surprise
in one so thin—weighty, sizable, crowned with nipples that came
out indigo on the Polaroid film. Maybe she'd painted them. Maybe the photographer painted them. She wore her black hair tautly
pulled back. A flamenco dancer. *She's* read her Ava Gardner. She
in fact did resemble the white Cuban women about whom Sabbath used to say to Ron, "They look Jewish but without the *ish*."
Nose job? Hard to tell. The nose was not the focus of the inquir-
ing photographer's curiosity. The picture Sabbath liked best was
the least anatomically detailed. In it Michelle was wearing nothing but soft brown kid boots widely cuffed at her upper thigh.
Elegance and filth, his bread and butter. The other pictures were
more or less standard issue, nothing mankind hadn't known since
Vesuvius had preserved Pompeii.

The edge of a chair on which she was seated in one picture, the
stretch of carpet across which she lay in another, the window
curtains to which she made love in a third . . . he could smell the
Lysol even from here. But as he knew from watching Drenka at
the Bo-Peep, the sleazy motel was a kick, too, a kick similar to
taking the lover's money as though he were just a john.

After inserting the photographs back into the envelope, he
helped Rosa up off the floor and handed her the envelope to
return to the drawer. He did the same with the money, counting
off the ten paper-clipped piles of bills to show her that he hadn't
slipped one up his sleeve. He then lifted the nightgowns off the
bed and, after holding them in his hands a minute—and shock-
ingly, to his surprise, failing to discover in the feel of them

sufficient reason to continue living—indicated that she should put them back atop the envelopes and shut the drawer.

So that's it. That's all. "Terminado," as the whores who pushed you off them would succinctly put it the split second after you'd come.

He surveyed the whole room now. All so innocent, this luxe I disparaged. Yes, a failure in every department. A handful of fairy-tale years, and the rest a total loss. He'd hang himself. At sea, with his dexterous fingers, he'd been an ace with knots. In this room or Deborah's? He looked for what best to hang himself from.

Thick grayish-blue wool carpet. Muted, pale plaid wallpaper. Sixteen-foot ceilings. Ornamented plaster. Pretty pine desk. Austere antique armoire. Comfortable easy chair in a darker plaid, one tone down from the gray plaid on the upholstered headboard of the king-size bed. Ottoman. Embroidered throw pillows. Cut flowers in crystal vases. Huge mirror in mottled pine frame on the wall back of the bed. A five-bladed ceiling fan hanging from a long stem above the foot of the bed. There it is. Stand up on the bed, tie the rope to the motor. . . . They'd catch sight of him first in the mirror, Manhattan south of 71st Street to frame his swinging corpse. An El Greco. Tormented figure in foreground, Toledo and its churches in the background, and my soul seen ascending to Christ in the upper right corner. Rosa will get me in.

He held his hands up before her eyes. There were bulging nodes behind each of his cuticles, the ring and little fingers of both hands he could hardly move at all on a morning like this one, and long ago both his thumbs had taken on the shape of spoons. He could imagine how, to a simple mind like Rosa's, his hands looked like the hands of someone bearing a curse. She might even be right—nobody really understands arthritis.

"Dolorido?" she asked sympathetically, attentively appraising the deformity of each finger.

"Sí. Muy dolorido. Repugnante."

"No, señor, no, no," even as she continued to examine him as she would a creature in a circus sideshow.

"Usted es muy simpática," he told her.

It now occurred to him that he and Ron had fucked Yvonne and the pregnant girl in the second whorehouse they'd visited that first night in Havana. What happened when they got off the ship was what happened back then in most of the places. Pimps or runners of some kind were there to urge you to the houses where they wanted to take you. They may have targeted us because we were young kids. The other sailors told them to piss off. So he and Ron were taken to a cruddy old decaying place with filthy tiled walls and tiled floors, into a salon practically barren of furniture, and out came a bunch of fat old women. That's who Rosa reminded him of—the whores in that shithole. Imagine my having the presence of mind, two months out of Asbury High, to say, "No, no, thanks," but I did. I said in English, "Young chickens. Young chickens." So the guy took them to the other place, where they found Yvonne de Carlo and the pregnant girl, young women who passed for good-looking in the Cuban marketplace. *You finished? Get off!*

"Vámonos," he said, and obediently Rosa followed him down the corridor to Deborah's bedroom, which did indeed look as though a thief had had at it. He wouldn't have been surprised to find a mound of warm feces on the top of the desk. The savage license taken here astonished even the perpetrator.

On Deborah's bed.

He seated himself at the edge of the bed while Rosa hung back by the disheveled closet.

"I will not tell what you did, Rosa. I will not tell."

"No?"

"Absolutamente no. Prometo." He indicated, with a gesture so painful it nearly made him retch, that it was between the two of them. "Nostro segreto."

"Secreto," she said.

"Sí. Secreto."

"Me promete?"

"Sí."

He pulled one of Norman's fifties out of his wallet and motioned for her to come and take it.

"No," said Rosa.

"I don't tell. You don't tell. I don't tell you showed the señora's money, the doctor's money, you don't tell you showed me her photographs. Her pictures. Comprende? Everything we forget. How do you say 'to forget' en español? 'To forget.'" He tried to indicate with a hand something flying out of his head. Oh, oh! Voltaren! *Volare!* The Via Veneto! The whores of the Via Veneto, as flavorful as the perfumed peaches he'd buy in Trastevere, half a dozen for a dime's worth of lira.

"Olvidar?"

"Olvidar! Olvidar todos!"

She came over and, to his delight, took the money. He clutched her hand with his deformed fingers while, with the other hand, he produced a second fifty.

"No, no, señor."

"Donación," he said humbly, holding on to her.

He remembered *donación,* all right. In the days of the Romance Run, each time you went back to the same whorehouses and you brought nylons to your favorite girls. The guys said, "You like her? Give her a little *donación.* Pick her up something, and when you come back you'll give it to her. Whether she remembers you or not is another matter. She'll be glad to take the nylons anyhow." The names of those girls? In the dozens and dozens of brothels in the dozens and dozens of places, there must have been a Rosa somewhere.

"Rosa," he murmured softly, trying to pull her so that she would slide between his legs, "para usted de parte mía."

"No, gracias."

"Por favor."

"No."

"De mí para tí."

A glare that was all blackness but that looked to be the go-ahead signal anyway—you win, I lose, do it and get it over with. On Deborah's bed.

"Here," he said and managed to wedge the mass of her lower torso between his widespread legs. He grasps the sword. He eyes the bull. *El momento de verdad.* "Take it."

Without speaking, Rosa did as she was told.

Secure it with a third fifty, or was agreement reached? *Cuánto dinero? Para qué cosa?* To be back there, to be seventeen in Havana and ramming it in! *Vente y no te pavonees.* That crone, that one old bitch, always sticking her head in my room and trying to hurry me up. A madam's hard eye, heavy makeup, a butcher's thick shoulders, and, after only fifteen minutes, the scornful harangue of the slavedriver. "Vente y no te pavonees!" 1946. Come and don't show off!

"Look," he said to her sadly. "The room. Chaos."

She turned her head. "Sí. Caos." She breathed deeply—resignation? disgust? If he slipped her the third fifty, would she just slide to her knees as easily as when she prayed? Interesting if she prayed and blew him both at once. Happens a lot in Latin countries.

"*I* made this caos," Sabbath told her, and when he rubbed the tip of a spoon-shaped thumb across the pockmarked cheeks, she offered no objection. "Me. Por qué? Because I lost something. I could not find something I lost. Comprende?"

"Comprendo."

"I lost my glass eye. Ojo artificial. This one." He drew her a little closer and pointed to his right eye. He began to smell her, armpits first, then the rest. Something familiar. It is not lavender. Bahia! "This isn't a real eye. This is a glass eye."

"Vidrio?"

"Sí! Sí! Este ojo, ojo de vidrio. Glass eye."

"Glasseye," she repeated.

"Glasseye. That's it. I lost it. I took it out last night to go to sleep, just as I usually do. But because I wasn't at home, a mi casa, I didn't put it in the usual place. You follow all this? I am a guest here. Amigo de Norman Cowan. Aquí para el funeral de señor Gelman."

"No!"

"Sí."

"El señor Gelman está muerto?"

"I'm afraid so."

"Ohhhhh."

"I know. But that's how I come to be here. If he hadn't died, we two would never have met. Anyhow, I took out my glasseye to sleep, and when I woke up I couldn't remember where I'd put it. I had to get to the funeral. But could I go to a funeral without an eye? Understand me? I was trying to find my eye and so I opened all the drawers, the desk, the closet"—feverishly he pointed around the room as she nodded and nodded, her mouth no longer grimly set but rather innocently ajar—"to find the fucking eye! Where had it gone? Looking everywhere, going crazy. Loco! Demente!"

Now she was beginning to laugh at the scene he was so slap-shtikishly playing out for her. "No," she said, tapping him disapprovingly on the thigh, "no loco."

"Sí! And guess where it was, Rosa? Guess. Dónde was the ojo?"

Sure a joke was on the way, she began shaking her head from side to side. "No sé."

Here he hopped energetically off the bed and, while *she* now sat on the bed to watch him, he began to mime for her how before going to sleep he popped the eye out of his head and, after looking and finding nowhere to put it—and fearful that someone who came in and saw it on Deborah's desk, say, would be horrified (this too he mimed for her, making her laugh a beguiling ripple of a girlish laugh)—he just dropped it into his trouser pocket. Then he brushed his teeth (showed her this), washed his face (showed her that), and came back into the bedroom to undress and stupidly—"Estúpido! Estúpido!" he cried, knocking his poor fists against the sides of his head and not even stopping to acknowledge the pain—hung his trousers on a pants hanger in Deborah's closet. He showed her a pants hanger on which were hanging a pair of Deborah's wide blue silk pants. Then he showed her how he had turned *his* pants upside down to hang them in the closet and how, of course, the *ojo* had fallen out of the pocket and into one of her running shoes on the floor. "Can you beat that? Into the kid's zapato! My eye!"

She was laughing so hard she had to squeeze herself with her arms as though to prevent her belly from splitting open. If you're going to fuck her, just step up to the bed and fuck her now, man. On Deborah's bed, the fattest woman you will have ever fucked. One last enormous woman, and then with a clear conscience you can hang yourself. Life won't have been for nothing.

"Here," he said and, taking one of her hands in his own, drew it toward his right eye. "Did you ever feel a glasseye before? Go ahead," he said. "Be gentle, Rosa, but go ahead, feel it. You may not have this chance again. Most men are ashamed of their infirmities. Not me; I love 'em. Make me feel alive. Touch it."

She shrugged uncertainly. "Sí?"

"Don't be afraid. It's all part of the deal. Touch it. Touch it gently."

She gasped, drawing in her breath as she laid the padded tip of her tiny pointing finger lightly on the surface of his right eye.

"Glass," he said. "Hundred percent glass."

"Feel real," she said and, indicating that it wasn't so spooky as she first had feared, looked eager to take another poke at the thing. Contrary to appearances, she was not a slow learner. And she was game. They're all game, if you take your time and use your brains—and aren't sixty-four years old. The girls! All the girls! It was killing to think about.

"Of course it feels real," he replied. "That's because it's a good one. The best. Mucho dinero."

Life's last fuck. Working since she was nine. No school. No plumbing. No money. A pregnant, illiterate Mexican out of some slum somewhere or up from peasant poverty, and weighing about the same as yourself. It couldn't have ended otherwise. Final proof that life is perfect. Knows where it's going every inch of the way. No, human life must not be extinguished. No one could come up with anything like it again.

"Rosa, will you be a good soul and clean the room? You *are* a good soul. You weren't trying to fool me down there praying to Jesus. You were just asking his forgiveness for your leading me into temptation. You just swung right into it the way you were taught. I admire that. I wouldn't mind somebody like Jesus to turn to. Maybe he could get me some Voltaren without a prescription. Isn't that one of his specialties?" He didn't know precisely what he was saying, because his blood began draining into his boots.

"No comprendo." But she wasn't frightened, for while smiling at her, he was barely speaking above a whisper and had weakly settled back down onto the bed.

"Make order, Rosa. Make regularidad."

"Okay," she said and began zealously to pick Deborah's things up off the floor instead of having to do what this madman with the white beard and the crazy fingers and the glass eye—and more than likely a loaded pistol—expected for two lousy fifties.

"Thank you, dear," said Sabbath woozily. "You've saved my life."

And then, while he was fortunately anchored to the edge of the bed, the vertigo took him by the ears, a shot of bile surged into his throat, and he felt as he had felt riding the waves as a kid after catching a big one too late and it broke over him like the chandelier at Asbury's palatial Mayfair, the great chandelier that, in dreams he'd been having for half a century, ever since Morty was killed in the war, was tearing loose from its moorings and falling on top of his brother and him as they sat there innocently, side by side, watching *The Wizard of Oz.*

He was dying, had given himself a heart attack by going all out for Rosa's amusement. Final performance. Will not be held over. Puppet master and prick conclude career.

Rosa was kneeling next to the bed now, stroking his scalp with one of her warm little hands. "Sick?" she asked.

"Low self-esteem."

"Want doctor here?"

"No, ma'am. Hands hurt, that's all." Did they! He assumed at first the pain-riddled fingers were causing him to shake. Then the teeth began to chatter as they had the evening before and he had suddenly to fight with all his fortitude to prevent himself from throwing up. "Mother?" No answer. Her silent act again. Or was she not there? "Mama!"

"Su madre? Dónde, señor?"

"Muerto."

"Hoy?"

"Sí. This morning. Questo auroro. Aurora?" Italian again. Italy again, the Via Veneto, the peaches, the girls!

"Ah, señor, no, no."

She kindly supported his hairy cheeks with her hands, and when she pulled him to her mountainous bosom, he let her; he'd let her take the pistol out of his pocket, if he had one, and shoot him right between the eyes. She could plead self-defense. Rape. He had a harassment record a mile long already. They'd string him up by his feet outside NOW. Roseanna would see they did it to him the way they'd done it to Mussolini. And cut off his prick, for good measure, like that woman who'd used a kitchen knife twelve inches long to slice the cock off her sleeping husband, an ex-Marine and a violent bastard, for fucking her up the ass down in Virginia. "You wouldn't do that to me, darling, would you?" "I would," said R. obligingly, "if you had one." She and all her progressive friends in the valley couldn't stop talking about this case. Roseanna didn't seem anything like so upset by it as she was by circumcision. "Jewish barbarism," she told him after attending the *bris* of a friend's grandson in Boston. "Indefensible. Disgusting. I wanted to walk out." Yet the woman who'd cut off her husband's cock seemed, from the excitement with which Roseanna spoke of her, to have become a heroine. "Surely," Sabbath suggested, "she could have registered her protest another way." "How? Dial 911? Try it and see where it gets you." "No, no, not 911. That's not justice. No, stick something unpleasant up *his* ass. One of his pipes, say, if he happens to be a smoker. Maybe even one that was lit. If he is not a smoker, then she could shove a frying pan up his ass. A rectum for a rectum. Exodus 21:24. But cutting his dick off—really, Rosie, life isn't just a series of pranks. We are no longer schoolgirls. Life is not just giggling and passing notes. We are women now. It's a serious business. Remember how Nora does it in *A Doll's House*? She doesn't cut off Torvald's dick—she walks out the fucking door. I don't believe you neces-

sarily have to be a nineteenth-century Norwegian to walk out a
door. Doors continue to exist. Even in America they are still more
plentiful than knives. Only doors take guts to walk out of. Tell
me, have you ever wanted to cut my dick off in the middle of the
night as an amusing way of settling scores?" "Yes. Often." "But
why? What did I ever do, or fail to do, to give you an idea like
that? I don't believe I ever once entered your anus without a
prescription from the doctor and written permission from you."
"Forget it," she said. "I don't know that it's a good idea for me to
forget it now that I know it. You have really had thoughts about
taking a knife—" "A scissors." "A scissors and cutting off my
cock." "I was drunk. I was angry." "Oh, that was just chardonnay talking tough back in the bad old days. So what about today?
What would you like to cut off now that you're 'in sobriety'?
What does Bill W. suggest? I offer my hands. They're no fucking
good anyway. I offer my throat. What is the overpowering sym-
bolism of the penis for you people? Keep this up and you'll make
Freud look good. I don't understand you and your friends. You
stage a sit-down strike in the middle of Town Street every time
the road crew goes near the limb of a sacred maple tree, you
throw your bodies in front of every twig, but when it comes to
this unfortunate incident, you're all gung ho. If the woman had
gone outside and sawed down his favorite elm for revenge, this
guy might have had a chance with you all. Too bad he wasn't
a tree. One of those irreplaceable redwoods. The Sierra Club
would have been out in force. She would have had her head
handed to her by Joan Baez. A redwood? You mutilated a redwood? You're as bad as Spiro Agnew! You're all so merciful and
tender, against the death penalty even for serial killers, judging
poetry contests for degenerate cannibals in maximum-security
prisons. How could you be so horrified about napalming the
Communist enemy in Southeast Asia and so happy about this
ex-Marine having his dick cut off right here in the USA? Cut mine
off, Roseanna Cavanaugh, and I bet you ten to one, a hundred
to one, you're back on the booze tomorrow. Cutting off a dick
isn't as easy as you think. It isn't just snip, snip, snip, like you're

darning a sock. It isn't just chop, chop, chop, like you're mincing an onion. It isn't an onion. It's a human dick. It's full of blood. Remember Lady Macbeth? They didn't have AA in Scotland, and so the poor woman went off her rocker. 'Who would have thought the old man to have had so much blood in him?' 'Here's the smell of the blood still. All the perfumes of Arabia will not sweeten this little hand.' She flips out—Lady Powerhouse Macbeth! So what's going to happen to you? That woman in Virginia *is* a heroine—as well as a despicable human being. But you don't have the guts, darling. You're just a schoolteacher in the sticks. We're talking about evil, Rosie. The worst you could do in life was become a wino. What the fuck's a wino? A dime a dozen. Any drunk can become a drunk. But not everybody can cut off a dick. I don't doubt that this splendid woman has given encouragement to dozens of other splendid women all around the country, but personally I don't think you've got anything like what it takes to get down there and do it. You'd vomit if you had to swallow my come. You told me that long ago. Well, how do you think you'd like to perform surgery on your loving husband without an anesthetic?" "Why not wait and see?" said Roseanna with a smile. "No. No. Let's not wait. I'm not going to live forever. I'll be seventy the day after tomorrow. And then you'll have missed your big chance to prove how courageous you are. Cut it off, Roseanna. Pick a night, any night. Cut it off. I dare you."

And wasn't that what he had run from and why he was here? There was a mammoth scissors in the utility closet. There was a much smaller scissors, shaped like a heron, in her sewing kit and an ordinary-size one with orange plastic handles in her middle desk drawer. There was a hedge clipper out in her potting shed. For weeks, ever since this case had begun to obsess her, he had been thinking of throwing them all in the woods up at Battle Mountain when he went at night to visit Drenka's grave. Then he remembered that her art classes were full of scissors; every kid had a pair, for cutting and pasting. And then the jury in Virginia declares this woman innocent on grounds of temporary insanity.

She went crazy for two minutes. Just about how long it took Louis to knock out Schmeling in that second fight. Barely enough time to cut it off and throw it away, but she managed, she did it—shortest insanity in world history. A record. The old one-two, and that's it. Roseanna and the peaceniks were on the phone all morning. They thought it was a great decision. That was enough warning for him. Great day for women's liberation but a black day for the Marine Corps and Sabbath. He would never sleep in that house of scissors again.

And who was his comforter now? She was cradling his head as though she intended to give him suck.

"Pobre hombre," she muttered. "Pobre niño, pobre madre. . . ."

He was weeping, to Rosa's surprise out of both eyes. She continued nonetheless to soothe his sorrows, talking softly in Spanish and stroking the scalp where the pitch-black hair that strikingly offset the hot green needles that were his eyes used to grow in profusion back when he was a seventeen-year-old in a sailor's cap and everything in life led to pussy.

"How do you have one eyes?" asked Rosa, gently rocking him to and fro. "Por qué?"

"La guerra," he moaned.

"It cry, glasseye?"

"I told you, it wasn't cheap."

And under the spell of her fleshiness, pressing against her pungency, his nose sinking deeper and deeper into the deep, Sabbath felt as though he were porous, as though the last that was left of the whole concoction that had been a self was running out now drop by drop. He wouldn't need to knot a rope. He would just drip his way into death until he was dry and gone.

So then, this had been his existence. What conclusion was to be drawn? Any? Who had come to the surface in him was inexorably himself. Nobody else. Take it or leave it.

"Rosa," he wept. "Rosa. Mama. Drenka. Nikki. Roseanna. Yvonne."

"Shhhh, pobrecito, shhhhh."

"Ladies, if I have put my life to an improper use . . ."

"No comprendo, pobrecito," she said, and so he shut up, because neither really did he. He was fairly sure that he was half faking the whole collapse. Sabbath's Indecent Theater.

2

TO BE
OR
NOT TO BE

. . .

Sabbath hit the street with the intention of spending the hours before Linc's funeral playing Rip Van Winkle. The idea revived him. He looked the part and had been out of it longer even than Rip. RVW merely missed the Revolution—from what Sabbath had been hearing over the years, he had missed the transformation of New York into a place utterly antagonistic to sanity and civil life, a city that by the 1990s had brought to perfection the art of killing the soul. If you had a living soul (and Sabbath no longer made such a claim for himself), it could die here in a thousand different ways at any hour of the day or night. And that was not to speak of unmetaphorical death, of citizens as prey, of everyone from the helpless elderly to the littlest of school-children infected with fear, nothing in the whole city, not even the turbines of Con Ed, as mighty and galvanic as fear. New York was a city completely gone wrong, where nothing but the subway was subterranean anymore. It was the city where you could obtain, sometimes with no trouble at all, sometimes at considerable expense, the worst of everything. In New York the good old days, the old way of life, was thought to have existed no further than three years back, the intensification of corruption and violence and the turnover in crazy behavior being that rapid. A showcase for degradation, overflowing with the over-flow of the slums, prisons, and mental hospitals of at least two hemispheres, tyrannized by criminals, maniacs, and bands of kids who'd overturn the world for a pair of sneakers. A city where the few who bothered to consider life seriously knew themselves to be surviving in the teeth of everything inhuman—or all too human: one shuddered to think that all that was abhorrent in the city disclosed the lineaments of mass mankind as it truly longed to be.

Now, Sabbath did not swallow these stories he continually heard characterizing New York as Hell, first, because every great city is Hell; second, because if you weren't interested in the gaudier abominations of mankind, what were you doing there in the first place?; and third, because the people he heard telling these stories—the wealthy of Madamaska Falls, the tiny professional elite and the elderly who'd retired to their summer homes there—were the last people on earth you'd believe about anything.

Unlike his neighbors (if Sabbath could be said to consider anyone anywhere a neighbor), he did not naturally shrink from the worst in people, beginning with himself. Despite his having been preserved in a northern icebox for the bulk of his life, during recent years he had been thinking that he, for one, could perhaps be something other than repelled by the city's daily terrors. He might even have left Madamaska Falls (and Rosie) to return to New York long ago if it had not been for his sidekicker. . . . and for the feelings still springing from Nikki's disappearance . . . and for the silly destiny that had been chosen for him instead by his tiresome superiority and threadbare paranoia.

Though his paranoia, he observed, shouldn't be exaggerated. It was never the poisoned spearhead of his thinking, never on the truly grand scale, needing absolutely nothing to unleash it. Certainly by now it was no more than a sort of everyman's paranoia, quarrelsome enough to rise to the bait but by and large frazzled and sick of itself.

Meanwhile he was trembling again, and without the comfort of Rosa's pungency and its nostalgic meaning. It seemed that once the thing had taken hold, as it had again earlier in Deborah's ransacked room, he was hard put to extinguish, by an act of will, the desire not to be alive any longer. It was walking along with him, his companion, as he headed toward the subway station. Though he hadn't walked them for decades, he saw nothing at all of those streets, so busy was he in staying abreast of his wish to die. He marched in unison with it step-by-step, keeping time to an infantry chant he'd had drummed into his head by the black cadre at Fort Dix when he was there training to be a killer of Communists after coming back from sea.

> You had a good home but you left—
> You're right!
> You had a good home but you left—
> You're right!
> Sound off, one-two,
> Sound off, three-four,
> Sound off, one-two-three-four—
> Three-four!

The-desire-not-to-be-alive-any-longer accompanied Sabbath right on down the station stairway and, after Sabbath purchased a token, continued through the turnstile clinging to his back; and when he boarded the train, it sat in his lap, facing him, and began to tick off on Sabbath's crooked fingers the many ways it could be sated. This little piggy slit his wrists, this little piggy used a dry-cleaning bag, this little piggy took sleeping pills, and this little piggy, born by the ocean, ran all the way out in the waves and drowned.

It took Sabbath and the-desire-not-to-be-alive-any-longer just the length of the ride downtown to together compose an obituary.

MORRIS SABBATH, PUPPETEER, 64, DIES

Morris "Mickey" Sabbath, a puppeteer and sometime theatrical director who made his little mark and then vanished from the Off Off Broadway scene to hide like a hunted criminal in New England, died Tuesday on the sidewalk outside 115 Central Park West. He fell from a window on the eighteenth floor.

The cause of death was suicide, said Rosa Complicata,

whom Mr. Sabbath sodomized moments before taking his life. Ms. Complicata is the spokesperson for the family.

According to Ms. Complicata, he had given her two fifty-dollar bills to perform perverse acts before his jumping out the window. "But he no have hard prick," said the heavyset spokesperson, in tears.

Suspended Sentence

Mr. Sabbath began his career as a street performer in 1953. Observers of the entertainment world identify Sabbath as the "missing link" between the respectable fifties and the rambunctious sixties. A small cult developed around his Indecent Theater, where Mr. Sabbath used fingers in place of puppets to represent his ribald characters. He was prosecuted on charges of obscenity in 1956, and though he was found guilty and fined, his sentence of thirty days was suspended. Had he served the time it might have straightened him out.

Under the auspices of Norman Cowan and Lincoln Gelman (for Gelman obituary see B7, column 3), Mr. Sabbath directed a notably insipid *King Lear* in 1959. Nikki Kantarakis was praised by our critic for her Cordelia, but Mr. Sabbath's performance as Lear was labeled "megalomaniacal suicide." Ripe tomatoes had been handed to all ticket holders as they entered the theater, and by the end of the evening Mr. Sabbath seemed to relish his besmirchment.

Pig or Perfectionist?

The RADA-trained Miss Kantarakis, star of the Bowery Basement Players and the director's wife, mysteriously disappeared from their home in November 1964. Her fate remains unknown, though murder has never been ruled out.

"The pig Flaubert murdered Louise Colet," said Countess du Plissitas, the aristocrat's feminist, in a telephone interview today. Countess du Plissitas is best known for fictionalizing biography. She is currently fictionalizing the biography of Miss Kantarakis. "The pig Fitzgerald murdered Zelda," the countess continued, "the pig Hughes murdered Sylvia Plath, and the pig Sabbath murdered Nikki. It's all there, all the different ways he murdered her, in *Nikki: The Destruction of an Actress by a Pig*."

Members of the original Bowery Basement Players contacted today agreed that Mr. Sabbath was merciless in his direction of his wife. They were all hoping that she would kill him and were disappointed when she disappeared without even having tried.

Mr. Sabbath's friend and coproducer, Norman Cowan—whose daughter, Deborah, a student in underclothing at Brown, played a starring role in the extravaganza *Farewell to a Half Century of Masturbation*, elaborately staged by Mr. Sabbath in the hours just before he leaped to his death—tells another story. "Mickey was a genuinely nice person," Mr. Cowan commented. "Never gave anybody any trouble. A bit of a loner, but always with a kind word for everyone."

First Whore Mean

Mr. Sabbath trained in the whorehouses of Central and South America, as well as the Caribbean, before establishing himself as a puppeteer in Manhattan. He never used a rubber and miraculously never contracted VD. Mr. Sabbath often recounted the story of his first whore.

"The one I chose was very interesting," he once told a person sitting next to him on the subway. "I'll never forget her as long as I live. You wouldn't forget your first one anyway. I chose her because she looked like Yvonne de Carlo, the actress, the movie actress. Anyway, here I am shaking like a leaf. This is in Old Havana. I remember how marvelous and romantic that was, decaying streets with balconies. Very first time. Never been laid in my life. So there I was with Yvonne. We both started getting undressed. I remember sitting in a chair by the door. The first thing and the most lasting thing of all is that she had red underwear, a red brassiere and underpants. And that was fantastic. The next thing I remember is being on top of her. And the next thing I remember is that it was all over and she said, 'Get off of me!' Slightly mean. 'Get off!' Now this doesn't happen every time, but since it was my first time, I thought it did and got off. 'You finished? Get off!' There are some nasty types even among whores. I'll never forget it. I thought, 'Okay, what do I care?' but it did strike me as unfriendly and even mean. How did I know, a kid from the boondocks, that one out of ten would be mean and tough like that, however pretty?"

Did Nothing for Israel

Not long after the alleged murder of his first wife, Mr. Sabbath made his way to the remote mountain village where he was supported until his death by a second wife, who dreamed for years of cutting off his cock and then taking sanctuary in her abused-women's group. During his three decades in hiding, aside from virtually making a prostitute of Mrs. Drenka Balich, a Croatian American neighbor, he seems to have worked on little else but a five-minute puppet adaptation of the hopelessly insane Nietzsche's *Beyond Good and Evil*. In his fifties he developed erosive osteoarthritis in both hands, involving the distal interphalangeal joints and the proximal interphalangeal joints, with relative sparing of the metacarpophalangeal joints. The result was radical instability and function loss from persistent pain and stiffness, and progressive deformity. Owing to his prolonged consideration of the advantages of arthrodesis against the advantages of implant arthroplasty, his wife became an expert in chardonnay. The osteoarthritis provided a wonderful pretext for being even more bitter about everything and devoting his entire day to thinking up ways to degrade Mrs. Balich.

He is survived by the ghost of his mother, Yetta, of Beth Something-or-other Cemetery, Neptune, New Jersey, who haunted him unceasingly during the last year of his life.

His brother, Lieutenant Morton Sabbath, was shot down
over the Philippines during the Second World War. Yetta
Sabbath never got over it. It is from his mother that Mr.
Sabbath inherited his own ability never to get over anything.

Also surviving is his wife, Roseanna, of Madamaska
Falls, with whom he was shacked up on the night that
Miss Kantarakis disappeared or was murdered by him
and her body disposed of. Mr. Sabbath is believed by
Countess du Plissitas to have coerced Mrs. Sabbath, the
former Roseanna Cavanaugh, into being an accomplice
to the crime, thus initiating her plunge into alcoholism.

Mr. Sabbath did nothing for Israel.

◆ ◆ ◆

a blur whizzing blur why now most unpleasant invention nobody
think ticker tape like this I don't head coming down here stupid
find what I lost idiocy Greek Village gyro sandwich souvlaki
sandwich baklava you know Nikki gypsy clothes spangles beads
angelically on Victorian boots never a fuck without a rape tossed
in no no not there but only way she came was there god forgive those dont fuck in the ass hey gyro you know Nikki souvlaki
you know Nikki St. Marks hotel $25.60 and up room rent you
know Nikki tattooed tubby you know Nikki garbage still from
when we left leather shops tie wrists ankles blindfold proceed
want to know a secret I want to know only secrets when you
use me like a boy Im your boy you are my girl my boy your
puppet hand puppet make me a hand puppet Ethnic Jewelry more
leather old people Im one Religious Sex Clothing Shop incense
Nikki always Nikki burning gift shops T-shirts incense never
out of incense fire escapes still need paint long hairs last out-
post movers movers movers red-faced brick broad women Polish-
American home cooking and what will I say other than why
so why bother theres less chance of her being here than my being her cant stand this there is god can those be ours in the window Nikki stained them hung them disappeared I left 120 bucks
of Salvation Army shit the wooden blinds she loved there they

are the red tapes faded slats missing thirty years later Nikkis blinds

"Smoke? Wanna smoke?"

"Not today, honey."

"Man, I'm starvin'. I got great smokes. The real McCoy. I ain't had no breakfast, ain't had no lunch. Been out here two hours. Ain't sold shit."

"Patience, patience. 'Nothing illegal is achieved without patience.' Benjamin Franklin."

"Ain't had fuck to *eat*, man."

"How much?"

"Five."

"Two."

"Shit. This is the real McCoy."

"But as you are the one starving, the leverage is mine."

"Fuck you, old man, old Jew man."

"Tut tut. That's beneath you. 'Neither a philo- nor an anti-Semite be; / And it must follow, as the night the day, / Thou canst not then be false to any man.'"

"Someday ain't gonna be out here beggin' and sellin' shit. Gonna be Jews out here beggin'. Wait'll all the beggars is Jews. You gonna like that."

"All the Jews will be begging when there is a black Mount Rushmore, my dear, and not a day sooner—when there is a black Mount Rushmore with Michael Jackson, Jesse Jackson, Bo Jackson, and Ray Charles carved upon its face."

"Two for five. I'm starvin', man."

"The price is right—a deal. But you must learn to think more kindly of Jews. You people were here long before we were. We did not have your advantages."

Nina Cordelia Desdemona Estroff Pharmacy still here my god Freie Bibliothek u. Lesehalle Deutsches Dispensary all basements Indian boutiques Indian restaurants Tibetan trinkets Japanese restaurants Ray's Pizza Kiev 24 hours 7 days a week introduction to Hinduism always she was reading dharma artha kama and moksha release from rebirth supreme goal death certainly a wor-

thy subject maybe the greatest certainly a solution for low self-esteem The Racing Form the Warsaw papers the bums the bums the
Bowery bums still in the stairwells head in hands piss gushing out
from their pockets

"I'm on a real guilt trip, man."

"Say that again, please?"

"Guilt trip. I need somethin' to eat. I ain't had breakfast or
lunch yet."

"Wouldn't worry. Nobody has."

"I'm innocent, man. I was framed. Somebody help me."

"I'll take your case, son. I believe in your innocence no less
than my own."

"Thanks, man. You a lawyer?"

"No, a Hindu. And you?"

"I'm Jewish. But I studied Buddhism."

"Yes, overachiever is written all over your jeans."

"What's it all like to a wise old Hindu?"

"Oh, not for everyone, but I happen to love hardship. Live
on plant foods from the forest. Seek constantly to achieve purity
and self-control. Practice restraint of the senses. Perform aus-
terities."

"I gotta eat somethin', man."

"Animal food is to be avoided."

"Shit, I don't eat animal food."

"Avoid actresses."

"How about shiksas?"

"For a Jew who studies Buddhism the shiksa is not forbidden
to eat. Ben Franklin: 'God forgive those who don't fuck in the
ass.'"

"You're nuts, baby. You're a great Hindu man."

"I have passed through life in the world and performed my
duties to society. Now I am reinitiated into the celibate state and
become like a child. I concentrate on internal sacrifices to the
sacred fires in my own self."

"Far out."

"I am seeking final release from rebirth."

lamppost sex sale naked girl silhouette phone number whats that say I speak Hindi Urdu and Bangla well that leaves me out shiksa Mount Rushmore Ava Gardner Sonja Henie Ann-Margret Yvonne de Carlo strike Ann-Margret Grace Kelly she is the Abraham Lincoln of shiksas

So Sabbath passeth the time, pretending to think without punctuation, the way J. Joyce pretended people thought, pretending to be both more and less unfixed than he felt, pretending that he did and did not expect to find Nikki down in a basement with a dot on her head selling saris or in her gypsy clothes roaming these streets of theirs in search of him. So passeth Sabbath, seeing all the antipathies in collision, the villainous and the innocent, the genuine and the fraudulent, the loathsome and the laughable, a caricature of himself and entirely himself, embracing the truth and blind to the truth, self-haunted while barely what you would call a self, ex-son, ex-brother, ex-husband, ex–puppet artist without any idea what he now was or what he was seeking, whether it was to slide headlong into the stairwells with the substrata of bums or to succumb like a man to-the-desire-not-to-be-alive-any-longer or to affront and affront and affront till there was no one on earth unaffronted.

At least he hadn't been witless enough to go find on Avenue C where he personally had handed tomatoes to all the first-nighters. It'd be another grim hole in the ground with Indian cuisine. Nor did he cut across Tompkins Park to where his workshop once had been, where they'd fucked so hard and so long that the couch would slide on its casters halfway to the door by the time he'd had to dress and race back to beat Nikki home from the theater. That bewitching bondage now seemed like the fantasy of a twelve-year-old boy. Yet it had happened, to him and to Roseanna Cavanaugh, fresh from Bennington College. When Nikki disappeared, aside from the grief and the tears and the torments of confusion, he was also as delighted as a young man could be. A trapdoor had opened and Nikki was gone. A dream, a sinister dream common to all. *Let her disappear. Let him disappear.* Only for Sabbath the dream came true.

◆ ◆ ◆

Dragging him down, spewing him forth, knocking him flat, beating him like the batter in his mother's Mixmaster. Then, for the finale, a breech delivery onto the shore, leaving him abraded and stinging from where he had been dragged across the pebbled shingle by the churning of the wave he'd mistimed. When he got up he didn't know where he was—he could be in Belmar. But out to the depths he savagely swam, back to where Morty had a gleaming arm stuck straight up and was shouting over the sound of the sea, "Hercules! Come on!" Morty caught every wave right; zinc-striped nose plowing the way, he'd ride a wave, when the tide was full, from way beyond the last rope to damn near up to the boards. They used to laugh at the Weequahic guys down from Newark. Those guys can't ride waves, they'd say. Those Newark Jewish kids were all escaping polio. If they were home they'd beg to go swimming at the amusement park pool up there in Irvington and as soon as they paid and got their ticket they immediately got polio. So their parents took them down the shore. If you were a Jew from Jersey City you went to Belmar, if you were a Jew from Newark you went to Bradley. We used to play blackjack with them under the boards. I was introduced to blackjack by those Weequahic guys, then developed my skills further at sea. Those blackjack games were legendary in our little backwater. Down for double! Up the shoot! Bai-*ja!* And the Jewish Weequahic broads at the Brinley Avenue beach in their two-piece suits, their Weequahic bellies bare. Loved it when they came in for the summer. Up till then all you did was listen to the radio and do your homework. A cloistered, quiet time. And suddenly everything was happening, the streets in Asbury were jammed with people, the boards in Bradley were jammed at night—from the moment the Memorial Day weekend began, our small-town life was over. Waitresses all over Asbury, college girls from all over the country lining up there to get a job. Asbury was the hub, next came Ocean Grove, the Methodist shtetl where you couldn't drive on Sundays, and then Bradley, and down on the beach Jewish girls from every part of Jersey. Eddie Schneer, the parking-lot thief Morty and I worked for, used to warn us, "Don't mess with Jewish girls. Save it for the shiksas. Never get nasty with Jewish girls." And the

Jewish city guys from Weequahic who we said couldn't ride the waves, we used to have wave-riding contests with them, bet them and ride waves for money. Morty always won. Our great summertimes before he joined the Air Corps.

And when the tide was out and the ailing and the arthritic old drifted down to dunk themselves at the water's rippling edge, where the sunburned kids with their leaky toy buckets were shoveling for sand crabs, Morty, his pals, and "Little Sabbath" carved a large rectangular court up on the beach, drew a line dividing it, and, three or four to a side, clad in their sopping suits, they played Buzz, a deceptively ferocious beach game devised by the daredevil shore kids. When you're "it" you have to go over and touch someone on the other side and get back before they pull your arms out of the sockets. If they catch you on the line, your team pulls you one way and the other team pulls you the other way. Much like the rack. "And what happens," Drenka asked him, "if they do catch you?" "They pull you down. If they catch you, they pull you down, they tackle you, and they sodomize you. Nobody gets hurt." Drenka laughed! How he could make Drenka laugh when she asked him to tell her about being an American boy at the shore. Buzz. Sand scratching your eyes, stuffing your ears, burning your belly, packing the crotch of your suit, sand between your buttocks, up your nose, a clump of sand, stained with blood, spat from between your lips, and then, together— "Geronimo!"—everyone out again to where the surf was calm now and you could sun yourself on your back, swaying sleepily, laughing at nothing, singing "opera" at the top of your lungs— "Toreador / Don't spit on the floor / Use the cuspidor / That's what it's for!"—and then, spurred by a sudden heroic impulse, spinning about onto your belly for the dive to the ocean floor. Sixteen, eighteen, twenty feet down. *Where's the bottom?* Then the lung-bursting battle up to the oxygen with a fistful of sand to show Morty.

On Morty's days off from being a lifeguard at the West End Casino, Mickey didn't leave his side, either on land or sea. What a pounding he could take! And how great that felt when he was a happy-go-lucky kid before the war letting himself go riding the waves.

Not so now. He clutched the edge of a street vendor's stand, waiting for the coffee to save him. Thought went on independently of him, scenes summoning themselves up while he seemed to wobble perilously on a slight rise between where he was and where he wasn't. He was trapped in a process of self-division that was not at all merciful. A pale, pale analog to what must have happened to Morty when his plane was torn apart by flak: living your life backward while spinning out of control. He had the definite impression that they were rehearsing *The Cherry Orchard* even as he carefully took the coffee cup in one disfigured hand and paid with the other. There was Nikki. This mark she had left on his mind could open out like the mouth of a volcano, and it was already thirty years now. There is Nikki, listening the way she listened when she was given even the minutest note—the look of voluptuous attention, the dark, full eyes without panic, tranquil as only they were when she was having to be someone other than herself, murmuring his words inwardly, brushing her hair off her ears so nothing was between his words and herself, breathing little sighs of defeat to acknowledge just how right he was, his state of mind her state of mind, his sense of things her sense of things, Nikki his instrument, his implement, the self-immolating register of his ready-made world. And rat-a-tat-tat Sabbath, the insuperable creator of her hiding place, born to deliver her from all losses and from all the fears they'd bred, missing not so much as the movement of an eye, punctilious to the point of madness, dangerously prodding the air with a finger so that nobody dared even to blink while he laid it out, every detail, in that overbearing way of his—how frightening he looked to her, a little bull with a big mind, a little keg filled to the spout with the intoxicating brandy of himself, his eyes *insisting* like that, warning, reminding, scolding, mimicking; it was all to Nikki like a ferocious caress, and she felt in her, overriding everything timorous, this stony obligation to be great. "*O my childhood. That's a question.* Don't lose that soft, questioning tone. Fill the speech with sweetness. To Trofimov: *You were only a boy then*, et cetera. Some sweet charm has gone there too. More playful, broken—charm him! Your entrance: vivacious, excited, generous—Parisian! The dance. *I can't sit still*, et cetera. Be sure to get rid of the cup long before this. Get up. The Parisian dance with Lopakhin takes you *down*stage, *down*stage. *Compliment* Lopakhin on this unexpected excellence in Parisian dancing. *You, Varya.* Wagging a finger at her. It's *mock* chastisement. Then teasing, quick, kissing both her cheeks, *You're just the same as ever.* The line *I don't quite follow you*—much dizzier. Laugh audibly after *mentioned in the encyclopedia*. Don't lose the laughing and the noises—make all the delicious noises you want; they're wonderful, they're Ranyevskaya! *Much* more teasingly provocative with Lopakhin when he goes on and on about the sale of the orchard—that's where you get your bigness. For you this business talk is just a marvelous occasion to bewitch a new man. Bewitch him! He's as much as invited you to by saying he loves you the very moment he lays eyes on you. Where are those teasing sounds? The seductive moan. The musical *Hmmmmm*. Chekhov: 'The important thing is to find the right smile.' Tender, Nikki, innocent, lingering, false, real, lazy, vain, habitual, charming—find *the smile*, Nikki, or you'll completely fuck up. Her vanity: powder your face, dab a little scent, straighten up your back to make yourself look beautiful. You are vain and you are aging. Imagine that: a corrupt and weary woman and yet as vulnerable and innocent as Nikki. *They're from Paris.* Let us see how lightly you take that—must see that *smile*. Three steps—*only three*—up from the torn telegram before you turn back and break down. Then let's *see* the breakdown as you retreat to the table. *If only this weight could be lifted from my heart.* Look at the floor. Musingly, gently, *If only I could forget my past. Keep* looking down, reflectively, through his line—then look up and you see your mother. IT IS MOTHER. Introduces the past, which magically then appears as Petya. She sees mother in a tree—but can't recognize Petya. Why does she give Petya the money? This is not convincing as you are doing it. Does he flirt with her? Charm her? Is he a great friend of old?

Something has to have been there *before* to make it credible *now.*
Yasha. Who is Yasha? What is Yasha? He is living proof of her
bad judgment. *There's no one there.* This whole speech, from
beginning to end, is as to a child. Including *It looks like a woman.*
Lopakhin's past is to be beaten with a stick—your childhood
Eden was his childhood hell. Consequently he does *not* make a
sentimental *tsimmes* out of purity and innocence. Unshrinkingly,
Nikki, *without shrinking,* you cry, *Look! It's mother walking in
the orchard!* But the last thing Lopakhin would want to see is his
drunken father resurrected. Think of the play as her dream, as
Lyuba's Paris dream. She is exiled in Paris, miserable with her
lover, and she dreams. I dreamed that I returned home and everything was as it used to be. Mother was alive, she was there—appeared right outside the nursery window in the form of a cherry
tree. I was a child again, a child of my own called Anya. And I was
being courted by an idealistic student who was going to change
the world. And yet at the same time I was myself, a woman with
all my history, and the serf's son, Lopakhin, himself grown now
too, kept warning me that if I didn't chop down the cherry orchard the estate was going to be sold. Of course I couldn't chop
down the cherry orchard, so I gave a party instead. But in the
middle of the dancing, Lopakhin burst in, and though we tried to
beat him back with a stick, he announced that the estate had
indeed been sold, and to him, to the serf's son! He drove us all out
of the house and began to chop down the orchard. And then I
awoke . . . Nikki, what are your first words? Tell me. *The nursery.*
Yes! It's to the *nursery* that she's returned. At the one pole the
nursery; at the other, Paris—the one a place impossible to retrieve,
the other impossible to manage. She fled Russia to elude the
consequences of her disastrous marriage; she flees Paris to leave
behind the disastrous affair. A woman in flight from disorder. In
flight from disorder, Nikoleta. Yet she carries the disorder within
her—she is the disorder!"

But I was the disorder. I am disorder.

• • •

According to Morty's Benrus, eternity was officially beginning for Linc Gelman at the Riverside Memorial Chapel on Amsterdam Avenue in just about half an hour. Yet dedicated as Sabbath was to seeing what a man could make of a wreck of a life if only he had the wherewithal, when he reached the Astor Place station, instead of hurrying down for the train, he became engrossed by a small company of gifted players enacting, with effectively minimalist choreography, the last degrading stages of the struggle for survival. Their amphitheater was this acre or two of lower Manhattan where everything running north, south, east, and west comes unstuck and together again in an intricate angling of intersections and odd-shaped oases of open space.

"Don't have to be a Rockefella to help a fella, don't have to be a Rockefella to help a fella—" A black tiny being with a bashed-in face hopped up with his cup to recite for Sabbath in a gentle singsong voice rather belying the chain of events three centuries long that had culminated in this pinprick of tormented existence. This guy was barely living and yet—thought Sabbath, counting how many others were working the adjoining territory with cups of their own—clearly he was Man of the Year.

Sipping at the dregs in his own cup, Sabbath at last looked up from the submerged blunder that was his past. The present happened also to be in progress, manufactured day and night like the troop ships at Perth Amboy during the war, the venerable present that goes back to antiquity and runs right from the Renaissance to today—this always-beginning, never-ending present was what Sabbath was renouncing. Its inexhaustibility he finds repugnant. For this alone he should die. So what if he has led a stupid life? Anyone with any brains knows that he is leading a stupid life even while he is leading it. Anyone with any brains understands that he is destined to lead a stupid life *because there is no other kind.* There is nothing personal in it. Nonetheless, childish tears well up in his eyes as Mickey Sabbath—yes, *the* Mickey Sabbath, of that select band of 77 billion prize saps who constitute human history—bids good-bye to his one-and-onlyness with a half-mumbled, heartbroken "Who gives a shit?"

A grizzled black face, wild and wasted, eyes bereft of any desire to see—blurred, muzzy eyes that Sabbath took to be at the twilight edge of sanity—appeared only inches from his own grizzled face. For such wretched affliction Sabbath had the stomach and so he did not turn away. His own anguish he knew to be but the faintest imitation of a sublife as abhorrent as this one. The black man's eyes were terrifying. If deep in that pocket his fingers are twisted around the handle of a knife, I may not be doing what I should be doing by holding my ground like this.

The beggar shook his cup like a tambourine, causing the change to rattle dramatically. A heavy odor of rot polluted his breath as into Sabbath's beard he whispered conspiratorially, "It's just a job, man—somebody's got to do it."

It *was* a knife. Jabbing into Sabbath's jacket, a knife. "What's the job?" Sabbath asked him.

"Bein' a borderline case."

Try to remain calm and to look unperturbed. "You do appear to have had your share of disappointment."

"America love me."

"If you say so." But when the beggar lurched heavily against him, Sabbath cried out, "Let's not have violence—you hear me? No violence!"

This provoked from his assailant a gruesome grin. "Vi-o-lence? *Vi-o-lence?* I *told* you—America *love* me!"

Now, if what Sabbath felt pushing into him was indeed the tip of a knife milliseconds from impaling his liver, if Sabbath truly had the-desire-not-to-be-alive-any-longer, why did he bring the heel of his big boot so forcefully down on that beloved American's foot? If he no longer gave a shit, why did he give a shit? On the other hand, if this limitless despair was only so much simulation, if he was not so steeped in hopelessness as he pretended to be, whom was he deceiving other than himself? His mother? Was a suicide required for his mother to understand that Mickey had amounted to nothing? Why else was she haunting him?

The black man howled and stumbled backward, whereupon Sabbath, fiery still with whatever impulse had saved his life, looked quickly down to discover that what he had taken for the tip of a knife was something in the shape of a grub or a slug or a maggot, a soft worm of a thing that looked as though it had been dipped in coal dust. It made you wonder what all the fuss was for.

In the meantime, nobody on those streets seemed to have noticed either the pecker that was nothing to write home about or the crazy bastard to whom it belonged and who, in what was admittedly a clumsy effort not entirely thought through, had wanted merely to become Sabbath's friend. Nor had anyone noticed Sabbath stomp him. The encounter that had left Sabbath in a sweat appeared to have been as good as invisible to two beggars who were no farther from the puppeteer than one corner of the boxing ring is from the other. They were intimately talking together across a supermarket cart and a load of transparent plastic bags stuffed to bursting with empty soda bottles and cans. The lanky one, who appeared, from the proprietary way he sprawled across it, to be the owner of the cart and its loot, was wearing a decent-enough sweat suit and sneakers that were practically brand-new. The other, shorter man was wrapped in rags that could well have been appropriated off the floor of an auto garage.

The more prosperous of the two spoke in a large, declamatory voice. "Man, there ain't enough hours in the *day* for me to do all the things I got scheduled."

"You fuckin' thief," replied the other weakly. Sabbath saw that he was weeping. "You stole it, you shitface."

"Sorry, man. I'd pencil you in, but my computers are down. The automatic car wash don't work. You don't do a drive-through at McDonald's in under seven minutes, and they get it all wrong anyway. Things we supposed to be really good at we ain't good at anymore. I call IBM. I ask them where I can buy one of them laptop computers. Call their 800 number. He says, 'I'm sorry, the computers are down.' IBM," he repeated, looking gleefully at Sabbath, "and *they* ain't got it together."

"I know, I know," said Sabbath. "The TV fucked it up."

"The TV fucked it up good, man."

"The challah machine," said Sabbath, "is the last thing that works. Look at a window full of challah. No two exactly alike, and yet all within the genre. And they still look like they're plastic. And that's what a challah wants to do. Wanted to look like plastic even before plastic. There's where they got the idea for plastic. From challahs."

"No shit. How you know that?"

"National Public Radio. They help you understand things. There's always National Public Radio to help me understand, no matter how confused I may be."

The only other white man anywhere nearby was standing in the middle of Lafayette Street, one of those bantamweight red-faced bums of indeterminate age and Irish descent who'd been making a home of the Bowery for decades now and so was familiar to Sabbath from back when he had lived in the neighborhood. He was clutching a bottle in a brown paper bag and talking quietly to a pigeon, a wounded pigeon that couldn't get itself up on its legs and take more than a wobbly step or two before keeling over on its side. In the midst of the early afternoon traffic it vainly fluttered its wings, trying to get moving. The bum stood straddling the pigeon, using his free hand to direct the cars to drive around and on through the intersection. Some drivers, angrily honking their horns, came perilously close to deliberately running him down, but the bum only cursed them and continued to stand guard over the bird. With the flapping sole of one of the sandals he was wearing, trying gently to help the pigeon find its equilibrium, he repeatedly nudged the bird up to its feet only to see it tumble to its side once the assistance was removed.

It looked to Sabbath as though the pigeon had been struck by a car or was ill and dying. He came over to the curb to watch as the bum with the bottle, wearing a red and white baseball cap with the logo "Handy Home Repair," leaned down toward the helpless creature. "Here," he said, "have a little ... have some ..." and he spilled a few drops from the mouth of the bottle onto the street. Though the pigeon obstinately worked to recover the power of self-locomotion, it was clear how with each succeeding effort its strength was ebbing away. So, too, was the magnanimity of the bum. "Here—here, it's vodka, take some." But the pigeon remained oblivious to the offering. It lay on its side barely stirring, its wings unable to do much more than intermittently twitch and collapse. The bum warned, "You're gonna get killed out here— *drink,* you fucker!"

Finally, when he could no longer endure the bird's indifference, he reared back and kicked the pigeon as hard as he could out of the path of the oncoming traffic.

It landed in the gutter only feet from where Sabbath was standing to watch. The bum marched over and kicked it again, and that took care of the problem.

Spontaneously Sabbath applauded. As far as he could tell, there were no longer street performers like himself—streets far too dangerous for that—the street performers now were homeless beggars and bums. Beggar's cabaret, beggar's cabaret that was to his own long-extinct Indecent Theater what the Grand Guignol was to the darling Muppets and their mouths, all the decent Muppets, making people happy with their untainted view of life: everything is innocent, childlike, and pure, everything is going to be okay—the secret is to tame your prick, draw attention away from the prick. Oh, the timidity! *His* timidity! Not Henson's, *his!* The cowardice! The *meekness!* Finally afraid to be utterly unspeakable, choosing to hide out in the hills instead! To everyone he had ever horrified, to the appalled who'd considered him a dangerous man, loathsome, degenerate, and gross, he cried, "Not at all! My failure is failing to have gone far *enough!* My failure is not having gone *further!*"

In response, a passerby dropped something into his coffee cup. "Cocksucker, I haven't finished!" But when he plucked the object out of the cup, it wasn't chewed chewing gum or a cigar butt—for the first time in four years, Sabbath had earned a quarter.

"God bless you, sir," he called after his benefactor. "God bless you and your loved ones and your cherished home with the electrical security system and the computer-accessed long-distance services."

At it again. How he'd begun was how he'd end, he who had gone gloomily around for years believing his life of adulteries and arthritis and professional embitterment to have been senselessly lived outside the conventions, without purpose or unity. But far from being disappointed at the malicious symmetry of his finding himself thirty years later once again on the street with his hat in his hand, he had the humorous sensation of having meandered blindly back into his own grand design. And you had to call that a triumph: he had perpetrated on himself the perfect joke.

By the time he went off to panhandle in the subway, his cup contained over two dollars in change. Clearly Sabbath had the touch, the look, the patter, the battered, capsized, repellent whatever-it-was that got under people's skins sufficiently fast for them to want to shut him down just long enough to scoot on by and never see him or hear him again.

Between Astor Place and Grand Central, where he had to change for the Suicide Express, he lumbered dutifully from car to car, shaking his cup and reciting from *King Lear* the role he hadn't had occasion to perform since he'd been assailed by his own tomatoes. A new career at sixty-four! Shakespeare in the subway, *Lear* for the masses—rich foundations love that stuff. Grants! Grants! Grants! At least let Roseanna see that he was out hustling, on his feet again, after the scandal that had cost them his twenty-five hundred a year. He was meeting her halfway. Financial equity between them was restored. Yet, even as he was regaining a working man's dignity, a residual sense of self-preservation cautioned him that he wasn't clowning on Town Street. In Madamaska Falls human corruption was considered to reside pretty much in him, Sabbath alone the menace, no one as dangerous anywhere around . . . no one but that midget Jap dean. He hated her fucking midget guts, not for her leading the coven that cost him his job—he hated the job. Not for losing the dough—he hated the dough, hated being an employee on a payroll who got a paycheck that he took to a bank where behind the counter there was a person they called a teller because she had it in her to tell even Sabbath to have a good day. He could not think of anything he hated more than endorsing that check, except perhaps looking at the stub where all the deductions were tallied up. It always got him, trying to figure out that stub, always pissed him off. Here I am at the bank endorsing my check—just what I always wanted.

No, it wasn't the job, it wasn't the money, it was losing those girls that killed him, a dozen of them a year, none over twenty-one, and always at least one. . . .

◆ ◆ ◆

That year—the fall of '89—it had been Kathy Goolsbee, a freckled redhead with the shiksa overbite, a hefty, big-limbed scholarship kid from Hazleton, PA, another of his treasured six-footers, a baker's daughter who'd worked in the shop after school from the time she was twelve and who pronounced *can* "kin" and *going to* the way Fats Waller did when he sang, "I'm gunna sit right down and write myself a lettuh." Kathy displayed an unlikely flair for meticulous puppet design that reminded him of Roseanna when she started out as his partner, and so more than likely it *would* have been Kathy that year had she not "accidentally" left on the sink of the second-floor women's room of the college library the tape that, unknown to her teacher, she had made of a phone conversation they'd had only days earlier, their fourth. She swore to him that all she intended to do was to take the tape into a toilet stall so she could listen there in privacy; she swore to him that she'd brought it with her to the library only because, since they'd got going together on the telephone, her head, even without her headset, was ablaze with little else. She swore to him that vengefully robbing him of his only source of income had never entered her mind.

It had all begun when Kathy phoned his home one evening to tell Professor Sabbath she had the flu and couldn't turn in her project the next day, and Sabbath, seizing on the surprising call to quiz her paternally about her "goals," learned that she was living with a boyfriend who tended bar at night in the student hangout and was at the library during the day writing a "poli sci" dissertation. They talked for half an hour, exclusively about Kathy, before Sabbath said, "Well, at least don't worry about the workshop—you stay in bed with that flu," and she replied, "I am." "And your boyfriend?" "Oh, Brian's at Bucky's, working." "So you're not only in bed, you're not only sick, you're all alone."

"Yeah." "Well, so am I," he said. "Where is your wife?" she asked, and Sabbath understood that Kathy was his nominee for the school year 1989–90. When you feel a strike like that at the end of the line, you don't have to be much of a fisherman to know you've hooked a beaut. You get a move on when a girl who speaks only in the stunted argot of her age-group asks in an uncharacteristically languid, slitheringly restless voice, with words that waft out of her more like an odor than a sound, "Where is your wife?"

"Out," he replied. "Hmmmm." "Are you warm enough, Kathy? Is it the chills making you make that noise?" "Uh-uh." "You must be sure you're warm enough. What are you wearing in bed?" "My pj's." "With the flu? That's all?" "Oh, I'm boiling in just these. I keep having flashes. Flushes." "Well," laughing, "I do, too—" and yet, even as he began to reel her in cautiously, gently, without haste, taking all the time in the world to haul her on board, big and speckled and thumpingly alive, inwardly Sabbath was so excited he did not begin to realize that it was he being guided up through leagues of lust by the hook with which she'd pierced *him*; had no idea, he who'd passed into his sixties only the month before, that it was he being craftily landed and that someday very soon now he would discover himself eviscerated, stuffed, and hung as a trophy on the wall above the desk of Dean Kimiko Kakizaki. All the way back in Havana, when Yvonne de Carlo had said to the young merchant seaman, "You finished? Get off!" he had come to understand that in dealing with the wayward you must never allow your cunning to be set aside along with your skivvies simply because of the mad craving to come . . . and yet it never occurred to Sabbath, no, not even to wily old Sabbath, cynical now for a good fifty years, that a big strapping Pennsylvanian with all those freckles could be quite so deficient in ideals as to be setting him up for bringing him down.

It was not three weeks after her first call that Kathy was explaining to Sabbath that she had begun her evening's work listening to their tape in the stacks, at a carrel piled high with books for "Western Civ," but that after only ten minutes, the tape had made her so wet she had left everything and taken off with the headset for the ladies' bathroom. "But how did the tape wind up on the sink," Sabbath asked, "if you were listening to it in a toilet stall?" "I was taking it out to put something else in." "Why didn't you do that in the stall?" "Because I would only have started listening again. I mean, I just didn't know what to do, basically. I thought, 'This is really crazy.' I was, like, so wet and swollen, how could I concentrate? I was in the library to research my paper, only I couldn't stop masturbating." "Everybody masturbates in libraries. That's what they're for. This does not explain to me why you walk away leaving a tape—" "Somebody came *in*." "Who? Who came in?" "It doesn't *matter*. Some *girl*. I got *confused*. By then I didn't even know what I was doing anymore. This whole thing has made me crazy. I was, like, afraid from getting so crazy from the tape, and so I just walked out. I felt really awful. I was gunna call. But I was, like, afraid of *you*." "Who put you up to this, Kathy? Who put you up to taping me?"

Now, however justified Sabbath's anger may have been by what was either an unforgivable oversight or an out-and-out betrayal, as Kathy sat sobbing in the front seat of his car, unburdening herself of the news, even he knew himself to be being less than ingenuous. (He had parked, fatefully enough, across from the Battle Mountain cemetery where Drenka's body would be laid to rest just a few years later.) The truth was that he, too, had taped their conversation, not only the conversation on the tape she'd left at the library but the three that preceded it. But then, Sabbath had been taping his workshop girls for years now and planned to leave the collection to the Library of Congress. Seeing to the collection's preservation was one of the best reasons he had— the only reason he had—to one day get a lawyer to draw up a will.

Including his four with Big Kathy, there were a total of thirty-three tapes, perpetuating the words of six different students who'd taken the puppetry workshop. All were locked away in the bottom drawer of an old file cabinet, stored in two shoeboxes marked "Corres." (A third shoebox, marked "Taxes 1984," contained Polaroids of five of the girls.) Each tape was dated and all were organized alphabetically—and responsibly—by Christian names only and filed chronologically within that classification. He kept the tapes in excellent order not only so that each was easy to locate when he needed it to hand but so that they could be quickly accounted for if he ever worried, as irrationally he sometimes did, that one or another had gotten misplaced. From time to time Drenka would like to listen to the tapes while sucking him off. Otherwise they never left the locked file cabinet, and whenever he took one of his favorites to play a patch for himself, he would double-lock the studio door. Sabbath knew the danger of what he had in those shoeboxes yet he could never bring himself either to erase the tapes or to bury them in garbage at the town dump. That would have been like burning the flag. No, more like defiling a Picasso. Because there was in these tapes a kind of *art* in the way that he was able to unshackle his girls from their habit of innocence. There was a kind of art in his providing an illicit adventure not with a boy of their own age but with someone three times their age—the very repugnance that his aging body inspired in them had to make their adventure with him feel a little like a crime and thereby give free play to their budding perversity and to the confused exhilaration that comes of flirting with disgrace. Yes, despite everything, he had the artistry still to open up to them the lurid interstices of life, often for the first time since they'd given their debut "b.j." in junior high. As Kathy told him in that language which they all used and which made him want to cut their heads off, through coming to know him she felt "empowered." "I still have moments when I'm uncertain and scared. But for the most part," she said, "I just want . . . I want to spend time with you. . . . I want—to take care of you." He laughed. "You think I need taking care of?" "I *mean* it," she said earnestly. "*What* do you mean?" "I mean I can care for you . . . I mean I can take care of your body. *And* your heart." "Yes? You've seen my EKG? You're afraid when I come I'll have a coronary?" "I don't *know*. . . . I mean . . . I don't know *what* I mean but I mean it. That's what I mean—what I just said." "And can I take care of you?" "Yeah. Yeah. You kin." "Which part of you?" "My body," she dared to reply. Yes, they experienced not merely their capacity for deviancy—that they'd known of since seventh grade—but the larger risks that deviancy entailed. His gifts as a theater director and a puppet master he poured without stinting into these tapes. Once he'd passed into his fifties, the art in these tapes—the insidious art of giving license to what was already there—was the only art he had left.

And then he got nailed.

The tape Kathy "forgot" had not only landed by morning in Kakizaki's office but was somehow hijacked and rerecorded, before it even reached the dean, by an ad hoc committee calling itself Women Against Sexual Abuse, Belittlement, Battering, and Telephone Harassment, whose acronym was formed from the last seven words. By dinnertime of the following day, SABBATH had opened up a phone line on which the tape was continuously played. The local phone number to call—722-2284, fortuitously enough S-A-B-B-A-T-H again—was announced by the committee's cochairpersons, two women, an art history professor and a local pediatrician, during an hour-long call-in show on the college radio station. The introduction prepared by SABBATH for the telephonic transmission described the tape as "the most blatantly vile example of the exploitation, humiliation, and sexual defilement of a college student by her professor in the history of this academic community." "You are about to hear," the introduction began, spoken by the pediatrician, and sounding to Sabbath appropriately clinical though lawyerly as well—lawyerly with palpable hatred—"two people talking on the telephone: one a man of sixty and the other a young woman, a college student, who has just turned twenty. The man is her teacher, acting in loco parentis. He is Morris Sabbath, adjunct professor of puppet theater in the four-college program. In order to protect her privacy—and her innocence—the name of the young woman has been bleeped wherever it appeared on the tape. That is the only alteration that has been made in the original conversation, which was secretly transcribed by the young woman in order to document what she had been subjected to by Professor Sabbath from the day she enrolled in his course. In a candid, confidential statement given voluntarily to the steering committee of SABBATH, the young woman revealed that this was not the first such conversation into which she had been lured by Professor Sabbath. Moreover, she turns out to have been only the latest of a series of students whom Professor Sabbath has intimidated and victimized during the years he has been associated with the program. This tape records the fourth such telephone conversation to which the student was subjected.* The listener will quickly recognize how by this point in his psychological assault on an inexperienced young woman, Professor Sabbath has been able to manipulate her into thinking that she is a willing participant. Of course, to get the woman to think that it is her fault, to get her to think that she is a 'bad girl' who has brought her humiliation on herself by her own cooperation and complicity . . ."

◆ ◆ ◆

The car descended the slope of Battle Mountain to the lonely spot where he'd arranged to pick her up, the crossroad separating the

---

*What follows is an uncensored transcription of the entire conversation as it was secretly taped by Kathy Goolsbee (and by Sabbath) and played by SABBATH for whoever dialed 722-2284 and took the thirty minutes to listen. In just the first twenty-four hours, over a hundred callers stayed on the line to hear the harassment from beginning to end. It wasn't long before tapes reproduced from the original began to turn up for sale around the state and, according to the *Cumberland Sentinel*, "as far afield as Prince Edward Island, where the tape is being used as an audio teaching aid by the Charlottetown Project on the State of Canadian Women."

What are you doing right now?
I'm on my stomach. I'm masturbating.
Where are you?
I'm home, I'm on my bed.
You all alone?
Ummmm.
How long are you alone for?
A long time. Brian's at a basketball game.
I see. How nice. You are all alone and on your own bed masturbating.

woods from the fields that led to West Town Street. All the way
down the eighteen hundred feet she wept with her whole body
shaking, immersed in pain, as though he were lowering her alive
into her grave. "Oh, it's unbearable. Oh, it hurts. I'm so unhappy.
I don't understand why this is happening to me." She was a big
girl whose production of secretions was considerable, and her
tears were no exception. He'd never seen tears so large. Someone
less of a connoisseur might have taken them for real.

"Extremely immature behavior," he said. "The Sobbing
Scene."

"I want to suck you," she managed to moan through her tears.

"The emotionality of young women. Why don't they ever come
up with something new?"

Across the road a couple of pickup trucks were parked in the
dirt lot of the roadside nursery whose greenhouses constituted
the first reassuring signs of the white man's intrusion into these
wooded hills (once the heartland of the Madamaskas, to whose

Well, I'm glad you called. What are you wearing?

(Babyish laugh) I'm wearing my clothes.

What clothes are you wearing?

I'm wearing jeans. And a turtleneck. Standard wear.

Yes, that's your standard wear, isn't it? I was very excited after I spoke
to you last time. You're very exciting.

Ummmm.

You are. Don't you know that?

But I felt bad. I felt like I disturbed you when I called at your house.

You didn't disturb me in terms of my not wanting to hear from you. I
just felt it was a good idea to stop that before it went any further.

Sorry. And I won't do it again.

Fine. You just misjudged. And why not? You're new to this. Okay.
You're alone and you're on your bed.

Yeah, and also, I wanted . . . Last time we talked you said . . . about
. . . I told you I felt disgusted, you know, when I get really disgusted . . .
and you said about what, and I said whatever I said, like I said, my lack
of ability in workshop . . . and then I think I was just very evasive, like,
I didn't really, like, I felt that I couldn't really tell you *(embarrassed
laugh)*. . . . It's much more specific. . . . I'm just, like . . . well, maybe it's

tribes the local falls were said—by those opposed to the profane installation of a parking lot and picnic tables—to have been sacred. It was in the numbingly cold pool of one of the remotest tributaries of those sacred falls, the brook that spilled down the rocky streamed beside the Grotto, that he and Drenka would gambol naked in the summer. See plate 4. Detail from the Madamaska vase of dancing nymph and bearded figure brandishing phallus. On bank of brook, note the wine jar, a he-goat, and a basket of figs. From the collection of the Metropolitan Museum. XX century A.D.).

"Get out. Disappear."

"I want to suck you hard."

A worker in coveralls was loading mulch sacks onto one of the trucks—otherwise there wasn't anyone in sight. Mist was rising beyond the woods to the west, the seasonal mist that to the Madamaskas undoubtedly meant something about reigning divinities or departed souls—their mothers, their fathers, their Morties,

---

just now . . . it's like I think about sex all the time *(confessional laugh)*.

Do you?

Yes, I do. I just feel I can't do anything about it. It's very . . . I mean, it's very . . . It's very good, sometimes. *(Laugh)*

You masturbate a lot?

Well, no.

No?

Well, I don't really have the opportunity. I'm in class. And it's all so boring and my mind is just elsewhere completely. And ummmm . . .

You have sex thoughts.

Yeah. Constantly. And I just . . . I think it's normal but sort of extreme. And I feel—guilty, I guess.

Really? What do you feel guilty about? Having sex thoughts all the time? Everybody does.

You think so? I don't think most people think like that.

You'd be surprised at what most people think like. I wouldn't worry about it. You're young and you're healthy and you're lovely and so why shouldn't you? Right?

I guess. I don't know. Sometimes I read in psych about people, you know, diagnosed, like, "hypersexual," and I'm, like, "Hey." Now I feel

their Nikkis—but to Sabbath recalled nothing more than the opening of "Ode to Autumn." He was not an Indian, and the mist was the ghost of no one he knew. This local scandal, remember, was taking place in the fall of 1989, two years before the death of his senile mother and four before her reappearance jolted him into understanding that not everything alive is a living substance. This was back when the Great Disgrace was still to come, and for obvious reasons he could not locate its origins in the sensuous stimulus that was the innocuously experimental daughter of the Pennsylvania baker with the foreboding surname. You besmirch yourself in increments of excrement—everyone knows that much about the inevitabilities (or used to)—but not even Sabbath understood how he could lose his job at a liberal arts college for teaching a twenty-year-old to talk dirty twenty-five years after Pauline Réage, fifty-five years after Henry Miller, sixty years after D. H. Lawrence, eighty years after James Joyce, two hundred years after John Cleland, three hundred years after John Wilmot,

---

I'm just gunna, like, you're gunna think I'm a nymphomaniac and I'm not. I don't . . . whatever . . . like, I'm not out having sex. I don't know. I think I just sexualize every interaction I have with people, and I feel guilty. I feel like this is . . . you know . . . no good.

You feel that with me?

Well, ummmm . . .

You sexualized our phone calls, I sexualized our phone calls—nothing wrong with that. You don't feel guilty about that, or do you?

Well, I mean . . . I don't know. I guess I don't feel guilty. I feel very empowered. But, nevertheless, I'm just, like, saying, like, in general I don't sit around thinking I lack ability. I sit around thinking, *What* is going on in my head? I can't stand it.

So you're going through the time when you're obsessed with sex. It happens to everybody. Especially as nothing in school is interesting you.

I think that's the problem. It's like I react to it. I have to rebel or something.

It doesn't engage your mind. And so your mind is empty and something moves in and what moves in—because you're frustrated, the thing that can answer the frustration is sex. It's very common. There's nothing on your mind, and it's filled by this thing. Don't worry about it. Okay?

second earl of Rochester—not to mention four hundred after
Rabelais, two thousand after Ovid, and twenty-two hundred after Aristophanes. By 1989 you had to be a loaf of Papa Goolsbee's
pumpernickel not to be able to talk dirty. If only you could run a
'29 penis on ruthless mistrust, cunning negativity, and world-
denouncing energy, if only you could run a '29 penis on relentless
mischief, oppositional exuberance, and eight hundred different
kinds of disgust, then he wouldn't have needed those tapes. But
the advantage a young girl has over an old man is that she is wet
at the drop of a hat, while to engorge him it is necessary at times
to drop a ton of bricks. Aging sets problems that are no joke. The
prick does not come with a lifetime guarantee.

The mist was rising preternaturally from the river, and the
pumpkins, ripe for carving, dotted like the freckles on Kathy's
face a big open field back of the greenhouse, and affixed to the
trees, wouldn't you know it, all the right leaves, every last one
tinted to polychromatic perfection. The trees were resplendent

---

(*Laugh*) Yeah. I'm glad. . . . You see, I feel like I could tell you this but
I couldn't tell anyone else.

You can tell me and you have told me and it's fine with me. You're in
Levi's and you've got on your turtleneck shirt.

Yeah.

Yeah?

Yeah.

You know what I want you to do?

What?

Unzip your Levi's.

Okay.

Undo the button.

Okay.

And unzip it.

Okay. . . . I'm in front of the mirror.

You're in front of the mirror?

Yeah.

Lying down?

Yeah.

Now pull your Levi's down. . . . Pull 'em down around your ankles.

precisely as they'd been resplendent the year before—and the year
before that—a perennial profusion of pigmentation to remind
him that by the waters of the Madamaskas he had every reason to
weep, because that was about as far as he could have got himself
from the tropical sea and the Romance Run and those grand cities
like Buenos Aires, where a common seaman of seventeen could
eat for peanuts in 1946 at the greatest steak houses along the
Florida—they called the main street in B.A. Florida—and then
cross the river, the famous Plata, to where they had *the best
places,* which meant the places where there were the most beautiful girls. And in South America that meant the most beautiful girls
in the world. So many hot, beautiful women. And he had seques-
tered himself in New England! Colorful leaves? Try Rio. They got
the colors too, only instead of on trees they're on flesh.

Seventeen. Three years Kathy's junior and no ad hoc committee
of mollycoddling professors to keep me from getting clap, getting
rolled, or getting stabbed to death, let alone getting my little ears

---

(Whispered) Okay.
And take them off. . . . I'll give you time. . . . Did you get them off?
Yeah.
What do you see?
I see my legs. And I see my crotch.
Do you have bikini underpants on?
Yes.
Take your hand and put your finger right on the crotch of your
underpants. Just on the outside of the underpants, rub it up and down.
Just rub it gently up and down. How does that feel?
Good. Yeah. It feels real good. It feels so nice. It's wet.
Is it wet?
It's really wet.
You're still outside the underpants. Just on the outside rub it. Rub it
up and down. . . . Now move the underpants aside. Can you do that?
Yeah.
And now put your finger on your clitoris. And just rub it up and
down. And tell me how that feels.
It feels good.
Make yourself excited that way. Tell me how that feels.

molested. I went there deliberately to get myself molly-bloomed!
That's what sevenfuckinteen is *for!*

Frost, he mused—thought Sabbath—passing the time until
Kathy got the idea that not even with *his* low standards would
he dare to risk his dick again with an out-and-out adder and that
she should just slither back to the Japanese viperina. The dim
meatballs who were the proud descendants of the settlers who'd
usurped these hills from the Original Goyim—an epithet historically more accurate than "Indians" and more respectful, too, as
Sabbath had explained to that pal of Roseanna's who taught
"Hunting and Gathering" as a literature course. . . . Where was I?
thought he, when once again the blandishments tumbling forth
from perfidious Kathy caused him to lose his . . . the dim meatballs, long now the Reigning Goyim, all crowing gaily—as in
"When Hearts Were Young and Gay"—about another frost,
lower temperatures than even the night before, when Roseanna,
wearing only a nightie, had been found by the state police at

---

I'm putting my finger in my cunt. I'm on top of my finger.
You on your belly or on your back?
I'm sitting up.
You're sitting up. And looking in the mirror?
Yeah.
And you're going in and out?
Yeah.
Go ahead. Fuck it with your finger.
I want it to be you, though.
Tell me what you want.
I want your cock. I'll get it really, really hard.
Want me to stick it in you?
I want you to stick it into me hard.
A nice stiff cock inside you?
Ummmm. Oh, I'm touching my breasts.
You want to take your turtleneck off?
I'm just lifting it up.
You want to put the nipple between your fingers?
Yeah.
How about wetting it? Wet it with your fingers. Wet your fingers with

three A.M. stretched on her back across Town Street, waiting to be run over.

An hour or so earlier she had left their house by car but had failed even to negotiate the first fifty feet of the hundred yards of curving dirt incline that lay between the carport and Brick Furnace Road. She had been speeding off not for town but for Athena, fourteen miles away, where Kathy shared an apartment with Brian a few blocks from the college, at 137 Spring. And despite having driven her Jeep into a boulder in the hay field that was their front yard, despite having to stumble without shoes or slippers two and a half miles down the twist of pitch-black lanes to the bridge that crossed the brook to Town Street, despite having lain on the asphalt insufficiently clad anywhere from fifteen minutes to half an hour before being spotted by the cop cruising by, she was clutching in one of her freezing hands a yellow Post-it note bearing—in a drunken scrawl legible by then not even to herself—the address of the girl who'd asked at the close of the

---

your tongue and then wet the end of your nipple. Is that good?

Oh, God.

Now fuck your cunt again. Fuck your cunt.

Ummmm.

And tell me what you want. Tell me what you most want.

I want you on top of my back. Your cock inside me. Oh, God. Oh, God, I want *you*.

What do you want, *(bleep)*? Tell me what you want.

I want your cock. I want it everywhere. I want your hands everywhere. I want your hands on my legs. On my stomach. My back. On my breasts, squeezing my breasts.

Where do you want my cock?

Oh, I want it in my mouth.

What are you going to do when it's in your mouth?

Suck it. Suck it really hard. I want to suck your balls. I want to lick your balls. Oh, God.

And what else?

Oh, I just want you to squeeze me. Then I want you to start pumping me.

Pump you? I'm pumping you right now. Tell me what you want.

tape, "When is your wife coming back?" Roseanna's intention was to tell this little whore in person just how fucking back she was, but having stumbled to the ground so many times without getting anywhere near Athena, Roseanna decided on Town that she'd be better off dead. That way the girl would never have to ask that question again. None of them would.

"I want to suck you right here."

Sabbath had not only driven some six hours that day—getting Roseanna to the private psychiatric hospital in Usher and then himself back in time to meet Kathy—but had been up confronting this newest upheaval since just after three in the morning, when he had been awakened by a loud knock at the side door and the astonishing news that it was the police returning the wife whom he had assumed was sleeping all the while in their king-size bed, not cuddled close to him, needless to say, but safely over at the far edge, where, admittedly, he had not journeyed for many a year. When they had moved up from queen-size he had remarked to a

---

I want you to pump me. Oh, I want you inside me.

What are you doing now?

I'm on my stomach. I'm masturbating. I want you to suck my breasts.

I'm sucking on them right now. I'm sucking your tits now.

Oh, God.

What else do you want me to do to you?

Oh, God. I'm going to come.

You're going to come?

I want to. I want you here. I want you on top of me. I want you on top of me right now.

I'm on top of you.

Oh. God. Oh, God. I have to stop.

Why do you have to stop?

Because—I'm afraid. I'm afraid to not be able to hear.

I thought no one was coming back. I thought he was playing basketball.

Well, you never know. Oh, God. Oh, God. Oh, God, this is awful. I have to stop. I want your cock. Pumping me hard. Digging into me. Oh, God. What are you doing right now?

I have my cock in my hand.

visitor that the new bed was so big he couldn't find Roseanna in it. Overhearing him from where she happened to be gardening just outside the kitchen window, she had shouted into the house, "Why don't you look?" But this was easily over a decade back, when he still spoke to people and she was drinking only a bottle a day and there was still a remnant of hope.

Yes, there at the door, earnestly polite now, stood Matthew Balich, whom his former art teacher had failed to recognize either because of the state trooper uniform or because of the booze. She had apparently whispered to Matthew, before he authoritatively made known his mission, that they must be very quiet to avoid awakening her hardworking husband. She had even tried to tip him. Heading for Kathy's in only a nightgown, she'd still had the percipience to take her purse in case she needed to buy a drink.

It had been a long night, morning, and afternoon for Sabbath. First the Jeep had to be towed off the boulder where she'd run

---

You squeezing it and rubbing it? I want you to rub it. Tell me. I want my mouth on it. I want to suck it. Oh, God, I want to kiss it. I want to put your cock in my ass.

What do you want to do with my cock right now?

I want to suck it right now. I want to be between your legs. You pull my head.

Hard?

No. Just gently. And then I'll move around. Let me suck you.

I'll let you. If you say please, I'll let you.

Oh, God. This is torture.

Is it? You got your finger in your cunt?

No.

It's not torture. Put your finger in your cunt, *(bleep)*. Put your finger in your cunt.

Okay.

Put your finger right up inside your cunt.

Oh, God, it's so hot.

Put it up there. Now move it up and down.

Oh, God.

Move it up and down, *(bleep)*. Move it up and down, *(bleep)*. Move aground, then arrangements had to be made through the family doctor to get her a bed at Usher, then the effort had to be undertaken to force her, hung over and hysterical though she was, to agree to twenty-eight days in Usher's rehab program, and then at last there was the six-hour round-trip to the hospital, Roseanna ranting at him from the backseat the whole way there, pausing only to instruct him angrily to pull over at each service station they passed so she could try to relieve herself of her cramps.

Why she had to get plastered by stages in those putrid restrooms instead of openly guzzling from the bottle in her purse Sabbath did not bother to inquire. Her pride? After last night, her pride? Nor did Sabbath do anything to stop her when she listed the ways in which a wife whose intentions had merely been to assist him at his work and to comfort him when there were setbacks and to look after him when the arthritis was most acute had herself been ruthlessly ignored, insulted, exploited, and betrayed.

---

it up and down, *(bleep)*. Fuck it, *(bleep)*. Come on, fuck it. Come on, fuck it.

Oh, God! Oh, God!

Go ahead, fuck it.

Oh! Oh! Oh! Mickey! Oh, my God! Ahh! Ahh! Ahh! Jesus Christ! Oh, my God! Jesus Christ! I want you so bad! Uhhh! Uhhh! Oh, God. . . . I just came.

Did you come?

Yeah.

Was that good?

Yeah.

Want to come again?

Uh-uh.

No?

No. I want you to come.

You want to make me come?

Yeah. I'm gunna suck your cock.

You tell me how you're going to make me come.

I'm gunna suck you. Slowly. Up and down. Slowly move my lips up and down your cock. Move my tongue. I'm gunna suck off the top of

Up front in the car Sabbath played the Goodman tapes to which he and Drenka used to dance together in the motel rooms he rented up and down the valley when first they'd become enraptured lovers. During the 130-mile drive west to Usher, the tapes more or less drowned out Roseanna's tirade and allowed Sabbath some respite from all that he'd been through since Matthew had kindly returned her. First they fucked, then they danced, Sabbath and Matthew's mom, and while Sabbath faultlessly sang the lyrics into her grinning, incredulous face, his come would leak out of her, making even more lubricious the inner roundness of her thighs. The come would stream all the way down to her heels, and after they'd danced he would massage her feet with it. Nestled down at the end of the motel bed, he would suck on her big toe, pretending it was her cock, and she pretended that his come was her own.

(And where did all those 78s disappear to? After I went to sea, what happened to the 1935 Victor recording of "Sometimes I'm

---

your cock. Really slowly. Ummm. Oh, God. . . . What do you want me to do?

Suck my balls.

Okay. Okay.

I want you to put your tongue on my ass. Want to do that?

Okay.

Make my asshole very excited with your tongue.

Yeah. I can do that.

Put your finger up my ass.

Okay.

Did you ever do that?

Nooo. Uh-uh.

Take your finger, while we're fucking. Gently put it on my asshole. And then fuck my ass with your finger. Do you think you'd like that?

Yeah. I want to make you come.

Play with it with your hand. And when a little drop comes out, you can smear the head of it with the drop. You like that?

Yeah.

Did you ever fuck a woman?

No.

Happy" that was Morty's treasure of treasures, the one with the
Bunny Berigan solo that Morty called "the greatest trumpet solo
ever, by anyone"? Who got Morty's records? What happened to
his things after Mother died? Where are they?) Stroking with one
spoon-shaped thumb the breadth of Croatian cheekbone while
with the other jiggling her on-off switch, Sabbath sang "Stardust"
to Drenka, not like Hoagy Carmichael, in English, but in French
no less—"Suivant le silence de la nuit / Répète ton nom . . ."—exactly the way it was sung for the prom crowds by Gene Hochberg,
who led the swing band in which Morty played clarinet (and who,
amazingly, would wind up just like Morty flying B-25s in the
Pacific and who Sabbath had always secretly wished had been the
one to be shot down). A bearded barrel he indisputably was, yet
Drenka cooed ecstatically, "My American boyfriend. I have an
American boyfriend," while the great Goodman performances of
the thirties transformed into the pavilion over the LaReine Avenue beach the room reeking of disinfectant that he had rented for

---

Didn't you?

No.

No? Just have to ask, you know.

(Laughter)

Nobody at school ever tried to fuck you? No woman ever tried to fuck
you in the four-college program?

Ummm, no.

Really?

Ummm, no. Not that I haven't thought about it.

You have thought about it?

Yeah.

What do you think?

I think about being on top of a woman and sucking her breasts. And
putting our cunts together—and rubbing. Kissing.

Never did it?

Uh-uh.

Did you ever fuck two men?

Uh-uh.

No?

Uh-uh. *(Laughing)* Did you?

six bucks in the name of Goodman's maniac trumpeter on "We
Three and the Angels Sing," Ziggy Elman. At the LaReine Avenue
pavilion Morty taught Mickey to jitterbug one August night in
1938, when the little boy who was his shadow was just nine. The
kid's birthday present. Sabbath taught the girl from Split how to
jitterbug on a snowy afternoon in 1981 in a motel in New England called the Bo-Peep. By the time they left at six to drive, in two
cars, the plowed roads home, she could tell Harry James's solos
from Elman's on "St. Louis Blues," she could imitate very funnily
Hamp going "Ee-ee" in that screechy way he did it in the final
solo of "Ding Dong Daddy," she could knowingly say about
"Roll 'Em" what Morty used to knowingly say to Mickey about
"Roll 'Em" after the boogie-woogie beginning starts petering out
in the Stacy solo: "It's really just a fast blues in F." She could even
bang out on Sabbath's hairy hindquarters the Krupa tom-tom
beat in her own accompaniment to "Sweet Leilani." Martha Til-
ton taking over from Helen Ward. Dave Tough taking over from

Not that I recall. You ever think about that?
Yeah.
About fucking two men.
Yeah.
You have fantasies about it?
Yeah. I guess so. I think about just sort of anonymous men. Fucking.
Did you ever fuck a man and a woman?
No.
Did you ever think about that?
I don't know.
No?
Maybe. Yeah. I guess so. Why are *you* asking all the questions?
Well, you can ask me questions if you want.
Did you ever fuck a man?
No.
Never?
No.
Really?
Yes.
Did you ever fuck two women?

Krupa. Bud Freeman coming over in '38 from the Dorsey band. Jimmy Mundy, from the Hines band, coming over as staff arranger. In one long winter afternoon at the Bo-Peep her American boyfriend taught Drenka things she could never learn from the devoted husband whose pleasure that day was to be out all alone in the snow, building stone walls until it got too dark even to see his own breath.

At Usher a kindly, handsome doctor twenty years Sabbath's junior assured him that if Roseanna cooperated with "the program" she would be home and on the path to sobriety in twenty-eight days. "Wanna bet?" Sabbath said, and drove back to Madamska Falls to kill Kathy. Ever since three A.M., when he learned how Roseanna, because of that tape, had stretched out on Town Street in her nightgown, waiting to be run over, he had been planning to take Kathy to the top of Battle Mountain and strangle her.

As a ripe, enormous pumpkin floated free from the darkening

Uh-huh.

Did you ever fuck a prostitute?

Uh-huh.

You did? Oh, my God *(laughing)*.

Yeah, I fucked two women.

Did you like it?

I loved it. I love it.

Really?

Yeah. They loved it, too. It's fun. I fucked the two of them. They fucked each other. And they both sucked me. And then I would suck one of them. While the other sucked me. That was good. I had my face in her cunt. And the other one would be sucking on my cock. And then the first one would be sucking on the other one's cunt. So everybody would be sucking everybody else. And sometimes one of them sucks you and makes you hard and then she puts it in the other one's cunt. How does that strike you?

It's good.

I like to watch them suck each other. That's always exciting. They make each other come. There are lots of things to do, aren't there?

Yeah.

field across from the car and the high drama of a full harvest moon began, Sabbath could not have said where he found the strength to refrain—as, for the fifth time in as many minutes, she extended yet again the offer to entrap him—from either commencing the strangulation with his once-powerful fingers or going ahead and taking it out in a car for the millionth time in this life.

"Kathy," he said, exhaustion giving him the sensation that he was glimmering and fading like a dying light bulb, "Kathy," he said, thinking as he watched the moon ascend that if only he'd had the moon on his side things would have turned out differently, "do us all a favor—do Brian instead. That may even be what he's angling for by turning into a deaf-mute. Didn't you say that the shock of hearing the tape has turned him into a deaf-mute? Well, go home and sign him that you're going to blow him and see if his face doesn't light up."

Not too hard on Sabbath, Reader. Neither the turbulent inner

Frighten you?

Yeah.

Does it really?

A little bit. But I want to fuck you. I want to fuck you. I don't want to fuck you with someone else.

I'm not asking you to. I'm just answering your questions. I just want to fuck you. I want to suck your cunt. Suck your cunt for an hour. Oh, *(bleep)*, I want to come all over you.

Come on my breasts.

You like that?

Yes.

You're a very hot girl, aren't you? Tell me what your cunt looks like now.

Uh-uh.

No? You're not going to tell me what it looks like?

Uh-uh.

I can imagine it.

(Laughter)

It's a beautiful cunt.

You know what happened?

talkathon, nor the superabundance of self-subversion, nor the years of reading about death, nor the bitter experience of tribulation, loss, hardship, and grief make it any easier for a man of his type (perhaps for a man of any type) to get good use out of his brain when confronted by such an offer once, let alone when it is made repeatedly by a girl a third his age with an occlusion like Gene Tierney's in *Laura*. Don't be too hard on Sabbath for beginning to begin to think that maybe she was *telling the truth*: that she *had* left the tape in the library accidentally, that it *had* fallen into the Kakumoto's hands accidentally, that she *had* been helpless to resist the pressures brought on her and had capitulated only to save her skin, as who among her "peers"—that was what she called her friends—would have done otherwise? She was really a sweet and decent kid, good-natured, involved, she had presumed, in some half-crazy but harmless extracurricular amusement, Professor Sabbath's Audio-Visual Club; a large, graceless girl, ill-educated, coarse, and incoherent in the preferred

---

What?

I had a gynecologist appointment. And I thought the gynecologist was coming on to me.

Was he?

She.

She was?

It was very different from anything that had ever happened to me before.

Tell me.

I don't know. She was just, like . . . She was very pretty. She was beautiful. She put the speculum in and she said, "Oh, my God, you have so much stuff in here." And she kept saying it. And she sort of lifted out this huge glob. I don't know. It was weird.

She touch you?

Yeah. She put her hand in me. I mean her fingers to do the exam.

Make you excited?

Yeah. She touched this . . . I have a little burn on my thigh, and she touched it, and she asked me what happened. I don't know. It was different. And that's when . . .

That's when what?

style of the late-twentieth-century undergraduate, but utterly without the shifty ruthlessness necessary for the vicious stunt he was charging her with. Maybe merely because he was so enraged and exhausted, a great misapprehension had taken hold of him and he was falling victim to another of his stupid mistakes. Why would she be crying so pitifully for so long if she was conspiring against him? Why would she cling to his side like this, if her true ties and affinities were with his supervirtuous antagonists and their angry, sinister fixed ideas about what should and should not constitute an education for twenty-year-old girls? She didn't begin to have Sabbath's skill at feigning what looked like genuine feeling . . . or did she? Why else would she be begging to blow someone wholly alien to her, inessential to her, someone who was already a month into his seventh decade on earth, if not to assert without equivocation that she was farcically, illogically, and incomprehensibly his? So little in life is knowable, Reader— don't be hard on Sabbath if he gets things wrong. Or on Kathy if

---

Nothing.

Tell me.

I just felt really good. I thought I was crazy.

You thought you were crazy?

Yeah.

You're not crazy. You're a hot kid from Hazleton and you're excited. Maybe you should fuck a girl.

Uh-uh *(laughing)*.

You can do whatever you want, you see? You want to make me come now?

Yeah. I'm all sweaty. It's cold here, too. Yeah, I want you to come. I want to suck your cock. I want it so bad.

Keep going.

You have your hand on it?

You bet.

Good. Are you rubbing it?

I'm jerking it.

You're jerking it?

I'm pumping it up and down. I'm pumping it up and down. I'm going to take my balls out. Oh, it feels good, *(bleep)*, it feels good.

she gets things wrong. Many farcical, illogical, incomprehensible transactions are subsumed by the manias of lust.

Twenty. Could I even survive saying no to twenty? How many twenties are left? How many thirties or forties are left? Under the sad end-of-days spell of the smoky dusk and the waning year, of the moon and its ostentatious superiority to all the trashy, petty claptrap of his sublunar existence, why does he even hesitate? The Kamizakis are your enemies whether you do anything or not, so you might as well do it. Yes, yes, if you can still do something, you *must* do it—that is the golden rule of sublunar existence, whether you are a worm cut in two or a man with a prostate like a billiard ball. If you can still do something, then you must do it! Anything living can figure that out.

In Rome . . . in Rome, he was now remembering while Kathy continued her sobbing beside him, an elderly Italian puppeteer said to have once been quite famous had come to the school to judge a competition that Sabbath proceeded to win, and after-

---

Where do you want me?

I want your cunt to sit right down on my cock. To slide on top of it. And to just start pumping up and down. To sit on it and go up on it.

Squeeze my breasts?

I'll squeeze 'em.

Squeeze my nipples?

Oh, I'll bite on your nipples. Your beautiful pink nipples. Oh, *(bleep)*. Oh, it's filling up with come now. It's filling up with hot, thick come. It's filling up with hot white come. It's going to shoot out. Want me to come in your mouth?

Yeah. I want to suck you right now. Very fast. I want to put you in my mouth. Oh, God. I'm sucking it hard.

Suck it, *(bleep)*. Suck me.

Faster and faster?

Suck me, *(bleep)*.

Oh, God.

Suck me, *(bleep)*. Want to suck my dick?

Yes, I want to suck you. I want to suck your cock.

Suck my stiff cock. Hard, stiff cock. Suck my hard, stiff cock.

Oh, God.

ward the puppeteer, having given a demonstration of stale wiz-
ardry with a puppet looking exactly like himself, had asked young
Sabbath to accompany him to a café in the Piazza del Popolo. The
puppeteer was in his seventies, small, pudgy, and bald with a
poor yellowish complexion, but so haughtily autocratic was his
bearing that Sabbath spontaneously followed the example of his
awestruck professor and, even enjoying for a change being deferential—albeit impudently so—he addressed the old man, whose
name meant nothing to him, as Maestro. In addition to his insufferable posturing there was an ascot that half hid a substantial
wattle, a beret that, out-of-doors, concealed the baldness, a stick
with which he tapped the table to draw the attention of the
waiter—and all of this readied Sabbath for a flood of boring old
bohemian self-adoration that he would just have to endure for
having won the prize. But instead, no sooner had the puppeteer
ordered cognac for both of them than he said, "Dimmi di tutte
le ragazze che ti sei scopato a Roma"—Tell me about all the girls

---

Oh, it's full of come, *(bleep)*. Oh, *(bleep)*, suck it now. Ahha! Ahh!
Ahh! Ahh! . . . Oh, my goodness. . . . Are you still there?
Yeah.
That's good. I'm glad it's you who's still there.
(Laughter)
Oh, sweetheart.
You're an animal.
An animal? You think so?
Yeah.
A human animal?
Yeah.
And you? What are you?
A bad girl.
That's a good thing to be. It's better than the opposite. You think you
have to be a good girl?
Well, it's what people expect.
Well, you be realistic and let them be unrealistic. Jesus. There's a mess
here.
(Laughter)
Oh, lovely *(bleep)*.

you fucked in Rome. And then while Sabbath answered, speaking plainly and freely of the arsenal of allurement Italy was to him, describing how more than once he had been provoked to emulate the locals and follow someone clear across the city to nail down a pickup, the master's eyes were eloquent with a sardonic superiority that caused even the ex–merchant seaman, a veteran six times over of the Romance Run, to feel a little like a model child. The old man's attention did not waver, however, nor did he interrupt other than to press for more elaboration than the American could always furnish in his limited Italian— and, repeatedly, to demand from Sabbath the precise age of each girl whose seduction he described. Eighteen, replied Sabbath obediently. Twenty, Maestro. Twenty-four. Twenty-one. Twenty-two . . .

Only when Sabbath had finished did the maestro announce to him that his own current mistress was fifteen. Abruptly he rose to leave—to leave the café and to leave Sabbath with the check—but not before adding, with a derisive flick of his cane, "Naturalmente la conosco da quando aveva dodici anni"—Of course I've known her since she's twelve.

And only now, practically forty years later, with Kathy still crying for him and the oblivious blank of a moon still rising for him, with folks here in the hills and down in the valley settling in by the fire for a pleasant fall evening of listening on the phone to Kathy and him coming, did Sabbath believe that the old puppeteer had been telling him the truth. Twelve. Capisco, Maestro. You might as well go for broke.

"Katherine," he said sadly, "you were once my most trusted accomplice in the fight for the lost human cause. Listen to me. Stop crying long enough to listen to what I have to say. Your people have on tape my voice giving reality to all the worst things

---

Are you still alone?
Yes. I'm still alone.
When's your wife coming back?

they want the world to know about men. They have got a hundred times more proof of my criminality than could be required
by even the most lenient of deans to drive me out of every decent
antiphallic educational institution in America. Must I now ejaculate on CNN? Where is the camera? Is there a telephoto lens in
that pickup truck over by the nursery? I've got my breaking point,
too, Kathy. If they send me up for sodomy, the result could be
death. And that might not be as much fun for you as you may
have been led to believe. You may have forgotten, but not even
at Nuremberg was everyone sentenced to die." On he continued—in the circumstances, a lovely speech; *it* should be taped,
thought he. Yes, on Sabbath went, developing with increasing
cogency the argument in support of a constitutional amendment
to make coming illegal for American men, regardless of race,
creed, color, or ethnic origin, until Kathy cried out, "I'm of age!"
and wiped her face dry of tears with the shoulder of her running
jacket.

"I do what I want," she angrily asserted.

Maestro, what would *you* do? To peer down at her head cradled in your lap, your cock encircled by her foaming lips, and to
watch her blowing you in tears, to patiently lather that undissipated face with that sticky confection of spit, semen, and tears, a
delicate meringue icing her freckles—could life bestow any more
wonderful last thing? She had never looked more soulful to Sabbath, and he pointed this out to the maestro. She had never before
looked soulful to Sabbath at all. But tears made her radiant, and
even to the jaded maestro she seemed to be digging into a spiritual
existence that was news to her, as well. She *was* of age! Kathy
Goolsbee had just grown up! Yes, not only something spiritual
but something primordial was going on, as there had been on that
hot summer day up in the picturesque brook beside the Grotto
when he and Drenka had pissed on each other.

"Oh, if only I could believe that you weren't in cahoots with
these filthy, lowlife, rectitudinous cunts who tell you children
these terrible lies about men, about the sinister villainy of what is
simply the ordinary grubbing about in reality of ordinary people

like your dad and me. Because that is who they are against, honey—me and your dad. That's what it comes down to: caricaturing us, insulting us, abhorring in us what is nothing more than the delightful Dionysian underlayer of life. Tell me, how can you be against what has been inherently human going back to *antiquity*—going back to the virginal peak of Western civ—and call yourself a civilized person? Maybe it's because she's Japanese that she doesn't dig the unparalleled mythologies of ancient Attica. I don't get it otherwise. How would they like you to be sexually initiated? Intermittently by Brian, while he takes poli sci notes at the library? Are they going to leave it to a dry-as-dust scholar to initiate a girl like you? Or are you supposed to pick it up on your own? But if you're not expected to pick up chemistry on your own, if you're not expected to pick up physics on your own, then why are you supposed to pick up the erotic *mysteries* on your own? Some need seduction and don't need initiation. Some don't need initiation but still need seduction. Kathy, *you needed both*. Harassment? I remember the good old days when *patriotism* was the last refuge of a scoundrel. Harassment? I have been Virgil to your Dante in the sexual underworld! But then, how would those professors know who Virgil is?"

"I want," she said yearningly, "to suck you so hard."

That "so"! And yet hearing the so intensifying "so," feeling the familiar, lifelong urge to crude, natural bodily satisfaction creep uncontrollably across every square inch of his two square yards of yearning old hide, Sabbath thought not, as he would have hoped, of his estimable mentor, the unplatitudinous maestro, obedient to the end to the edict of excitement, but of his sick wife suffering in the hospital. Of all people! It isn't fair! The '29 as stiff as a horse's and who should he start thinking about but Roseanna! He saw before him the little cell of a room to which they'd assigned her after admission, a room beside the nurse's station, where she could be conveniently observed during the twenty-four-hour detox watch. They would take her blood pressure every half hour and do what they could for the shakes she was going to have because she had been drinking steadily for the previous three days—drinking hard right up to the hospital door. He saw her standing beside that narrow bed with the sad chenille spread, so stoop-shouldered that she looked no taller than he was. On the bed lay her suitcases. Two pleasant un-uniformed nurses, who had asked her politely to open them for inspection, meticulously went through her things, removing her eyebrow tweezers, her nail scissors, her hair dryer, her dental floss (so she wouldn't stab, electrocute, or hang herself), impounding a bottle of Listerine (so she would not drink it all down in desperation or smash the bottle to use the shards to slit her wrists or cut her throat), examining everything in her wallet and extracting from it her credit cards, driver's license, and all her cash (so she could not buy contraband whiskey smuggled into the hospital or wander off grounds to a bar in Usher village or jump-start a staff member's car and head home), rummaging through all the jeans, sweaters, underwear, and jogging stuff; and all the while Roseanna, lost, lifeless, immensely alone, hollowly looked on, her aging folksingerish good looks demolished—a woman decarnalized: simultaneously a pre-erotic juvenile and a post-erotic wreck. She might have been living all these years, not in a simple box of a house where every fall the deer fed off the apple trees in the hillside orchard beyond the screen porch, but locked away inside an automatic car wash, where there was no hiding from the battering rain and the big turning brushes and the gaping blowers pouring forth their hot air. Roseanna restored to its roots in stripped-to-its-skin, nickel-and-dime, down-to-earth reality the exalted phrase "the bludgeonings of fate."

"The cause," sobbed Roseanna, "goes free, the effect goes to jail." "Isn't that life exactly," he agreed. "Only it's not jail. It's a hospital, Rosie, and a hospital that doesn't even look like one. As soon as you stop suffering, you'll see that it's very pretty, like a big country inn. There are a lot of trees and nice walks to walk on with your friends. I noticed driving in that there is even a tennis court. I'll send your racket Federal Express." "Why are they taking my Visa card!" "Because you don't pay nightmare by nightmare and tremor by tremor; as your Catholic upbringing should have taught you, you pay through the nose at the end." "It's *your* things they should be searching! They'd come up with enough to put *you* away for good!" "Do you want the nurses to do that, to search me? For what?" "The handcuffs you use on your teenage whore!" Twenty, Sabbath thought to inform the two nurses, no longer a teenager, unfortunately; but neither nurse appeared the least bit amused or appalled by the Sabbaths' farewell banter and so he didn't bother. Foul language and loud shouting the nurses had heard before. The drunk frenetic, terrified, extremely angry at the mate, the mate even angrier with the drunk. Husbands and wives yelling and screaming and accusing were nothing new to them, nothing new to anyone—you don't have to work in a mental hospital to know about husbands and wives. He watched the nurses dutifully checking each and every pocket of all of Roseanna's jeans for a stray joint or a razor blade. They impounded her keys. Good. That was in her own best interest. Now there was no chance of her bursting unannounced into the house. He wouldn't have wanted Roseanna, in her condition, to have to deal with Drenka, too. Let's deal first with the addiction. "*You* should be locked up, Mickey—and everyone who knows you knows it!" "I'm sure one day they *will* lock me up, if that is truly the consensus. But let the others see to that. You just get sober real quick now, ya hear?" "You don't *want* me s-s-sober! You *prefer* a drunk. S-so you can s-s-s—" "Seem," he whispered, to help her over the hump. Her *s*'s always bested her when she mixed her rage with more than a quart of vodka. "S-seem to be the long s-s-s—" "Long-suffering husband?" "Yes!" "No. No. Sympathy isn't my bag. You know that. I don't ask to be s-s-seen as anything other than what I am. Though tell me again what that is—I wouldn't want to forget during the days we're apart." "A failure! A fucking nons-s-s-stop failure! A s-s-s-scheming, lying, s-s-s-sick, deceiving total failure who lives off his wife and fucks *children!* He's the one," she weepingly told the nurses, "who *put* me here. I was *fine* till I met him. I wasn't this at *all!*" "And," he rushed to reassure her, "in only twenty-eight days it'll all be over and you'll be just the way you were before I made you into 'this.'" He raised his hand beside his face to shyly wave good-bye. "*You cannot leave me here!*" she cried. "The doctor said I get to see you after the first two weeks." "But what if they give me shock treatment!" "For drinking? I don't think they do that—do they, nurse? No, no. All they give you is a new outlook on life. I'm sure all they want you to do is to drop your illusions and adapt to reality like me. Bye-bye. Two little weeks." "I'll be counting the days," said Rosie's old self, but then, when she saw that he was really going to leave her there, something from within contorted her spiteful smile into a knotted lump and she began to wail.

This sound accompanied Sabbath along the corridor and down the flight of stairs and out the main hospital door, where a group of patients were having a smoke and looking upstairs to see in which of the rooms the new wailer was suffering. It accompanied him to the parking lot and into the car and then out onto the highway, and it was with him all the way back to Madamaska Falls. Louder and louder Sabbath played the tapes, but even Goodman couldn't cancel it out—even Goodman, Krupa, Wilson, and Hampton in their heyday, breaking loose with "Running Wild," even Krupa opening dramatically out with the bass drum on that last great chorus couldn't obliterate Roseanna's eight-bar solo flourish. A wife going off like a siren. The second crazy wife. Was there any other kind? Not for him. A second crazy wife who'd begun life hating her father and then discovered Sabbath to hate instead. But then Kathy *loved* her protective, self-sacrificing dad, who'd worked day and night in the bakery to put three Goolsbee kids into college, and a lot of good it did her. *Or* Sabbath. I can't win. No one can, when they follow Father with me.

If it was Roseanna's wail earlier in the day that gave Sabbath the determination to decline what he had never before declined in his life, then that was a truly record-breaking wail.

"Time to go home to blow Brian."

"But this isn't *fair.* I didn't *do* anything."

"Go home or I'll kill you."

"Don't say that—my God!"

"You would not be the first woman I killed."

"Uh-huh. Sure. Who was?"

"Nikki Kantarakis. My first wife."

"That's not funny."

"True enough. Murdering Nikki constitutes my sole claim to real gravitas. Or *was* it pure fun? I'm never entirely convinced by my assessment of anything. That ever happen to you?"

"Jesus! Like, what are you even *talking* about?"

"I'm only talking about what everybody talks about. You know what they say at the college. They say I had a wife who disappeared but that she didn't *just* disappear. Can you deny you've heard 'em say it—can you, Kathy?"

"Well . . . people say everything—don't they? I don't even remember. Who even *listens?*"

"Sparing my feelings, isn't that nice. But you needn't. You learn by sixty to accept in a sporting spirit the derision of virtuous bystanders. Besides, they happen to have it right. Thus proving that if, when speaking of a fellow creature, you give continual expression to your antipathy, a strange kind of truth may unfold."

"Why don't you say anything *seriously* to me!"

"I have never said anything more seriously to anyone: I killed a wife."

"*Please* stop this."

"You telephoned to play doctor on the phone with somebody who killed his wife."

"I did *not.*"

"What drives you, anyway? At the highest levels of higher education, my identity as a murderer has been laid bare, and you phone to tell me that you are in your pj's, all alone in bed. What's inside of *you* scorching *you?* Your bondage is bondage to *what?* I am a notorious killer-diller *who strangled his wife.* Why else would I have to live in a place like this if I hadn't strangled somebody? I did it with these very hands while we were rehearsing in our bedroom, on our bed, the final act of *Othello.* My wife was a young actress. *Othello?* It's a play. It's a play in which an

African Venetian strangles his white wife to death. You never heard of it because it perpetuates the stereotype of the violent black male. But back in the fifties, humanity hadn't figured out yet what was important, and students fell prey in college to a lot of wicked shit. Nikki was terrified of every new role. She suffered insufferable fears. One was of men. Unlike you, she was not wily in the ways of men. This made her perfect for the part. We rehearsed beforehand alone in our apartment to try to reduce Nikki's fears. 'I can't do it!' This I heard from her many times. I played the stereotypical violent black male. In the scene in which he murders her I did it—I went ahead and murdered her. Got carried away by the spell of her acting. It just opened something up in me to see it. Someone to whom the tangible and the immediate are repugnant, to whom only the illusion is fully real. This was the order Nikki made of her chaos. And you, what is the order you make of yours? Talking about your tits to an old man on the phone? You elude description, at least by me. Such a shameless creature and yet so bland. Perverse and treacherous, the French kiss of death, already deep into the disreputable thrills of a double life—and *bland*. As chaos goes, yours seems decidedly unchaotic. The chaos theorists ought to study you. How deep does what Katherine does or says reach down into Katherine? Whatever you want, however dangerous or deceitful, you pursue, like, impersonally, you know?"

"Okay. How *did* you kill her?"

Lifting his hands, he said, "I used these. I told you. 'Put out the light, and then put out the light.'"

"Whatja do with the body?"

"I rented a boat at Sheepshead Bay. A harbor in Brooklyn. I was a sailor boy once. I loaded the body down with bricks and dumped Nikki overboard out at sea."

"And how did you get a dead body to Brooklyn?"

"I was always carrying things around. I had an old Dodge in those days and I was always shoving into the trunk my portable stage and my props and my puppets. The neighbors saw me coming and going all the time like that. Nikki was a stringbean. She didn't weigh much. I stuffed her doubled-over into my seaman's bag. No big deal."

"I don't believe you."

"Too bad. Because I've never told anyone before. Not even Roseanna. And now I've told you. And as our little scandal teaches us, telling you isn't exactly observing the dictates of prudence. Who do you tell first? Dean Kuziduzi, or will you go straight to the Japanese high command?"

"Why must you be so racially prejudiced against Japanese!"

"Because of what they did to Alec Guinness in *The Bridge on the River Kwai*. Putting him in that fucking little box. I hate the bastards. Who will you tell first?"

"No one! I'm not telling anyone, because it's not *true!*"

"And if it were? Would you tell anyone then?"

"What? If you really were a murderer?"

"Yes. And if you knew I was. Would you turn me in the way you turned in the tape?"

"I *forgot* the tape! I left the tape *accidentally!*"

"Would you turn me in, Kathy? Yes or no?"

"Why must I answer these questions!"

"Because it's indispensable to my finding out just who the fuck you are working for."

"No one!"

"Would you turn me in? Yes or no? If it were true that I was a murderer."

"Well . . . you want a serious answer?"

"I'll take what I get."

"Well . . . it would depend."

"On?"

"On? Well, on our relationship."

"You might not turn me in if we had the right relationship? And what would that be? Describe it."

"I don't know. . . . I guess love."

"You would protect a murderer if you loved him."

"I don't *know*. You never murdered anyone. These questions are *stupid*."

"*Do* you love me? Don't worry about my feelings. Do you love me?"

"In a way."

"Yes?"

"Yes."

"Old and loathsome as I am?"

"I love . . . I love your mind. I love how you expose your mind when you talk."

"My mind? My mind is a murderer's mind."

"Stop *saying* that. You're *scaring* me."

"My mind? Well, this is quite a revelation. *I* thought you loved my ancient penis. My *mind?* This is quite a shock for a man of my years. Were you really only in it for my mind? Oh, no. All the time I was talking about fucking, you were watching me expose my mind! Paying unwanted attention to my *mind!* You dared to introduce a mental element into a setting where it has no place. Help! I've been mentally harassed! Help! I am the victim of mental harassment! God, I am getting a gastrointestinal disorder! You have extracted mental favors from me without my even knowing and against my will! I have been belittled by you! My *dick* has been belittled by you! Call the dean! My dick has been disempowered!"

With this, Kathy finally found the initiative to push open the door, but so frantically, with such force, that she tumbled from the car to the shoulder of the road. But she was up on her Reeboks almost immediately and, through the windshield, could be seen speeding north toward Athena. Puppets can fly, levitate, twirl, but only people and marionettes are confined to running and walking. That's why marionettes always bored him: all that walking they were always doing up and down the tiny stage, as though, in addition to being the subject of every marionette show, walking were the major theme of life. And those strings—too visible, too many, too blatantly metaphorical. And always slavishly imitating human theater. Whereas puppets . . . shoving your hand up a puppet and hiding your face behind a screen! Nothing like it in the animal kingdom! All the way back to Petrushka, anything goes, the crazier and uglier the better. Sabbath's cannibal puppet that won first prize from the maestro in Rome. Eating his enemies on the stage. Tearing them apart and talking about them all the while they were chewed and swallowed. The mistake is ever to think that to act and to speak is the natural domain of anyone other than a puppet. Contentment is being hands and a voice—looking to be more, students, is madness. If Nikki had been a puppet, she might still be alive.

And down the road, Kathy fleeing by the oversize light of the preposterous moon. And the smokers now gathered in moonlight, too, beneath the cell of the detoxing Roseanna, whose wailing could still be heard 130 miles away. . . . Oh, she was in for it tonight, up against an even more horrifying trial than being married to him. The doctor had warned Sabbath that she might telephone to beg him to come get her out. He counseled Sabbath to ignore the bidding of compassion and tell her no. Sabbath promised to do his best. Rather than head home to hear her ringing, he sat a while longer in the car, where, for reasons he couldn't figure out right off, he was remembering the guy who'd given him those books to read on the Standard Oil tanker, remembering how they unloaded through that great piping system at Curaçao and how that guy—one of those gentlemanly, quiet types who mysteriously spend their lives at sea when you would expect them to wind up as teachers or even maybe ministers—had given him a book of poems by William Butler Yeats. A loner. A self-educated loner. The guy's silences gave you the creeps. Another American type. One met all our American types at sea. Even by that time, a good many of them Hispanic—tough, really tough Latino types. I remember one who looked like Akim Tamiroff. All kinds of our colored brothers, every type you can think of—sweet men, not so sweet men, everybody. There was a big, fat black cook on that ship where the guy who gave me that book started me off reading. I'd be lying in my top bunk with a book, and this cook would always come in and grab my balls. And start laughing. I'd have to wrestle him away. Guess that makes me "homophobic." He didn't make any more aggressive moves but would have been very

pleased if I'd responded, no doubt about that. Interesting thing
was that I used to see him in the whorehouses. Now, the guy who
gave me the poetry was out-and-out queer yet never laid a glove
on me, pretty green-eyed lad though I was. Told me which poems
to read. Gave me a lot of books. Awfully nice of him, really. Guy
from Nebraska. I'd memorize the poems on my watch.

Of course! Yeats to Lady Goolsbee:

> I heard an old religious man
> But yesternight declare
> That he had found a text to prove
> That only God, my dear,
> Could love you for yourself alone
> And not your yellow hair.

In only a few hours Kathy would be crossing the finish line. He
could see her taping her breasts and falling into the embrace of
the Immaculate Kamizoko. Breasting the tape. Kakizomi. Kazi-
komi. Who could remember their fucking names. Who wanted
to. Tojo and Hirohito sufficed for him. Sobbing hysterically, she
would tell the dean of his terrifying confession. And the dean might
not resist believing it as Kathy had pretended to do.

Driving home he played "The Sheik of Araby." Few things in
this world as right as those four zippy solos. Clarinet. Piano.
Drums. Vibes.

How come nobody hates Tojo anymore? Nobody remembers
that killer except me. They think Tojo's a car. But ask the Koreans
about the Japanese sitting on their faces for thirty-five years. Ask
the Manchurians about the civility of their conquerors. Ask the
Chinese about the wonderful understanding shown them by those
little flat-faced imperialist bastards. Ask about the brothels the
Japs stocked for their soldiers with girls just like you. Younger.
The dean thinks *I'm* the enemy. Ho, ho! Ask her about the boys
back home and how they bravely fucked their way through Asia,
the foreign women they enslaved and made into whores. Ask 'em
in Manila about the bombs, tons of bombs dropped by Japs *after*
Manila was an open city. Where is Manila? How would you

know? Maybe one day Teacher will take an hour off from harassment lessons to mention to all her spotless lambs a little horror called World War II. The Japan*eez*. As racially arrogant as anyone anywhere—beside them the Ku Klux Klan is . . . But how would you know about the Ku Klux Klan? How would you know anything, given whose clutches you're in? You want the lowdown on the Japan*eez*? Ask my mother, also a woman harassed in life. Ask her.

Expansively he sang along with the quartet, pretending to be Gene Hochberg, who could really get a crowd of kids up and swingin'; delighting himself, Sabbath was, not just in the multidemeaning lyric of the old twenties anthem celebrating date rape and denigrating Arabs but in the unending, undecorous, needling performance, the joy of the job of being their savage. How could the missionaries puff themselves up without their savage? Their naive fucking impertinence about carnal lusting! Seducer of the young. Socrates, Strindberg, and me. Yet feeling great all the same. The glassy chiming of Hampton's hammering—that could fix about anything. Or maybe it was having Rosie out of the way. Or maybe it was knowing that he'd never had to please and wasn't starting now. Yes, yes, yes, he felt uncontrollable tenderness for his own shit-filled life. And a laughable hunger for more. More defeat! More disappointment! More deceit! More loneliness! More arthritis! More missionaries! God willing, more cunt! More disastrous entanglement in everything. For a pure sense of being tumultuously alive, you can't beat the nasty side of existence. I may not have been a matinee idol, but say what you will about me, it's been a real human life!

> I'm the Sheik of Araby,
> Your love belongs to me.
> At night when you're asleep,
> Into your tent I'll creep.
> The stars that shine above,
> Will light our way to love.
> You'll rule the land with me,
> I'm the Sheik of Araby.

Life *is* impenetrable. For all Sabbath knew, he had just thrown over a girl who had neither betrayed nor bebitched him and never could—a simple, adventurous girl who loved her father and would never deceive any grown man (except Father, with Sabbath); for all he knew he had just frightened off the last twenty-year-old into whose tent he would ever again creep. He had mistaken innocent, loving, loyal Cordelia for her villainous sisters Goneril and Regan. He'd got it as backward as old Lear. Lucky for his sanity there was some consolation to be had in the big bed up on Brick Furnace Road by fucking Drenka there that night and the twenty-seven nights to follow.

◆ ◆ ◆

The only communication Sabbath received during the two weeks before he was allowed to visit Roseanna was a resoundingly factual postcard sent to him from Usher at the end of her first week there: no salutation and mailed simply to their street address in Madamaska Falls—she would not even write his name. "Meet me at Roderick House, 23rd, 4:30 p.m. Dinner at 5:15. I have AA meeting 7–8 p.m. Stay Ragged Hill Lodge in Usher if you don't want to drive home same night. R.C.S."

Just as he was getting into the car at 1:30 on the 23rd, the phone rang in the house and he raced back through the kitchen door, thinking that it must be Drenka. When he heard Roseanna, reversing the charges, he figured she was calling to ask him not to come. He'd phone Drenka with the news as soon as she hung up.

"How are you, Roseanna?"

Her voice, never highly inflected, was ironed flat, stern and angry and flat. "Are you coming?"

"I was just getting into the car. I had to run back to the house to get the phone."

"I want you to bring something. Please," she added, as though someone were there instructing her on what to say and how to say it.

"Bring something? Of course," he said. "Anything."

Her reply to this was a harsh, unscripted laugh. Followed icily by "In my file. Top drawer at the back. A blue three-ring binder. I have to have it."

"I'll bring it. But I'll have to get into the file."

"You'll need the key." More icily still, if that could be possible.

"Yes? Where would I find it?"

"In my riding boots. . . . The left boot."

But over the years he'd searched through all her boots, shoes, and sneakers. She must have moved it there recently from wherever it had been hidden from him before.

"Go get it now," she said. "Find it now. It's important. . . . Please."

"Sure. Okay. The right boot."

"The *left!*"

No, it wasn't hard to make her lose hold. And that was with two weeks already under her belt and only two to go.

He found the key and, from the file, got the blue three-ring binder and came back to the phone to assure her he had it.

"Did you lock the file?"

He lied and said yes.

"Bring the key with you. The file key. Please."

"Of course."

"And the binder. It's blue. There are two elastic bands around it."

"Got it right here."

"Please don't lose it!" she exploded. "It is a matter of life or death!"

"Are you sure you really want it?"

"Don't *argue* with me! Do as I ask you! It's not easy for me even to *talk* to you!"

"Would you rather I didn't come?" He wondered if it would be safe at this hour to drive by the inn and blow the horn twice, their signal for Drenka to meet him at the Grotto.

"If you don't want to come," she said, "don't. You're not doing anyone a favor. If you're not interested in seeing me, *that is fine with me.*"

"I am interested in seeing you. That's why I was in the car when you called. How do you feel? Are you any better?"

She answered in a wavering voice, "It isn't easy."

"I'm sure it isn't."

"It's damn hard." She began to cry. "It's *impossibly* hard."

"Are you making headway at all?"

"Oh, you don't understand! You'll never understand!" she shouted, and hung up.

In the binder were the letters that her father had sent her after she had left him to go to live with her mother, following her mother's return from France. He'd written a letter to Roseanna every single day right up to the evening that he killed himself. The suicide letter was addressed both to Roseanna and to the younger sister, Ella. Roseanna's mother had gathered the letters to her daughters together and had kept them for them until she herself had died after a long ordeal with emphysema the year before. The binder had been bequeathed to Roseanna along with her mother's antiques, but she had never been able even to remove the elastic bands holding it shut. For a while she was determined to throw it out, but she could not do that either.

Halfway to Usher, Sabbath stopped at a highway diner. He held the binder in his lap until the waitress brought him coffee. Then he removed the elastic bands, placed them carefully in his jacket pocket, and opened to the letters.

The letter written only hours before he hanged himself was headed "My beloved children, Roseanna and Ella," and dated "Cambridge, Sept. 15, 1950." Rosie was thirteen. Professor Cavanaugh's last letter Sabbath read first:

> Cambridge, Sept. 15, 1950
>
> My beloved children, Roseanna and Ella,
>
> I say *beloved* in spite of everything. I have always tried to do my best, but I have failed completely. I have failed in my marriages and I have failed in my work. When your mother left us, I became a broken man. And when even you, my beloved children, abandoned me, everything

ended. Since then I have had total insomnia. I have no strength any longer. I am exhausted and I am ill from all the sleeping pills. I cannot go on any longer. God help me. Please do not judge me too harshly.

Live happily!
Dad

Cambridge, Feb. 6, 1950

Dear little Roseanna!

You cannot imagine how I miss my beloved little darling. I feel completely empty inside and I don't know how I'll get over it. But at the same time I feel that it was important and necessary that it happen. I have seen the change in you since May of last year. I was terribly worried since *I could not help you* and you did not wish to confide in me. You bottled yourself up and pushed me away. I did not know that you had such a hard time in school but I suspected as much since your classmates never visited you. Only pretty little Helen Kylie came sometimes and picked you up in the morning. But my little dear one, the fault was yours. You felt superior and you showed it maybe more than you knew yourself. This is exactly the same thing that happened to your mother with her friends here. Dear little Roseanna, I do not say this to accuse you but so that you can think through all of this and eventually discuss it with your mother. And then you'll learn that in life one must not be selfish. . . .

Cambridge, Feb. 8, 1950

. . . you had lost contact with your father and I could no longer penetrate the armor by which you surrounded yourself. It worried me so deeply. I understood that you needed a mother, I even tried to get you one but that failed totally. Now you have your real mother back, whom you so long have missed. Now you have all the possibilities again to become well. This will give you new courage to live. And you'll be happy again with school. In intelligence you are way, way above the average. . . .

Your father's home remains open for you, whenever you want to return, for a shorter or longer period of time. You are my most beloved child and the emptiness is enormous without you. I shall try to gain solace thinking that what happened was best for you.

Please write me something as soon as you are settled. Good-bye, my little darling! A thousand loving kisses from your lonely

Dad

Cambridge, Feb. 9, 1950

Dear little Roseanna!

I ran into Miss Lerman on the street. She was sad that you left the school. She said that all the teachers liked you so much. But she understood that you had a difficult time lately, infections, et cetera, which forced you to be absent for long periods. She also noted that lately you hadn't been together with Helen Kylie or your other nice friends, Myra, Phyllis, and Aggie. But she said these girls were committed to their studies while Roseanna has lost the desire to succeed. She hoped that you would get over your difficulties in a few years. She had seen many similar cases, she said. She also felt strongly, as I do, that a girls' school is better for girls in puberty. Unfortunately your mother does not seem to share Miss Lerman's opinion. . . .

. . . yes, dear little Roseanna, I hope you'll soon be as happy as when you were my sunshine, truthful and straightforward. But then our problems began. I wanted to help you but I couldn't since you didn't want my help. You couldn't confide your worries to me any longer. Then you needed a mother but then you did not have a mother, unfortunately. . . .

A huge hug from
Dad

Cambridge, Feb. 10, 1950

Dear Roseanna!

You promised to call and write often to me when you left. You were so sweet and open and I believed you. But love is blind. Now five days have passed since you left and I have not had one line from you. Neither did you want to speak to me last night, even though I was home. I am beginning to understand, my eyes are opening. Do you have a bad conscience? Can you no longer look your father in the eye? Is that the thank-you for all I have done for you during these five years when I alone had to take care of my children? It is cruel. It is horrible. Can you ever again come home to your father and look him in the eye? I can hardly grasp this. But I do not judge you. I understand that lately you have been under hypnosis. Your mother seems to have made it her mission to harass me to the utmost. Her only interest is my defeat. She does not seem to have changed as much as you children seem to think.

Maybe you will write a few lines and tell me what I should do. Shall I clean out your room and try to forget that you ever existed?

Why did you lie to me at the stationery store about the ten dollars? It was unnecessary. Not a beautiful last memory.

Dad

Cambridge, Feb. 11, 1950

Dearest little Roseanna!

A thousand thank-yous for your longed-for letter today! It made me so happy that I now feel like another person. The sun is shining again over my broken life. Please forgive my last letter. I was so depressed when I wrote it that I barely believed I could stand up again. But today everything feels different. Irene has now become so kind that I would even say she is *sweet*. She has probably helped me over the worst crisis—your departure. . . .

Of course you are welcome so long as you do not completely cut off contact with your father. And now, since things here at home are calm and peaceful again, your letters will be heartily welcome to us *all*. Please write as often as you can to us. It doesn't have to be a long epistle but just a short greeting that you are fine. Though sometimes you must write some lines to your father telling him how you feel in the depths of your soul, especially when sorrows drag you down.

Dearest dearest dearest regards from us all, but especially from your loving

Dad

This was the way the letters went from the February day in 1950 when Roseanna moved from Cambridge with Ella to live with her mother through the end of April, which was as far as Sabbath was able to read if he intended to be on time for dinner at the hospital. And he was sure to hear the same despondent message being beeped right on down to the end anyway—the world against him, obstructing him, insulting and crushing him. *Shall I clean out your room and try to forget that you ever existed?* From bleeding Professor Cavanaugh to his thirteen-year-old beloved after not having heard from her for five days. The suffering, crazy drunk—couldn't have been battle-free one day of his life, until the day the stone was lifted. *Please do not judge me harshly. Live happily! Dad.* And then, no longer out of tune with a thing. Everything at last under control.

Sabbath pulled into the hospital parking lot just before five. On foot he made his way up a circular drive that separated a wide bowl of green lawn from a long three-storied white clapboard house with black-shuttered windows at the top of the hill, the hospital's main building, designed, coincidentally enough, very much in the style of the Baliches' colonial-style inn overlooking Lake Madamaska. In the last century there'd been a lake here, too, where now there was the lakelike lawn, and looming above it a massive Gothic mansion that had fallen into ruin after the death of the childless owners. First the roof gave way, then the stone walls, until, in 1909, the lake was drained and the spookily picturesque pile was pushed into the hole with a steam shovel and covered over to make way for a TB sanatorium. Today the old sanatorium was the main building of Usher Psychiatric Hospital but continued to be referred to as the Mansion.

Doubtless because the dinner hour was approaching, the crowd of smokers gathered outside the front door of the Mansion numbered twenty or twenty-five, a handful of them surprisingly young, boys and girls in their teens who were dressed like the students in the valley, the boys with their baseball caps on backward and the girls in college T-shirts, running shoes, and jeans. He asked the prettiest of the girls—who would also have been the tallest if only she had stood up straight—to direct him to Roderick House and observed, when she raised her arm to point the way, a horizontal slash mark across her wrist that looked to be only recently healed.

An ordinary autumn late afternoon—which is to say, radiant and extraordinary. How horrible, how *dangerous* this beauty must be to someone suicidally depressed, yet the kind of day, thought Sabbath, that perhaps makes it possible for a garden-variety depressive to believe that the cavern through which he is crawling may be leading in the direction of life. Childhood at its very best is recalled, and the abatement, if not of adulthood, at least of dread seems for the moment possible. Autumn at the psychiatric hospital, autumn and its famous meanings! How can it be autumn if I am here? How can I be here if it is autumn? *Is* it autumn? The year again in magical transition and it does not even register.

Roderick House lay just off the bottom of a turning of the road that ringed the lawn and led back out to the county highway. The house was a smaller, two-story version of the Mansion, one of seven or eight such houses set irregularly back among the trees, each with an open veranda and a grassy front yard. Coming upon Roderick from the rise of the drive, Sabbath saw four women sitting on outdoor furniture pulled close together on the lawn. The one reclining in the white plastic chaise was his wife. She was wearing sunglasses and lying perfectly still, while around her the others were in lively conversation. But then something so funny was said by someone—perhaps even by Roseanna—that she sprang to a sitting position and clapped her hands together with joy. Her laugh was more spontaneous than he'd heard it for years. They were all still laughing when Sabbath appeared, walking across the lawn. One of the women leaned toward Roseanna. "Your visitor," she whispered.

"Good day," said Sabbath and formally bowed to them. "I am the beneficiary of Roseanna's nest-building instinct and the embodiment of all the resistance she encounters in life. I am sure that each of you has an unworthy mate—I am hers. I am Mickey Sabbath. Everything you have heard about me is true. Everything is destroyed and I destroyed it. Hello, Rosie."

It did not astonish him when she failed to pop up out of the chair to embrace him. But when she took off the sunglasses and shyly said, "Hi," . . . well, the voice on the phone had not led him to expect such loveliness. Only fourteen days off the sauce and away from him, and she looked thirty-five. Her skin was clear and tawny, her shoulder-length hair shone more golden than brown, and she seemed even to have recovered the width of her mouth and that appealing width between her eyes. She had a notably broad face but her features had been vanishing within it for years. Here lay the simple origin of their suffering: her knockout girl-next-door looks. In just fourteen days she had cast off two decades of bungled life.

"These," she said awkwardly, "are some residents of the house." *Helen Kylie, Myra, Phyllis, Aggie* . . . "Would you like to see my room? We've got a little time." She was now an utterly disconcerted child, too embarrassed by a parent's presence to be anything but miserable so long as he remained among her friends.

He followed Roseanna up the stairs to the veranda—three smokers out there, youngish women like the ones on the lawn—and into the house. They passed a small kitchen and turned down a corridor lined with notices and newspaper clippings. To one side the corridor opened onto a small, dark living room where another group of women were watching TV, and to the other onto the nurse's station, partitioned in glass and cheerily hung with "Peanuts" posters above the two desks. Roseanna pulled him halfway through the door. "My husband's here," she said to the young nurse on duty. "Fine," replied the nurse and nodded politely to Sabbath, whom Roseanna immediately dragged away before he told the nurse, too, that everything was destroyed and he had destroyed it, right on the money though that indictment might be.

"Roseanna!" a friendly voice called from the living room. "Roseanna Banana!"

"Hi."

"Back to Bennington," said Sabbath.

Bitterly she jumped on him. "Not *quite!*"

Her room was small, freshly painted a sparkling white, with two curtained windows looking onto the front yard, a single bed, an old wooden desk, and a dresser. All anyone needed, really. You could live in a place like this forever. He stuck his head into the bathroom, turned on a tap—"Hot water," he said approvingly— and then, when he came out, saw on the desk three framed photographs: the one of her mother wrapped in a fur coat in Paris just after the war, the old one of Ella and Paul with their two plump, blond children (Eric and Paula) and a third (Glenn) plainly on the way, and a photograph that he had never seen before, a studio portrait of a man in a suit, tie, and starched collar, a stern, broad-faced middle-aged man who did not look at all "broken" but could be no one but Cavanaugh. There was a composition notebook open on the desk, and Roseanna closed it with one quivering hand while she nervously circled the room. "Where's the binder?" she said. "You forgot the binder!" She was no longer the sylph in sunglasses he'd seen on the lawn, merrily laughing with Helen, Myra, Phyllis, and Aggie.

"I left it locked in the car. It's under the seat. It's safe."

"And what," she cried in all seriousness, "if somebody steals the car?"

"Is that likely, Roseanna? That car? I was hurrying to be on time. I thought we'd get it after dinner. But I'll leave whenever you want me to. I'll get the binder and leave now if you want me to. You looked great until two minutes ago. I'm no good for your complexion."

"I planned to show you the place. I wanted to take you around. I *did.* I wanted to show you where I swim. Now I'm confused. Terribly. I feel hollow. I feel awful." Sitting on the edge of her bed, she began to sob. "It's, it's a thousand dollars a day here" were the words she managed finally to utter.

"Is that what you're crying about?"

"No. The insurance covers it."

"Then what is making you cry?"

"Tomorrow . . . tomorrow night, at the meeting, I have to tell 'My Story.' It's my turn. I've been making notes. I'm terrified. For days I've been making notes. I'm nauseated, my stomach hurts. . . ."

"Why be terrified? Pretend you're talking to your class. Pretend they're just your kids."

"I'm not terrified of *speaking*," she replied angrily. "It's what I'm *saying*. It's my saying the *truth*."

"About?"

She couldn't believe his stupidity. "About? *About?* Him!" she cried, pointing to her father's picture. "That man!"

So. It's *that* man. It's *him*.

Innocently enough, Sabbath asked, "What did he do?"

"Everything. *Everything*."

The dining room, on the first floor of the Mansion, was pleasant and quiet and bright with light from the bay windows that looked out across to the lawn. The patients sat where they liked, mostly at oak tables large enough for eight, but a few stayed apart at tables along the wall that seated two. Again he was reminded of the inn at the lake and the pleasant mood of the dining room there when Drenka officiated as high priestess. Unlike the customers at the inn, the patients served themselves from a buffet table where tonight there were french fried potatoes, green beans, cheeseburgers, salad, and ice cream—thousand-buck-a-day cheeseburgers. Whenever Roseanna got up to refill her glass of cranberry juice, one or another of those drying out and crowded together at the juice machine smiled at her or spoke to her, and as she passed with yet another full glass, someone at a table took hold of her free hand. Because tomorrow night she had to tell "My Story" or because tonight "he" was here? He wondered if anybody at Usher—patient, doctor, or nurse—had as yet dialed across the state line to get an earful of what had put her here.

Only it was the father who had done everything who had put her here.

But how come she'd never told him of this "everything" before? Hadn't she dared to speak of it? Hadn't she dared to remember it? Or did the charge so clarify for her the history of her misery that whether it was truly rooted in fact was a cruelly irrelevant question? At last she possessed the explanation that was at once exalted and hideous and, by zeitgeist standards, more than reasonable. But where—if anywhere any longer—was a true picture of the past?

You cannot imagine how I miss my beloved little darling. I feel completely empty inside and I don't know how I'll ever get over it. You are my most beloved child and the emptiness is enormous without you. Only pretty little Helen Kylie came sometimes. When you were my sunshine, truthful and straightforward. You were so sweet and open and I believed you. But love is blind. Do you have a bad conscience? Can you no longer look your father in the eye? Your longed-for letter. The sun is shining again over my broken life.

Who had hanged himself in that Cambridge attic, a bereft father or a spurned lover?

At dinner, by talking continuously, she seemed able to pretend that Sabbath wasn't there or that whoever was sitting opposite was somebody else. "See the woman," she whispered, "two tables behind me, petite, thin, glasses, early fifties?" and she synopsized the story of *her* marital disaster—a second family, a twenty-five-year-old girlfriend and two little children three and four, the husband had secretly stashed away in the next town. "See the girl with the braids? Red-haired . . . lovely, smart kid . . . twenty-five . . . Wellesley . . . construction worker boyfriend. Looks like the Marlboro man, she says. Throws her up against the wall and down the stairs, and she can't stop phoning him. Phones every night. Says she's trying to get him to feel some remorse. No luck yet. See that dark, youngish guy, working-class? Two tables to your left. A glazier. Sweet guy. Wife hates his family and won't let him take the children to see them. Wanders around all day talking to himself. 'It's useless . . . it's hopeless . . . it's never going to

change . . . the shouting . . . the scenes . . . can't take it.' All you
hear in the morning are people crying in their rooms, crying and
saying 'I wish I were dead.' See the guy there? Tall, bald, big-
nosed guy? In the silk robe? Gay. Room full of perfumes. Wears
his robe all day. Always carrying a book. Never comes to program. Tries to kill himself every September. Comes here every
October. Goes home every November. He's the only man in
Roderick. One morning I passed his room and heard him sobbing
inside. I went in and sat down on the bed. He told me his story.
His mother died three weeks after he was born. Rheumatic heart.
He didn't know how she died until he was twelve. She was
warned beforehand about pregnancy but had him anyway and
died. He thought he killed her. His first memory is of sitting in a
car with his father, being driven from one home to another. They
changed residences all the time. When he was five his father
moved in with a couple, friends. His father stayed there thirty-
two years. Had a secret affair with the wife. The couple had two
daughters he considers his sisters. One *is* his sister. He's an archi-
tectural draftsman. Lives by himself. Sends for pizza every night.
Eats it watching television. Saturday nights he makes himself
something special, a veal dish. He stammers. You can barely hear
him when he speaks. I held his hand for about an hour. He was
crying and crying. Finally he says, 'When I was seventeen, my
mother's brother came, my uncle, and he . . .' But he couldn't
finish. He can't tell anybody what happened when he was seventeen. Still can't, and he's fifty-three. That's Ray. One person's story
is worse than the next. They want internal quiet and all they get's
internal noise."

So she continued till they had finished their ice cream, whereupon she jumped to her feet, and together they headed for her
father's letters.

Walking rapidly beside her down the drive to the parking lot,
Sabbath spotted a modern building of glass and pink brick on a
crest off to the back of the Mansion. "The lockup," Roseanna
told him. "It's where they detox the ones that come in with d.t.'s.
It's where they give you shock. I don't even like to look at it. I said

to my doctor, 'Promise me you'll never send me to the lockup. You can't ever send me to the lockup. I couldn't take it.' He said, 'I cannot make you any such promise.'"

"Surprise," said Sabbath. "They only stole the hubcaps."

He opened the car door, and the moment he took the binder (with the thick elastic bands back in place) out from under the front seat and handed it to her, she was sobbing again. Somebody else every two minutes. "This is *hell*," said Roseanna, "the turbulence doesn't *stop!*" and, turning away from him, she ran back up the hill, clutching the binder to her chest as though it alone would spare her from the lockup. Should he spare her the further agony of his presence? If he left now he'd be home before ten. Too late to get to Drenka, but how about Kathy? Take her to the house, dial S-A-B-B-A-T-H, listen to the tape while they went down on each other.

It was twenty to seven. Roseanna's meeting began in the Mansion "lounge" at seven and ran until eight. He strolled across the green bowl of the lawn, still impersonating—though for how much longer who could tell?—a guest. By the time he had got to Roderick, Roseanna had called the nurse on duty from a Mansion phone to ask her to tell him to wait in the room until she got back from AA. But that had been his plan, whether he was invited or not, ever since he'd seen on her desk the composition notebook in which she was readying her revelation for the next night.

Maybe Roseanna had forgotten where she'd left it; maybe from merely having to lay eyes on him again (and here, without the helping hand of the drink whose beneficent properties as a marital booster are celebrated even in Holy Scripture*), she'd been unable to think straight and had left a message with the nurse that made no sense at all. Or maybe she actually wanted him to sit

---

*"Give strong drink unto him that is perishing, and wine unto the distressed in soul: Let him drink and forget his misery and remember his sorrow no more!" (Proverbs 31.6–7)

alone in her room and read all that her agony had written there. But to get him to see what? She had wanted him to provide her with this while she provided him with that, and, of course, he had no intention of being party to any such arrangement, because, as it happened, he had wanted her to provide him with that while he provided her with this. . . . But why, then, remain married? To tell the truth, he didn't know. Sitting it out for thirty years is indeed inexplicable until you remember that people do it all the time. They were not the only couple on earth for whom mistrust and mutual aversion furnished the indestructible foundation for a long-standing union. Yet, how it seemed to Rosie, when her endurance had reached its limit, was that they *were* the only ones with such wildly contradictory cravings, they *had* to be: the only couple who found each other's behavior so tediously antagonizing, the only couple who deprived each other of everything each of them most wanted, the only couple whose battles over differences would never be behind them, the only couple whose reason for coming together had evaporated beyond recall, the only couple who could not sever themselves one from the other despite ten thousand grievances apiece, the only couple who could not believe how much worse it got from year to year, the only couple between whom the dinner silence was freighted with such bitter hatred. . . .

He had imagined her journal as mostly a harangue about him. But there was nothing about him. The notes were all about the other him, the professor in the starched collar whose picture she was forcing herself to face in the morning when she awoke and at night when she went to sleep. There was something in her existence worse than Kathy Goolsbee—Sabbath *himself* was beside the point. The last thirty *years* were beside the point, so much futile churning about, so much festering of the wound by which— as she portrayed it here—her soul had been permanently disfigured. He had his story; this was Roseanna's, the official in-the-beginning story, when and where the betrayal that is life was launched. *Here* was the frightful lockup from which there was no release, and Sabbath was not mentioned once. What a bother we are to one another—while actually nonexistent to one another, unreal specters compared to whoever originally sabotaged the sacred trust.

We had different women, housekeepers, who would live with us, that would help to make the dinner. My father also did the cooking. A little bit vague in my memory. The housekeeper would sit with us too. I don't remember the dinners that well.

He was not there after school. I had a key. I would go to the store and buy myself some food. Pea soup. Cake and cookies that I liked. My sister would be home. We would take a snack in the afternoon, and then we would go out and play with our friends.

Recollection of his snoring loudly. Had to do with his drinking. Find him in the morning fully dressed, sleeping on the floor. So drunk he would miss the bed.

He wouldn't drink during the week but on weekends. We had a sailboat for a while and we would go out in the summertime on the boat. He was overpowering. Wanted his way. And he wasn't a terrific sailor. As he got a little bit more drunk he would lose control and walk and turn his pockets inside out to show us he had no money. And then he would be clumsy, and if we had a friend along, he embarrassed me terribly. Very disgusted by him physically when he did these things.

I needed clothes so he would take me to the clothing store. I was very embarrassed by having a father to do that. He didn't have the taste for it and sometimes he made me buy clothes that I didn't like and forced me to wear them. I remember a loden jacket that I hated. I hated it with a passion. I felt very tomboyish because I didn't have women who could take care of me and give me advice. That was very hard.

He would have the housekeepers and several of them
wanted to marry him. I remember one who was an educated woman and she cooked very well and she wanted so
much to marry the professor. But it always ended in catastrophe. Ella and I would listen through the doors to follow
the romantic developments. We knew exactly when they
were fucking. I don't imagine he was a good fuck, drunk
as he was. But we would always listen from behind the
door and were aware of everything going on. But then the
reality set in, his bossing them around, telling them even
how to do the dishes. He was a professor of geology and
so he knew how to wash the dishes better than they did.
There would be arguments and screaming, and I don't
think he hit the women but there was always an unpleasant ending. When they left it was always a crisis. And for
me there was always the expectation of the crisis. And
when I was twelve and thirteen and grew more interested
in going out and meeting boys, and I had a gang of girlfriends, he took that very hard. He would sit drinking his
gin by himself and fall asleep that way. I can't think of
him, that isolated person who could not manage by himself, without crying, as I am doing now.

She left in 1945, when I was eight years old. I don't remember when she left, I just remember being left. And
then I remember when she came back the first time, 1947,
at Christmas. She brought some toy animals that made
noises. My sense of desperation. I wanted my mother
back. Ella and I were again listening, now to what she and
our father were talking about behind the doors. Maybe
they were fucking too. I don't know. But what went on
behind the doors we tried to listen to. There were intense
whispers and sometimes very loud arguments. My mother
was there for two weeks and it was a great relief when she
left because the tension was so awful. She was a striking-
looking woman, well dressed, so worldly to me from living in Paris.

He used to have a locked desk. Ella and I knew how to
open it with a knife, so we always had access to his secrets.

We found letters from the different women. We laughed and thought it was a big joke. One night my father came into my room and he said, "Oh, I'm falling in love." I pretended that I knew nothing. He said he was going to get married. I thought, "Wonderful, now I can be relieved of my duty of caring for him." She was a widow, already sixty, and he thought she had some money. No sooner had they married than the arguments started, the same as with the other women. This time I felt myself in the middle of the whole thing, responsible for the fact that they had married! My father came to me and said it was terrible because she was older than she said and she didn't have the money she said she had. An enormous calamity. And she began bad-mouthing me. Complaining that I didn't study, that I was spoiled, I wasn't reliable, I was messy, I didn't clean up my room, a hopeless brat and I never told the truth or listened to what she said.

I was taking a bath in my mother's place and the phone rang and I heard my mother screaming. My first thought was that my father had killed my stepmother. But my mother came into the bathroom and she said, "Your father is dead. I have to go Cambridge." I said, "What about me?" She said, "You have to study and I don't think you should go." But I insisted that this was important for me and so she let me come with her. Ella didn't want to come, she was afraid to, but I made her come. He had left a letter to Ella and me. I still have that letter. I have all the letters he sent me when I went to live with my mother. I haven't read them since he died. When I got them in the mail I couldn't read them. To receive a letter from my father made me nauseated all day. My mother would finally make me open it. I would read it in her presence or she would read it to me. "Why haven't you written your father who misses you?" In the third person. "Why haven't you written to your father who loves you so much? Why did you lie to me about the money?" Then the next day, "Oh, my beloved Roseanna, I did receive a letter from you and I'm so happy."

I didn't hate him but he was a giant discomfort for me. He had gigantic power over me. He wasn't drunk every day because he had to teach. It was when he was drunk that he would come into my room late at night and lie in bed beside me.

In February '50 I moved into my mother's apartment with Ella. I saw my mother as my rescuer. I adored her and looked up to her. I thought she was beautiful. My mother made me into a doll. Overnight I became a popular young girl, with all the boys after me, and I got tall practically overnight. There was even a "Roseanna Club," the boys told me. But the attention I got, I couldn't take in. I wasn't there. I was someplace else. It was hard. But I do remember that I suddenly became very prim-looking, striped little dresses, and petticoats, and a rose in my hair for parties. My mother's mission in life was to justify her leaving. She said he would have killed her. Even when she picked up the phone to talk to him, she was afraid of him—her veins would stick out and she'd go white. I think I heard it every day, one way or another, her justification for running away. She too hated when his letters would come but she was too afraid of him not to make me read them. And there was a struggle over money. He didn't want to pay if I didn't live with him. It was always me, never Ella. I had to live with him or he wouldn't pay for me. I don't know how they resolved it, all I know is that there was always a struggle over money and me.

There was something physically disgusting about him. The sexual part. I had then and I have still a strong physical distaste for him. For his lips. I thought they were ugly. And the way he held me, even in public, like a woman he loved instead of like a young girl. When he took me on his arm to take a walk, I felt I was in a grip I could never get out of.

I got so frantic and busy doing other things that I was able for a while to forget about him. I went to France that next summer after his death and at fourteen I had a love affair. I stayed with a friend of my mother's and there were all these boys . . . so I did forget him. But I was in a daze for years. I've been in a daze always. I don't know why he comes to haunt me now that I'm a woman in her fifties, but he does.

I prepared myself to read his letters last summer by picking some flowers and making it pleasant and when I started reading I had to stop.

I drank to survive.

On the page following, every line of her handwriting had been scratched out so heavily that barely anything remained legible. He searched for the words to amplify "It was when he was drunk that he would come into my room late at night and lie in bed beside me," but all he could distinguish, even with microscopic scrutinizing, were the words "white wine," "my mother's rings," "a torture day" . . . and these were part of no discernible sequence. What she'd written here was not for the ears of the patients at that meeting or for the eyes of anyone, herself included. But then he turned the page and found some kind of exercise written out quite legibly, perhaps one she had been assigned by her doctor.

Reenactment of leaving my father at age thirteen, 39 years ago, in February. First as I remember it and then as I would have liked it to happen.

As I remember it: My father had picked me up at the hospital where I'd checked in a few days earlier to have a tonsillectomy. In spite of all my fear of him, I could tell that he was very happy to have me home, but I felt as I often did with him—I can't quite pinpoint it, but made terribly uncomfortable by his breathing and his lips. I have no recollection of the act itself. Just the vibrations set off in me by his breathing and his lips. I never told Ella. I haven't to this day. I have told no one.

Daddy told me that he and Irene did not get along very well. That she continued to complain about me, that I was a slob and didn't study or listen to what she had to say. Best for me to stay away from her as much as possible. . . . Daddy and I were sitting in the living room after lunch. Irene was cleaning up in the kitchen. I felt weak and tired but determined. I had to tell him now that I was leaving him. That everything was already planned. My mother had agreed to take me as long as—she stressed this repeatedly—it was my will to come and not her coercion that had made me. Legally my father had custody over us. Rather unusual at that time. My mother had given up all claims on us, since she felt we children should not be separated and she had few resources to bring us up. Besides, Daddy was likely to kill us all if we all left him. It's true that he had commented after reading in the newspaper about family tragedies where a husband actually killed everyone, including himself, that that was the right thing to do.

I remember my father standing in front of me looking much older than fifty-six, bushy white hair and a worn face, slightly stooped over but still tall. He was pouring coffee into a cup. I told him boldly that I was leaving. That I had talked to my mother and she had agreed to let me come to her. He almost dropped his cup and his face became ashen. Everything went out of him. He sat down, speechless. He did not frighten me by getting angry, which I had feared. Although I often defied him, I was always deadly afraid of him. But not this time. I knew I had to get out of there. If I didn't, I was dead. All he could say was, "I understand, but we must not let Irene know. We will only tell her that you are going to your mother to recuperate." Less than six months later he hanged himself. How could I not believe I was responsible?

As I would have liked it to happen: Feeling rather weak but happy that the surgery was over, I was glad to be going home. My father had picked me up at the hospital. It was a sunny January day. Daddy and I sat in the living room after finishing lunch. With my sore mouth I could only drink liquids. I had no appetite and I was also worried about starting to bleed. I had gotten scared in the hospital seeing other patients being readmitted because of slow bleeding. I was told you could bleed to death if it wasn't discovered in time. Daddy sat next to me on the sofa. He told me that he wanted to talk to me. He told me that my mother had called and told him that I might want to move to her now that I was a grown girl. Daddy said that he understood I was having a hard time. This had been a difficult year for everyone. There had been a lot of unhappiness between him and Irene and he knew it had spilled over on me. His marriage was not working out the way he hoped, but I, who was his daughter and still a child—now a teenager but still a child—had absolutely no responsibility for the way things were at home. He told me that it was unfortunate that I had been in the middle, with Irene coming to complain about him and he coming to complain about her. He felt guilty about this, and therefore, though it was hard for him to see me go since he loved me dearly, he felt that should I want to go it was probably a good idea. Of course he would pay child support for me if I moved to mother. He truly wanted what was best for me. He went on to tell me that he had not been feeling well for a long time, often suffering from insomnia. I felt enormously relieved that he understood my problems. I would now at last have a mother to guide me. Also I could come back any time I wanted, my room would always be there.

Dear Father,

Today, while waiting for your letters to me to arrive at the hospital, I've decided to write a letter to you. The pain I felt then, the pain I feel now—are they the same? I would hope not. Yet they feel identical. Except today I am tired of hiding from my pain. My old hiding skill (being drunk) won't ever work again. I am *not* suicidal, the way you were. I only wanted to die because I wanted the past to leave me alone and go away. Leave me alone, Past, let me just sleep!

So here I am. You have a daughter in a mental hospital. You did it. Outside it is a beautiful fall day. Clear blue sky. The leaves changing. But within I am still terrified. I will not say that my life has been wasted but do you know that I was robbed by you? My therapist and I have talked about it and I know now that I was robbed by you of the ability to have a normal relationship with a normal man.

Ella used to say that the best thing you did was to commit suicide. That's how simple it is for Ella, my unmolested sister with all her lovely children! What a strange family I come from. Last summer when I was at Ella's I visited your grave. I had never been back since your funeral. I picked some flowers and put them on your stone. There you lay next to Grandpa and Grandma Cavanaugh. I wept for you and for the life that ended so horribly. You nebulous figure, so abstract and yet so crucial to me, please let God watch over me when I have to undertake my task tomorrow night!

Your daughter in a mental hospital,

Roseanna

By eight-ten he had read everything three times over and she still had not returned to the room. He studied the father's photo, looking in vain for a visible sign of the damage done him and the damage he'd done. In the lips she hated he could see nothing extraordinary. Then he read as much as he could stand of *A Step-by-Step Guide for Families of Chemically Dependent Persons,* a paperback book on the table beside her pillow that was undoubtedly intended to brainwash him once she had returned home to displace Drenka from their bed. Here he was introduced to Share and Identify, who soon were to become household helpers, like Happy or Sleepy or Grumpy or Doc. "Emotional pain," he read, "can be broad and deep. . . . It hurts to become involved in arguments. . . . And what about the future? Will things keep getting worse?"

He left on the desk the file cabinet key that he'd found in her riding boot. But before he went down to the nurse's station to ask where Roseanna might be, he returned to her notebook and took fifteen more minutes to make a contribution of his own directly below the letter she had written to her late father earlier that day. He did nothing to disguise his handwriting.

Dear little Roseanna!

Of course you are in a mental hospital. I warned you again and again about separating yourself from me and separating me from pretty little Helen Kylie. Yes, you are mentally ill, you have completely lost yourself to drink and cannot retrieve yourself on your own, but your letter today still gave me a real shock. If you want to take legal action, go ahead, even though I am dead. I never did expect that death would bring me any peace. Now, thanks to you, my beloved little darling, being dead is as awful as being alive was. *Take* legal action. You who abandoned your father have no position at all. For five years I lived entirely for you. Because of the expenses of your education and your clothes, etc., I was never able to be secure on a professor's salary. For my own part, during those years I bought nothing, not even clothes. I even had to sell the boat. Nobody can say that I did not sacrifice everything to taking loving care of you, even though one can argue about different methods of upbringing.

I don't have time to write any more. Satan is calling me to my session. Dear little Roseanna, cannot you and your husband be happy in the end? If not, the fault is entirely your mother's. Satan agrees. He and I have talked in therapy about the husband you chose and I know for sure that I have nothing to be guilty about. If you did not marry a normal man it is entirely your mother's fault for sending you to a coeducational school during the dangerous years of puberty. All the pain in your life is entirely her responsibility. My anxiety, which has its roots way back when I was alive, will not disappear even here, because of what your mother did to you and what you did to me. In our group there is another father who had an ungrateful daughter. He shared about his agony and we identified. It was very helpful. I learned that I cannot change my ungrateful daughter.

Only how much farther do you want to push me, my little one? Didn't you push me far enough? You judge me entirely by your pain, you judge me entirely by your holy feelings. But why don't you judge me for a change by *my* pain, by *my* holy feelings? How you cling to your grievance! As though in a world of persecution you alone have a grievance. Wait till you're dead—death is grievance and only grievance. Perennial grievance. It is despicable of you to continue this attack on your dead father—I will be in therapy here forever because of you. Unless, unless, dear little Roseanna, you were somehow to find it in you to write just a few thousand pages to grieving Papa to tell him how remorseful you are for everything you did to ruin his life.

Your father in Hell,

Dad

"Probably still at the Mansion," said the nurse, consulting her watch. "They hang around to smoke. Why don't you go over there? If she's headed this way, you'll pass her on the drive."

But at the Mansion, where smokers were indeed gathered once again outside the main door, he was told that Roseanna had gone to the gym with Rhonda to take a swim. The gym was a low, sprawling building down the lawn and across the road—they told him he could see the pool through the windows.

There was no one swimming there. It was a big, well-lit pool, and, after peering through the misty windows, he went inside to see if perhaps she was at the bottom of it, dead. But the young woman attendant, sitting at a desk next to a pile of towels, said no, Roseanna hadn't been there tonight. She'd done her hundred laps that afternoon.

He proceeded back up the dark hill to the Mansion to look in the lounge where the meeting had been held. He was guided to it by the glazier, who'd been reading a magazine in the parlor while someone at the piano—the Wellesley girlfriend of the Marlboro man—was tapping out "Night and Day" with one hand. The lounge was along a broad corridor with a pay phone at either end. Standing at one of them was a small, skinny Hispanic kid of about twenty who Roseanna had told him at dinner was an addict who dealt cocaine. She was wearing a colorful nylon sweat suit and had a headset over her ears even as she loudly argued over the phone in what Sabbath figured to be either Puerto Rican or Dominican Spanish. From what he understood, she was telling her mother to fuck herself.

In the lounge, a large room with a television screen at the far end, there were couches and lots of easy chairs scattered about, but it was empty now except for two elderly women quietly playing cards at a table beside a standing lamp. One was a gray-haired patient, dumpy but with a becoming air of antique jadedness, whom several of the patients had jokingly applauded when she'd appeared, twenty minutes late, in the dining room doorway. "My public," she had said grandly in her high-born New England accent, and curtsied. "This is the P.M. performance," she announced, fluttering into the room on her toes. "If you're lucky you can come to the A.M. performance." The woman playing cards with her was her sister, a visitor, who must also have been in her late seventies.

"Have you seen Roseanna?" Sabbath called over to them.

"Roseanna," replied the patient, "is seeing her doctor."

"It's eight-thirty at night."

"The suffering that is the hallmark of human affairs," she informed him, "does not diminish at eventide. To the contrary. But you must be the husband who is of such importance to her. Yes. Yes." Cannily sizing him up—girth, height, beard, baldness, costume—she said with a gracious smile, "That you are a very great man is unmistakable."

On the second floor of the Mansion, Sabbath made his way

past a row of patients' rooms to the end of the corridor and a nurse's station that was about twice the size of the one at Roderick, a lot less bright and cheery, but mercifully without the "Peanuts" posters. Two nurses were doing some paperwork, and atop a low file cabinet, swinging his legs and drinking what looked from both the plastic sack full of Pepsis at his side and the wastebasket at his feet to be his sixth or seventh soda, sat a muscular young man with a dark chin beard wearing black jeans, a black polo shirt, and black sneakers, who vaguely resembled the Sabbath of some thirty years ago. He was expounding to one of the nurses in an impassioned voice; from time to time she glanced up to acknowledge what he was saying but then went right back to her paperwork. She herself couldn't have been more than thirty, chunky, robust, clear-eyed, with dark hair clipped neatly short, and she gave Sabbath a friendly wink when he appeared at the door. She was one of the two nurses who had searched Rosie's suitcases the afternoon they arrived.

"Ideological idiots!" proclaimed the young man in black. "The third great ideological failure of the twentieth century. The same stuff. Fascism. Communism. Feminism. All designed to turn one group of people against another group of people. The good Aryans against the bad others who oppress them. The good poor against the bad rich who oppress them. The good women against the bad men who oppress them. The holder of the ideology is pure and good and clean and the other is wicked. But do you know who is wicked? Whoever imagines himself to be pure is wicked! I am pure, you are wicked. How can you swallow that stuff, Karen?"

"I don't, Donald," the young nurse replied. "You know I don't."

"*She* does. My ex-wife does!"

"I am not your ex-wife."

"There *is* no human purity! It does not exist! It cannot exist!" he said, kicking the file cabinet for emphasis. "It must not and *should* not exist! Because it is a lie! Her ideology is like all ideologies—founded in a lie! Ideological tyranny. It's the disease of the century. The ideology *institutionalizes* the pathology. In twenty years there will be a new ideology. People against dogs. The dogs are to blame for our lives as people. Then after dogs there will be what? Who will be to blame for corrupting our purity?"

"I hear where you're coming from," mumbled Karen while attending to the work on her desk.

"Excuse me," said Sabbath. He leaned into the room. "I don't mean to interrupt a man whose aversions I wholeheartedly endorse, but I am looking for Roseanna Sabbath and I have been told she is seeing her doctor. Any way this can be established as fact?"

"Roseanna's in Roderick," said the Donald in black.

"But she's not there now. I can't find her. I came all this way and I've lost her. I am her husband."

"Are you? We've heard so many wonderful things about you in group," Donald said, again whacking both sneakers against the file cabinet and reaching into the plastic sack for a Pepsi. "The great god Pan."

"The great god Pan is dead," a deadpan Sabbath informed him. "But I see"—stentorian now—"that you are a young fellow unafraid of the truth. What are you doing in a place like this?"

"Trying to leave," said Karen, rolling her eyes like an exasperated kid. "Donald's been trying since nine this morning. Donald's been graduated but he can't go home."

"I have no home. The bitch destroyed my home. Two years ago," he told Sabbath, who by now had come into the room and taken the empty chair beside the wastebasket. "I came back from a business trip one night. My wife's car isn't in the driveway. I go into the house and it's empty. All the furniture is gone. All she left was the album with the wedding pictures. I sat on the floor and looked at the wedding pictures and cried. I came home from work every day and looked at the wedding pictures and cried."

"And like a good boy, drank your dinner," said Karen.

"The booze was only to quell the depression. I got over that. I'm in the hospital," he told Sabbath, "because she is getting married today. *Got* married today. She married another woman. A *rabbi* married them. And my wife is not Jewish!"

"Ex," said Karen.

"But the other woman is Jewish?" asked Sabbath.

"Yeah. The rabbi was there to please the other woman's family. How's that?"

"Well," said Sabbath gently, "rabbis occupy an exalted position in the Jewish mind."

"Fuck that. *I'm* Jewish. What the fuck is a rabbi doing marrying two lesbos? You think in Israel a rabbi would do it? No, only in Ithaca, New York!"

"To embrace humanity in all its glorious diversity," asked Sabbath, professorially stroking his beard, "is that a long-standing peculiarity of the Ithaca rabbinate?"

"Fuck no! They're rabbis! They're assholes!"

"Language, Donald." It was the other nurse speaking now, clearly a tough one—seasoned, hardened, and tough. "It's time for vital signs, Donald. It'll be time for meds soon. We're going to get busy here. What are your plans? Have you made any plans?"

"I'm leaving, Stella."

"Good. When?"

"After vital signs. I want to be sure to say good-bye to everybody."

"You have been saying good-bye to everybody all day long," Stella reminded him. "Everybody in the Mansion has taken you for a walk and told you you can make it. You *can* make it. You are *going* to make it. You won't stop at a bar to have a drink. You will drive straight to your brother's in Ithaca."

"My wife is a lesbian. Some asshole rabbi married her today to another woman."

"You don't know this for sure."

"My sister-in-law was *there,* Stella. My ex-wife stood under the *chuppa* with this broad, and when the time came she broke the glass. My wife is a shiksa. The two of them are lesbians. This is what Judaism has come to? I can't believe it!"

"Donald, be kind," said Sabbath. "Don't disparage the Jews for wanting to be with it. Even the Jews are up against it in the Age of Total Schlock. The Jews can't win," Sabbath said to Stella, who looked to be Filipino and was, like himself, an older and wiser person. "Either they're mocked because they're still wearing their beards and waving their arms in the air or they are ridiculed by people like Donald here for being up-to-the-minute servants of the sexual revolution."

"What if she'd married a zebra?" Donald asked indignantly. "Would a rabbi have married her to a zebra?"

"Zebra or *zebu*?" asked Sabbath.

"What's a zebu?"

"A zebu is an east Asian cow with a large hump. Many women today are leaving husbands for zebus. Which did you say?"

"Zebra."

"Well, I think not. A rabbi wouldn't touch a zebra. Can't. They don't have cloven hooves. For a rabbi to officiate at the marriage of a person to an animal, the animal has to chew its cud *and* have a cloven hoof. A camel. A rabbi can marry a person to a camel. A cow. Any kind of cattle. Sheep. Can't marry someone to a rabbit, however, because even though a rabbit chews its cud, it doesn't have a cloven hoof. They also eat their own shit, which, on the face of it, you might think a point in their favor: chew their food *three* times. But what is required is *twice*. That's why a rabbi can't marry a person to a pig. Not that the pig is unclean. That's not the problem, never has been. The problem with the pig is, though it has a cloven hoof, it doesn't chew its cud. A zebra may or may not chew its cud—I don't know. But it doesn't have a cloven hoof, and with the rabbis, one strike and you're out. The rabbi can marry a person to a bull, of course. The bull is like a cow. The divine animal, the bull. The Canaanite god El—which is where the Jews got El-o-him—is a bull. Anti-Defamation League tries to down-play this, but like it or not, the El in Elohim, a bull! Basic religious passion is to worship a bull. Damn it, Donald, you Jews ought to be *proud* of that. *All* the ancient religions were obscene. Do you know how the Egyptians imagined the origins of the universe? Any kid can read about it in his encyclopedia. God masturbated. And his sperm flew up and created the universe."

The nurses did not look happy with the turn given to the

conversation by Sabbath, and so the puppeteer decided to address them directly. "God's jerking off alarms you? Well, gods are alarming, girls. It's a god who commands you to cut off your foreskin. It's a god who commands you to sacrifice your firstborn. It's a god who commands you to leave your mother and father and go off into the wilderness. It's a god who sends you into slavery. It's a god who *destroys*—it's the spirit of a god that comes down to *destroy*—and yet it's a god who gives life. What in all of creation is as nasty and strong as this god who gives life? The God of the Torah embodies the world in all its horror. And in all its truth. You've got to hand it to the Jews. Truly rare and admirable candor. What other people's national myth reveals their God's atrocious conduct *and* their own? Just read the Bible, it's all there, the backsliding, idolatrous, butchering Jews and the schizophrenia of these ancient gods. What is the archetypal Bible story? A story of betrayal. Of treachery. It's just one deception after another. And whose is the greatest voice in the Bible? Isaiah. The mad desire to obliterate all! The mad desire to save all! The greatest voice in the Bible is the voice of somebody who has lost his mind! And that God, that Hebrew God—you can't escape Him! What's shocking is not His monstrous features—plenty of gods are monstrous, it seems almost to have been a prerequisite—but that there's no recourse from Him. No power beyond *His*. The most monstrous feature of God, my friends, is the *totalitarianism*. This vengeful, seething God, this punishment-ordaining bastard, is *ultimate!* Mind if I have a Pepsi?" Sabbath inquired of Donald.

"Awesome," said Donald, and thinking perhaps, as Sabbath was thinking, that this was the way people in a madhouse were *supposed* to talk, he took a cold can out of the plastic sack and even opened the tab for Sabbath before handing it on to him. Sabbath took a long swig just as the baby cocaine dealer came in to have her vital signs checked. She was listening to the music on her headset and singing along with the lyrics in a flattish, unvarying, throaty tone. "Lick it! Lick it! Lick it, baby, lick it, lick it, lick it, lick it!" When she saw Donald, she said, "Ain't you goin'?"

"I wanted to see them take your blood pressure one last time."

"Yeah, that make you hot, Donny?"

"What *is* her pressure?" asked Sabbath. "What would you think?"

"Linda? Doesn't make much difference to Linda. Her pressure isn't the big thing in Linda's life."

"How do you feel, Linda?" Sabbath asked her. "Estas siempre enfadada con tu mama?"

"La odio."

"Por qué, Linda?"

"Ella me odia a *mí*."

"Her pressure's 120 over 100," said Sabbath.

"Linda?" said Donald. "Linda's a kid. 120 over 70."

"Wanna bet the spread?" said Sabbath. "A buck on the spread, another buck if you hit the diastolic or the systolic, three if you nail 'em both." He took a wad of singles out of his pants pocket, and when he smoothed them into a pile on the palm of one hand, Donald took some bills out of his wallet and said to Karen, who was standing holding the blood pressure cuff beside the chair where Linda was seated, "Go ahead. I'll play him."

"What's going on here?" Karen asked. "Play *what*?"

"Go ahead. Take her pressure."

"Jesus," Karen said and put the cuff on Linda, who was singing along with the tape again.

"Shut *up*," said Karen. She listened through the stethoscope, made a recording in the ledger, and then took Linda's pulse.

"What was it?" said Donald.

Karen was silent as she entered the pulse rate in the ledger.

"Oh fuck, Karen—what *was* it?"

"120 over 100," Karen said.

"Shit."

"Four bucks," said Sabbath, and Donald peeled off the money and gave it to him. "Next." Sciarappa the barber, back in Bradley.

In the doorway was Ray in his silk robe. He went silently to the chair and rolled up his left sleeve.

"140 over 90," said Sabbath.

"160 over 100," said Donald.

Ray nervously tapped the book in his hand until Karen touched his fingers and made him relax them. Then she took his pressure. Linda, leaning against the door frame, was waiting to see who was going to win all the money. "This is great," she said. "This is crazy."

"150," said Karen, "over 100."

"I got you on the spread," said Sabbath, "you got me on the diastolic. It's a wash. Next."

His next was the young woman with the scar on her wrist, the tall, pretty blond who slouched and who had given Sabbath directions to Roderick House before dinner. She said to Donald, "Aren't you ever leaving?"

"If you come with me, Madeline. You look good, honey. You're almost standing straight."

"Don't get alarmed—it's the same old me," she said. "Listen to what I found in the library today. I was reading the journals. Listen." She took a piece of paper out of the pocket of her jeans. "I copied it from a journal. Word for word. *Journal of Medical Ethics.* 'It is proposed that *happiness*'"—glancing up, she said, "Their italics"—"'it is proposed that *happiness* be classified as a psychiatric disorder and be included in future editions of the major diagnostic manuals under the new name: major affective disorder, pleasant type. In a review of the relevant literature it is shown that *happiness* is statistically abnormal, consists of a discrete cluster of symptoms, is associated with a range of cognitive abnormalities, and probably reflects the abnormal functioning of the central nervous system. One possible objection to this proposal remains—that *happiness* is not negatively valued. However, this objection is dismissed as scientifically irrelevant.'"

Donald looked pleased, proud, beguiled, as though the reason for his stalling around was indeed to run off with Madeline. "You make that up?"

"If I'd made it up it would be clever. Nope. A psychiatrist made it up. That's why it's not."

"Oh bullshit, Madeline. Saunders isn't stupid. He used to be an analyst," he told Sabbath, "the guy who runs the place, and now he's, like, this cool-guy psychiatrist who tries to be relaxed about everything—not too analytic. He's into this big cognitive behavioral thing. Trying to make yourself stop if you're having obsessive ruminations. Just train yourself to say 'Stop!'"

"That's not stupid?" asked Madeline. "And meanwhile, what am I supposed to do about my rage and having no confidence? Nothing is easy. Nothing is pleasant. What am I supposed to do about this idiotic therapist I had this morning for Assertiveness Training? I had her again this afternoon—we had to sit through a videotape on medical aspects of addiction and afterwards she led the discussion. And I raised my hand, I said, 'There are some things that I don't understand about this tape. You know, when they have the experiment on the two different mice—' And the idiot therapist says, 'Madeline, this is not a discussion about that. This is a discussion about your feelings. How did the tape make you feel about your alcoholism?' I said, 'Frustrated. It raised more questions than it answered.' 'Okay,' she said in that perky way she has, 'Madeline feels frustrated. Anyone else? What do *you* feel, Nick?' So we go around the room, and so I raise my hand again and I said, 'If we could ever just for a minute shift the discussion from the level of feelings to the level of information—' 'Madeline,' she says, 'this is a discussion of people's feelings in response to this tape. If you have a need for information, I suggest you go to the library and look things up.' That's how I wound up in the library. My feelings. Who *cares* how I feel about my addiction?"

"If you will only keep monitoring your feelings," said Karen, "that is what is going to keep you from *being* addicted."

"It's not worth it," said Madeline.

"It is," said Karen.

"Yeah," said Donald, "you're an addict, Madeline, because you're not connected to people, and you're not connected to people because you haven't told them your *feelings*."

"Oh, why can't things just be nice?" asked Madeline. "I just want to be told what to do anyway."

"I like when you say that," said Donald. "'I just want to be told what to do.' It's a turn-on in that little voice."

"Ignore his negativity, Madeline," Karen the nurse told her. "He's just pulling your chain."

But Madeline appeared unable to ignore anything. "Well," she said to Donald, "in certain situations I do like to be told what to do. And in certain other situations I like to make demands."

"So there you go," said Donald. "It's all too fucking complicated."

"I had art therapy this afternoon," Madeline told him.

"Did you draw a picture, dear?"

"I did a collage."

"Somebody interpret it for you?"

"They didn't need to."

Donald, laughing, started on another Pepsi. "And how's your crying going?"

"I'm in a real slump of a day. I woke up crying this morning. I cried all morning long. I cried in Meditation. I cried in group. You'd think it would dry up."

"Everybody cries in the morning," Karen said. "Just part of getting under way."

"I don't know why today should be worse than yesterday," Madeline told her. "I think all the same dark thoughts but they're not any darker today than they were yesterday. In Meditation, guess who we read from in our little daily meditation book? Shirley MacLaine. And this morning I went to the sharps nurse to get my tweezers. I said, 'I need my tweezers out of the sharps closet.' And she said, 'You have to use them here, Madeline. I don't want you to take them back to your room.' And so I said, 'If I'm going to kill myself, I'm not going to do it with my *tweezers.*'"

"Tweeze yourself to death?" said Donald. "Hard to do. How do you do that, Karen?"

Karen ignored him.

"I got very angry," said Madeline. "I told her, 'I can crack the light bulb and swallow it, too. Give me my tweezers!' But she wouldn't, just because I was crying."

"At AA," Donald said to Sabbath, "they go around at the beginning of the meeting. Everybody has to introduce himself.

'Hi, my name is Christopher. I'm an alcoholic.' 'Hi, my name is Mitchell. I'm an alcoholic.' 'Hi, I'm Flora. I'm cross-addicted.'"

"Cross-addicted?" Sabbath asked.

"Who knows—some Catholic thing. I think she's in the wrong group. Anyway, they get to Madeline. Madeline gets up. 'My name is Madeline. What's your red wine by the glass?' How's your smoking?" he asked her.

"I am basically smoking like a fiend."

"Tsk-tsk," said Donald. "Smoking is just another of your defenses against intimacy, Madeline. You know nobody wants to kiss a smoker anymore."

"I'm smoking even more than when I came in. A couple months ago I really thought I had it . . ."

"*Licked?*" said Donald. "Could the word be *licked?*"

"I was going to, but I thought, I'm just not using that word around him. You know, nothing *is* easy—*nothing*. And it's making me nervous. Press 1 for this, press 2 for that. What am I supposed to do about being left on hold all day? Everything is such a fight. I'm still fighting my managed care from the first time I was here. They keep telling me I should have called them when I was admitted to the Poughkeepsie ICU. I was in a fucking *coma*. It's hard to push 1 and push 2 when you're in a coma. And even if you could, they don't *have* phones in the ICU."

"You were in a coma?" asked Sabbath. "What is that like?"

"You're in a coma. You're out," said Madeline in the voice that *didn't* sound as though it had seen much change since she was a ten-year-old. "You're unresponsive. It's not like anything."

"This gentleman is Roseanna's husband," Donald said to her.

"Ah," said Madeline, her eyes widening.

"Madeline is an actress. When she's not in a coma she's in the soaps. She's a very wise girl who wants from life no more than to die by her own hand. She left her family an endearing suicide note. Ten words. 'I don't know what I did to deserve this gift.' Mr. Sabbath wants to bet on your blood pressure."

"Under the circumstances, that is very kind of him," she replied.

"120 over 80," said Sabbath.

"And what do you bet?" Madeline asked Donald.

"I bet low, honey. I bet 90 over 60."

"Hardly living," said Madeline.

"Wait a minute," said Stella, the Filipino nurse. "What *is* this?" She got up from the desk to confront the gamblers. "Usher is a *hospital*," she said, glaring directly at Sabbath. "These people are *patients*. . . . Donald, show a little mental toughness, Donald. Get in your car and go home. And you, did you come here to play games, or did you come here to see your wife?"

"My wife is hiding from me."

"You get out. You leave."

"I can't find my wife."

"Beat it," she told him. "Go reside with the gods."

Sabbath waited around the corner from the nurse's station until Madeline's blood pressure had been taken and she appeared in the corridor alone. "Can you lead me to Roderick House again?" he asked her.

"Sorry, I can't go outside."

"If you could just get me aimed in the right direction . . ."

Together they walked down the staircase to the first floor; she went as far as the porch, where, from the top of the steps, she pointed to the lights of Roderick House.

"It's a beautiful fall night," said Sabbath. "Walk me there."

"I can't. I'm a high-risk person. For a psychiatric hospital you have a lot of freedom here. But after dark I'm not allowed outside. I'm only a week out of ACU."

"What's ACU?"

"Acute care unit."

"The place on the hill?"

"Yeah. A Holiday Inn you can't get out of."

"Were you the most acute person there?"

"I don't really know. I wasn't paying much attention. They won't let you have caffeine after breakfast so I was busy storing up tea from morning. So pathetic. I was too busy working out the caffeine smuggling to make many friends."

"Come. We'll find you a Lipton's tea bag to suck on."

"I can't. I have program tonight. I think I have to go to Relapse Prevention."

"Aren't you a bit ahead of yourself?"

"Actually, no. I've been planning my relapse."

"Come with me."

"I really should go and work on my relapse."

"Come on."

She hurried down the steps and started with him along the dark drive to Roderick House. He had to move fast.

"How old are you?" Sabbath asked.

"Twenty-nine."

"You look ten."

"And I tried not to look too young tonight. Didn't it work? I get carded all the time. They're always asking for my ID. Whenever I have to wait in a doctor's office, the receptionist gives me a copy of *Seventeen*. Aside from how I look, I act younger than I am, too."

"That you can expect to get worse."

"Whatever. The harsh reality."

"Why did you try to kill yourself?"

"I don't know. The only thing that doesn't bore me. The only thing worth thinking about. Besides, by the middle of the day I think the day has just gone on long enough and there's only one way to make the day go away, and that is either booze or bed."

"And that does it?"

"No."

"So next you try suicide. *The* taboo."

"I try it because I'm confronting my own mortality *ahead* of my time. Because I realize it's the critical question, you see. The messiness of marriage and children and career and all that—I've already realized the futility of it all without having had to go through it all. Why can't I just be fast-forwarded?"

"You've got a mind, don't you? I like the mosaic it makes."

"I'm wise and mature beyond my years."

"Mature beyond your years and immature beyond your years."

"What a paradox. Well, you can only be young once, but you can be immature forever."

"The too-wise child who doesn't want to live. You're an actress?

"Of course not. Donald's humor—Madeline's life is soap opera. I think he anticipated something of a romantic nature between us. There was an element of seduction, which was sort of touching in its own little way. He said lots of glowing and flattering things about me. Intelligent. Attractive. He told me I should stand up straight. To do something about my shoulders. 'Elongate, honey.'"

"What happens when you stand up straight?"

Her voice was soft and the answer that she muttered now he couldn't even hear. "You must speak up, dear."

"I'm sorry. I said nothing happens."

"Why do you speak so quietly?"

"Why? That's a good question."

"You don't stand up straight and you don't speak loud enough."

"Oh, just like my father. My high, squeaky voice."

"Is that what he tells you?"

"All my life."

"Another one with a father."

"Yes indeed."

"How tall *are* you when you stand up straight?"

"Just under five ten. But it's hard to stand up straight when you're at the lowest point of your life."

"Also hard when you went through high school not only five ten, not only with a conspicuously active mind, but flat-chested to boot."

"Golly, a man understands me."

"Not you. Tits. I understand tits. I have been studying tits since I was thirteen years old. I don't think there's any other organ or body part that evidences so much variation in size as women's tits."

"I *know*," replied Madeline, openly enjoying herself suddenly and beginning to laugh. "And why is that? Why did God allow this enormous variation in breast size? Isn't it amazing? There are women with breasts ten times the size of mine. Or even more. True?"

"That is true."

"People have big noses," she said. "I have a small nose. But are there people with noses ten times the size of mine? Four or five, max. I don't know why God did this to women."

"The variation," Sabbath offered, "accommodates a wide variety of desires, perhaps. But then," he added, thinking again, "breasts, as you call them, are not there primarily to entice men— they're there to feed children."

"But I don't think size has to do with milk production," said Madeline. "No, that doesn't solve the problem of what this enormous variation is *for*."

"Maybe it's that God hasn't made up his mind. That's often the case."

"Wouldn't it be more interesting," asked Madeline, "if there were different *numbers* of breasts? Mightn't that be more interesting? You know—some women with two, some with six . . ."

"How many times have you tried to commit suicide?"

"Only twice. How many times has your wife tried?"

"Only once. So far."

"Why?"

"Forced to sleep with her old man. As a kid, her father's girl."

"Was she really? They all say that. The simplest story about yourself that explains everything—it's the house specialty. These people read more complicated stories in the newspaper every day, and then they're handed this version of their lives. In Courage to Heal they've been trying for three weeks to get me to turn in my dad. The answer to every question is either Prozac or incest. Talk about boring. All the false introspection. It's enough in itself to make you suicidal. Your wife is one of the two or three I can even stand to listen to. She's elegant-minded by comparison with the others. Her desire is passionate to face the losses. She doesn't back

away from the excavation. But you, of course, find nothing redeeming in these reflections back on origins."

"Don't I? I wouldn't know."

"Well, they're trying to confront this awful stuff with their raw
souls, and it's way, way beyond them, and so they say all those
stupid things that don't sound much like 'reflections.' Still, there's
something about your wife that, in its own way, has a certain
heroism. The way she stood up to an excruciating detox. There's
a kind of deliberateness to her that I sure don't have: running
around here collecting the shards of her past, struggling with her
father's letters. . . ."

"Don't stop. *You* get more and more elegant-minded by the
moment."

"Look, she's a drunk, drunks drive people nuts, and to the
husband that's the crux. Fair enough. She's putting up a struggle
that you disdain for its lack of genius. She doesn't have your wit
and so forth and so she can't have the penetrating cynicism. But
she has as much nobility as someone can within the limits of her
imagination."

"How do you know she does?"

"I don't. I just made it up. I make it up as I go along. Doesn't
everyone?"

"Roseanna's heroism and nobility."

"I mean it's clear to me that she did suffer a great blow and that
she earned her pain, that's all. She came by her pain honestly."

"How?"

"Her father's suicide. The awful way in which he suffocated
her. Her father's effort to become the great man in her life. And
then the suicide. Wreaking that vengeance on her just for saving
her own life. That was a huge blow for a young girl. You couldn't
really ask for a bigger one."

"So you believe he fucked her or you don't?"

"I don't. I don't believe it, because it's not necessary. She had
enough without it. You're talking about a little girl and her father.
Little girls love their fathers. There's enough going on there. The
courting is all you need. It doesn't require a seduction. Could be

he killed himself not because they had consummated it but so that they wouldn't. A lot of suicides, gloomy people with guilty ruminations, think their families would be better off without them."

"And did you think like that, Madeline?"

"Nope. I thought I might be better off without my family."

"If you know all this," said Sabbath, "or know enough to make it up, how come I'm meeting you here?"

"You're meeting me here *because* I know all this. Guess who I'm reading in the library? Erik Erikson. I'm in the intimacy-versus-isolation stage, if I understand him correctly, and I think really not coming out ahead. You are in the generativity-versus-stagnation stage, but you are very quickly approaching the integrity-versus-despair stage."

"I have no children. I haven't generated shit."

"You'll be relieved to learn that the childless can generate through acts of altruism."

"Unlikely in my case. What is it, again, I have to look forward to?"

"Integrity versus despair."

"And how do things look for me, from what you've read?"

"Well, it depends whether life is basically meaningful and purposeful," she said, bursting out laughing.

Sabbath laughed too. "What's so funny about 'purposeful,' Madeline?"

"You do ask tough questions."

"Yeah, well, it's amazing what you find out when you ask."

"Anyway, I don't have to worry yet about generativity. I told you: I'm in intimacy versus isolation."

"And how are you doing?"

"I think it's questionable how I'm doing on the intimacy question."

"And on the isolation one?"

"I get the feeling they're somewhat meant by Dr. Erikson to be polar opposites. If you're not doing well in one, you must be scoring fairly high in the other."

"And you are?"

"Well, I guess mainly in the romantic arena. I didn't realize, until I read Dr. Erikson, that this was my 'developmental goal,'" she said, starting to laugh again. "I guess I haven't achieved it."

"What's your developmental goal?"

"I suppose a stable little relationship with a man and all his fucking complex needs."

"When was the last time you had that?"

"Seven years ago. It hasn't been an *abysmal* failure. I can't really tell objectively how sorry I should feel for myself. I don't give the same credibility to my being that other people give to theirs. Everything feels acted."

"Everything *is* acted."

"Whatever. With me there's some glue missing, something fundamental to everyone else that I don't have. My life never seems real to me."

"I have to see you again," Sabbath said.

"So. This *is* a flirtation. I wondered but couldn't believe it. Are you always attracted to damaged women?"

"I didn't know there were any other kind."

"Being called damaged is a lot worse than being called cuckoo, isn't it?"

"I believe you were called damaged by yourself."

"Whatever. That's the risk you take talking. In high school I was called ditsy."

"What's 'ditsy' mean?"

"Kind of an airhead. Call Mr. Kasterman, my math teacher. He'll tell you. I'd always be coming in from cooking class with flour all over me."

"I never slept with a girl who tried to commit suicide."

"Sleep with your wife."

"*That* is ditsy."

Her laugh was very sly now, a delightful surprise. A delightful person, suffused by a light soulfulness that wasn't at all juvenile, however juvenile she happened to look. An adventurous mind with an intuitive treasure that her suffering hadn't shut down, Madeline displayed the bright sadder-but-wiser outlook of an

alert first grader who'd discovered the alphabet in a school where
Ecclesiastes is the primer—life is futility, a deeply terrible experience, but the really serious thing is *reading*. The sliding about
of her self-possession was practically visible as she spoke. Self-
possession was not her center of gravity, nor was anything else
of hers that was on display, other perhaps than a way of saying things that was appealing to him for being just a little imper-
sonal. Whatever had denied her a woman's breasts and a woman's
face had made compensation of sorts by charging her mind with
erotic significance—or so at least its influence swept over Sabbath, ever vigilant to all stimuli. A sensual promise that perme-
ated her intelligence disarranged pleasantly his hard-on's time-
worn hopes.

"What would it be like for you," she asked him, "sleeping with
me? Like sleeping with a corpse? A ghost? A corpse resurrected?"

"No. Sleeping with somebody who took the thing to the final
step."

"The adolescent romanticism makes you look like an asshole,"
said Madeline.

"I've looked like an asshole before. So what? What are you so
bitter about at your age?"

"Yes, my retrospective bitterness."

"What's it about?"

"*I* don't know."

"But you do."

"You just like to dig right on in there, don't you, Mr. Sabbath?
What am I bitter about? All those years I worked and planned for
things. It all seems . . . I'm not sure."

"Come down to my car."

She gave the suggestion serious consideration before she replied, "For a quart of vodka?"

"A pint," he said.

"In return for sexual favors? A quart."

"A fifth."

"A quart."

"I'll get it," he said.

"You do that."

Sabbath ran to the parking lot, in a frenzy drove the three miles
to Usher, found a liquor store, bought *two* quarts of Stolichnaya,
and drove back to the parking lot, where Madeline was to be
waiting. He'd done the whole thing in twelve minutes but she
wasn't there. She wasn't among the smokers outside the Mansion,
she wasn't in the Mansion lounge playing cards with the two old
ladies or in the parlor, where the battered Wellesley girl was now
doggedly trying her luck with "When the Saints Go Marching
In," and, when he retraced their steps, she was not anywhere
along the route to Roderick House. So there he was, alone in the
shadows on a beautiful fall night, two quarts of the best hundred-
proof Russian vodka in a brown paper bag beneath his arm,
stood up by someone whom he'd had every reason to trust, when
a guard appeared behind him—a very large black man in a blue
security officer's uniform and carrying a walkie-talkie—and asked
him politely what his business was. The explanation having
proved inadequate, two more guards appeared, and though no
one assaulted him physically, there were insults to be endured
from the youngest and most vigilant of the guards while Sabbath
voluntarily allowed himself to be escorted to his car. There the
three examined his license and registration by flashlight, wrote
down his name and his out-of-state license number, and then took
the car keys and got in the car, two in the back with Sabbath and
the Stolichnaya and one up front to drive the car off the grounds.
Mrs. Sabbath would be questioned before she went to bed and a
report filed with the chief doctor (who happened to be Roseanna's
doctor) first thing in the morning. If the patient had arranged for
her visitor to bring her the alcohol, his wife would be ejected on
the spot.

He arrived in Madamaska Falls close to one A.M. Exhausted as
he was, he drove to the lake and then followed Fox Run Crossing
up past the inn to where the Baliches lived atop the hill overlooking the water, in a new house as spacious and lavish as any on the
mountain. The house was the realization for Matija of a dream—
the dream of a grand family castle that was a country unto itself—

and the dream dated back to elementary school, when, for homework, he had to write about his parents and tell the teacher
truthfully, like a good Pioneer, what their relationship was to the
regime. Matija had even brought a blacksmith over from Yugoslavia, an artisan from the Dalmatian coast, to stay for six months
in the inn's annex and work at a forge near Blackwall where he
made the outdoor railings for the vast green terrace that looked
onto the sunsets staged at the western end of the lake, the indoor
banisters for the wide central staircase that twisted up toward a
dome ceiling, and the filigreed iron entrance gates operated elec-
tronically from the house. The iron chandelier had come by sea
from Split. Matija's brother was a contractor and he had bought it
from gypsies who sold all that kind of antique stuff. The chain
forged for the chandelier by the resident blacksmith hung menac-
ingly down the two stories from the sky-blue dome into a foyer
where there were leaded stained-glass window panels to either
side of a mahogany double door. Through the doorway you could
have driven a horse-drawn carriage onto the marble floor (cut
especially for the house after Matija had gone to Vermont to
inspect the quarry). It seemed to Sabbath—the first day that Matija had taken Silvija to see the sights, and Drenka was fucked on
Silvija's bed in Silvija's dirndl—that no two rooms in the house
were level with each other but had to be reached by going up or
down three, four, or five highly varnished, broad steps. And there
were wood carvings of kings on pedestals beside the stairways
between the rooms. A Boston antiques dealer had found them in
Vienna—seventeen medieval kings who, together, had to have
beheaded at least as many of their subjects as Matija had beheaded chickens for his popular chicken paprikash with noodles.
There were six beds in the house, all with brass frames. The pink
marble Jacuzzi could seat six. The modernistic kitchen with the
state-of-the-art cooking island at its heart could seat sixteen. The
dining room with the tapestried walls could seat thirty. Nobody,
however, used the Jacuzzi or entered the dining room, the Baliches
slept in just one claustrophobic bed, and the prepared food they
carried up from the inn late at night, they ate in front of a TV

console installed on four empty egg crates in a room as barren and humble as any you could have found in a worker's housing block built by Tito.

Because Matija was fearful lest his good fortune arouse envy in his guests no less than in his staff, the house had deliberately been situated behind a triangular expanse of firs said to be as old as any in New England. The stand of trees pointed dramatically heavenward, stately schooner masts that had been spared the colonial ax, and yet the roof lines of Matija's million-dollar house—conforming to his fanciful immigrant aim—looked at first glance to be going in every direction *except* up. Strange. The tamed, abstemious, frugal foreigner, beneficiary not merely of his own dedicated hard work but of the fat-cat blowout of the eighties, conceives for himself a palace of abundance, as grand a manifestation as he can imagine of his personal triumph over Comrade Tito, while his wife's intemperate lover, the native-born American hog, lives in a four-room little box built without a basement in the 1920s, a pleasant enough house by now but one that only Roseanna's ingenuity with a paintbrush and a sewing machine, and a hammer and nails, had been able to salvage from the dank Tobacco Road horror it was when, in the mid-sixties, Roseanna came up with the bright idea of domesticating Sabbath. Home and Hearth. The woods, the streams, the snow, the thaw, the spring, New England's spring, that surprise that is among the greatest reinvigorators of humankind on record. She pinned her hopes on the mountainous north—and a child. A family: a mother, a father, cross-country skis, and the kids, a lively, healthy band of shrieking kids, running unmenaced all over the place, enabled, by the very air they breathed, to avoid growing up like their malformed parents, entirely at the mercy of living. Rural domestication, the city dweller's old agrarian dream of "Live Free or Die" license plates on the Volvo, was the purifying rubric not simply by which she hoped and prayed she could put to rest her father's ghost but by which Sabbath could silence Nikki's. Little wonder Roseanna was in orbit from there on out.

There were no lights on at the Baliches', at least not that Sabbath could see through the fir-tree wall. He tapped twice on the horn, waited, tapped twice, and then sat for ten minutes till it was time to tap the horn once again and allow her five minutes more before driving away.

Drenka was a light sleeper. She'd become a light sleeper when she became a mother. The smallest noise, the tiniest cry of distress from little Matthew's room, and she was out of the bed and had him in her arms. She told Sabbath that when Matthew was a baby she would lie down and sleep on the floor beside his crib to be certain that he didn't stop breathing. And even when he got to be four and five, she would sometimes be seized in her bed by fears for his safety or his health and spend the night on the floor of his room. She had done her mothering the way she did everything, as though she were breaking down a door. Lead her into temptation, into motherhood, into software, you got the impress of all of her, all that rash energy without a single restraint. In full force this woman was extraordinary. To whatever was demanded, she had no aversion. Fear, of course, plenty of fear; but aversions, none. An amazing experience, this thoroughly unaloof Slav for whom her existence was a great experiment, the erotic light of his life, and he had found her not dangling a little key from her finger on Rue St. Denis between Châtelet and the archway of the Porte St. Denis but in Madamaska Falls, capital of caution, where the local population is content to be in raptures about changing the clock twice a year.

He rolled down the window and heard the Baliches' horses breathing in the paddock across the road. Then he saw two of them looming up by the fence. He opened a Stolichnaya bottle. He'd been drinking some since he went to sea but never like Roseanna. That moderation—and circumcision—were about all he had to show for being a Jew. Which was probably the best of it, anyway. He took two drinks and there she was, in her nightgown, with a shawl drawn around her shoulders. He reached out the window and there *they* were. Two hundred and sixty miles round-trip, but it was worth it for Drenka's breasts.

"What is it? Mickey, what's wrong!"

"Not much chance of a blow job, I guess."

"Darling, *no*."

"Get in the car."

"No. No. Tomorrow."

He took her flashlight out of her hand and shined it into his lap.

"Oh, it's so big. My darling! I can't now. Maté—"

"If he wakes up before I come, fuck it, we'll run away, we'll do it—I'll just turn on the motor and off we go like Vronsky and Anna. Enough of this hiding-out shit. Our whole *lives* are hiding."

"I mean Matthew. He's working. He could come by."

"He'll think we're kids necking. Get in, Drenka."

"We *can't*. You're crazy. Matthew knows the car. You're drunk. I have to go back! I love you!"

"Roseanna may be out tomorrow."

"But," she exclaimed, "I thought two more *weeks!*"

"What am I supposed to do with this thing?"

"You know what." Drenka leaned in through the open window, squeezed it, jerked it once—"Go *home*," she pleaded and then ran for the path back to the house.

On the fifteen-minute drive to Brick Furnace Road, Sabbath saw only one other vehicle on the road, the state police cruiser. That's why she was up—listening to the scanner. Warming to the biblical justice of being taken in for adulterous sodomy by her son, he sounded his horn and flashed his brights; but for the time being, the run of bad luck appeared to have ended. Nobody came tearassing after the county's leading sex offender and had him pull over to surrender his license and registration; no one invited him to justify how he came to be driving with a vodka bottle in his steering hand and a dick in the other, his focus not at all on the highway, not even on Drenka, but on that child's face that masked a mind whose core was all clarity, on that lanky blond with the droopy shoulders and the delicate voice and the freshly sliced wrist, who was just three weeks clear of going completely off the rails.

• • •

"'Pray, do not mock me. / I am a very foolish fond old man, / Four score and upward, not an hour more nor less, / And, to deal plainly, I fear I am not in my perfect mind. / Methinks . . .'"

Then he lost it, one stop north of Astor Place went completely dry. Yet remembering even that much while begging in the subway on the way to Linc's funeral after the soft-porn drama with the Cowans' Rosa was a huge mnemonic surprise. Methinks what? Methinking methoughts shouldn't be hard. The mind is the perpetual motion machine. You're not ever free of anything. Your mind's in the hands of *everything*. The personal's an immensity, nuncle, a constellation of detritus that doth dwarf the Milky Way; it pilots thee as do the stars the blind Cupid's arrow o' wild geese that o'erwing the Drenka goose'd asshole as, atop thy cancerous Croatian, their coarse Canadian honk thou libid'nously mimics, inscribing 'pon her malignancy, with white ink, thy squandered chromosomal mark.

Back up, back way, way up. Nikki says, "Sir, do you know me?" Lear says, "You are a spirit, I know. Where did you die?" Cordelia says blah, blah; the doctor says blah, blah; I say, "Where have I been? Where am I? Fair daylight? I am mightily abused . . . blah, blah, blah." Nikki: "O look upon me, sir, / And hold your hand in benediction o'er me. / No, sir, you must not kneel." And Lear says it was a Tuesday in December 1944, I came home from school and saw some cars, I saw my father's truck. Why is that there? I knew something was wrong. In the house I saw my father. In terrible pain. In terrible pain. My mother hysterical. Her hands. Her fingers. Moaning. Screaming. People there already. A man had come to the door. "I'm sorry," he said and gave her the telegram. Missing in action. Another month before the second telegram arrived, a tentative, chaotic time—hope, fear, searching for any story we could get, the phone ringing, never knowing, stories reaching us that he had been picked up by friendly Filipino guerrillas, someone in his squadron said he passed him in the flight, he was going on the last run, the flak got very bad and Morty's plane went down, but in friendly territory . . . and Lear replies, "You do me wrong to take me out o' the grave," but Sabbath is remembering the second telegram. The month before was terrible but not as terrible as this: the death notice was like losing *another* brother. Devastating. My mother in bed. Thought *she* was dying, afraid she was going to die too. Smelling salts. The doctor. The house filling up with people. It's hard to be clear about who was there. It's a blur. Everybody was there. But life was over. The family was finished. I was finished. I gave her smelling salts and they spilled and I was afraid I killed her. The tragic period of my life. Between fourteen and sixteen. Nothing to compare with it. It didn't just break her, it broke us all. My father, for the rest of his life, completely changed. He was a reassuring force to me, because of his physique and because he was so dependable. My mother was always the more emotional one. The sadder one, the happier one. Always whistling. But there was an impressive sobriety in my father. So to see *him* fall apart! Look at my emotions now—I'm fifteen remembering this stuff. Emotions, when they're revved up, don't change, they're the same, fresh and raw. Everything passes? *Nothing* passes. The same emotions are here! He was my *father,* a hardworking guy, out in the truck to the farmers at three in the morning. When he came home at night he was tired and we had to be quiet because he had to get up so early. And if he was ever angry—and that was rare—but if he was ever angry, he was angry in Yiddish and it was terrifying because I couldn't even be sure what he was angry about. But after, he was never angry again. If only he had been! After, he became meek, passive, crying all the time, crying everywhere, in the truck, with the customers, with the Gentile farmers. This fucking thing *broke* my father! After the *shiva* he went back to work again, after the year of official mourning he stopped crying, but there was always that personal, private misery that you could see a mile away. And I didn't feel so terrific myself. I felt I lost a part of my body. Not my prick, no, can't say a leg, an arm, but a feeling that was physiological and yet an interior loss. A hollowing out, as though I'd been worked on with a chisel. Like the horseshoe-crab shells lying along the beach, the armature intact and the inside empty. All of it gone. Hollowed out. Reamed out. Chiseled away. It was so oppressive. And my mother going to bed—I was *sure* I was going to lose my mother. How will she survive? How will any of us survive? There was such an emptiness everywhere. But I had to be the strong one. Even *before* I had to be the strong one. Very tough when he went overseas and all we knew was his APO number. The anxiety. Excruciating. Worried all the time. I used to help my father with the deliveries the way Morty did. Morty did things that nobody in his right mind would have done. Clambering around up on the roof fixing something. On his back, shimmying all the way into the dark crud under the porch, wiring something. Every week he washed the floors for my mother. So now I washed the floors. I did a lot of things to try to calm her down after he shipped out to the Pacific. Every week we used to go to the movies. They wouldn't go near a war movie. But even during an ordinary movie, when something suddenly cropped up about the war or somebody just said something about somebody overseas, my mother would get upset and I would have to calm her down. "Ma, it's just a movie." "Ma, let's not think about it." She would cry. Terribly. And I'd leave with her and walk her around. We used to get letters through the APO. He'd do little cartoons on the envelope sometimes. I'd looked forward to the cartoons. But the only one they cheered up was me. And once he flew over the house. He was stationed in North Carolina and he had to make a flight to Boston. He told us, "I'm going to fly over the house. In a B-25." All the women were outside in the street in their aprons. In the middle of the day my father came home in the truck. My friend Ron was there. And Morty did it—flew over and dipped his wings, those flat gull wings. Ron and I were waving. What a hero he was to me. He was incredibly gentle with me, five years younger—he was just so gentle. He had a real physique. A shot-putter. A track star. He could heave a football almost the whole length of the field; he had a tremendous capacity to toss a ball or to put the shot—to throw things, that was his skill, to throw them far. I would think of that after he was missing. In school I would be thinking that throwing things far might help him survive in the jungle. Shot down on the twelfth of December and died of wounds on the fifteenth. Which was another misery. They had him in a hospital. The rest of the crew was killed instantly, but the plane was shot down over guerrilla territory and the guerrillas got him out and to a hospital and he lived for three days. That made it even worse. *The crew was killed immediately and my brother lived three more days.* I was in a stupor. Ron came. Usually he as good as lived at our house. He said, "Come on out." I said, "I can't." He said, "What happened?" I couldn't talk. It took a few days before I could tell him. But I couldn't tell people at school. I couldn't do it. Couldn't *say* it. There was a gym teacher, a big, strong guy who had wanted Morty to give up track and train as a gymnast. "How's your brother?" he would ask me. "Fine," I'd say. I couldn't say it. Other teachers, his shop teacher, who always gave him A's: "How's your brother doing?" "Fine." And then they finally knew, but I never told them. "Hey, how's Morty doing?" And I perpetuated the lie. This went on and on with the people who hadn't heard. I was in my stupor for a year at least. I even got scared for a while of girls' having lipstick and having tits. Every challenge was suddenly too great. My mother gave me his watch. It nearly killed me, but I wore it. I took it to sea. I took it to the Army. I took it to Rome. Here it is, his GI Benrus. Wind it daily. All that's changed is the strap. Stop function on the second hand still working. When I was on the track team I used to think about his ghost. That was the first ghost. I was like my father and him, always strong up top. Besides, Morty threw the shot, so I *had* to. I *imbued* myself with him. I used to look up at the sky before I threw it and think that he was looking over me. And I called for strength. It was a state meet. I was in fifth place. I knew the unreality of it but I just kept praying to him and I threw it farther than I ever did before. I still didn't win, but I had got his strength!

I could use it now. Where is it? Here's the watch, but where's the strength?

In the seat to the right of where Sabbath had gone blank on "Methinks . . ." was what had caused him to go blank: no more than twenty-one or -two, sculpted entirely in black—turtleneck sweater, pleated skirt, tights, shoes, even a black velvet headband keeping her shining black hair back from her forehead. She had been gazing up at him, and it was the gaze that had stopped him, its meek, familiar softness. She sat with one arm resting on the black nylon backpack by her side, silently watching as he worked to recall the last scene of act four: Lear is carried sleeping into the French camp—"Ay, madam; in the heaviness of sleep / We put fresh garments on him"—and there to wake him is Cordelia— "How does my royal lord? How fares your majesty?" And it is then Lear replies, "You do me wrong to take me out o' the grave...."

The girl with the gaze was speaking, but so softly at first that he couldn't hear her. She was younger than he'd thought, probably a student, probably no more than nineteen.

"Yes, yes, speak up." What he was always telling Nikki whenever she said something she was afraid to say, which was half the time she spoke. She had driven him crazier with each passing year, saying things so that he couldn't hear them. "What did you say?" "It doesn't matter." Drove him *nuts*.

"'Methinks,'" she said, quite audibly now, "'I should know you, and know this man....'" She'd given him the line! A drama student, on her way uptown to Juilliard.

He repeated, "'Methinks I should know you, and know this man,'" and then on his own momentum proceeded. "'Yet I am doubtful; for I am mainly ignorant / What place this is; and all the skill I have...'" Here he *pretended* not to know what was next. "'And all the skill I have...'" Feebly, twice, he repeated this and looked to her for assistance.

"'Remembers not these garments,'" prompted the girl, "'nor I know not...'"

She stopped when, with a smile, he indicated that he believed he could himself once again pick up from there. She smiled back. "'Nor I know not / Where I did lodge last night. Do not laugh at me, / For, as I am a man, I think this lady...'"

Is Nikki's daughter.

Not impossible! Nikki's beautifully imploring eyes, Nikki's perplexingly, perpetually uncertain voice... no, she was not merely some tenderhearted, overimpressionable kid who would excitedly tell her family tonight that a white-bearded old bum had been reciting to her from *Lear* on the Lexington IRT and that she had dared to help him remember the lines—*she was Nikki's daughter.* The family she was going home to tonight was *Nikki's!* Nikki was alive. Nikki was in New York. This girl was hers. And if hers, somehow his, whoever the father might be.

Sabbath was hovering directly above her now, his emotions an avalanche rolling across him, sweeping him beneath them, uprooting the little rootedness still holding him to himself. What if they were *all* alive and at Nikki's house? Morty. Mom. Dad. Drenka. Abolishing death—a thrilling thought, for all that he wasn't the first person, on or off a subway, to have it, have it desperately, to renounce reason and have it the way he did when he was fifteen years old and they *had* to have Morty back. Turning life back like a clock in the fall. Just taking it down off the wall and winding it back and winding it back until your dead all appear like standard time.

"'For, as I am a man,'" he said to the girl, "'I think this lady / To be my child Cordelia.'"

"'And so I am, I am.'" Undesigning Cordelia's unguarded response, the poignantly simple iambic trimeter that Nikki had uttered in a voice one-tenth a lost orphan's and the rest a weary, teetering woman's, spoken by the girl whose gaze was Nikki's exactly.

"Who is your mother?" Sabbath whispered to her. "Tell me who your mother is."

The words made her go pale; her eyes, Nikki's eyes, which could hide nothing, were like those of a child who's just been told something terrible. All her horror of him came right up to the surface, as it would, sooner or later, in Nikki, too. To have been moved by this mad monstrosity because he could quote Shakespeare! To have become entangled on the subway with someone unmistakably crazy, capable of *anything*—how could she be so idiotic!

Simple as it was to read her thoughts, Sabbath declaimed, no less brokenly than Lear, "You are the daughter of Nikki Kantarakis!"

Frantically pulling open the straps of her knapsack, the girl tried to locate her purse and find money to give him, money to make him *go away.* But Sabbath had to see once more the fact that was indisputable—that Nikki lived—and turning her face with his crippled hand, *feeling Nikki's living skin,* he said, "Where is your mother hiding from me?"

"Don't!" she screamed, "don't touch me!" and was swatting at his arthritic fingers as though a swarm of flies had attacked her when somebody came up from behind him and with jarring force hooked Sabbath under the arms.

A business suit was all he could see of his powerful captor. "Calm down," he was being told, "calm down. You shouldn't drink that stuff."

"What *should* I drink? I'm sixty-four years old and I've never been sick a day in my life! Except my tonsils as a child! *I drink what I want!*"

"Calm *down,* Mac. Cut it out, calm down, and get yourself to a shelter."

"I caught lice in the shelter!" Sabbath boomed back. "'Do not abuse me'!"

"*You* abuse *her*—you're the abuser, chief!"

The train had reached Grand Central. People rushed for the open doors. The girl was gone. Sabbath was freed. "'Pray you now,'" shouted Sabbath as he wandered off the train alone, looking in all directions for Nikki's daughter. "'Pray you now,'" he exclaimed to those standing back from him as he strode majestically along the platform, shaking his cup out before him, "'pray you now . . .'" and then, without even Nikki's daughter to prompt him, he remembered what is next, words that could have meant nothing at all to him in the theater of the Bowery Basement Players in 1961: "'Pray you now, forget and forgive. I am old and foolish.'"

This was true. It was hard for him to believe that he was simulating any longer, though not impossible.

> Thou'lt come no more;
> Never, never, never, never, never.

Destroy the clock. Join the crowd.

It was Michelle Cowan, Norman's wife, who'd got the fifty tablets of Voltaren sent over from a pharmacy on Broadway and written him a prescription for four refills, and so he was in great form over dinner that evening because he knew that he'd soon be getting some relief from the pain in his hands, and also because Michelle was nothing like so gaunt as she'd looked in the Polaroid photos hidden beneath her lingerie along with that envelope of a hundred hundred-dollar bills. She was a nicely fleshed-out woman very much in the mold of Drenka. And she laughed so easily— so quick to be amused and entertained by him. And she'd done nothing at all to indicate distress after he stealthily hunted down beneath the table her unshod foot and lightly laid upon it the sole of his slipper.

The slippers were on loan from Norman. Norman had also sent his secretary out to an army-navy store to buy Sabbath a change of clothes. Two pairs of khakis, a couple of work shirts, some socks, undershirts, and briefs were all in a big paper bag on Debby's bed when they got home from the funeral. Even handkerchiefs. He looked forward to organizing his new things in among Debby's later that night.

Michelle's hidden Polaroids had to be at least five years old. Mementos of an old affair. Ready for a new one? She looked ripish all right, though maybe because she'd let herself go, gotten heavier, figuring it was over with men. Probably about Drenka's age but living with a husband who, of course, in no way resembled Drenka's Matija. Though sooner or later all husbands resemble Drenka's Matija, do they not?

The previous night Norm had described the antidepressant he was taking as not a "dick-friendly" drug. So here there was nobody fucking her, that much was clear. Not that Sabbath was about to take up the slack if she was getting a thousand bucks a shot. Though maybe it wasn't men who gave her the money but Michelle who gave money to men. Young men. In her laugh was the lowdown trace of a coarse rumble that made him want to believe that. Or maybe the cash was for the day she packed up and left.

The plan to leave. Who didn't have one? It evolves as tortuously as the wills of propertied people, rewrites and revisions every six months. I'll go stay with this one; no, I'll go stay with that one; this hotel, that hotel, this woman, that woman, two different women, with *no* woman, no woman ever again! I'll open a secret account, hock the ring, sell the bonds. . . . Then they get to be sixty, sixty-five, seventy, and what difference does it make anymore? They're going to leave all right, but this time they're *really* going to leave. For some people this is the best thing to be said for death: finally out of the marriage. And without having to wind up in a hotel. Without having to live through those miserable Sundays alone in a hotel. It's the Sundays that keep these couples together. As if Sundays alone could be any worse.

No, this is not a good marriage. You wouldn't be far off guessing that much no matter whose table you happened to be eating at, but Sabbath could tell from that laugh—if not from the fact that he was being permitted to play footsie with her only ten minutes into the meal—that something had turned out wrong. In her laugh was the recognition that she was no longer in charge of the forces at work. In her laugh was the admission of her captivity: to Norman, to menopause, to work, to aging, to everything that could only deteriorate further. Nothing unforeseen that happens is likely ever again to be going to be good. What is more, Death is over in its corner doing deep knee bends and one day soon will leap across the ring at her as mercilessly as it leaped upon Drenka—because even though she's at her heaviest ever, weighing in at around one thirty-five, one forty, Death is Two-Ton Tony Galento and Man Mountain Dean. The laugh said that everything had shifted on her while her back was turned, while she was facing the other way, the *right* way, her arms open wide to the dynamic admixture of demands and delights that had been the daily bread of her thirties and forties, to all that assiduous activity, all the extravagant, holidaylike living—so inexhaustibly *busy* . . . with the result that in no more time than it took for the Cowans to cross the ocean on the Concorde for a long weekend in Paris, she was fifty-five and seared with hot flashes, and her daughter's was now the female form exuding the magnetic currents. The laugh said that she was sick of staying, sick of plotting leaving, sick of unsatisfied dreams, sick of satisfied dreams, sick of adapting, sick of not adapting, sick of just about everything except existing. Exulting in existing while being sick of everything—*that's* what was in that laugh! A semidefeated, semiamused, semiaggrieved, semiamazed, seminegative, hilarious big laugh. He liked her, liked her enormously. Probably just as insufferable a mate as he was. He could discern in her, whenever her husband spoke, the desire to be just a little cruel to Norman, saw her sneering at the best of him, at the very best things in him. If you don't go crazy because of your husband's vices, you go crazy because of his virtues. He's on Prozac because he can't win. Everything is leaving her except for her behind, which her wardrobe informs her is broadening by the season—and except for this steadfast prince of a man marked by reasonableness and ethical obligation the way others are scarred by insanity or illness. Sabbath understood her state of mind, her state of life, her state of suffering: dusk is descending, and sex, our greatest luxury, is racing away at a tremendous speed, *everything* is racing off at a tremendous speed and you wonder at your folly in having ever turned down a single squalid fuck. You'd give your right arm for one if you are a babe like this. It's not unlike the Great Depression, not unlike going broke overnight after years of raking it in.

"Nothing unforeseen that happens," the hot flashes inform her, "is likely ever again to be going to be good." Hot flashes mockingly mimicking the sexual ecstasies. Dipped, she is, in the very fire of fleeting time. Aging seventeen days for every seventeen seconds in the furnace. He clocked her on Morty's Benrus. Seventeen seconds of menopause oozing out all over her face. You could baste her in it. And then it just stops like a tap that's been shut. But while she is in it, he can see how it seems to her that there's no bottom to it—that this time they're out to cook her like Joan of Arc.

Nothing quite touches Sabbath like these aging dishes with the promiscuous pasts and the pretty young daughters. Especially when they've still got it in them to laugh like this one. You see all they once were in that laugh. I am what's left of the famous motel fucking—hang a medal on my drooping boobs. It's no fun burning on a pyre at dinner.

And Death, he reminded her by evenly pressing down on her naked instep with the ball of his foot, on top of us, over us, ruling us, Death. You should have seen Linc. You should have seen him all quieted down like a good little boy, a good little boy with green skin and white hair. Why was he green? He wasn't green when I knew him. "It's frightening," Norman had said after quickly identifying the corpse. They walked out into the street and over to a coffee shop for a Coke. "It's spooky," said Norman, with a shudder. Yet Sabbath enjoyed it. Exactly what he'd driven all this way to see. Learned a lot, Michelle. You lie in there like a good little boy who does what he is told.

And as if pressing Michelle Cowan's foot beneath his own wasn't sufficient reason to live, there were his new khaki trousers and his new Jockey briefs. A big bagful of clothes such as he had not thought to buy for himself in years. Even handkerchiefs. Long time between handkerchiefs. All the tattered shit he wore, the T-shirts yellowing under the arms, the boxer shorts with the elasticity shot, the unmatched remnants that were his socks, the big-tipped boots he sported like Mammy Yokum twelve months a year. . . . Were the boots what they call a "statement"? This fucking way they talk made him feel like a curmudgeon. Diogenes in his tub? Making a statement! He'd noticed that the college girls down in the valley were all now wearing clodhoppers not unlike his own, kind of lace-up construction boots, along with lacy maiden-aunt dresses. Feminine in the dress but not conventionally feminine, because there's something else there in the shoes. The shoes say, "I'm tough. Don't mess with me," while the lacy, long, old-fashioned dress says . . . so that altogether we've got ourselves a *statement,* something like, "If you would be kind enough, sir, to try to fuck me, I'll kick your fucking head in." Even Debby, with her low self-esteem, gets burnished up like Cleopatra. Haute couture has been passing me by, along with everything else. Wait'll I hit the streets in my khakis. Manhattan, let me in!

He was sublimely effervescent about not being the good little boy in the box doing what he was told. Also over not having been turned in by Rosa. She'd said nothing to anyone about their morning. The mercy there is in life, and none of it deserved. All our crimes against each other, and still we get another shot at it in a new pair of pants!

Outside the funeral home, after the service, Linc's eight-year-old grandson, Joshua, had said to his mother—whose hand was in Norman's—"Who were the people talking about?"

"Grandpa. Linc was his name. You know that. Lincoln."

"But that wasn't Grandpa," the boy said. "That wasn't what he was like."

"Wasn't it?"

"No. Grandpa was like a baby."

"But not always, Josh. When he got sick he became like a baby. But before, he was just as all his friends described him."

"That wasn't Grandpa," he replied, determinedly shaking his head. "Sorry, Mom."

Linc's littlest grandchild named Laurie. A tiny, energetic girl with large, dark, sensual eyes who raced up to Sabbath on the pavement after the service and said, "Santa, Santa, I'm three! They put Grandpa in a box!"

The box that never failed to impress. Whatever your age, the sight of that box never lost its power. One of us takes up no more room than that. You can store us like shoes or ship us like lettuce. The simpleton who invented the coffin was a poetic genius and a great wit.

"What would you like for Christmas?" Sabbath asked the child, kneeling to satisfy her desire to touch his beard.

"Chanukah!" Laurie shouted with great excitement.

"It's yours," he told her and restrained the impulse to touch with a crooked finger her clever little mouth and thereby wind up where he began.

Where he began. That indeed was the subject. The obscene performance with which he'd begun.

It was Norman who'd started it off, describing for Michelle the skit that had got Sabbath arrested out in front of the gates of Columbia back in 1956, that skit in which the middle finger of his left hand would beckon a pretty young student right up to the screen and then enter into conversation with her while the five fingers of the other hand had begun deftly to unbutton her coat.

"Describe it, Mick. Tell Shel how you got arrested."

Mick and Shel. Shel and Mick. A duo if ever there was one. And Norman seemed to recognize that already, to understand after less than half an hour at the dinner table that in Sabbath's down-and-outness there might be more to stir his wife than in all his own orderly success. There was in the aging Sabbath's failure a threat of disarray not unlike the danger there used to be to Norman in young Sabbath's eruptive-disruptive vitality. My misbehaving always imperiled him. He should know what it's done to me. This mighty fortress built to withstand the remotest intimation of mayhem, and yet here near the end, as at the beginning, he continues to be humbled by the stinky little mess I make of things. I frighten him. As my father said, "*Bolbotish.*" This generous, lovely, *bolbotish* success continues to kowtow to a putz. You'd think I'd burst forth in a boiling blaze, incandescent from Pandemonium, instead of having driven down 684 in an ancient Chevy with a busted tailpipe.

"How I got arrested," Sabbath said. "Four decades, Norm.

Almost forty years. I don't know that I remember anymore how I got arrested." He did, of course. Had never forgotten any of it.

"You remember the girl."

"The girl," he repeated.

"Helen Trumbull," Norman said.

"That was her name? Trumbull? And the judge?"

"Mulchrone."

"Yes. Him I remember. Gave a great performance. Mulchrone. The cop was Abramowitz. Right?"

"Officer Abramowitz, yes."

"Yes. The cop was a Jew. And the prosecutor another Irishman. That kid with the crew cut."

"Just out of St. John's," said Norman. "Foster."

"Yes. Very disagreeable, Foster. Didn't like me. Outraged. Genuinely outraged. How can anyone do this? Yes. Guy from St. John's. That's right. Crew cut, rep tie, his father's a cop, he never thinks he'll earn more than ten thousand dollars a year and he wants to send me up for life."

"Tell Shelly."

Why? What's he up to, showing me in my best light or in my worst? Turning her on to me or turning her off? It had to be off, because before dinner, alone in the living room with Sabbath, he had lavished on his wife and her work a uxorious deluge of admiration—what Roseanna had been dying for, thirsting for, all her married life. While Michelle was showering and changing for dinner, Norman had shown him, in a recent alumni magazine from the University of Pennsylvania dental school, a photograph of Michelle and her father, an old man in a wheelchair, one of several pictures illustrating a story about parents and children who were Penn dental school graduates. Before his stroke and well into his seventies, Michelle's father had been a dentist in Fairlawn, New Jersey, according to Norman an overbearing bastard whose own father had been a dentist and who had pronounced at Michelle's birth, "I don't give a shit that she's a girl— this is a dental family, and she's going to be a dentist!" As it turned out, she had not merely gone to his dental school but

outdone the hard-driving son of a bitch by taking two more years
to become a periodontist and ending up at the top of her class. "I
can't tell you," said Norman, nursing the evening glass of wine he
said he was allowed while on Prozac, "what a physical trial being
a periodontist is. Most days she gets home just like tonight, beat.
Imagine going with an instrument and trying to clean the back
outer corner of an upper second or third molar and trying to get
up into that pocket there, up in the gum. Who can see? Who can
reach? She's physically amazing. Over twenty years of this. I've
said to her, why don't you think of cutting the practice back to
three days a week? With periodontal disease you see your patients
year after year, forever—her patients will wait for her. But no,
she's out every morning at seven-thirty and isn't home until seven-
thirty, and some weeks she's even in there on Saturdays." Yes,
Saturday, Sabbath was thinking, must be a big day for Shelly . . .
while Norman was explaining, "If you're meticulous in the way
that Michelle is, and you've got to do a cleaning around every
surface of every tooth in unreachable places . . . Granted, she's got
instruments with curves that help; she's got these instruments she
cleans these roots with called scalers and curettes, because she's
not just dealing with the crown portion like a hygienist. She's got
to do this up to the root surfaces if there are pockets, if there is
bone loss—" How he praises her! How much he cares! How
much he knows—and doesn't. Before dinner, Sabbath had been
wondering whether the encomium was designed to keep him at
bay or whether it was the drug speaking. I may be listening to
Prozac. Or maybe I am merely listening to his wife's elaborate
excuses for Working Late at the Office—to somebody lamely repeating, as if he believed it, something somebody else told them to
believe about them. "Because up there," Norman continued, "is
where the action is. It's not just to shine the enamel and make
pretty teeth. It's to pick the tartar, which can be very adherent—
and I've seen her come home *limp* after a day of this stuff—it's to
snap the tartar off the roots. Sure, there are ultrasonic instruments that help. They use an ultrasonic device, runs on an electrical current, emits ultrasonic energy, goes up into the pocket there

to help crack off all the crap. But so it doesn't overheat, there's of course a water spray, and it's like living in a fog, with that water spray. Living in the mist. It's like spending twenty years in the rain forest. . . ."

So she was an Amazon, was that it? Daughter of a once-terrifying tribal chief whom she had conquered and gone beyond, an Amazon warrior, emitting ultrasonic energy, armed against barnacled tartar with stainless steel scalers and curving curettes . . . what *was* Sabbath to conclude? That she was too much for Norman? That he was as perplexed by her as he was proud of her—and overpowered? That now that the youngest child was off at college and it was just him and the dental dynasty heiress alone together side by side . . . Sabbath didn't know what to think in the living room, before dinner, any more than he did at the table, with Norman urging him to tell the story of the defiant outsider that he'd been in his twenties, so unlike Norman himself starting out, the well-groomed, well-mannered Columbia-educated son of the jukebox distributor whose croaking voice and crude success had shamed Norman throughout his youth. The son and the daughter of two brutes. Only I had the gently loving father, and look how it all turned out.

"Well, so there I am. 1956. On 116th and Broadway, just by the university gates there. Twenty-seven years old. The cop has been standing around for days watching. There are usually about twenty, twenty-five students. Some passersby, but mostly students. Afterward I pass the hat. The whole thing takes less than thirty minutes. I think I got a breast out once before. To get a kid to go that far with me, rare in those days. I didn't expect it. The idea of the act was that I *couldn't* get that far. But this time it happened. The tit is out. It's out. And the cop comes up and he says, 'Hey, you, you can't do that.' He's calling this down to me back of the screen. 'It's all right, Officer,' I tell him, 'it's part of the show.' I stayed down and the middle finger said it to him, the one that had been talking to the girl. I figure, 'Great, now I've got a cop in the show.' The kids watching aren't sure he *isn't* part of the show. They start laughing. 'You can't do that,' he tells me. 'There are children here. They can see the breast.' 'There aren't any children here,' the finger says. 'Get up,' he tells me, 'stand up. You can't expose that breast on the street. You can't have a breast exposed in the middle of Manhattan at twelve-fifteen at 116th Street and Broadway. And also, you're taking advantage of this young woman. Do you want him to do this to you?' the cop asks her. 'Is there a sexual molestation charge here?' 'No,' she says, 'I permitted him to do it.'"

"The girl's a student," Michelle said.

"Yep. Barnard student."

"Brave," said Michelle. "'I permitted him to do it.' What'd the policeman do?"

"He says, 'Permitted? You were hypnotized. This guy hypnotized you. You didn't know he was doing it to you.' 'No,' she says to him defiantly, 'it was okay.' She was frightened when the cop came but there she was with all the other students, and students are generally anti-cop, so she just picked up the mood and she went with it. She said, 'It's all right, Officer—leave him alone. He wasn't doing anything wrong.'"

"Sound like Debby?" Michelle said to Norman.

Sabbath waited to see how the Prozac would field that one. "Let him go on," Norman said.

"So the cop says to the girl, 'I can't leave him alone. There could be kids here. What would people say about the police if they just allowed blouses to be opened and breasts to be out on the street and someone publicly twisting a nipple? You want me to let him do it in Central Park? Have you done it,' he asks me, 'in Central Park?' 'Well,' I said, 'I have my show in Central Park.' 'No, no,' he says to me, 'you can't do this. People are complaining. The guy who owns the drugstore over there is complaining, get these people away from here, it's not good for his business.' I told him I wasn't aware of that—if anything, I felt the drugstore hurt *my* business. This got a rise from the kids, and now he's getting pissed off. 'Listen, this young woman didn't want her breast out and she wasn't even aware of it until I pointed it out to her. She was hypnotized by you.' 'I *was* aware of it,' the girl says, and all the kids applaud her—they're really impressed by her. 'Officer, listen,' I said, 'what I did was okay. She agreed to it. It was just fun.' 'It was not fun. It's not my idea of fun. It's not that druggist over there's idea of fun. You can't use that kind of behavior here.' 'Okay, so okay,' I said, 'now what are you going to do about it? I can't stand around talking all day. I got a living to make.' The kids love this, too. But the cop remains decent, given the circumstances. All he says is, 'I want you to tell me you're not going to do it again.' 'But it's my act. It's my art.' 'Oh, don't give me that shit about your art. What does playing with a nipple have to do with art?' 'It's a new art form,' I tell him. 'Oh, bullshit, bullshit, you bums are always telling me about your art.' 'I'm not a bum. This is what I do for my livelihood, Officer.' 'Well, you're not doing this livelihood in New York. You have a license?' 'No.' 'Why don't you have a license?' 'You can't get a license for it. I'm not selling potatoes. There is no license for a puppeteer.' 'I don't see puppets.' 'I carry my puppet between my legs,' I said. 'Watch it, shorty. I don't see puppets. I just see fingers. And there *is* a license for a puppeteer—there's a street license for acting—' 'I can't get that.' 'Of course you can get it,' he tells me. 'I *can't*. And I can't go down there and wait four or five hours to find out I can't.' 'Okay,' says the cop, 'so you're vending without a license.' 'There's no vending license,' I tell him, 'for touching women's breasts on the street.' 'So you *admit* that's what you do.' 'Oh, shit,' I say, 'this is ridiculous.' And the whole thing starts to get belligerent and he tells me he's going to take me in."

"And the girl?" Michelle again.

"The girl's good. The girl says, 'Hey, leave him alone.' And the cop says, 'You trying to interfere with this arrest?' 'Leave him alone!' she tells him."

"This *is* Debby," Michelle laughed. "Absolutely Deborah."

"Is it?" Sabbath asked.

"To a T." She's proud.

"The cop grabs me because I'm starting to be a real pain in the ass. I say, 'Hey, I'm not going in. This is silly,' and he says, 'You are,' and the girl says, 'Leave him alone,' and he says, 'Listen, if you keep doing this, I'll take you in also.' 'This is crazy,' the girl says, 'I just came from my physics class. I didn't do anything.' Things get out of control and the cop pushes her out of the way, and so I start shouting, 'Hey, don't push her.' 'Oh,' he says to me, 'Sir Galahad.' In 1956 a cop could still say something like that. This was before the decline of the West spread from the colleges to the police departments. Anyway, he takes me in. He lets me get all my apparatus together and he takes me in."

"With the girl," Michelle said.

"No. Just took me. 'I want to book this guy,' he tells the booking officer. The precinct station on 96th Street. I got scared, of course. When you walk into a station, there's a big desk up front with a booking officer, and this big desk scares you. I said, 'This is absolutely *bullshit*,' but when Abramowitz says, 'This guy should be booked for vending without a license, disorderly conduct, harassment, assault, and obscenity. And resisting arrest. And obstruction of justice,' when I heard this, I think I'm going to serve for the rest of my life and I went nuts. 'This is all bullshit! I'll get the ACLU! This'll be the end of you!' I tell the cop. I'm shitting my pants but that's what I'm shouting. 'Yeah, the ACLU,' Abramowitz says, 'those Red bastards. Great.' 'I'm not going to say anything till I get a lawyer from the ACLU!' Now the cop is shouting, 'Fuck them. Fuck you. We don't need a lawyer. We're just going to arrest you now, shorty—you bring a lawyer here when you got to be in court.' The desk sergeant is listening to all this. He says to me, 'Tell me what happened, young man.' I don't know from shit what it means, but I just say again and again, 'I'm not going to tell you till I get a lawyer!' And Abramowitz is now deep in the fuck-you mode. But the other guy says, 'What happened, son?' I think, Tell him; he's not a bad guy. So I said, 'Listen, this is all that happened. And he went crazy. He went crazy because he saw a breast. It happens all the time. Kids are making out on the street. This guy lives in Queens—he doesn't know what's happening. Does he ever see the way girls walk around here in the summer? Everybody on the street knows except this guy who lives in Queens. An exposed breast is no big deal.' So Abramowitz says, 'It's not just an exposed breast. You don't know her, you never met her, you unnippled it, you unbuttoned it, she really didn't know what was going on, you were distracting her with the finger and you hurt her.' '*I* didn't hurt her—*you* hurt her. You *pushed* her.' The desk sergeant says, 'You mean to say you totally undressed a woman on Broadway?' 'No! No! All I did was this.' And I explained again. The guy was fascinated. 'How could you, on an open street, with a woman you never met before?' 'My art, Sergeant. That's my art.' This breaks him up," said Sabbath, seeing it breaking Michelle up, too. And Norman, so happy! Watching from a foot away while I seduce his wife. This Prozac is some drug.

"'Harry,' the desk sergeant says to Abramowitz, 'why don't you leave the kid alone? He's not a bad kid. All he did was his art.' He's still laughing. 'Finger painting. Baby shit. What's the difference? He has no record. He's not going to do it again. If the kid had seventeen molestation charges . . .' But Abramowitz is furious now. 'No! That's my street. Everybody knows me there. He was abusive to me.' 'How?' 'He pushed me away.' 'He touched you? He touched a police officer?' 'Yeah. He touched me.' So now I'm not up for touching the girl; now I'm up for touching the cop. Which I never did, but of course the desk sergeant, after trying to placate Harry, switches and goes over to Harry's side. To the arresting officer's side. And so they charge me with all this stuff. The cop makes out an affidavit as to what happened. And a complaint is issued against me. Seven charges. I can get a year for each. I'm commanded to appear at Sixty Centre Street—that it, Norm? Sixty Centre?"

"Sixty Centre Street, in Part Twenty-two, at two-thirty in the afternoon. You remember everything."

"So how did you get a lawyer?" Michelle asked him.

"Norman. Norman and Linc. I got a phone call, either from Norm or Linc."

"Linc," said Norman. "Poor Linc. In that box."

Got him, too. And it's only a box. Never seems to become clichéd.

"Linc said, 'We understand you got arrested. We've got a lawyer for you. Not a little shmegeggy just out of law school but some guy who's been around for a while. Jerry Glekel. He's done fraud cases, assault and battery, robbery, burglary. He does organized-crime work. It pays very well but the work is not marvelous, and this he's willing to do as a favor to me.' Right, Norm? A favor to Linc, whom he somehow knows. Glekel says this is all bullshit and in all probability it'll be dismissed. I talk to Glekel. I'm still hot on the ACLU, so he goes to the Civil Liberties Union and tells them this is a case he thinks they should support. I'll represent him, he says. You should support him, submit an amicus brief. We'll make it an ACLU-sponsored case. Glekel's got it all figured out. What it deals with really is artistic freedom on the streets, arbitrary control by the police of the streets. Who controls the streets? The people or the police force? Two people doing something that's innocuous, that's playful—the defenses are all obvious, just another case of police abuse. Why should a kid like this have to spend X and Y and Z, et cetera? So we came to trial. About twenty-two people show up at the trial. Lost in the big courtroom. The civil rights student group from Columbia. About twelve kids and their adviser. Somebody from the *Columbia Spectator*. Somebody from the Columbia radio station. They're not there because of me. They're there because this girl, Helen Trumbull, is saying that I did nothing wrong. In 1956, this creates a tiny stir. Where'd she get the guts? This is still years before Charlotte Moorman is playing the cello bare-breasted down in the Village, and this is just a kid, not a performer. There's even somebody sitting there from the *Nation*. They got wind of it. And there's the judge. Mulchrone. Old Irish guy, former prosecutor. Tired. Very tired. He doesn't want to hear this shit. He doesn't care. There are murders and killings in the street, and here he is wasting his time with a guy who twisted a nipple. So he's not in the best of moods. The prosecutor is the young boy from St. John's, who wants to put me behind bars for life. The trial starts at two, two-thirty, and about an hour before, he has the witnesses down in his office running them through the lies. And then they get on the stand and they do their stuff. Three of them, as I remember it. Some old lady who says the girl kept trying to push my hand away but I wouldn't stop. And the druggist, the Jewish druggist, humanistically outraged as only a Jewish druggist can be. He could only see the back of the woman but he testified that she was upset. Glekel cross-examines him, contending that the druggist couldn't have seen it, because the girl had her back to him. Twenty minutes of his Jewish druggist lies. And the cop testifies. He's called at the beginning. He testified, and I'm nuts— I'm angry, I'm squirming, I'm furious. Then I got up and testified. The prosecutor asks me, 'Did you ever ask the woman if you could unbutton her shirt?' 'No.' '*No?* Did you know who was in the audience at the time?' 'No.' 'Did you know that there were kids in the audience?' 'There were no kids in the audience.' 'Can you state under oath, as a matter of certainty, that there were no kids in the audience? You're down *there* and they're up *here*. Didn't you see seven kids walking at the back there?' And the druggist, you see, will testify that there were seven kids, and the old lady, too, all of them, you see, they all want to hang me because of the tit. 'Look, this is a form of art.' This gets a rise every time. The kid from St. John's makes a face. 'Art? What you did was you unbuttoned a woman's breast, and that's art? How many other women's dresses have you unbuttoned?' 'Actually it rarely has ever happened that I've got that far. Unfortunately. But that's the art. The art is being able to get them into the act.' The judge, Mulchrone, the first thing he says, he says now. Flat voice. 'Art.' Like he's just been wakened from the dead. 'Art.' The prosecutor won't even get into the dialogue, it's so absurd. Art! He says to me, 'You have any kids?' 'No.' 'You don't care about kids. You have a job?' 'This is my job.' 'You don't have a job. Have a wife?' 'No.' 'Ever had a job that lasted more than six months?' 'Merchant seaman. U.S. Army. GI Bill in Italy.' So he's got me nailed. He delivers his shot. 'You call yourself an artist. I call you a drifter.' Then my lawyer calls the professor from NYU. Big mistake. This was Glekel's idea. They had professors to argue the *Ulysses* case, they had professors to argue the 'Miracle' case— why shouldn't we have a professor to argue *your* case? I didn't want it. The professors are as full of shit on the stand as the druggist and the cop. Shakespeare was a great street artist. Proust was a great street artist. And so on. He was going to compare me and my act to Jonathan Swift. The professors are always schlepping in Swift to defend some *farshtunkeneh* nobody. Anyway, in about two seconds the judge learns he's not a witness—he's an *expert* witness. To Mulchrone's credit, he is baffled. 'What's he an expert on?' 'That street art is a valid form of art,' my lawyer says, 'and what they were doing, this interplay on the streets, is traditional.' The judge covers his face. It's three-thirty in the afternoon and the man has heard a hundred and twelve cases before me. He is seventy years old and he has been on the bench all day. He says, 'This is absolute nonsense. I'm not going to listen to a professor. He touched a breast. What happened is he touched a breast. I don't need any testimony from a professor. The professor can go home.' Glekel: 'No, Your Honor. There is a larger perspective to this case. And the larger perspective is that there is legitimate street art and what happens in street art is that you can engage people in a way that you can't engage them in a theater.' And all the time Glekel is speaking, the judge is still covering his face. The judge covers his face even when he himself is speaking. The whole of *life* makes him want to cover his face. He's right, too. He was a wonderful man, Mulchrone. I miss him. He knew the score. But my lawyer goes on, Glekel goes on. Glekel is sick of doing organized-crime work. He has higher aspirations. I think mostly now he is directing his argument to the reporter from the *Nation*. 'It's the intimacy of street art,' he says, 'that makes it unique.' 'Look,' Mulchrone says, 'he touched a breast on the street in order to get some laughs or in order to get some attention. Isn't that right, sonny?' So the prosecutor has three witnesses and the cop against me, and we don't have the professor, but we've got the girl. We've got Helen Trumbull. The wild card is this girl. It was unusual that she should come down there. Here's the alleged victim testifying for the perpetrator. Though Glekel is saying this is a victimless crime. In fact, the victim, if there even is one, is coming his way, but the prosecutor says no, the victim is the public. The poor public, getting the shaft from this fucking drifter, this *artist*. If this guy can walk along the street, he says, and do this, then little kids think it's permissible to do this, and if little kids think it's permissible to do this, then they think it's permissible to blah blah banks, rape women, use knives. If seven-year-old kids—the seven nonexistent kids are now seven seven-year-*old* kids—are going to see that this is fun and permissible with strange women . . ."

"And what happened with the girl?" Michelle asked. "When she testified."

"What do you want to have happened?" Sabbath asked her.

"How did she hold up?"

"She's a middle-class girl, a nervy girl, a terrific, defiant girl, but once she gets in the court, how do you expect she held up? She gets scared. Out on the street, she was a good kid, she had guts—116th Street and Broadway is a young people's world—but here in the courtroom, the alliance is the cops, the prosecutor, and the judge . . . it's their world, they believe each other, and you've got to be blind not to see it. So how does she testify? In a scared voice. Goes there meaning to help me, but once she walks into the courtroom, a big room, big walls, JUSTICE FOR ALL written up there in wood—she gets scared."

"Debby," said Michelle.

"The girl testifies that she didn't scream. The druggist said she screamed and she says she never screamed. 'You mean to say a man is touching your breast in the middle of Manhattan, doing this, and you didn't scream out?' See, sounds like she's a whore. That's what he wants to establish, that Debby," says Sabbath, altogether deliberately, but pretending not even to have heard his own error, "is a whore." Nobody corrects him. "'How often do men touch your breasts in the middle of the street?' 'Never.' 'Were you surprised, were you upset, were you shocked, were you this, were you that?' 'I didn't notice.' 'You didn't *notice*?' The kid is getting nervous as hell but she hangs in. 'It was part of the game.' 'Do you generally have men play games with your breasts in the middle of the street? A man you didn't know, a man you'd never spoken to, a man whose face you couldn't see?' 'But he testified I screamed,' Debby says; 'I *never* screamed.'"

"Helen," Norman said.

"Trumbull," Sabbath said. "Helen Trumbull."

"You said Debby."

"No, I said Helen."

"It doesn't matter," Michelle said. "What happened to her?"

"Well, he really goes to work on her. For old St. John's. For his father the cop. For morality. For America. For Cardinal Spellman. For the Vatican. For Jesus and Mary and Joseph and all the gang there in the manger, for the donkeys and the cows there in the manger, for the wise men and the myrrh and the frankincense, for the whole fucking Catholic schmeer that we all need like a fucking hole in the head, this kid from St. John's really tears into Debby's ass. He brutalizes her. He kicks her every fucking which way. I twist nipples out on the street, but this guy goes right for the cunt. Remember? Yeah, I remember, Norm. A real clitorectomy, the first I ever had the privilege to see. He cut her little fucking weenie right off her, right there, right under where it says JUSTICE FOR ALL, and the judge and the cop and the druggist ate it up. Yeah, he really broke her down. 'Have you ever walked into class with your breasts exposed?' 'No.' 'When you were at Bronx Science high school, before you came to Barnard to become a defender of artistic freedom, did anybody at Bronx Science ever touch your breasts in full view of the other students?' 'No.' 'But weren't some of those students friends of yours? Isn't it less embarrassing to do it in front of friends than in front of strangers in the street?' 'No. Yes. I don't know.' Uh-oh—score this round for the gang in the manger. He's finally got her thinking that she may be *in the wrong.* Have you ever exposed your breasts on 115th Street, 114th Street, 113th Street—and what about the little kids who were watching? 'There *were* no little kids.' 'Listen, you're standing *here,* this guy is performing *there*—this whole thing took a minute and a half. Did you see who was walking behind you during that minute and a half? Yes or no?' 'No.' 'It's noon. Kids are on lunch hour. You have kids from the music school up there, you have kids from private schools. Do you have a brother or a sister?' 'Yes. Both.' 'How old are they?' 'Twelve and ten.' 'Your sister is ten. How would you like your ten-year-old sister to know what you allowed a man you didn't know to do to you in full view of 116th Street and Broadway, with dozens of cars passing, hundreds of people walking around? For you to be standing there while this man is twisting your nipple—how do you feel about telling that to your sister?' Debby tries to brazen it out. 'I wouldn't mind.' I wouldn't mind. What a girl! If I could find her today and if she would let me, I'd get down on 116th Street and Broadway and lick the soles of her feet. *I wouldn't mind.* In 1956. 'And how about if he did it to your sister?' This gets her back up. 'My sister's only ten,' she says. 'Have you told this to your mother?' 'No.' 'Have you told this to your father?' 'No.' 'No. And so isn't it true, then, that the reason you're testifying for him is that you feel sorry for him? It's not because you think what he did was right, is it? Is it? Is it, Debby?' Well, by now she's in tears. They did it. They've done it. They've pretty well proved that this girl is a whore. I went nuts. Because the basic lie in this case is that there are kids there. And what if there even were? I stood up, I screamed, 'If there are so many kids, why aren't there any kids testifying here!' But the prosecutor likes that I screamed. Glekel is trying to get me to sit down but the prosecutor says to me, and the voice is *very* holy, he says, 'I wasn't going to drag kids in here and expose them to this. I'm not you.' 'Fuckin' A, you're not! And if kids wander by, what are they going to do—drop dead? *This is part of the show!*' Well, shouting like that, I didn't do my cause much more good than the girl did. She goes off in tears, and the judge asks if anybody has any more witnesses. Glekel: 'I'd like to sum up, Your Honor.' The judge: 'I don't need it. It's not that complicated. You're telling me that, if this guy is having intercourse with her in the middle of the street, that's also art? And I can't do anything about it because it has antecedents in Shakespeare and the Bible? Come on. Where do you draw the line between this and intercourse in the street? Even if she consents.' So I got convicted."

"On which grounds?" Michelle asked. "All of them?"

"No, no. Disorderly conduct and obscenity. Obscene performance on the street."

"What *is* 'disorderly conduct' anyway?"

"I am disorderly conduct. The judge can sentence me anywhere up to a year for each offense. But he's not a bad guy. It's almost four o'clock now in the afternoon. He looks out into the courtroom and he's got twelve more cases out there, or twenty, and he wants to go home and have a drink in the worst way. He looks like he's four hundred miles southwest of the nearest drink. He does not look good. I didn't know what arthritis was then. Today my heart goes out to him. He's got it all over and the pain is driving him nuts, but still he says to me, 'Are you going to do this again, Mr. Sabbath?' 'It's how I make my living, Your Honor.' He covers his face and tries me a second time. 'Are you going to do this again? I want you to promise me that, if I don't put you in jail, you won't do this and you won't touch that and you won't touch this.' 'I can't,' I say. St. John's sneers. Mulchrone: 'If you're telling me that you committed a crime and you're going to do it again, I'm going to give you thirty days in jail.' Here Jerry Glekel, my ACLU lawyer, whispers in my ear, 'Say you won't do it. Fuck him. Just say it.' Jerry leans over and says, 'Fuck him—let's get out of here.' 'Your Honor, I won't do it.' 'You won't do it. That's wonderful. Thirty days, sentence suspended. A fine of one hundred dollars, payable now.' 'I have no money, Your Honor.' 'What do you mean, you don't have any money? You have a lawyer, you pay for a lawyer.' 'No, the ACLU gave me this lawyer.' 'Your Honor,' Jerry says, 'I'll put up the hundred dollars, I'll pay the hundred dollars, and we all go home.' And then on the way out, St. John's passes by us and says, so nobody but us can hear, 'And which of you gets to screw with the girl?' I said to him, 'You mean, which of us Jews? We all do. We all get to screw the girl. Even my old zaydeh gets to screw her. My rabbi gets to screw her. Everybody gets to screw her except you, St. John's. You get to go home and screw your wife. That's what you're sentenced to— screwing for life Mary Elizabeth, who worships her older sister, the nun.' So there was the flare-up, a fight mercifully cut short by Linc and Norm and Glekel, and this cost another hundred bucks, which Glekel paid, and then Linc and Norm paid Glekel back, and in all I got off lucky. It didn't have to be an Enlightenment

philosopher like Mulchrone up there. I could have got Savon-
arola."

I did, thought Sabbath. Thirty-three years later, I got Savona-
rola dressed up to look like a Japanese woman. Helen Trumbull. Kathy Goolsbee. The Savonarolas break them down. They
don't want my foot on hers or on anyone else's. They want my
foot like Linc's in the casket, touching nothing and dead to the
touch.

Not for a second had Sabbath let her foot be. So close already
to copulation! Not once throughout the entire performance did
he lose her—unlike Norman, she was too entertained by him to
seize up even momentarily each time he called Helen Debby or
when, for her benefit, he put in the bit about licking the girl's feet.
She was right at his side, from the farce out on the street to the
playground finale in Mulchrone's courtroom, her large, plump
laugh filled half with her earthy happiness and half with her wild
distress. She was thinking, like Lear, "Let copulation thrive!" She
was thinking (thought Sabbath) that in cahoots with this loathsome freak there might yet be a use to which she might put her old
propensities and her pendulating breasts, still a chance for the old
juicy way of life to make one big, last thumping stand against the
inescapable rectitude, not to mention the boredom, of death. Linc
did look bored. Good and green and bored. Don't admonish me,
Drenka—you'd do it in a shot. This is the crime we were wedded
to. I'll be as bored as you and Linc soon enough.

◆　◆　◆

Everybody went to bed early. Sabbath knew enough not to get
right into Debby's things, and sure enough, only ten minutes after
the dinner dishes had been cleared away and they'd all said good
night, Norman had knocked at the door to give him a bathrobe
and to ask if he wanted to see last Sunday's *Times* before they
threw it away. Had numerous sections of it clutched in his arms,
and Sabbath decided to accept them, if for no other reason than
so Norman could deceive himself, assuming he was so inclined,
into thinking that the *chazerai* in the Sunday papers was the

soporific his guest was using to put himself to sleep. It was probably no less dependable than ever, but Sabbath had a better idea. "I haven't seen last Sunday's *Times* for over thirty years," Sabbath said, "but why not?" "Don't you get the New York papers up there?" "I don't get anything up there. If I read the New York papers, I'd be on Prozac too." "Can you at least get a bagel on a Sunday morning?" "Any morning. We were a bagel-free zone for a very long time. One of the last. But now, except for a county in Alabama where the citizens voted no on a referendum, I believe the poor goy cannot elude the bagel anywhere in America. They're everywhere. They're like guns." "And you don't read the papers, Mickey? This is unimaginable to me," Norm said. "I gave up reading the papers when I found that every day there was another story about the miracle of Japan. I can't take the photographs of all those Japs wearing suits. What happened to their little uniforms? They must do a quick change for the photographer. When I hear the word *Japan,* I reach for my thermonuclear device." Now that should send him packing . . . but no, he'd gone so far as to cause Norman to worry again. They were in the doorway of Debby's room still and Sabbath could see that Norman, tired as he was, was about to come in now and have a talk—probably again about going to Graves. The guy's name was Graves. Sabbath had begged off after the funeral, said he'd think about seeing the doctor another day. "I know what you're wondering," Sabbath quickly put in, "you're wondering where do I get my news from—from television? No. Can't. They've got Japs on TV too. All over the screen, little Japs holding elections, little Japs buying and selling stock, little Japs even shaking hands with our president—with the president of the United States! In his grave Franklin Roosevelt is spinning like an atomic dreydl. No, I prefer to live without the news. I got all the news I need about those bastards a long time ago. Their prosperity creates difficulties for my sense of fair play. The Land of the Rising Nikkei Average. I'm proud to say I still have all my marbles as far as racial hatred is concerned. Despite all my many troubles, I continue to know what matters in life: profound hatred. One of the

few remaining things I take seriously. Once, at my wife's suggestion, I tried to go a whole week without it. Nearly did me in.
Week of great spiritual tribulation that was for me. I'd say hating
the Japanese plays a leading role in every aspect of my life. Here,
of course, in New York, you New Yorkers love the Japanese
because they brought you raw fish. The great bonanza of raw fish.
They serve raw fish to people of our race, and, as though we were
prisoners on the Bataan death march who have no choice, who
would starve to death otherwise, the people of our race eat it. And
pay for it. Leave *tips*. I don't get it. After the war was over we
shouldn't have allowed them ever to fish again. You lost the right
to fish, you bastards, on December 7, 1941. Catch one fish, *one,*
and we will show you the *rest* of the arsenal. Who else would so
relish eating fish raw? Between their cannibalism and their prosperity, they affront me, you know? His Highness. Do they still
have 'His Highness'? Do they still have their 'glory'? Are they still
glorious, the Japanese? I don't know, for some reason all my
racial hatred leaps to the fore just thinking about how glorious
they are. Norman, I have so much to put up with in life. Professional failure. Physical deformity. Personal disgrace. My wife is
a recovering alcoholic who goes to AA to learn how to forget
to speak English. Never blessed with children. Children never
blessed with me. Many, many disappointments. Do I have to put
up with the prosperity of the Japanese, too? That could really
push me over the edge. Maybe it's what did it to Linc. What the
yen has done to the dollar, who knows if that didn't do it to him.
Me it kills. Oh, it kills me so much I wouldn't mind—what's the
expression they use now when they want to bomb the shit out of
someone? 'Send them a message.' I'd like to send them a message
and rain just a little more terror down on their fucking heads. Still
great believers, are they, in taking things by force? Still inspired,
are they, by the territorial imperative?—" "Mickey, Mickey,
Mickey—whoa, slow down, cool it, Mick," pleaded Norman.
"Do they still have that fucking flag?" "Mick—" "Just answer
that. I'm asking a guy who reads the New York *Times* a question.
You read the 'News of the Week in Review.' You watch Peter

Jennings. You're an up-to-the-minute guy. Do they still have that flag?" "Yes, they have that flag." "Well, they shouldn't have a flag. They shouldn't be allowed to fish and they shouldn't have a flag, and they shouldn't come over here and shake *anybody's* hand!" "Kid, you're off and runnin' tonight, you haven't stopped," Norman said, "you're—" "I'm fine. I'm just telling you why I gave up on the news. The Japs. That's it in a nutshell. Thanks for the paper. Thanks for everything. The dinner. The handkerchiefs. The money. Thanks, buddy. I'm going to sleep." "You should." "I will. I'm beat." "Good night, Mick. And slow down. Just slow down and get some sleep."

Sleep? How could he ever sleep again? *There they are.* Sabbath tossed the heap of paper onto the bed, and what slides out of the center but the business section—and there they are! Big headline running across all but one column of the page: "The Men Who Really Run Fortress Japan." *That* can gall ya! Fortress Japan! And under it, "Bad news for business: The Prime Minister is quitting. But the bureaucrats not." Headlines, photos, paragraph after infuriating paragraph not only dominating the front of the business section but running over and taking up most of page 8, where there's a graph, and another photo of another Jap, and that headline again, ending with "Fortress Japan." Three of them on the front page, each with his own picture. None of them wearing their little uniforms. All of them in ties and shirts, pretending to be ordinary peace-loving people. They've got mock-ups of offices behind them, so as to make the readers of the *Times* think they work in offices like human beings and aren't flying around conquering countries in their fucking Zeroes. "They are among an intellectually nimble, hard-working elite of 11,000 sitting atop Japan's million or so national civil servants. They oversee perhaps the most closely regulated economy in . . ." The caption beneath one of the photographs—Sabbath could not believe it. According to the caption, the Jap in the photograph "says he was burned by U.S. negotiators. . . ." Burned? His skin burned? How much of it? Morty's burns covered eighty percent of his body. How much of his body did the U.S. negotiators burn on this son of a bitch?

Doesn't look very burned to me. I don't see any burns at all. We've got to give our negotiators more kerosene—we've got to get negotiators who know how to build a fire under these bastards! "What has gone wrong? Japanese officials say that the United States has demanded too much. . . ." Oh, you fuckers, you filthy, fanatical, fucking imperialist Jap fuckers . . .

His speaking aloud must have been what prompted the knock on the door. But when he opened it once again to assure Norman that he was fine, just reading the Japanese papers, there was Michelle. At dinner she'd been wearing black tights and a narrow rust-colored velvety top that came down to her thighs: sham waifdom. Intended to awaken what fantasy in me? Or maybe she was confiding in him an original of her own: I am Robin Hood; I give to the poor. At any rate, she had changed now into—Christ, a kimono. Flowers all over it. Those wide sleeves. Into a Japanese kimono down to her feet. Yet the abhorrence inflamed by that paper's contemptible paean to Fortress Japan was subsumed instantaneously in his excitement. Beneath the kimono there appeared to be only her biography. He liked the extreme boyish way her hair was cut. Big tits and a boy's short haircut. And a well-worn woman's lines around the eyes. This look took a firmer hold on him than the first, the Central Park West Peter Pan. Something French now wafting around her. You get this look in Paris. You get this in Madrid. You get this in Barcelona, in the really classy places. There were a few times in my life, in Paris and other places, where I liked her so well that I gave her my number and my address and I said, "Anytime you come to America, look me up." I remember one said she was going to do some traveling. I've been waiting for that whore to call ever since. Michelle's family background was, in fact, French—Norman had told him so before dinner. Maiden name Boucher. And she looked it now, too, whereas in the dirty pictures, with her hair tautly back and the body unsurpassingly gaunt, she had looked to him like some rich Jewish husband's Canyon Ranch Carmen. The middle-aged dieters from the spa down in Lenox sometimes came to Madamaska Falls to visit the Indian sites when they were bored with their tofu at a hundred smackers a plate. Some ten years back he'd made a stab at picking up two of them who'd driven all the way out from Canyon Ranch for an afternoon of sightseeing. But when he offered—admittedly, early in the game—to guide them along the falls to the ridge where the Madamaskas used to initiate their maidens into the sacred mysteries with a gourd, all their anthropological ignorance was glaringly revealed and they drove off. "It wasn't my idea," he called after the Audi, "it was *theirs*, the Native Americans'!" He'd be hearing from those two when he heard from that whore.

But here was the former Mademoiselle Boucher, New Jersey's Colette, brimming over with boredom. She did not love her husband and she had come to a decision. Thus the kimono. Nothing Japanese about it at all—it was the most scandalous thing she could get away with in the circumstances. She was shrewd. He knew her lingerie drawer. He knew she could do better. He knew she would, too. Isn't it something the way the course of a life can change overnight? Never, never would he voluntarily depart this stupendous madness over fucking.

She said she had forgotten earlier to give him the prescription for Zantac. Here it was. Zantac was what he took to try to control the stomach pains and the diarrhea produced by the Voltaren that lessened the pain in his hands, providing he didn't use a knife and fork, drive a car, tie his shoelaces, or wipe his ass. If only he had the money, he could go out and hire some enterprising Jap to wipe his ass, one of the intellectually nimble, hardworking elite of 11,000 sitting atop—"sitting atop." They know how to write in those enlightened papers. I should start taking the *Times*. Hep me with learn Engwish so no more get me burn by U.S. My brother's legs were two charred timbers. Had he even lived, he would have been legless. The legless track star of Asbury High.

Pills and pain. Aldomet for my blood pressure and Zantac for my gut. A to Z. Then you die.

"Thanks," he said. "Never before received a prescription from a doctor in a kimono."

"Our era has lost much to commercial inelegance," she replied, pleasing him no end with a geisha bow. "Norman thinks you might want to have those pants of yours dry-cleaned." She pointed to his corduroys. "And that jacket, the mackinaw, that odd thing you wear with the pockets."

"The Green Torpedo."

"Yes. Maybe the Green Torpedo could use a cleaning."

"You want the trousers now?"

"We are not children, Mr. Sabbath."

He retreated into Debby's bedroom and slipped off his pants. Norman's robe, a colorful full-length velour robe with a belt long enough to hang himself, was still where he'd dropped it beside his jacket on the carpet. He returned to her, enwrapped in the robe, to make an offering of his dirty clothes. The robe trailed behind him like a gown. Norman was six two.

She took the clothes without a word, without the slightest manifestation of the squeamishness she had every right to feel. Those pants had had an active life during the last several weeks, a real full life such as would leave an ordinary person exhausted. Every indignity he had ever suffered seemed collected and preserved in the loose-fitting seat of those old pants, their cuffs encrusted with mud from the cemetery. But they did not appear to repel her, as he had momentarily feared while undressing. Of course not. She deals with dirt all day. Norman had narrated the whole saga. Pyorrhea. Gingivitis. Swollen gums. One *schmutzig* mouth after another. *Schmutz* is her métier. Crud is what she works away at with her instruments. Drawn not to Norman but to crud. Scrape the tartar. Scrape the pockets. . . . Seeing Michelle so enthrallingly kimono'd, his *schmutzig* clothes balled up under her arm—and with her geisha boy haircut lending just the right touch of transsexual tawdriness to the whole slatternly picture— he knew he could kill for her. Kill Norman. Push him out the fucking window. All that marmalade, mine.

So. Here we are. The moon is high, somewhere there's music, Norman's dead, and it's just me and this betitted pretty-boy in his flowered kimono. Missed my chance with a man. That Ne-

braska guy who gave me the books on the tanker. Yeats. Conrad.
O'Neill. He would have taught me more than what to read if I'd
let him. Wonder what it's like. Ask her, she'll tell you. The only
other people who fuck men are women.

"Why do you like to look this way?" she asked, patting the
dirty clothes.

"What other way is there to look?"

"Norman says that, when you were young, to look at you was
to die. He says Linc used to say, 'There's a bull in Sabbath. He
goes all out.' He says people couldn't take their eyes off of you. A
force. A free spirit."

"Why would he say that? To justify having seated at your
dinner table a nobody nobody can possibly take seriously? Who
of your social class can take seriously someone like me, steeped in
selfishness, and with my terrible level of morality, and lacking all
the appurtenances that go with all the right ideals?"

"You have great eloquence at your command."

"I learned early on that people seem more easily to pass over
how short I am when I am linguistically large."

"Norman says you were the most brilliant young fellow he ever
met."

"Tell him he doesn't have to."

"He adored you. He still has a lot of feeling for you."

"Yeah, well, a lot of well-bred people need their real-lifer. Normal enough. I'd been to sea. I'd been to Rome. Whores on more
than one continent—a laudable achievement in those years.
Showed 'em I'd escaped the bourgeois trammels. Educated bour-
geoisie like to admire someone who's escaped the bourgeois trammels—reminds them of their college ideals. When I got written up
in the *Nation* for taking a tit out on the street I was their noble
savage for a week. Today they'd excoriate my balls off for so
much as thinking about it, but in those days that made me heroic
to all right-thinking people. Dissenter. Maverick. Menace to society. Great. I would bet you that even today part of being a culti-
vated millionaire in New York is having an interest in a disgrace-
ful person. Linc and Norm and their friends got a big kick then

out of just saying my name. Gave them a spacious feeling of being illegit. A puppeteer who takes tits out on the street—like knowing a boxer, like helping a convict publish his sonatinas. To add to the fun I had a crazy young wife. An actress. Mick and Nikk, their favorite pathological couple."

"And she?"

"I murdered she."

"Norman says she disappeared."

"No. I murdered her."

"How much does this act cost you? How much of an act do you really need?"

"What other way is there for me to be? If you know, I'd like you to tell me. There is no stupidity that fails to interest me," he said, feigning anger only a little—the "really" had been a cheap shot. "What other way is there to act?"

He liked that she did not appear intimidated. Refused to back off. That was good. Well schooled by her old man. Nonetheless, suppress the inclination to undo the kimono. Not yet.

"You'll do anything," she said, "not to be winning. But why *do* you behave this way? Primal emotions and indecent language and orderly complex sentences."

"I'm not big on oughts, if that's what you mean."

"I don't entirely believe that. As much as he wants to be the Marquis de Sade, Mickey Sabbath is not. The degraded quality is not in your voice."

"Neither was it in the Marquis de Sade's. Neither is it in yours."

"Freed from the desire to please," she said. "A giddy feeling. What has it got you?"

"What has it got *you?*"

"*Me?* I'm pleasing people all the time," she said. "I've been pleasing people since I was born."

"Which people?"

"Teachers. Parents. Husband. Children. Patients. All people."

"Lovers?"

"Yes."

Now.

"Please me, Michelle," and, taking her by one wrist, he tried to pull her into Debby's room.

"Are you crazy?"

"Come on, you've read Kant. 'Act as if the maxim from which you act were to become through your will a universal law.' *Please me.*"

Her arms were strong from scraping all that crud away and his were no longer a seaman's. No longer even a puppeteer's. He could not budge her.

"Why were you pressing Norman's foot throughout dinner?"

"No."

"Yes," she whispered—and that laugh, that laugh, a mere *tendril* of it was marvelous! "You were playing footsie with my husband. I expect an explanation."

"No."

And now she gave over the whole provocative thing—softly, because they were only down the hall from the conjugal bed, but the whole branching tangle of contradictions that was her laugh. "Yes, yes." The kimono. The whispering. The haircut. The laugh. And so little time left.

"Come *in.*"

"Don't be insane."

"You're great. You're a great woman. *Come inside.*"

"Unbridled excess knows no limit in you," she said, "but I suffer from a severe predilection not to ruin my life."

"What did Norman say about my foot? How come he didn't just throw me out?"

"He thinks you're having a breakdown. He thinks you're cracking up. He thinks you don't know what you're doing or why you're doing it. He's intent on getting you to his psychiatrist. He says you need help."

"You're all I thought you were. You're more, Michelle. Norman told me the whole story. Those upper third molars. Like cleaning windows at the top of the Empire State Building."

"Your mouth could *use* a little going-over. The interdental papilla? That little piece of flesh that sticks out between each tooth? Red. Swollen. Might want to investigate that further."

"Then come in, for God's sake. Investigate the papilla. Investigate the molars. Pull 'em out. Whatever makes you happy. I want to make you happy. My teeth, my gums, my larynx, my kidneys— if it works and you like it, take it, it's yours. I cannot believe that I was playing with Norman's foot. It felt so good. Why didn't he say anything? Why didn't he get down there under the table and pick it up and place it where it was supposed to be? I thought he was such a great host. I thought he had all this feeling for me. Yet he placidly sits there and allows my foot *not* to be where he knows full well I *want* it to be. And at *his* dinner table. Where I am an invited guest. I didn't beg to eat here, he *asked* me to. I'm really surprised at him. I want *your* foot."

"Not now."

"Don't you find that the simplest formulations in English are barely endurable? 'Not now.' Say that again. Treat me like shit. Temper me like steel—"

"Calm down. Control yourself. Quiet, *please.*"

"Say it again."

"Not now."

"When?"

"Saturday. Come to my office Saturday."

"Today's Tuesday. Wednesday, Thursday, Friday—no, no. Absolutely not. I'm sixty-four years old. Saturday's too late."

"*Calm.*"

"If Yahweh wanted me to be calm, he would have made me a goy. Four days. No. *Now.*"

"We *can't,*" she whispered. "Come Saturday—I'll give you a periodontal probe."

"Oh, okay. You've got a customer. Saturday. Okay. Wonderful. How do you do it?"

"I've got an instrument for it. I stick my instrument into your periodontal pocket. I enter the gingival crevice."

"More. More. Speak to me about the business end of your instrument."

"It's a very fine instrument. It won't hurt. It's slender. It's flat. It's about a millimeter wide. Perhaps ten millimeters long."

"You think metrically." Drenka.

"It's the only area in which I think metrically."

"Will I bleed?" he asked.

"Just a drop or two."

"That's all?"

"Christ . . ." she said and allowed her forehead to fall forward onto his. To rest there. It was a moment unlike any he'd had all day. Week. Month. Year. He calmed down.

"How," she asked, "did we arrive at this so soon?"

"It's a consequence of living a long time. There isn't forever to fuck around."

"But you are a maniac," she said.

"Oh, I don't know. It takes two to tangle."

"You do a lot of things that most people don't do."

"What do I do that you don't do?"

"Express yourself."

"And you don't do that?"

"Hardly. You have the body of an old man, the life of an old man, the past of an old man, and the instinctive force of a two-year-old."

What is happiness? The substantiality of this woman. The compound she was. The wit, the gameness, the shrewdness, the fatty tissue, the odd indulgence in high-flown words, that laugh marked with life, her responsibility to everything, not excluding her carnality—there was stature in this woman. Mockery. Play. The talent and taste for the clandestine, the knowledge that everything subterranean beats everything terranean by a mile, a certain physical poise, the poise that is the purest expression of her sexual freedom. And the conspiratorial understanding with which she spoke, her terror of the clock running down . . . Must everything be behind her? No! No! The ruthless lyricism of Michelle's soliloquy: and no I said no I will No.

"Adultery is a tough business," he whispered to her. "The main thing is to be clear about wanting it. The rest is incidental."

"Incidental," she sighed.

"God, I'm fond of adultery. Aren't you?" He dared to take her face in his crippled hands and to trace the boyish haircut around at the neckline with that middle finger for which they had once arrested him, the middle finger whose sweet talk was thought to have traumatized or hypnotized or tyrannized Helen Trumbull. Yeah, they had it all figured out in 1956. They still have. "The softness it brings to the hardness," he went on. "A world without adultery is unthinkable. The brutal inhumanity of those against it. Don't you agree? The sheer fucking depravity of their views. The *madness*. There is no punishment too extreme for the crazy bastard who came up with the idea of fidelity. To demand of human flesh fidelity. The cruelty of it, the mockery of it, is simply unspeakable."

He would never let her get away. Here was Drenka, only instead of the colloquialisms that she fucked up in her ardor to engage the teacher and enjoy his games, speaking charmingly humorous, delectable English. Drenka, it's *you*, only from suburban New Jersey instead of Split. I know because this high degree of excitement I experience with no one *but* you—this is your warm body resurrected! Out o' the grave. Morty next.

He chose then to undo his own robe rather than hers—the six-footer's velour robe, with the Paris label, that made him look like the Little King in the old comic strip—to introduce her to his hard-on. They should meet. "Behold the arrow of desire," said Sabbath.

But one glimpse caused her to recoil. "Not *now*," she warned again, and this breathy utterance won his heart. Even better was watching her run off. Like a thief. Running but willing. Running but ready.

He had a reason to live until Saturday. A new collaborator to replace the old one. The vanishing collaborator, indispensable to Sabbath's life—it wouldn't have been Sabbath's life otherwise: Nikki disappearing, Drenka dying, Roseanna drinking, Kathy indicting him . . . his mother . . . his brother. . . . If only he could stop replacing them. Miscasting them. Since the latest loss, he'd really been out there calibrating the dread. And to think that as a puppeteer he could do it without even a puppet, a full life with just his fingers.

Saturday, he decided, we'll make the quick reassessment. No shortage of sharp objects lying about in her dental tray. He'd swipe a curette, end it that way, if, that is, it all went nowhere. Let the adventure occur, O Lord Dionysus, Noble Bull, Mighty Maker of the Sperm of All Male Creatures. It's not life repossessed that I expect to encounter. That exaltation is long gone. It's more what Krupa used to call to Goodman when Benny was ridin' solo on "China Boy." "Take one more, Ben! Take one more!"

Providing she doesn't come to her senses, the last of the collaborators. Take one more.

◆ ◆ ◆

Of the second night that Sabbath spent in Debby's room, suffice it to say—before moving on to the crisis of the morning—that his thoughts were of both mother and daughter, singly and together. He was under the spell of the tempter whose task it is to pump the hormone preposterone into the male bloodstream.

In the morning, after a leisurely bath in Debby's tub, he took a wonderful crap in her toilet—satisfying stools easily urged forth, density, real dimension, so unlike the sickbed stuff that, on an ordinary day, streamed intermittently out of him because of the agitating action of Voltaren. He bequeathed unto the bathroom a big, trenchant barnyard bouquet that filled him with enthusiasm. The robust road again! I have a mistress! He felt as overcome and nonsensical as Emma Bovary out riding with Rodolphe. In the masterpieces they're always killing themselves when they commit adultery. He wanted to kill himself when he couldn't.

After meticulously returning to the dresser and the closet every stitch of Debby's he'd venerated during the night, adorned for the first time in decades in all new clothes, he came stomping into the kitchen to find the party was over. Norman had delayed his departure to tell Sabbath that he was to get out after breakfast.

Michelle was off at work but her instructions were that Sabbath be ejected immediately. Norman told him to go ahead and have breakfast but to leave after that. In the jacket Sabbath had given Michelle to send to the cleaners, she'd found a bag of crack, which Norman had in front of him on the table. Sabbath remembered having bought it the morning before on the streets of the Lower East Side, bought it for a joke, for no reason at all, because he was getting a kick out of the dealer.

"And these. In your trousers."

The father was holding in his hand the daughter's floral underpants. During all of the day's excitements and difficulties, when exactly had Sabbath forgotten that the panties were in his pocket? He could clearly remember, at the funeral, rolling them around in his pocket through the two-hour amusement of the eulogies. Who wouldn't have? Overflow crowd. Broadway and Hollywood people—Linc's most famous friends—each in turn recollecting the corpse. The predictable torrent of claptrap. The two sons spoke and the daughter—the architect, the lawyer, the psychiatric social worker. I knew nobody and nobody knew me. Except Enid, heavyset, white-haired, dowagerly, as unrecognizable to him at first as he was to her. "It's Mickey Sabbath," Norm had said to her. He and Sabbath, after identifying Linc's body, had come back to the anteroom where Enid sat alone with the family. "He drove down from New England." "My God," said Enid, and clutching Sabbath's hand she began to cry. "And I haven't shed a tear all day," she told Sabbath with a helpless laugh. "Oh, Mickey, Mickey, I did a terrible thing just three weeks ago." Hadn't seen Sabbath in over thirty years, and yet to him she confessed the terrible thing she had done. Because he knew what it was to do terrible things? Or because terrible things had been done to him? Most likely the former. Reaching into my pocket, knowing they were there, silk putty to knead painfully while each of the eulogists stood across from the coffin and described the suicide's comic antics, how he loved to play with children, how everybody's kids loved him, how endearingly, wonderfully eccentric he was. . . . Then the young rabbi. Take the beauty out of the tragedy. Half an hour to explain to us how that's done. Lincoln isn't really dead, in our hearts this love lives on. True, true. Yet at the open coffin, when I asked, "Linc, what would you like for dinner tonight?" I got no answer. That proves something, too. Guy next to me, without a pocketful of panties to ease the pain, couldn't resist the anti-clerical aperçu. "He plays it a little girlish for my taste." "I think he's auditioning," I replied. He liked that. "I'm not going to mind never seeing him again," the guy whispered. I thought he meant the rabbi, only out on the street realized that he'd meant the deceased. A young TV star gets up, sleek in a black sheath dress, smiling to beat the band, and she tells everybody to hold hands with everybody else and observe a minute of silence remembering Linc. I held the hand of the nasty guy next to me. Had to take a hand out of my pocket to do it—and *that's* when I forget the underpants! Then Linc: green. The man was green. Then my hideous fingers clasped in Enid's while she confessed the terrible thing she'd done. "I couldn't take the tremor any longer and I hit him. I hit him, with a book, and I shouted, 'Stop shaking! Stop shaking!' There were some times when he *could* stop—he would bring all his strength to bear on it and the shaking would stop. He'd hold out his hands for me to see. But if he succeeded in doing that, he couldn't do anything else. All his systems had to be recruited to stop shaking. The result was he couldn't talk, he couldn't walk, he couldn't answer the simplest question." "Why was he shaking?" I asked her, because just that morning, in Rosa's embrace, I'd been shaking myself. "Either the medication," she said, "or the fear. They released him from the hospital when he could eat again and sleep again, and they said he was no longer suicidal. But he was still depressed and frightened and crazy. And he had the tremor. I couldn't live with him any longer. I moved him to an apartment around the corner a year and a half ago. I phoned him every day, but this last winter three months went by when I didn't see him. He phoned me. Sometimes ten times a day he phoned me. To see if I was all right. He was terrified that I was going to get sick and disappear. When he saw me he'd burst into tears. He was always the crier in the family, but this was something else. This was ultrahelplessness. He cried from the pain—from the terror. It never let up. But still I thought he was going to get better. I thought, Someday it's going to be the way it used to be. He'll make us all laugh." "Enid, do you know who I am," asked Sabbath, "who you are telling all this to?" But she did not even hear his words, and Sabbath understood that she was telling this to everyone. He was just the last one to hit the anteroom. "Three months in the hospital with a lot of crazy people," she said. "But after the first week he felt safe there. The first night they put him in bed next to a man who was dying—it terrorized him. Then in a room with three others, truly screwy people. Near the end of his stay I took him out to lunch twice, but apart from that he never left the hospital. Bars on the windows. The suicide watch. Seeing his face behind the barred windows, waiting for us to come—" She told him so much, she held him to her so long, that in the end he forgot what in his pocket he had been clinging to. Then at dinner he started telling *his* story. . . .

So, during the night, lust and treachery gunned down by her prudence, by foresight—by her brains. *That's* what happened. Don't blame Enid. Nor was it jealousy of the kid. If she'd wanted to probe his papilla on Saturday, the kid's stolen panties would only have turned her on more. She would have worn them for him. She would have got herself up in Debby's stuff for him. She's done it before, along with everything else. But she was using the underpants to get him out before he ruined everything she had going for her. The underpants to inform him that there would be no wavering, that should he try to bring pressure there'd be an even more resourceful authority than Officer Abramowitz to crush him. It wasn't the underpants, the crack, even the Green Torpedo—it was *Sabbath*. Maybe he could still tell a story, but otherwise nothing remotely alluring left, not even the hard-on he'd showed her. All that remained of his *going all out* was repellent to her. Crude she was herself, besmirched, wily, connubially half-crazed, but not yet uncontrollably desperate. Hers was the ordinary automatic dishonesty. She was a betrayer with a small *b*, and small-*b* betrayals are happening all the time—by now Sabbath could pull them off in his sleep. That wasn't what was at the center for him: this guy is *spinning;* he wants *to die.* Michelle had enough equilibrium to reach a sensible decision. The maniacal intoxicant to put the enchantment back in life is not me. She will be better off shopping around, scenting out somebody less clamorously kaput. And he'd thought he was going to gorge himself. It was bursting time again. You great big infant. That you could still believe that it could go on forever. Maybe now you've got a better picture of what's up. Well, let it come. I know what's up. Let it come.

Eat breakfast and go. This is an amazing moment. *It's over.*

"How could you take Debby's underwear?" Norman asked.

"How could I not is the question."

"It was irresistible to you."

"What a strange way to put it. Where does resistance even enter in? We're talking about thermodynamics. Heat as a form of energy and its effect on the molecules of matter. I am sixty-four, she is nineteen. It's only natural."

Norman was dressed like the connoisseur of fine living that he was: double-breasted chalk-stripe suit, maroon silk tie with matching breast-pocket handkerchief, pale blue shirt monogrammed at the pocket NIC. All of his considerable dignity was on display, not simply in his clothing, but in his distinctive face, a lean, long, intelligent face with gentle dark eyes and a becoming kind of baldness. That he had less hair even than Sabbath made him a thousand times more attractive. Without the hair you saw unveiled all the mind in that skull, the introspection, the tolerance, the acuity, the reason. And a manly skull it was, finely made yet almost ostentatiously determined—none of its delicacy suggested weakness of will. Yes, the whole figure emanated the ideals and scruples of humanity's better self and it wouldn't have been hard for Sabbath to believe that the office for which Norman shortly would be leaving in a limo had spiritual aims loftier even than those of a theatrical producer. Secular spirituality, that's what he exuded—maybe they all did, the producers, the agents, the mega-deal lawyers. With the aid of their tailors, Jewish cardi-

nals of commerce. Yeah, now that I think of it, very much like
them sharpies surrounding the pope. You'd never guess that the
jukebox distributor who paid for it all dealt at the edges of the
Mob. You're not supposed to guess. He'd made himself into that
impressive American thing, a nice guy. It all but says he's one on
his shirt. A nice rich guy with some depth, and dynamite on the
phone at the office. What more can America ask of its Jews?

"And at dinner last night," Norman said, "was it only natural
to want to play with Michelle's foot under the table?"

"I didn't want to play with Michelle's foot under the table. I
wanted to play with your foot under the table. *Wasn't* that your
foot?"

He registers neither antipathy nor amusement. Is it because he
knows where we're headed or because he doesn't know? I surely
don't know. Could be anywhere. I'm beginning to smell Sopho-
cles in this kitchen.

"Why did you tell Michelle you killed Nikki?"

"Should I try to hide it from her instead? Am I supposed to be
ashamed of that too? What is this shame kick you're on?"

"Tell me something. Tell me the truth—tell me if you believe
that you murdered Nikki. Is this something you *believe?*"

"I see no reason why I shouldn't."

"I do. I was there. I do because I was with you when she
disappeared. I saw what you went through."

"Yeah, well, I'm not saying it was easy. Going to sea doesn't
prepare you for everything. The color she turned. That came as a
surprise. Green, like Linc. With strangulation the primitive satis-
factions are all built in, of course, but if I had it to do over again
I'd opt for one of the more expeditious modes. I'd have to. My
hands. How do you plan to kill Michelle?"

Some emotion stirred up by Sabbath's question made Norman
look to Sabbath as though he were afloat or flying, drifting away
from the entire orientation of his life. An exciting silence ensued.
But in the end Norman did no more than to put Debby's underpants into the pocket of his own pants. The words he next spoke
were not without a tinge of menace.

"I love my wife and children more than anything in this world."

"I take that for granted. But how do you plan to kill her? When you find out she is fucking your best friend."

"Don't. Please. We all know how you are a man on the super-human scale, who has no fear of verbal exaggeration, but not everything is worth saying, even to a successful person like me. Don't. Not necessary. My wife found our daughter's underpants in your pocket. What do you expect her to do? How do you expect her to respond? Don't degrade yourself further by defiling my wife."

"I wasn't degrading myself. I wasn't defiling your wife. Norman, aren't the stakes too high for us to bow to convention? I was just wondering how you think about killing her when you think about killing her. Okay, let's change the subject. How do you think she thinks about killing you? Do you imagine her content, when you fly off to L.A., just to kind of hope American Airlines will take care of it for her? Too mundane for a Michelle. The plane will crash and I'll be free? No, that's how the secretaries solve their problems on the subway. Michelle's a doer, her father's daughter. If I know anything about periodontists, she's thought of strangling you more than once. In your sleep. And she could do it. Got the grip for it. So did I once upon a time. Remember my hands? My old hands? All day you work as a seaman on deck, chipping, chipping, chipping—the constant work of the ship. A metal drill, a hammer, a chisel. And then the puppets. The *strength* in those hands! Nikki never knew what hit her. She was a long time looking up at me with those imploring eyes, but actually I would think a coroner would have said that she was brain-dead in sixty seconds."

Leaning back in his chair at the breakfast table, Norman crossed an arm over his chest and, with the other arm resting on it, let his forehead drop forward onto his fingertips. Exactly how Michelle's forehead dropped onto mine. I can't believe the panties did it. I can't believe this truly superior aging woman could have been daunted by that. This isn't happening! This is a fairy tale! This is *true* depravity, this genteel shit!

"What the hell has become of your mind?" Norman said. "This is awful."

"What is awful?" Sabbath asked. "The kid's underpants wrapped around my dick to help me through the night after the day that I'd been through? That's so awful? Come off it, Norm. Panties in my pocket at a funeral? That's *hope*."

"Mickey, where are you going to go after you leave here? Are you going to drive home?"

"It's always been hard for you, Norman, hasn't it, to imagine me? How does he do it without protection? How do any of them do it without protection? Baby, there *is* no protection. It's all wallpaper, Norman. Look at Linc. Look at Sabbath. Look at Morty. Look at Nikki. *Look,* tiresome and frightening as looking may be. What we are in the hands of *is not protection*. When I was on the ships, when we got to port, I always liked to visit the Catholic churches. I always went by myself, sometimes every day we were in port. You know why? Because I found something terrifically erotic about watching kneeling maidens at prayer, asking forgiveness for the wrong things altogether. Watching them seeking protection. It made me very hot. Seeking protection against the other. Seeking protection against themselves. Seeking protection against everything. *But there isn't any.* Not even for you. Even you are exposed—what do you make of that? Exposed! Fucking naked, even in that suit! The suit is futile, the monogram is futile—nothing will do it. *We have no idea how it's going to turn out.* Christ, man, *you* can't even protect a pair of your daughter's—"

"Mickey," he said softly, "I take your point. I get the philosophy. It's a fierce one. You're a fierce man. You've let the whole creature out, haven't you? The deeper reasonability of seeking danger is that there is, in any event, no escaping it. Pursue it or be pursued by it. Mickey's view, and, in theory, I agree: there *is* no escaping it. But in practice I proceed differently: if danger's going to find me anyway, I needn't pursue it. That the extraordinary is assured Linc has convinced me. It's the ordinary that escapes us. I do know that. But that doesn't mean I care to abandon the portion of the ordinary I've been lucky enough to corral and hold on to. I want you to go. It's time for you to go. I'm getting your things out of Debby's room and then you're to go."

"With or without breakfast?"

"I want you *out* of here!"

"But what's eating you? It can't just be the underwear. We go too far back for that. Is it that I showed my dick to Michelle? Is that the reason I can't have my breakfast?"

Norman had risen from the table—he was not as yet shaking like Linc (or Sabbath with Rosa), though there *was* a seizure of sorts in his jaw.

"Didn't you know? I can't believe she didn't tell you. 'There's a bull in Sabbath. He goes all out.' The underpants are nothing. I just thought the only fair thing was to take it out. Before we met on Saturday. In case it wasn't to her taste. She invited me Saturday for a periodontal probe. Don't tell me you didn't know that either. Her office. Saturday." When Norman remained, without moving, on his side of the table, Sabbath added, "Just ask her. That was the plan. We had it all set up. That's why, when you said I couldn't stay to have breakfast, I figured it was because I was going to her office on Saturday to fuck her. *Plus* my taking out my dick. That it's only the panties . . . no, I don't buy that."

And this Sabbath meant. The husband understood the wife better than he let on.

Norman reached up to one of the cabinets above the serving counter and took down a package of plastic garbage sacks. "I'm going to get your things."

"Whatever you say. *May* I eat the grapefruit?"

Without again bothering to respond, Norman left Sabbath alone in the kitchen.

The half grapefruit had been segmented for Sabbath. The segmented grapefruit. Fundamental to their way of life—as fundamental as the Polaroids and the ten thousand bucks. Do I have to tell him about the money, too? No, he knows. Bet he knows everything. I do like this couple. I think the more I come to understand the chaos churning about here, the more I admire how he holds it together. The soldierly way he stood there while I

briefed him on last night. He knows. He's got his hands full.
There is something in her that is always threatening to undo it all,
the warmth, the comfort, the whole wonderful eiderdown that
is their privileged position. Having to deal with all that she is
while holding to his civilized ideals. Why does he bother? Why
does he keep her? The past, for one thing. So much of it. The
present—so much of *it*. The machine that it all is. The house on
Nantucket. The weekends at Brown as Debby's parents. Debby's
grades would tailspin if they split up. Call Michelle a whore,
throw her the hell out, and Debby would never make it to med
school. And there's the *fun* besides: the skiing, the tennis, Europe,
the small hotel they love in Paris, the Université. The repose when
all is well. Somebody there while you wait for the biopsy report to
come back from the lab. No time left for settlements and lawyers
and starting again. The courage of putting up with it instead—the
"realism." And the dread of no one at home. All these rooms
at night and no one else home. He's fixed in this life. His *talent*
is for this life. You can't start dating at the twilight of life. And
then menopause is on his side. If he continues to let her get
away with it, if he never goes the distance with being fed up,
it's because soon enough menopause will do her in anyway. But
neither does Michelle go the distance—because she's not just
one thing, either. Norman understands (if menopause doesn't do
it, that understanding of his will)—minimize, minimize. I never
learned that: work it out, ride it out, cool it down. She is as
indispensable to the way of life as the segmented grapefruit. She *is*
the segmented grapefruit: the partitioned body and the piquant
blood. The unholy Hostess. The holy Hotness. This is as close
to eating Michelle as I will come. It's over. I am a *meshuggeneh*
cast-off shoe.

"You live in the world of real love," he said when Norman
came back into the kitchen holding in one hand the sack stuffed
with everything except for Sabbath's jacket. The Green Torpedo
Norman handed to him at the table.

"And what do you live in?" Norman inquired. "You live in the
failure of this civilization. The investment of everything in eroti-

cism. The final investment of everything in sex. And now you reap the lonely harvest. Erotic drunkenness, the only passionate life you can have."

"And is it even that passionate?" asked Sabbath. "You know what Michelle would have told her therapist had we gone ahead and got it off? She would have said, 'A nice enough man, I suppose, but he has to be kept fresh by ice.'"

"No, kept fresh by provoking. Kept fresh by means of anarchic provocation. We are determined by our society to such an extent that we can only live as human beings if we turn anarchic. Isn't that the pitch? Hasn't that always been the pitch?"

"You're going to feel dashed by this, Norman, but on top of everything else I don't have, I don't have a pitch. You have kind-hearted liberal comprehension but I am flowing swiftly along the curbs of life, I am merely debris, in possession of nothing to interfere with an objective reading of the shit."

"The walking panegyric for obscenity," Norman said. "The inverted saint whose message is desecration. Isn't it tiresome in 1994, this role of rebel-hero? What an odd time to be thinking of sex as rebellion. Are we back to Lawrence's gamekeeper? At this late hour? To be out with that beard of yours, upholding the virtues of fetishism and voyeurism. To be out with that belly of yours, championing pornography and flying the flag of your prick. What a pathetic, outmoded old crank you are, Mickey Sabbath. The discredited male polemic's last gasp. Even as the bloodiest of all centuries comes to an end, you're out working day and night to create an erotic scandal. You fucking relic, Mickey! You fifties antique! Linda Lovelace is already light-years behind us, but you persist in quarreling with society as though Eisenhower is president!" But then, almost apologetically, he added, "The immensity of your isolation is horrifying. That's all I really mean to say."

"And there you'd be surprised," Sabbath replied. "I don't think you ever gave isolation a real shot. It's the best preparation I know of for death."

"Get out," Norman said.

Deep in the corner of one of his front pockets, those huge pockets in which you could carry a couple of dead ducks, Sabbath came upon the cup that he'd pushed in there before entering the funeral home, the beggar's cardboard coffee cup, still containing the quarters, nickels, and dimes that he'd managed to panhandle down in the subway and on the street. When he'd given his stuff over to Michelle to send out with the dry cleaning, he'd forgotten the cup, too.

The cup did it. Of course. The beggar's cup. That's what terrified her—the begging. Ten to one the panties took her to a new edge of excitement. It's the cup that she shrank from; the social odium of the cup went beyond even her impudence. Better a man who didn't wash than a man who begged with a cup. That was farther out than even she wished to go. There was stimulation for her in many things that were scandalous, indecent, unfamiliar, strange, things bordering on the dangerous, but there was only steep effrontery in the cup. Here at last was degradation without a single redeeming thrill. At the beggar's cup Michelle's daring drew the line. The cup had betrayed their secret hallway pact, igniting in her a panicked fury that made her physically ill. She pictured in the cup all the lowly evils leading to destruction, the unleashed force that could wreck everything. And probably she wasn't wrong. Stupid little jokes can be of great moment in the struggle not to lose. Was how far he had fallen with that cup entirely clear to *him?* The unknown about any excess is how excessive it's been. He really couldn't detest her as much for throwing him out because of the cup as he had when he'd thought that to her the treacherous villainy was jacking off in the panties, a natural enough human amusement and surely, for a houseguest, a minor misdemeanor.

At the thought that he had lost his last mistress before he'd even had the chance of wholeheartedly appropriating her secrets—and all because of the magical lure of begging, not just the seductiveness of a self-mocking joke and the irresistible theatrical fun in that but the loathsome rightness of its exalted wrongness, the grand *vocation* of it, the opportunity its encounters offered his despair to work through to the unequivocal end—Sabbath fell faint to the floor.

The fainting was a little like the begging, however, neither wholly rooted in necessity nor entirely unentertaining. At the thought of all that the cup had destroyed, two broad black strokes did indeed crisscross his mind from one edge of the canvas to the other—yet there was also in him the *wish* to faint. There was craft in Sabbath's passing out. The tyranny of fainting did not escape him. That was the last observation integrated into his cynicism before he hit the floor.

Things wouldn't have worked better had he planned them down to the smallest detail—a "plan" wouldn't have worked at all. He found himself laid out, still living, amid the pale plaids of the Cowans' room. It was criminal for his un-dry-cleaned beggar's jacket to be flush with their bedcover, but then, it was Norman who had put him there. Drizzle beading the big windows and a mist whose milkiness obliterated everything above the treetops of the park: a rumble not quite so low as the rumble in Michelle's laugh rolled in from beyond the windows, thunder summoning up for Sabbath his years and years of exile beside the Madamaskas' sacred falls. The haven of the Cowans' bed made him feel oddly lonely for Debby's and the barely discernible (perhaps even imaginary) impress of her torso along the mattress's spine. Only a day, and Debby's bed had become a home away from home. But her room was shut down like La Guardia. No more flying in and out.

Sabbath could hear Norman on the phone with Dr. Graves, talking about getting him into the hospital, and it did not sound as though he was encountering opposition. Norman couldn't bear to see what he was seeing, this guy now on the heels of Linc. . . . Sounded as though he'd set his mind to taking charge of Sabbath's deformities and restoring to him a harmonious being such as Sabbath had last known in third grade. Forgiving, compassionate, determined, indefatigable, almost irrationally humane—every person should have a friend like Norman. Every wife should have a husband like Norman, revere a husband like Norman instead of battering on his decency with her low-minded delights. Marriage is not an ecstatic union. She must be taught to renounce the great narcissistic illusion of rapture. Her lease on rapture is hereby revoked. She must be taught, before it's too late, to renounce this callow quarrel with life's limits. Sabbath owed Norman no less than that for sullying the Cowan home with his piddling vices. He must think selflessly only of Norman now. Any attempt to save Sabbath would plunge Norman into an experience he hardly deserved. The man to save was Norman—he was the indispensable one. And the power to save him is mine. The deed will crown my visit here, repaying as straightforwardly as I know how my debt for all the unwise ardor with which he invited me in. I am called to enter the realm of virtue.

Nothing was clearer to Sabbath than that Norman must never lay eyes on those Polaroids. And if ever he were to come upon the cash! On the heels of this friend's suicide and that friend's collapse, finding the pictures or the money or both would turn the last of his illusions to ashes, smash his orderly existence to bits. Ten thousand in cash. For buying what? For selling what? Who and what is she working for? Her pussy photographed for posterity by whom? Where? Why? To commemorate what? No, Norman must never know the answers, let alone get round to the questions.

The maneuverings necessary to hospitalize Sabbath were being finalized on the phone when he crossed the carpet to Michelle's dresser, reached into the bottom drawer and, from beneath the lingerie, removed the manila envelopes. He stuffed both into his jacket's big, waterproof interior pocket and, in their place, stowed his beggar's cup, change and all. When she next wished to bestir herself with a reminder of the other half of her story, it would be his cup that she'd find secreted in her drawer, his cup to shock her with the horrors she'd been spared. She'd count her blessings when she saw that cup . . . and cleave unto Norman, as she ought.

Seconds later, speeding out the apartment door, he ran into Rosa arriving for the day. He pressed his fingertip to the raised curve of her lips and signaled with his eyes that she should be quiet—the *señor* was home, on the phone, important *trabajo*. How she must love Norman's suave civility—and hate Michelle's betrayal of him. Hates her for everything. "Mi linda muchacha—adiós!" and then, even while Norman was nailing down a bed in Payne Whitney for him, Sabbath made haste for his car and the Jersey shore, to arrange there for his burial.

TUNNEL, TURNPIKE, parkway—the shore! Sixty-five minutes south and there it was! But the cemetery had disappeared! Asphalt laid over the graves and the cars *parking* there! A cemetery plowed under for a supermarket! *People were shopping at the cemetery.*

His agitation did not compel the manager's attention when he rushed through the outer door and made directly past the long daisy chain of empty shopping carts (the century was nearing its end, the century that had virtually reversed human destiny, but the shopping cart was what still signified to Sabbath the passing of the old way of life) for the crow's nest office overseeing the registers, to find out who was responsible for this insane desecration. "I don't know what you're talking about," the manager said. "What are you shouting for? Look in the yellow pages."

But it was a *cemetery*, didn't have a phone. A phone at a cemetery would be ringing off the hook. If you could get them on the *phone* . . . Besides, my family lies beneath that spit where you are roasting chickens. "Where the hell did you put them?"

"Put who?"

"The dead. I am a mourner! Which aisle?"

He drove in circles. He stopped to inquire at gas stations, but he didn't even know the place's name. Not that B'nai This or Beth That would have enlightened the black kids manning the pumps.

He only knew where it was—and there it wasn't. Here, at the outlying frontier of the county, where as recently as when his mother had died there'd been miles of sea-level brush, there was now risen everywhere something with which somebody hoped to advance his interest, and nothing that didn't say, "Of all our ideas, this is the worst," nothing that didn't say, "The human love for the hideous—there is no keeping up with it." Where'd they put them? What a demented civic project, to relocate the dead. Unless they'd obliterated them totally, to end the source of all uncertainty, to dispose of the problem entirely. Without them around, maybe it won't be so lonely. Yes, it's the dead who are standing in our way.

Only through the lucky accident of getting caught in a turning lane behind a car full of Jews on their way to bury someone did Sabbath find it. The chicken farmers were gone—that explained how he'd got so lost—and the triangular site half the size of an oil tanker was now bounded along its hypotenuse by a sprawling one-story "colonial" warehouse erected back of a high chain fence. An ominous conglomeration of pylons and power cables had been massively raised along the second side, and on the third a final resting place had been established by the local populace for box springs and mattresses that had met a violent end. Other household remains were scattered across the field or lying, just dumped there, at the edge of it. And it hadn't stopped raining. Mist and a drizzling rain to ensure the picture's permanent place in the North American wing of his memory's museum of earthly blight. The rain bestowed more meaning than was necessary. That was realism for you. More meaning than was necessary was in the nature of things.

Sabbath parked close beside the rusted picket fence opposite the pylons. Beyond a low iron gate hanging half off its hinges there stood a red brick house, a tilting little thing with an air conditioner that looked itself to be somebody's tomb.

ATTENTION GRAVEOWNERS
Leaning or incorrectly
set headstones are
DANGEROUS

Repairs must be made or
headstones will be removed

WARNING
Lock your car and protect your
valuables while visiting cemetery

Two dogs were chained to the house, and the men standing
and talking beside them were all three wearing baseball caps,
maybe because it was a Jewish cemetery or maybe because that is
what gravediggers wear. One, who was smoking, threw away his
cigarette as Sabbath approached—gray hair brutally cut, a green
work shirt and dark glasses. His tremor suggested that he needed
a drink. A second guy, in Levi's and a red and black flannel shirt,
couldn't have been more than twenty, a kid with the big-eyed,
sad-eyed Italian face of all the Casanova types at Asbury High,
the lovers in the Italian crowd who probably wound up selling
rubber tires for a living. They considered it a great coup to grab
a Jewish girl, all the while the Asbury High Jewboys were thinking, "The little wop girls, the ginzo cheerleaders, those are the
hot ones, the ones that, if you're lucky . . ." The Italians used
to call the colored kids *moolies, moolenyams*—Sicilian dialect,
Calabrian maybe, for eggplant. Hadn't been tickled by the comical dumbness of that word for years, not until he'd pulled up at
the Hess station to ask where there was a Jewish cemetery nearby,
an inquiry the mooly working there had taken for some bearded
white guy's weirdo joke.

The boss was obviously the big older man with the belly, who
walked with a limp and waved his arms about in dismay and
whom Sabbath asked, "How do I find Mr. Crawford?" A. B.
Crawford was the name affixed to the two warning signs nailed
up on a post by the gate. Identified as "Superintendent."

The dogs had begun needling Sabbath as soon as he entered the
cemetery and didn't let up while he spoke. "Are you A. B. Crawford? I'm Mickey Sabbath. My parents are over there somewhere"—he pointed to a distant corner across from the dump,
where the paths were wide and grassy and the stones didn't yet

look weatherworn—"and my grandparents are over in there."
Here he motioned to the other end of the cemetery, backing now
onto the storage facility across the road. The graves in that section were laid out in tightly interlaced, unbroken rows. The detritus, if that, of the shore's first Jews. Their stones had darkened
decades ago. "You've got to find a place for me."

"You?" said Mr. Crawford. "You're young yet."

"Only in spirit," replied Sabbath, feeling suddenly very much
at home.

"Yeah? I've got sugar," Crawford told him. "And this place is
the worst place in the world for it. Constant aggravation. This is
the worst winter we ever, ever put in."

"Is that right?"

"The frost in the ground was sixteen inches deep. *This*," he
gestured dramatically across his domain, "was a sheet of ice. You
couldn't get to a grave over there that somebody'll fall down."

"How did you bury people?"

"We buried 'em," he answered wearily. "They gave us a day
to knock out the frost and then we bury them the next day.
Jackhammers and stuff. Rough, rough winter. And water in the
ground? Forget it." Crawford was a sufferer. The métier made no
difference. Someone who cannot get out from under. A problem
of disposition. Unalterable. Sabbath sympathized.

"I want a plot, Mr. Crawford. The Sabbaths. That's my
family."

"You hit me at a bad time because I'm gonna have a funeral
pretty soon."

The hearse had arrived and people were assembling around it.
Umbrellas. Women carrying infants. Men with yarmulkes on.
Children. Everyone waiting back in the street only yards away
from the cables and pylons. Sabbath heard a chuckle from the
crowd, somebody saying something funny at a funeral. It always
happens. The small man who'd just arrived must be the rabbi. He
was holding a book. Immediately he was offered shelter beneath
an umbrella. Another chuckle. Hard to tell what that meant
about the person who died. Nothing probably. It was just that the

living were living and couldn't help it. Wit. As delusions go, not the worst.

"Okay," said Mr. Crawford, quickly estimating the size of the crowd, "they're still coming. Let's take a walk. Rufus," he called to the trembling drunk, "watch the dogs, huh?" But the going-over they'd been giving Sabbath erupted into vicious snapping when their master limped off with him. Crawford swiftly turned back and aimed a threatening finger toward the sky. *"Stop it!"*

"Why do you have dogs?" Sabbath asked as they resumed along a path that led around the gravestones to the Sabbath plot.

"They broke into the building four times already. To steal equipment. They robbed all the tools. Machinery that costs three, four hundred dollars. Gasoline-driven hedge shears and all that other kind of stuff that's over there."

"Don't you have insurance?"

"No. No insurance. Forget about that. It's me!" he said excitedly. "It's me! It's out of my pocket! I buy all the equipment and all that. This association here gives me nine hundred dollars a month—see? I have to pay all the help out of that—see? In the meantime, I just turned seventy and I dig all the graves, I put in all the foundations, and it's an absolute joke. The help you get to-day—you have to tell them every goddarn thing to do. And nobody wants to do this work anymore. I'm one man short. I'm going over to Lakewood and bringing a Mexican down here. You got to get a Mexican. It's a joke. Six months ago somebody was up here visiting a grave and a *schvartze* goes ahead and puts a gun to the people's head. Ten o'clock in the morning! That's why I got the dogs over here—they warn me if somebody is outside, if you're sittin' here by yourself."

"How long have you been here?" Sabbath asked, though he knew the answer already: long enough to learn to say *schvartze*.

"Too long," replied Crawford. "I been here I would say maybe close to forty years. I've had it right to here. The cemetery is broke. I know they're broke. There ain't no money in the cemetery business. The money is in the monument business. I got no pension. Nothin'. I just juggle back and forth. When I have a funeral, see, that you get a few extra dollars, and that goes toward the payroll, but it's just a, just a . . . I don't know, a problem."

Forty years. Missed Grandma and Morty, but got everybody else. And now he gets me.

Crawford was lamenting, "And nothing to show for it. Nothin' in the bank. *Nothin'.*"

"There's a relative of mine right there." Sabbath pointed to a stone marked "Shabas." Must be Cousin Fish, who'd taught him to swim. "The old-timers," he explained to Crawford, "were Shabas. They wrote it all kinds of ways: Shabas, Shabbus, Shabsai, Sabbatai. My father was Sabbath. Got it from relatives up in New York when he came to America as a kid. We're over here, I think."

In search of the graves he was growing excited. The last forty-eight hours had been replete with theatrics, confusion, disappointment, adventure, but nothing with a power as primary as this. His heart had not sounded as loud even while he was stealing from Michelle. He felt himself at last inside his life, like someone who, after a long illness, steps back into his shoes for the first time.

"One grave," Crawford said.

"One grave."

"For yourself."

"Right."

"Where did you want this grave?"

"Near my family."

Sabbath's beard was dripping, and after wringing it out with one hand, he left it looking like a braided candlestick. Crawford said, "Okay. Now where is your family?"

"There. There!" and walls of embitterment were crashing down; the surface of something long unexposed—Sabbath's soul? the film of his soul?—was illuminated by happiness. As close as a substanceless substance can come to being physically caressed. "They're *there!*" All in the ground *there*—yes, living together there like a family of field mice.

"Yeah," said Crawford, "but you need a single. This here is the single section. Against the fence here." He was pointing along a portion of badly neglected wire-mesh fence across the road from the worst of the dump. You could crawl through the fence, step right over it, or, without even wire cutters or a pliers, just peel away with your hand what remained affixed to the railings. A standing lamp had been pushed out of a car across the way, so that the lamp was not even in the dump but lying in the gutter like somebody gunned down in his tracks. Probably it needed nothing more than new wiring. But its owner obviously hated that lamp and drove it out to do it in across from the Jews' cemetery.

"I don't know if I can give you a grave here or not. This last one by the gate here is the only space I see and it could be reserved, you know. And from here on, the other side of the gate, there's four-grave plots. But maybe you got a grave over with your folks and don't even know it."

"That's possible," said Sabbath, "yes," and now that Crawford had raised that possibility he remembered that when they buried his mother there *was* an empty plot beside her.

There had been. Occupied. According to the dates on the stone, two years back they had put Ida Schlitzer in the family's fourth plot. His mother's maiden sister from the Bronx. In the whole of the Bronx no room left, not even for a half-pint like Ida. Or had everybody forgotten the second son? Maybe they thought he was still at sea or already dead because of his way of life. Buried in the Caribbean. In the West Indies. Should have been. On the island of Curaçao. Would have liked it down there. No deep-water port in Curaçao. There was a long, long pier, seemed like a mile long then, and at the end of it the tanker tied up. Never forget it, because there were horses and there were runners—pimps, if you like—but they were kids, little kids who had the horses. And they swat the goddamn horse and the horse takes you right to the whorehouse. Curaçao was a Dutch colony, the port called Willemstad, a bourgeois colonial port, men and women in tropical gear, white people in pith helmets, a pleasant little colonial town, and the cemetery just down from those beautiful hills where there was a complex of whorehouses bigger than any I had ever seen in all my days at sea. The crews of God knows how many ships tied up at this port, and all of them up there fucking. And the good men of the town up there fucking. And me asleep in the pretty cemetery below. But I missed my chance at Willemstad by giving up the whores for puppets. And so now Aunt Ida, who never dared say boo to anyone, has screwed me out of my plot. Displaced by a virgin who typed all her life for the Department of Parks and Recreation.

Beloved son and brother
Killed in Action in the
Philippines
April 13, 1924—December 15, 1944
Always in our hearts
Lt. Morton Sabbath

Dad to one side of him, Mother to the other, and, to Mother's side, Ida instead of me. Not even the memories of Curaçao could compensate for this. King of the kingdom of the unillusioned, emperor of no expectations, crestfallen man-god of the double cross, Sabbath had *still* to learn that nothing but *nothing* will ever turn out—and this obtuseness was, in itself, a deep, deep shock. Why does life refuse me even the *grave* I want! Had I only marshaled my abhorrence in a good cause and killed myself two years ago, that spot next to Ma's would be mine.

Looking over the Sabbath burial plot, Crawford suddenly announced, "Oh, I know them. Oh, they were good friends of mine. I knew your family."

"Yes? You knew my old man?"

"Sure, sure, sure, a good guy. A real gentleman."

"That he was."

"In fact, I think the daughter or someone comes out. You have some daughters?"

No, but what was the difference? He was only salving emotional wounds and trying to pick up a few bucks on the side. "Sure," said Sabbath.

"Well, yeah, she comes out a lot. See that," said Crawford, pointing to the shrubbery thickly covering all four graves, ever-green crew-cut to about six inches high, "you don't need work on that plot, no sir."

"No, that's nice. It looks very nice."

"Look, the only possible thing is if I can give you a grave over there." Where the triangle came to a point and the two potholed streets beyond intersected, there was an empty expanse within the sagging wire fence. "See? But you'd have to go for two graves up there. Anyplace but the single section you have to buy at least two graves. Want me to show you where the two-graves are?"

"Sure, why don't we do that, since I'm here now and you've got the time."

"I ain't got the time but I'll make the time."

"That's good, that's kind of you," Sabbath said, and together they started off through the drizzle toward where the cemetery looked like an abandoned lot, already in mid-April choked with unmown weeds.

"This is a nicer section," Crawford told him, "than with the singles. You'd be facing the road. Somebody going past would see your stone. Two roads join up there. Traffic from two directions." Banging the wet ground with the muddy boot on his good leg, he proclaimed, "I would say *right here*."

"But my family is way over there. And my back would be to them, right? I'm facing the wrong way here."

"Then take the other, with the singles. If it's not reserved."

"I don't have that good a shot at them from there either, frankly."

"Yeah, but you're across from a very fine family. The Weiz-mans. You're looking onto a very good family over there. Every-body's proud of the Weizmans. That woman that's in charge of this cemetery, her name is Mrs. Weizman. We just put her hus-band in here. Her whole family is buried in there. We just buried her sister in there. It's a good section, and right across from them is the single section."

"But how about along the fence over there, where it's not that far from my family? You see where I mean?"

"No, no, no. Them graves is sold to somebody already. And that's a *four*-grave section. You follow me?"

"Okay, I do," said Sabbath. "The single section, the two-graves, and the rest is all four-grave plots. I get the picture. Why don't you look and see whether that single is reserved or not? Because that's a little closer to my folks."

"Well, I can't do it now. I got a funeral."

Together they worked their way back through the rows of graves toward the little brick house where the dogs were chained up.

"Well, I'll wait," said Sabbath, "till the funeral is over. I can visit with my family, and you can tell me after if it's available and what the cost is."

"The cost. Yeah. Yeah. They ain't really that much. How much could it be? Four hundred, something like that. The most it could be. Maybe four fifty. I don't know. I have nothing to do with selling the graves."

"Who does?"

"The lady at the organization. Mrs. Weizman."

"And that's who pays you, the organization?"

"Pay me," he said in disgust. "It's a joke what they pay me. A hundred and a quarter a week I clear for myself. And from there over to there, it takes a man three days to cut the grass without anything else. For a hundred and a quarter a week, that's all. I've got no pension. I got sugar and no pension and all this aggravation. Social Security and that's all. So what do you want, do you think—the one grave or the two? I would rather see you up with the two. You won't be crammed in up there. It's a nicer section. But it's up to you."

"There's definitely more legroom," said Sabbath, "but it's so far from everyone. And I'm going to be lying there a long time. Look, see what's available. We'll talk together after you're done. Here," he said, "thanks for making time." He'd changed a hundred of Michelle's to get gas from the moolies, and he handed Crawford twenty bucks. "And," he said, slipping him a second twenty, "for taking good care of my family."

"My pleasure. Your father was a real gentleman."

"So are you, sir."

"Okay. You just look around and see where you'll be comfortable."

"That's what I'll do."

The lone plot that might or might not be available to him in the single section was beside a tombstone with a large Star of David carved at the top and four Hebrew words beneath it. Interred there was Captain Louis Schloss. "Holocaust Survivor, VFW, Mariner, Businessman, Entrepreneur. In Loving Memory Relatives and Friends May 30, 1929–May 20, 1990." Three months my senior. Ten days shy of sixty-one. Survived the Holocaust but not the business. A fellow mariner. Mickey Sabbath, Mariner.

They were rolling the plain pine box in now, Crawford pulling at the front, in the lead, limping at a rapid pace, and the two helpers at either side steering, the drunk with the green work shirt checking his pockets for the cigs. It hasn't even begun and he can't wait till it's over to light up. The smallish rabbi, his hands in front of him holding the book, was talking to Mr. Crawford as he hastened to keep abreast of him. They brought the box up to the open grave. Very clean, that wood. Must put in my order. Pay for that today. Plot, coffin, even a monument—get everything in order, courtesy of Michelle. Buttonhole this rabbi before he leaves and slip him a hundred to come back for me and read from that book. Thus do I cleanse her money of its frivolous history of illicit gratification and reintegrate this stash of bills into the simple and natural business of the earth.

The earth. Very much in evidence here today. Only a few steps behind him there was a raw mound of the earth piled up where somebody had recently been buried in it, and across the way from that were two graves freshly dug into the earth, side by side. Expecting twins. He walked over to take a look inside one, a little window-shopping. The clean way each was cut into the ground smacked of a solid achievement. The sharp spaded corners and the puddly bottom and the ripply deep sides—you had to hand it to the drunk, the Italian kid, and Crawford: there was the magnificence of centuries in what they did. This hole goes all the way back. As does the other. Both dark with mystery and fantastic. The right people, the right day. This weather told no lies about his situation. It put to him the grimmest of questions about his intentions, to which his answer was "Yes! Yes! Yes! I will emulate my failed father-in-law, a successful suicide!"

But am I playing at this? Even at this? Always difficult to determine.

In a wheelbarrow left out in the rain (more than likely by the drunk—Sabbath knew this from living with one) there was a conical pile of wet dirt. Sabbath, with a tinge of ghoulish pleasure, forced his fingers through the gritty goop until they all disappeared. If I count to ten and then extract them, they'll be the old fingers, the old, provocative fingers with which I pulled their tail. Wrong again. Have to go down in the dirt with more than these fingers if I hope ever to make straight in me all that is crooked. Have to count to ten ten billion times, and he wondered how high Morty had counted by now. And Grandma? And Grandpa? What is the Yiddish for zillion?

Getting to the old graves, to the burial ground established in the early days by the original seashore Jews, he gave the funeral in progress a wide berth and was careful to steer clear of the watchdogs when he passed the little red house. These dogs had not yet been made conversant with the common courtesies, let alone the ancient taboos that obtain in a Jewish cemetery. Jews guarded by dogs? Historically very, very wrong. His alternative was to be buried bucolically on Battle Mountain as close to Drenka as he could get. This had occurred to him long before today. But whom would he talk to up there? He had never found a goy yet who could talk fast enough for him. And there they'd be slower than usual. He would have to swallow the insult of the dogs. No cemetery is going to be perfect.

After ten minutes of rambling about in the drizzle, searching for his grandparents' graves, he saw that only if he traveled methodically up and down, reading every headstone from one end of each row to the other, could he hope to locate Clara and Mordecai Sabbath. Footstones he could ignore—they mostly said "At

Rest"—but the hundreds upon hundreds of headstones required his concentration, an immersion in them so complete that there would be nothing inside him but these names. He had to shrug off how these people would have disliked him and how many of them he would have despised, had to forget about the people they had been alive. Because you are no longer insufferable if you are dead. Goes for me, too. He had to drink in the dead, down to the dregs.

Our beloved mother Minnie. Our beloved husband and father Sidney. Beloved mother and grandmother Frieda. Beloved husband and father Jacob. Beloved husband, father, and grandfather Samuel. Beloved husband and father Joseph. Beloved mother Sarah. Beloved wife Rebecca. Beloved husband and father Benjamin. Beloved mother and grandmother Tessa. Beloved mother and grandmother Sophie. Beloved mother Bertha. Beloved husband Hyman. Beloved husband Morris. Beloved husband and father William. Beloved wife and mother Rebecca. Beloved daughter and sister Hannah Sarah. Our beloved mother Klara. Beloved husband Max. Our beloved daughter Sadie. Beloved wife Tillie. Beloved husband Bernard. Beloved husband and father Fred. Beloved husband and father Frank. My beloved wife our dear mother Lena. Our dear father Marcus. On and on and on. Nobody beloved gets out alive. Only the very oldest recorded all in Hebrew. Our son and brother Nathan. Our dear father Edward. Husband and father Louis. Beloved wife and mother Fannie. Beloved mother and wife Rose. Beloved husband and father Solomon. Beloved son and brother Harry. In memory of my beloved husband and our dear father Lewis. Beloved son Sidney. Beloved wife of Louis and mother of George Lucille. Beloved mother Tillie. Beloved father Abraham. Beloved mother and grandmother Leah. Beloved husband and father Emanuel. Beloved mother Sarah. Beloved father Samuel. And on mine, beloved what? Just that: Beloved What. David Schwartz, beloved son and brother died in service of his country 1894–1918. 15 Cheshvan. In memory of Gertie, a true wife and loyal friend. Our beloved father Sam. Our son, nineteen years old, 1903–1922. No name, merely "Our son." Beloved wife and dear mother Florence.

Beloved brother Dr. Boris. Beloved husband and father Samuel. Beloved father Saul. Beloved wife and mother Celia. Beloved mother Chasa. Beloved husband and father Isadore. Beloved wife and mother Esther. Beloved mother Jennie. Beloved husband and father David. Our beloved mother Gertrude. Beloved husband, father, brother Jekyl. Beloved aunt Sima. Beloved daughter Ethel. Beloved wife and mother Annie. Beloved wife and mother Frima. Beloved father and husband Hersch. Beloved father . . .

And here we are. Sabbath. Clara Sabbath 1872–1941. Mordecai Sabbath 1871–1923. There they are. Simple stone. And a pebble on top. Who'd come to visit? Mort, did you visit Grandma? Dad? Who cares? Who's left? What's in there? The box isn't even in there. You were said to be headstrong, Mordecai, bad temper, big joker . . . though even you couldn't make a joke like this. Nobody could. Better than this they don't come. And Grandma. Your name, the name also of your occupation. A matter-of-fact person. Everything about you—your stature, those dresses, your silence—said, "I am not indispensable." No contradictions, no temptations, though you were inordinately fond of corn on the cob. Mother hated having to watch you eat it. The worst of the summer for her. It made her "nauseous." I loved to watch. Otherwise you two got along. Probably keeping quiet was the key, letting her run things her way. Openly partial to Morty, Grandpa Mordecai's namesake, but who could blame you? You didn't live to see everything shatter. Lucky. Nothing big about you, Grandma, but nothing small either. Life could have marked you up a lot worse. Born in the little town of Mikulice, died at Pitkin Memorial. Have I left anything out? Yes. You used to love to clean the fish for us when Morty and I came home at night from surf casting. Mostly we came home with nothing, but the triumph of walking home from the beach with a couple of big blues in the bucket! You'd clean them in the kitchen. Fillet knife right at the opening, probably the anus, slit it straight up the center till you got behind the gills, and then (I liked watching this part best) you would just put your hand in and grab all the good stuff and throw it away. Then you scaled. Working against the scales and somehow without getting them all over the place. It used to take me fifteen minutes to clean it and half an hour to clean up after. The whole *thing* took you ten minutes. Mom even let you cook it. Never cut off the head and the tail. Baked it whole. Baked bluefish, corn, fresh tomatoes, big Jersey tomatoes. Grandma's meal. Yes, yes, it was something down on the beach at dusk with Mort. Used to talk to the other men. Childhood and its terrific markers. From about eight to thirteen, the fundamental ballast that we have. It's either right or it's wrong. Mine was right. The original ballast, an attachment to those who were nearby when we were learning what feeling was all about, an attachment maybe not stranger but stronger even than the erotic. A good thing to be able to contemplate for a final time—instead of racing through with it and getting out of here—certain high points, certain human high points. Hanging out with the man next door and his sons. Meeting and talking in the yard. Down on the beach, fishing with Mort. Rich times. Morty used to talk to the other men, the fishermen. Did it so easily. To me everything he did was so authoritative. One guy in brown pants and a short-sleeve white shirt and with a cigar always in his mouth used to tell us he didn't give a shit about catching fish (which was lucky, since he rarely pulled in more than a sand shark)—he told us kids, "The chief pleasure of fishing is getting out of the house. Gettin' away from women." We always laughed, but for Morty and me the bite was the thrill. With a blue you get a big hit. The rod jolts in your hand. Everything jolts. Morty was my teacher fishing. "When a striper takes the bait, it'll head out. If you stop the line from paying out it'll snap. So you just have to let it out. With a blue, after the hit, you can just reel in, but not with a striper. A blue is big and tough, but a striper will fight." Getting blowfish off the hook was a problem for everybody but Mort—spines and quills didn't bother him. The other thing that wasn't much fun to catch was rays. Do you remember when I was eight how I wound up in the hospital? I was out on the jetty and I caught a huge ray and it bit me and I just passed out. Beautiful, undulating swimmers but predatory sons of bitches, very mean with their sharp teeth. Ominous. Looks like a flat shark. Morty had to holler for help, and a guy came and they carried me up to the guy's car and rushed me to Pitkin. Whenever we went out fishing, you couldn't wait for us to get back so you could clean the catch. Used to catch shiners. Weighed less than a pound. You'd fry four or five of them in a pan. Very bony but great. Watching you eat a shiner was a lot of fun, too, for everyone but Mother. What else did we bring you to clean? Fluke, flounder, when we fished Shark River inlet. Weakfish. That's about it. When Morty joined the Air Corps, the night before he left we went down to the beach with our rods for an hour. Never got into the gear as kids. Just fished. Rod, hooks, sinkers, line, sometimes lures, mostly bait, mostly squid. That was it. Heavy-duty tackle. Big barbed hook. Never cleaned the rod. Once a summer splashed some water on it. Keep the same rig on the whole time. Just change the sinkers and the bait if we wanted to fish on the bottom. We went down the beach to fish for an hour. Everybody in the house was crying because he was going to war the next day. You were already here. You were gone. So I'll tell you what happened. October 10, 1942. He'd hung around through September because he wanted to see me bar mitzvahed, wanted to be there. The eleventh of October he went to Perth Amboy to enlist. The last of the fishing off the jetties and the beach. By the middle, the end of October, the fish disappear. I'd ask Morty—when he was first teaching me off the jetties with a small rod and reel, one made for fresh water—"Where do the fish go to?" "Nobody knows," he said. "Nobody knows where the fish go. Once they go out to sea, who knows where they go to? What do you think, people follow them around? That's the mystery of fishing. Nobody knows where they are." We went down to the end of the street that evening and down the stairs and onto the beach. It was just about dark. Morty could throw a rig a hundred and fifty feet even in the days before spin casting. Used the open-faced reels. Just a spool with a handle on it. Rods much stiffer then, much less adroit reel and a stiffer rod. Torture to cast for a kid. In the beginning I was always snarling the line. Spent most of the time getting it straightened out. But eventually I got it. Morty

said he was going to miss going out fishing with me. He'd taken
me down to the beach to say so long to me without the family
carrying on around us. "Standing out here," he told me, "the sea
air, the quiet, the sound of the waves, your toes in the sand, the
idea that there are all those things out there that are about to bite
your bait. That thrill of something being out there. You don't
know what it is, you don't know how big it is. You don't even
know if you'll ever see it." And he never did see it, nor, of course,
did he get what you get when you're older, which is something
that mocks your opening yourself up to these simple things, something that is formless and overwhelming and that probably is
dread. No, he got killed instead. And that's the news, Grandma.
The great generational kick of standing down on the beach in the
dusk with your older brother. You sleep in the same room, you get
very close. He took me with him everywhere. One summer when
he was about twelve he got a job selling bananas door-to-door.
There was a man in Belmar who sold only bananas, and he hired
Morty and Morty hired me. The job was to go along the streets
hollering, "Bananas, twenty-five cents a bunch!" What a great
job. I still sometimes dream about that job. You got paid to shout
"Bananas!" On Thursdays and Fridays after school let out for the
day, he went to pluck chickens for the kosher butcher, Feldman. A
farmer from Lakewood used to call on Feldman and sell him
chickens. Morty would take me along to help him. I liked the
worst part best: spreading the Vaseline all the way up our arms to
stymie the lice. It made me feel like a little big shot at eight or nine
not to be afraid of those horrible fucking lice, to be, like Mort,
utterly contemptuous of them and just pluck the chickens. And he
used to protect me from the Syrian Jews. Kids used to dance on
the sidewalk in the summertime outside Mike and Lou's. Jitterbug
to the jukebox music. I doubt you ever saw that. When Morty
was working at Mike and Lou's one summer he'd bring home his
apron and Mom would wash it for him for the next night. It
would be stained yellow from the mustard and red from the
relish. The mustard came right with him into our room when he
came into our room at night. Smelled like mustard, sauerkraut,

and hot dogs. Mike and Lou's had good dogs. Grilled. The Syrian guys used to dance outside Mike and Lou's on the sidewalk, used to dance by themselves like sailors. They had a little kind of Damascus mambo they did, very explosive steps. All related they were, clannish, and with very dark skin. The Syrian kids who joined our card games played a ferocious blackjack. Their fathers were in buttons, thread, fabrics then. Used to hear Dad's crony, the upholsterer from Neptune, talking about them when the men played poker in our kitchen on Friday nights. "Money is their god. Toughest people in the world to do business with. They'll cheat you as soon as you turn around." Some of these Syrian kids made an impression. One of them, one of the Gindi brothers, would come up to you and take a swing at you for no reason, come up and kill you and just look at you and walk away. I used to be hypnotized by his sister. I was twelve. She and I were in the same class. A little, hairy fireplug. Huge eyebrows. I couldn't get over her dark skin. She told him something that I said, so once he started to rough me up. I was deathly afraid of him. I should never have looked at her, let alone said *anything* to her. But the dark skin got me going. Always has. He started to rough me up right in front of Mike and Lou's, and Morty came outside in his mustard-stained apron and told Gindi, "Stay away from him." And Gindi said, "You gonna make me?" And Morty said, "Yes." And Gindi took one shot at him and opened up Morty's whole nose. Remember? Isaac Gindi. His form of narcissism never enchanted me. Sixteen stitches. Those Syrians lived in another time zone. They were always whispering among themselves. But I was twelve, inside my pants things were beginning to reverberate, and I could not keep my eyes off his hairy sister. Sonia was her name. Sonia had another brother, as I recall, Maurice, who was not human either. But then came the war. I was thirteen, Morty was eighteen. Here's a kid who never went away in his life, except maybe for a track meet. Never out of Monmouth County. Every day of his life he returned home. Endlessness renewed every day. And the next morning he goes off to die. But then, death is endlessness par excellence, is it not? Wouldn't you agree? Well, for whatever it is

worth, before I move on: I have never once eaten corn on the cob
without pleasurably recalling the devouring frenzy of you and
your dentures and the repugnance this ignited in my mother. It
taught me about more than mother-in-laws and daughter-in-laws;
it taught me everything. This model grandmother, and Mother
had all she could do not to throw you out into the street. And my
mother was not unkind—you know that. But what affords the
one with happiness affords the other with disgust. The interplay,
the ridiculous interplay, enough to kill all and everyone.

Beloved wife and mother Fannie. Beloved wife and mother
Hannah. Beloved husband and father Jack. It goes on. Our beloved mother Rose. Our beloved father Harry. Our beloved husband, father, and grandfather Meyer. People. All people. And here
is Captain Schloss and there . . .

In the earth turned up where Lee Goldman, another devoted
wife, mother, and grandmother, had just been united with one of
her family, a beloved one as yet unidentified, Sabbath found peb-
bles to place on the stones of his mother, his father, and Morty.
And one for Ida.

Here I am.

◆ ◆ ◆

Crawford's office was barren of everything except a desk, a
phone, a couple of battered chairs, and, inexplicably, a content-
less vending machine. A smell of wet dog fur soured the air, and
there was no reason not to think that the desk and two chairs had
been culled from the inventory of the improvised dump across the
way. On the desk a piece of glass, crisscrossed with masking tape
to hold it together, served the cemetery superintendent as a writing surface; a slew of old business cards had been pushed beneath
the glass along its four edges. The card that Sabbath saw first
read, "The Good Intentions Paving Company, 212 Coit Street,
Freehold, New Jersey."

To enter the brick tomblike building, Sabbath had had to shout
for Crawford to come out and calm the dogs. April 13, 1924—
December 15, 1944. Morty would be seventy. Today would be his

seventieth birthday! He'll be dead in December *fifty years.* I won't be here for the commemoration. Thank God none of us will.

The funeral was by then long over and the rain had stopped. Crawford had phoned Mrs. Weizman to get the costs for Sabbath and to see if the single was reserved, and for nearly an hour now he had been waiting for Sabbath to come to the office so he could report her prices, as well as the good news about the single. But each time Sabbath started away from the family plot, he'd turn around and go back. He didn't know whom he would be depriving of what by walking away after ten minutes of standing there, but he couldn't do it. The repeated leaving and returning did not escape his mockery, but he could do nothing about it. He could not go and he could not go and he could not go, and then—like any dumb creature who abruptly stops doing one thing and starts doing another and about whom you can never tell if its life is all freedom or no freedom—he could go and he went. And no lucidity to be derived from any of this. Rather, there was a distinctly assertive quickening of the great stupidity. If there was ever anything to know, now he knew he never had known it. And all this while his fists had been clenched, causing arthritic agony.

Crawford's face didn't make as much sense indoors as it had outside. Without his Phillies cap, he was revealed to be all burgeoning chin, bridgeless nose, and narrow expanse of forehead—it was as though, having given him this chin curved unmistakably in the shape of a shovel, God had marked baby Crawford at birth as a cemetery superintendent. It was a face on the evolutionary dividing line between our species and the subspecies preceding ours, and yet, from behind the desk with the fractured legs and the broken glass top, he established quickly a professional tone appropriate to the gravity of the transaction. To keep pictorially at the forefront of Sabbath's mind all the impertinences in store for his carcass, there was the wild snarling of the dogs. Rattling their chains beneath Crawford's window, they sounded all stoked up with Jew-hating dreams. Moreover, there were dog chains and leashes scattered about on the unswept, beat-up floor of dark checkerboard linoleum, and on Crawford's desk, to hold his pencils, his pens, his paper clips, and even some paperwork, he used the empty Pedigree dog food cans from which the dogs had been fed. A carton half full of unopened dog food had to be removed from the seat of the room's other chair before Sabbath could sit down across from Crawford's. Only then did he notice the transom over the front door, a rectangular window of colored glass scribed with the Star of David. This place had been built as the cemetery prayer house where the mourners gathered with the casket. It was a doghouse now.

"They want six hundred dollars for the single," Crawford told him. "They want twelve hundred for the two graves over there, and I chopped them down to eleven hundred. And I would suggest that the two graves would be the best thing for you over there. A nicer section. You'll be better off. The other you got the gate swinging next to you, you got the traffic in and out there—"

"The two graves are too far away. Give me the one next to Captain Schloss."

"If you think you'll be better off . . ."

"And a monument."

"I don't sell 'em. I told you."

"But you know somebody in the business. I want to order a monument."

"There are a million kind."

"Just like Captain Schloss's will do. A simple monument."

"That's not a cheap stone. That's about eight hundred. In New York they would charge you twelve hundred. More. There is a matching base. There is the foundation fee—concrete feet. The lettering I gotta bill you separate, a separate charge."

"How much?"

"Depends how much you want to say."

"As much as Captain Schloss says."

"He's got a lot written there. That's gonna cost you."

Sabbath removed from his interior pocket the envelope with Michelle's money, feeling to be sure the envelope of Polaroids was still there as well. From the money envelope he took six hundred for the plot and eight for the stone and put the bills on Crawford's desk.

"And three hundred more," asked Sabbath, "for what I want to say?"

"We're talkin' over fifty letters," said Crawford.

Sabbath counted out four hundred-dollar bills. "One is for you. To take care that everything is done."

"You want planting? On top of you? Yeco trees is two hundred and seventy-five dollars, for the trees and the work."

"Trees? I don't need trees. I never heard of yeco trees."

"That is what is on your family plot. That is yeco trees."

"Okay. Give me the same as theirs. Give me some yeco trees."

He reached in for three more of the hundreds. "Mr. Crawford, all my next of kin are here. I want you to run the show."

"You're ill."

"I need a coffin, buddy. One like I saw today."

"Plain pine. That one was four hundred. I know a guy can do the same for three fifty."

"And a rabbi. That short guy will do. How much?"

"Him? A hundred. Let me find you somebody else. I'll get you somebody just as good for fifty."

"A Jew?"

"Sure a Jew. He's old, that's all."

The door beneath the Star of David transom was pushed open, and just as the Italian kid came walking in, one of the dogs darted in alongside him and surged on his chain to within inches of Sabbath.

"Johnny, for Christ's sake," said Crawford, "shut the door and keep the dog outside."

"Yeah," said Sabbath, "you wouldn't want him to eat me yet. Wait'll I sign on."

"No, this one here won't bite you," Crawford assured Sabbath. "The other one, he can jump on you, but not this one. Johnny, get the dog out!"

Johnny dragged the dog backward by the chain and forced him, still snarling at Sabbath, out the door.

"The help. You can't sit here and say, 'Here, go do this job over there.' They don't know how. And now I'm going to have to get a Mexican? And he's gonna be any better? He's gonna be worse. Did you lock your car?" he asked Sabbath.

"Mr. Crawford, what am I leaving out of my plans?"

Crawford looked down at his notes. "Burial costs," he said. "Four hundred."

Sabbath counted out four hundred more and added the bills to the stack already on the desk.

"The instructions," Crawford told him. "What you want on the monument."

"Give me paper. Give me an envelope."

While Crawford prepared the bills—everything with carbon and in triplicate—Sabbath outlined on the back of Crawford's paper (the front was an invoice form, "Care of Grave," et cetera) the shape of a monument, drew it as naively as a child draws a house or a cat or a tree and felt very much the child while he did it. Within the outline he arranged the words of his epitaph as he wished them to appear. Then he folded the paper in thirds and slipped it into the envelope and sealed it. "Instructions," he wrote across the face of the envelope, "for inscription on the monument of M. Sabbath. Open when necessary. M.S. 4/13/94."

Crawford, contemplative, was a long time completing the paperwork. Sabbath enjoyed watching him. It was a good show. He formed every letter of every word on every document and receipt as though each were of the utmost importance. Suddenly he seemed to be inspired by a profound reverence, perhaps only for the money he had overcharged Sabbath but perhaps a little for the ineluctable meaning of the formalities. So these two shrewdies sat across that battered desk from each other, aging men mistrustfully interlinked—as one is, as we are—each of them drinking whatever still bubbled into his mouth out of the fountain of life. Mr. Crawford carefully rolled up the office copies of the invoices and filed the neat cylinder of papers in an empty dog food can.

Sabbath returned one last time to stand at the family plot, his heart both leaden and leaping, and tearing from within him the last of his doubt. *At this I will succeed. I promise you.* Then he went to look at his own plot. On the way there, he passed two gravestones he hadn't seen before. Beloved son and dear brother killed in action at Normandy July 1, 1944 age 27 years you will always be remembered Sergeant Harold Berg. Beloved son and brother Julius Dropkin killed in action Sept. 12, 1944 in southern France age 26 years always in our heart. They got these boys to die. They got Dropkin and Berg to die. He stopped and cursed on their behalf.

Despite the dump across the street and the damaged fence to the back and the corroded, fallen-down iron gate to one side, pride of ownership welled up in him, however mean and paltry that sandy bit of soil happened to look, there at the edge of the line of singles consigned to the cemetery's fringe. They can't take that away from me. So pleased was he with a prudent morning's work—the scrupulous officializing of his decision, the breaking of bonds, the shedding of fear, the bidding adieu—he whistled some Gershwin. Maybe the other section *was* nicer, but if he stood on his toes he could see through from here to his family's plot, and there were all the inspiring Weizmans just across the path, and immediately to the right of him—to his left, lying down—was Captain Schloss. He slowly read once again the substantial portrait of his eternal neighbor-to-be. "Holocaust Survivor, VFW, Mariner, Businessman, Entrepreneur. In Loving Memory Relatives and Friends May 30, 1929–May 20, 1990." Sabbath remembered only some twenty-four hours earlier reading the sign in the window of the salesroom abutting the funeral home where Linc had been eulogized. A nameless gravestone stood on display, beside it was a sign, headed "What Is a Monument?" and, beneath that, simple, elegant script avowing that a monument "is a symbol of devotion . . . a tangible expression of the noblest of all human emotions—LOVE . . . a monument is built because there was a life, not a death, and with intelligent selection and proper guidance, it should inspire REVERENCE, FAITH and HOPE for the living . . . it should speak out as a voice from yesterday and today to the ages yet unborn. . . ."

Beautifully put. I'm glad they have clarified for us what is a monument.

Beside the monument to Captain Schloss, he envisioned his own:

Morris Sabbath
"Mickey"
Beloved Whoremonger, Seducer,
Sodomist, Abuser of Women,
Destroyer of Morals, Ensnarer of Youth,
Uxoricide,
Suicide
1929–1994

◆ ◆ ◆

. . . and that was where Cousin Fish lived—and that finished the tour. The hotels were gone, replaced along the oceanfront by modest condos, but back down the streets the little houses still squarely stood, the wooden bungalows and stucco bungalows where everyone had lived, and as though on the recommendation of the Hemlock Society, he had driven past them all, final remembrance and farewell. But now he could think of no further procrastination that he might construe as a symbolic act of closure; now it was time to get a move on and get the damn thing done, the great big act that will conclude my story . . . and so he was leaving Bradley Beach forever when there on Hammond Avenue materialized the bungalow that had been Fish's.

Hammond ran parallel to the ocean but up by Main Street and the railroad tracks, a good mile or so from the beach. Fish must be dead many years now. His wife got the tumor when we were boys. A very young woman—not that we grasped that then. On the side of her head, a potato growing beneath the soil of her skin. She wore kerchiefs to hide the unsightliness, but even so, a sharp-eyed kid could see where the potato was flourishing. Fish sold us vegetables from his truck. Dugan for cake, Borden for milk, Pechter for bread, Seaboard for ice, Fish for vegetables. When I saw the potatoes in the basket, I would think of you-know-what. A dead mother. Inconceivable. For a while I couldn't eat a potato. But I got older and hungrier and it passed. Fish raised the two kids. Brought them with him to the house the nights the men played cards. Irving and Lois. Irving collected stamps. Had at least one from every country. Lois had boobs. At ten she had them. In grade school, boys used to throw her coat over her head, squeeze 'em, and run. Morty told me I couldn't do it, because she was our cousin. "*Second* cousin." But Morty said no, it was against some Jewish law. Our last names were all but the same. Thanks to the alphabet, I sat a mere eighteen inches away from Lois. Very trying, those classes. The pleasure was difficult—my first lesson in that. At the end of the hour I had to carry my notebook in front of my pants while leaving the room. But Morty said not to—even at the height of the sweater era, no. The last person I ever listened to in that department. Should have told him off at the cemetery: "What Jewish law? You made it up, you son of a bitch." Would have handed him a laugh. Rapture itself, to reach out my hand and give him a laugh, a body, a voice, a life with some of the fun in it of being alive, the fun of existing that even a flea must feel, the pleasure of existence, pure and simple, that practically anyone this side of the cancer ward gets a glimmer of occasionally, uninspiring as his fortunes overall may be. Here, Mort, what we call "a life," the way we call the sky "the sky" and the sun "the sun." How nonchalant we are. Here, brother, a living soul—for whatever it's worth, take mine!

Okay. Time to marshal the state of mind necessary to carry it off. That it would require of him a state of mind and *more*—littleness, greatness, stupidity, wisdom, cowardice, heroism, blindness, vision, everything in the arsenal of his two opposing armies united as one—this he knew. Swill about the fun that even a flea must feel was not going to make it any easier. Stop thinking the wrong thoughts and think *the right one*. And yet Fish's house—of all the houses! His own family's house, fussily kept up now by a Hispanic couple whom he had seen gardening on their knees along the edge of the driveway (no longer sand but asphalt), had worked beautifully on his resolve, causing all his misery to cohere around his decision. The new stuff, the glass sunporch and the aluminum siding and the scalloped metal shutters, made it ludicrous to think of the house as *theirs*, as ludicrous as to think that the cemetery was *theirs*. But *this* ruin, Fish's, had significance. That unaccountable exaggeration, significance: in Sabbath's experience invariably the prelude to missing the point.

Where there were shades, they were torn; where there were screens still hanging, they were rent and slit; and where there were steps, they did not look as though they could support a cat. Fish's badly dilapidated house looked to be uninhabited. How much, Sabbath wondered—before committing suicide—to buy it? He did have seventy-five hundred dollars left—and he had *life* left, and where there's life there's mobility. He got out of the car, and, grasping a railing that looked to be adhering to the steps by nothing more solid than a thought, he made his way to the door. Cautiously—lacking utterly the freedom of a man for whom the preservation of life and limb had ceased to be of concern.

Like Mrs. Nussbaum from the old *Fred Allen Show*—Fish's favorite—he called out, "Hello, is anybody?" He knocked on the living room windows. It was difficult to see inside because of the dreary day and because hanging across each window were mummy wrappings that had once been the curtains. He went around to the side and into the backyard. Splotches of grass and weed, nothing there but a beach chair, a sling beach chair that looked as though it had not been taken in out of the weather since the June afternoon he'd gone over to see Irving's stamps (purportedly) and from Irving's upstairs window watched Lois sunning below in her swimsuit, her body, her body, the vineyard that was her body taking up every inch of that very chair. The sun cream. Come from a tube. She rubbed it all over herself. It looked like come to him. She had a husky voice. Covered with come. His cousin. When someone only twelve has to live with all that, it is almost too much to ask. There was no Jewish law, you bastard.

He came around to the front to look for a For Sale sign. Where could he inquire about the house? "Hello?" he shouted from the bottom step, and from across the street he heard a voice call back, a woman's voice, "You looking for the old man?"

There was a black woman waving at him—youngish, smiling, nice and round in a pair of jeans. She was standing on the top step of the porch, where she'd been listening to the radio. When Sabbath was a boy the few blacks he saw were either in Asbury or over in Belmar. The blacks in Asbury were mostly dishwashers at the hotels, domestic servants, menial odd-jobs people, living over by Springwood Avenue, down from the chicken markets, the fish markets, and the Jewish delis where we went with an empty jar my mother gave us and they filled it up with sauerkraut when it was in season. A black bar there,too, a hot place during the war, Leo's Turf Club, full of bimbos and dandies in zoot suits. The guys stepped out in their fine duds on Saturday night and got *shicker*. The best music around at Leo's. Great sax players, according to Morty. Blacks weren't antagonistic to whites in Asbury then, and Morty got to know some of the musicians and took me there a couple of times when I was still a kid to hear that jivey jazz stuff. My appearance used to crack up Leo, the big Jewish guy who owned the place. He'd see me coming in and he'd say, "What the hell are you doin' in here?" There was a black saxophonist who was the brother of the star hurdler on the Asbury track team that Morty threw the discus and the shot for. He'd say, "What's happenin', Mort? What's up wit *dju*?" Dju! I loved *dju* for every possible reason and drove Morty crazy repeating it all the way home. The other black bar had the dreamier name—The Orchid Lounge—but it didn't have live music, only a jukebox, and we never went inside. Yes, Asbury High in Sabbath's day was Italian, some djus, these few blacks, and a smattering of what the hell do you call 'em, Protestants, white Protestants. Long Branch strictly Italian then. Longa Branch. Over in Belmar a lot of the blacks worked at the laundry and lived around 15th Avenue, 11th Avenue. There was a black family across the street from the synagogue in Belmar who came over for Shabbos to turn the lights on and off. And there was a black iceman around for a few years, before Seaboard monopolized the summer trade. He always puzzled Sabbath's mother, not so much because he was a Negro selling ice, the first and last anyone ever saw, but because of how he sold it. She would ask for a twenty-five-cent piece of ice and he would cut a piece and put it on the scale and say, "Dat's it." And she would bring it inside and over dinner that evening she would say to the family, "Why does he put it on the scale? I never see him add a piece or chop off a piece. Who is he fooling putting it on the scale?" "You," Sabbath's father said. She would get ice from him twice a week until one day he just disappeared. Maybe this is his granddaughter, the granddaughter of the iceman Morty and I called Dat's It.

"We ain't seen him in a month," she said. "Somebody ought to check him. You know?"

"That's what I'm here to do," Sabbath said.

"He can't hear. You got to bang real hard. Don't stop bangin'."

He did better than bang hard and long—he pulled open the rusted screen door and turned the knob of the front door and walked inside. Unlocked. And there was Fish. There was Cousin Fish. Not at the cemetery under a stone but sitting on a sofa by the side window. Clearly he neither saw nor heard Sabbath enter. Awfully small for Cousin Fish but that was who it was. The resemblance to Sabbath's father was still there in the wide bald skull, the narrow chin, the big ears, but more so in something not so easily describable—the family look that that whole generation of Jews had. The weight of life, the simplicity to bear it, the gratitude not to have been entirely crushed, the unwavering, innocent trust—none of that had left his face. Couldn't. Trust. A great endowment for this mortuary world.

I should go. He looks as though to extinguish him it wouldn't take more than a syllable. Whatever I say is liable to kill him. But this is Fish. Back then I thought that he got his name because he sometimes dared to go out at night on the party boats with the working-class goyim to fish. Not many Jewish guys with accents went out with those drunks. Once, when I was a little kid, he took Morty and me. Fun to go out with a grown man. My father didn't fish *or* swim. Fish did both. *Taught* me to swim. "Fishing you

usually don't catch," he explained to me, the smallest person on
the boat. "You don't catch more than you catch. Every once in a
while you get a fish. Sometimes you get a school and you get a lot
of fish. But that don't happen much." One Sunday early in September there was a terrific thunderstorm, and as soon as it was
over, Fish raced up in the empty vegetable truck with Irving and
told Morty and me to get in the back with our rods, and then he
drove like mad down to Newark Avenue beach—he knew just
which beach to go to. In the summertime, when there's a thunderstorm and the water temperatures change and the water gets very
turbulent, the schools come in after the minnows and you can see
the fish; they're right out there in the waves. And they were. And
Fish knew. See them on the waves coming out of the water. Fish
caught fifteen fish in thirty minutes. I was ten, and even I caught
three. 1939. And when I was older—this was after Morty went
away; I was about fourteen—I was missing Morty, and Fish
learned about it from my father and took me out on the beach for
the whole night with him one Saturday. After blues. He had a
thermos of tea that we shared. I cannot commit suicide without
saying good-bye to Fish. If my speaking up startles him and he
drops dead, they can just carve "Geriacide" on the stone.

"Cousin Fish—remember me? I'm Mickey Sabbath. I'm Morris. My brother was Morty."

Fish hadn't heard him. Sabbath would have to approach the
sofa. He'll think, when he sees the beard, that I'm Death, I'm a
thief, a burglar with a knife. And I have not felt less sinister since
I was five. Or happier. This is Fish. Uneducated, well mannered,
something of a jokester, but stingy, oh so stingy, said my mother.
True. The dread about money. But the men had that. How could
they not, Mom? Intimidated, outsiders in the world, yet with
wellsprings of resistance that were a mystery even to them, or that
would have been, had they not been mercifully spared the terrible
inclination to think. Thinking was the last thing they felt to be
missing from their lives. It was all more basic than that.

"Fish," he said, advancing with his arms extended, "I'm
Mickey. It's Mickey Sabbath. Your cousin. The son of Sam and

Yetta. Mickey Sabbath." His shouting got Fish to look up from
two pieces of mail that he was fiddling with in his lap. Who
mailed him anything? I hardly get mail. More proof he's not dead.

"You? Who are you?" Fish asked. "Are you from the newspaper?"

"I'm not from the newspaper. No. I'm Mickey Sabbath. *Sabbath.*"

"Yes? I had a cousin Sabbath. On McCabe Avenue. That's not
him, is it?"

The accent and syntax the same, but no longer the muscular
voice for shouting from the street into the houses and all the way
back to the yards, "Veg-e-tables! Fresh veg-e-tables, ladies!" In
the tonelessness, the hollowness, you heard not only how deaf he
was and how alone he was but that this was not one of his life's
great days. A mere mist of a man. And at those card games, when
he won, the delight was violent—repeatedly he smacked the oilcloth of the kitchen table as he laughed and raked in the dough.
Later my mother explained that this was because of how greedy
he was. Flypaper dangled from the kitchen fixture. The short-cir-
cuited *bzzz* of a fly fitfully dying over their heads was all that was
to be heard in the kitchen while they concentrated on what they'd
been dealt. And the crickets. And the train, that not very sonorous
sound which can strip a youngster in his bed right out of his skin
and down to his nerve endings—in those days, at least, peel a boy
down to expose every inch of him to living's high drama and
mystery—the whistle in the dark of the Jersey Shore freight line
tearing through the town. And the ambulance. In the summertime, when the old people were in for their week to escape the
North Jersey mosquitoes, the ambulance siren every night. Two
blocks south, over at the Brinley Hotel, somebody dying just
about every night. Splashing with the grandchildren by the
water's edge at the sunny beach and, at night, talking in Yiddish
on the benches at the boards and then, stiffly, together, back to the
kosher hotels, where, while getting ready for bed, one of them
would keel over and die. You'd hear it on the beach the next day.
Just keeled over on the toilet and died. Only last week he saw one

of the hotel employees shaving on Saturday and complained to the owner—and today he's gone! At eight and nine and ten I couldn't stand it. The sirens terrified me. I'd sit up in bed and holler, "No! No!" This would wake Morty in the twin bed beside mine. "What is it?" "I don't want to die!" "You won't. You're a kid. Go to sleep." He'd get me through it. Then *he* died, a kid. And what in Fish so antagonized my mother? That he could survive and laugh without a wife? Maybe there were girlfriends. Mingling on the street with the ladies all day long, bagging vegetables, maybe he bagged a couple of them ladies. This could explain why Fish is still here. A gonadal disgrace can be a dynamic force, hard to stop.

"Yes," said Sabbath. "That was my father. On McCabe. That was Sam. I'm his son. My mother was Yetta."

"They lived on McCabe?"

"That's right. The second block. I'm their son Mickey. Morris."

"The second block on McCabe. I swear I don't remember you, honest."

"You remember your truck, don't you? Cousin Fish and his truck."

"The truck I remember. I had a truck then. Yes." He seemed to understand what he'd said only after he said it. "Hah," he added—some wry recognition of something.

"And you sold vegetables from the truck."

"Vegetables. Vegetables I know I sold."

"Well, you sold them to my mother. Sometimes to me. I came out with her list and you'd sell them to me. Mickey. Morris. Sam and Yetta's son. The younger son. The other was Morty. You used to take us fishing."

"I swear I don't remember."

"Well, that's all right." Sabbath came around the coffee table and sat beside him on the sofa. His skin was very brown, and behind large horn-rimmed glasses, the eyes looked to be getting signals from the brain—up close Sabbath saw more clearly that somewhere back there things still converged. This was good.

They could actually talk. To his surprise, he had to overcome a desire to take Fish and pick him up and put him on his lap. "It's wonderful to see you, Fish."

"Nice to see you, too. But I still don't remember you."

"It's okay. I was a boy."

"How old were you then?"

"At the vegetable truck? It was before the war. I was nine, ten years old. And you were a young fellow in your forties."

"And I used to sell vegetables to your mother, you said?"

"That's right. To Yetta. It doesn't matter. How do you feel?"

"Pretty good, thank you. All right."

That politeness. Must have got the ladies, too, a virile specimen with muscles, manners, and a couple of jokes. Yes, that's what made my mother angry, no doubt about it. The ostentatious virility.

Fish's pants were streaked with urine stains and his cardigan sweater was a color that was indescribable where it was thickly caked with food at the front—particularly rich it was along the ribbon of the buttonholes—but his shirt seemed fresh and he did not smell. His breath, astonishingly, was sweet: the smell of a creature that survives on clover. But could those big, crooked teeth be his own? Had to be. They don't make dentures that look like that except maybe for horses. Sabbath again overcame the impulse to bodily lift him onto his lap and contented himself with swinging an arm around the back of the sofa so that it rested partly on Fish's shoulder. The sofa had much in common with the cardigan. Impasto, the painters call it. The way a young girl might present her lips—or did in a fashion long out-of-date—Fish offered his ear up to Sabbath, the better to hear him when he spoke. Sabbath could have eaten it, hairs and all. He was getting steadily happier by the moment. The ruthless hunger to win at cards. Fondling a customer behind the truck. The gonadal disgrace with the teeth of a horse. The incapacity to die. Sitting it out instead. This thought made Sabbath intensely excited: *the perverse senselessness of just remaining, of not going.*

"Can you walk?" Sabbath asked him. "Can you take a walk?"

"I walk around the house."

"How do you eat? You make your own food?"

"Oh, yeah. I cook myself. Sure. I make chicken . . ."

They waited while Fish waited for something to come after "chicken." Sabbath could have waited forever. I could move in here and feed him. The two of us having our soup. That black girl from across the street coming over for dessert. Don't stop bangin'. Wouldn't mind hearing that from her every day.

"I have, what you call it. Applesauce I have. For dessert."

"What about breakfast? Did you eat breakfast this morning?"

"Yeah. Breakfast. I made my cereal. Cook my cereal. I make oatmeal. The next day I make . . . what you call it. Cereal—what the hell you call it?"

"Cornflakes?"

"No, I don't have cornflakes. No, I used to have cornflakes."

"And Lois?"

"My daughter? She died. You knew her?"

"Of course. And Irv?"

"My son, he passed away. Almost a year ago. He was sixty-six years old. Nothing. He passed away."

"We were in high school together."

"Yes? With Irving?"

"He was a little ahead of me. He was between my brother and me. I used to envy Irving, running from the truck to carry the bags for the ladies right to their doors. When I was a kid, I thought Irving was somebody because he worked with his father up on the truck."

"Yes? You live here?"

"No. Not now. I did. I live in New England. Up north."

"So what made you come down here?"

"I wanted to see people I knew," Sabbath said. "Something told me you were still alive."

"Thank God, yes."

"And I thought, 'I would like to see him. I wonder if he remembers me or my brother. My brother, Morty.' Do you remember Morty Sabbath? He was your cousin too."

"A poor memory. I remember little. I been here about sixty

years. In this house. I bought it when I was a young man. I was
about thirty. Then. I bought a home and here it is, the same
place."

"Can you still manage stairs by yourself?" At the other end of
the living room, by the door, was a stairway Sabbath used to race
up with Irving so he could look down from the back bedroom on
Lois's body. Sea & Ski. Was that what she squirted out of the tube,
or was Sea & Ski later? It's a shame she didn't live to know how it
nearly killed me to watch her rub it on. Bet she'd like to hear it
now. Bet our friend decorum doesn't mean much to Lois now.

"Oh, yeah," Fish said. "I manage. I go upstairs, sure. I manage
to walk up. My bedroom is upstairs. So I gotta go upstairs. Sure. I
go up once a day. I go up and come down."

"Do you sleep much?"

"No, that's my trouble. I'm a very poor sleeper. I hardly sleep. I
never slept in my life. I can't sleep."

Could this be everything that Sabbath thought it was? It wasn't
considered characteristic of him to extend himself this way. But he
hadn't had as interesting a conversation—barring last night's in
the hallway with Michelle—in years. The first man I've met since
going to sea who doesn't bore me stiff.

"What do you do when you don't sleep?"

"I just lie in bed and think, and that's all."

"What do you think about?"

A bark came out of Fish, sounding like a noise coming out of a
cave. Must be what he remembers of a laugh. And he used to
laugh a lot, laugh like mad whenever he won that pot. "Oh,
different things."

"Do you remember anything, Fish, about the old days? Do you
remember the old days at all?"

"Such as what?"

"Yetta and Sam. My parents."

"They were your parents."

"Yes."

Fish was trying hard, concentrating like a man at stool. And
some shadowy activity did appear momentarily to be transpiring

in his skull. But finally he had to reply, "I swear I don't remember."

"So what do you do all day, now that you don't sell vegetables?"

"So I walk around. I exercise. I walk around the house. When the sun is out, I'm outdoors in the sun. Today is the thirteenth of April, right?"

"Right. How do you know the date? Do you follow the calendar?"

The indignation was genuine when he said, "No. I just *know* today's the thirteenth of April."

"Do you listen to the radio? You used to listen to the radio with us sometimes. To H. V. Kaltenborn. To the news from the front."

"Did I? No, I don't. I got a radio in there. But I don't bother with it. My hearing is bad. Well, I'm getting on in years. How old do you think I am?"

"I know how old you are. You're a hundred years old."

"So how do you know?"

"Because you were five years older than my father. My father was your cousin. The butter-and-egg man. Sam."

"He sent you over here? Or what?"

"Yeah. He sent me over here."

"He did, eh? He and his wife, Yetta. Do you see them often?"

"Occasionally."

"He sent you over to me?"

"Yes."

"Isn't that remarkable?"

The word gave Sabbath an enormous boost. If he can deliver "remarkable," then it, the brain, can come up yet with the things I want. You are dealing with a man on whom his life has left an impression. It's in there. It's just a matter of staying on him, staying with him, until you can take an impression of the impression. To hear him say, "Mickey. Morty. Yetta. Sam," to hear him say, "I was there. I swear I remember. We all were alive."

"You look pretty good for a man who's a hundred years old."

"Thank God. Not bad, no. I feel all right."

"No aches or pains?"

"No, no. Thank God, no."

"A lucky man you are, Fish, not to have pain."

"Thank God, sure. I am."

"So what do you enjoy to do now? Do you remember the card games with Sam? Do you remember the fishing? From the beach? From the boat with the goyim? It used to give you pleasure to visit our house at night. You would see me sitting there and you would squeeze my knee. You would say, 'Mickey or Morris, which is it?' You don't remember any of this. You and my father used to speak Yiddish."

"*Vu den?* I still speak Yiddish. I never forgot that."

"That's good. So you speak Yiddish sometimes. That's good. What else do you do that gives you pleasure?"

"For pleasure?" He is astonished that I can ask such a question. I ask about pleasure and for the first time it occurs to him that he may be dealing with a crazy person. A madman has come into the house and there is reason to be terrified. "What kind of pleasure?" he said. "I'm just around the house and that's all. I don't go to see no movies or anything like that. I can't. I wouldn't be able to see anything anyway. So what's the use?"

"Do you see any people?"

"Ummm." People. There is a big blot there, obscuring the answer. People. He thinks, though what that entails I have no idea—like trying to get wet kindling to light. "Hardly," he says at last. "I got my neighbor next door I see. He's a goy. A Gentile."

"Is he a nice fellow?"

"Yeah, yeah, he's nice."

"That's good. As it should be. They're taught to love their neighbors. You're probably lucky it's not a Jew. And who cleans for you?"

"I have a woman cleaning up a couple of weeks ago."

Yeah, well, she is out on her ass when I take over. The filth. The dirt. The living room is little more than a floor—besides the sofa and the coffee table there is only a broken, armless upholstered chair by the stairs—and the floor is like the floor of a monkey's cage I once saw in a zoo in a town in the boot of Italy, a zoo I've never forgotten. But the debris and the dust are the least of it. Either the woman is blinder than Fish or she is a crook and a drunk. She goes.

"There's nothing here to clean," Fish said. "The bed, it's in good shape."

"And who does your washing? Who washes your clothes for you?"

"The clothes . . ." That's a hard one. They're getting harder. Either he is tiring or he is dying. If it's death, Fish's long-deferred death, it wouldn't be inappropriate if what he hears last is "Who washes your clothes?" Tasks. These men *were* tasks. The men and the tasks were one.

"Who does your laundry?"

"Laundry" works. "A few little things. I do it myself. I haven't got much laundry. Just an undershirt and the shorts, and that's all. There isn't much to do. I wash it out in the basin, in the sink. And hang it on the line. And—it dries!" For comic effect, a pause. Then triumphantly—"it dries!" Yes, Fish is coming over; he always says something to make Mickey laugh. It didn't take much, but there was humor in him, all right, about the miracles and the gifts. It dries! "But he's so stingy. Before she passed away, poor woman, he never bought her a thing." "Fischel is a lonely man," my father says; "let him enjoy a family for ten minutes at night. He loves the boys. More than his own. I don't know why it's so, but he does."

"You ever go and take a look at the ocean?" Sabbath asked.

"No. I can't go anymore. That's out now. Too far to walk. Good-bye, ocean."

"Your mind's all right, though."

"Yeah, my mind is all right. Thank God. It's okay."

"And you still have the house. You made a good living selling vegetables."

Indignant again. "No, it *wasn't* a good living, it was a *poor* living. I used to peddle around. Asbury Park. Belmar. Belmar I used to go. In my truck. I had an open truck. All the baskets lined up. Used to be a market here. A wholesale market. And then years ago there used to be farmers. The farmers used to come in. It's a long time ago. I forgot about it even."

"You spent your whole life being a vegetable man."

"Mostly, yes."

Push. It's like single-handedly freeing a car from the banked-up snow, but the spinning tires are taking hold, so *push*. Yes, I remember Morty. Morty. Mickey. Yetta. Sam. He can say it. Get him to do it.

Do what? What can be done for you at this late hour?

"Do you remember your mother and father, Fish?"

"If I remember them? Sure. Oh, yes. Of course. In Russia. I was born in Russia myself. A hundred years ago."

"You were born in 1894."

"Yeah. Yeah. You're right. How did you know?"

"And do you remember how old you were when you came to America?"

"How old I was? I remember. Fifteen or sixteen years old. I was a young boy. I learned English."

"And you don't remember Morty and Mickey? The two boys. Yetta and Sam's boys."

"You're Morty?"

"I'm his kid brother. You remember Morty. An athlete. A track star. You used to feel his muscles and whistle. The clarinet. He played the clarinet. He could fix things with his hands. He used to pluck chickens for Feldman after school. For the butcher who played cards with you and my father and Kravitz the upholsterer. I would help him. Thursdays and Fridays. You don't remember Feldman either. It doesn't matter. Morty was a pilot in the war. He was my brother. He died in the war."

"During the war it was? The Second World War?"

"Yes."

"That was quite a few years ago, isn't it?"

"It's fifty years, Fish."

"That's a long time."

A dining room opened out back of the living room, and its

windows looked onto the yard. In the winter, on weekends, they used to catalog Irving's stamps on the dining room table, study the perforations and watermarks for as many centuries as it took before Lois came into the house and went up the stairs to *her room*. Sometimes she went to *the toilet*. The sounds of the water flowing through the pipes overhead Sabbath studied harder than he studied the stamps. The dining room chairs on which he and Irv sat were now buried away beneath clothing, draped with shirts, sweaters, pants, coats. Too blind for closets, the old man maintained his wardrobe here.

Against the length of one wall there was a sideboard that Sabbath, who had been staring at it intermittently ever since sitting down beside Fish, at last recognized. Maple veneer with rounded corners—it was his mother's, his own mother's treasured sideboard, where she kept the "good" dishes they never ate from, the crystal goblets they never drank from; where his father kept the tallis he used twice a year, the velvet bag of tefillin he never prayed with; and where once Sabbath had found, beneath the pile of "good" tablecloths too good for the likes of them to eat off of, a book bound in blue cloth consisting of instructions on how to survive the wedding night. The man was to bathe, powder himself, wear a soft robe (preferably silk), shave—even if he had already shaved in the morning—and the woman was to try not to pass out. Pages and pages, nearly a hundred of them, in which Sabbath could not find a single word he was looking for. The book was mostly about lighting, perfume, and love. Must have been a great help to Yetta and Sam. I only wonder where they got the cocktail shaker. No smells were involved, according to this book—not a single smell listed in the index. He was twelve. The smells he would have to come by beyond his mother's sideboard, sometimes grandly called the credenza.

When, four years before her death, his mother had gone into the rest home and he'd sold the house, the stuff must have been distributed around or stolen. He'd thought that lawyer had arranged an auction to pay the bills. Maybe Fish had bought the piece. Out of feeling for those evenings in our house. He would already have been ninety. Maybe for twenty bucks Irving had bought the sideboard for him. Anyway, here it is. Fish here, the sideboard here—what more is here?

"Remember, Fish, how during the war the lights were out on the boardwalk? Remember they had the blackout?"

"Yeah. The lights were out. I also remember when the ocean was so rough it picked up the whole boardwalk and put it on Ocean Avenue. It raised it up twice in my life. A big storm."

"The Atlantic is a powerful ocean."

"Sure. Picked up the whole boardwalk and put it on Ocean Avenue. Happened twice in my life."

"You remember your wife?"

"Of course I remember her. I came down here. I got married. A very fine woman. She passed away, it's about thirty, forty years ago. Since then I'm alone. It's no good to be alone. It's a lonely life. So what are you going to do? Nothing you can do about it. Make the best of it. That's all. When it's sunny out, the sun, I go out in the back. And I sit in the sun. And I get nice and brown. That's my life. That's what I love. The outdoor life. My backyard. I sit there mostly all day when the sun is out. You understand Yiddish? 'You're old, you're cold.' Today it's raining."

To get over to that sideboard. But by now Fish has put his hands on my thighs, they are resting on me while we talk, and not even Machiavelli could have got up at that moment, even if he knew, *as I did,* that inside that sideboard was everything he had come looking for. I knew this. Something is there that is not my mother's ghost: she's down in the grave with her ghost. Something is here as important and as palpable as the sun that turns Fish brown. Yet I couldn't move. This must be the veneration that the Chinese have for the old.

"You fall asleep out there?"

"Where?"

"In the sunshine."

"No. I don't sleep. I just look. I close my eyes and I look. Yeah. I can't sleep there. I told you before. I'm a very poor sleeper. I go upstairs in the evening, about four or five o'clock. I go to bed. So I rest in the bed, but I don't sleep. A very poor sleeper."

"Do you remember when you first came down the shore by yourself?"

"When I came to the shore? What do you mean, from Russia?"

"No. After New York. After you left the Bronx. After you left your mother and father."

"Oh. Yeah. I came down here. You're from the Bronx?"

"No. My mother was. Before she married."

"Yes? Well, I just got married and I came down here. Yeah. I married a very fine woman."

"How many children did you have?"

"Two. A boy and a girl. My son, the one who died not long ago. An accountant. A good job. With a retail concern. And Lois. You know Lois?"

"Yes, I know Lois."

"A lovely child."

"That she is. It's very nice to see you, Fish." Taking his hands in mine. About time.

"Thank you. It's a pleasure seeing you, I'm sure."

"You know who I am, Fish? I'm Morris. I'm Mickey. I'm Yetta's son. My brother was Morty. I remember you so well, on the street with the truck, all the ladies coming out of the houses—"

"To the truck."

He's with me, he's back there—and squeezing my hands with a strength greater even than what I have left in my own! "To the truck," I said.

"To buy. Isn't that remarkable?"

"Yes. That's the word for it. It was all remarkable."

"Remarkable."

"All those years ago. Everyone alive. So can I look around your house at the photographs?" There were photographs arranged along the top of the sideboard. No frames. Just propped up against the wall.

"You want to take a picture of it?"

I *did* want to take a picture of the sideboard. How did he know? "No, I just want to look at the photographs."

I lifted his hands from my lap. But when I got up, he got up and followed me into the dining room, walked very well, right at my heels, followed me to the sideboard like Willie Pep chasing some little *pisher* around the ring.

"Can you see the pictures?" he asked.

"Fish," I said, "this is you—with the truck!" There was the truck, with the baskets lined up along the slanting sides and Fish on the street next to the truck, standing at military attention.

"I think so," he said. "I can't see. It looks like me," he said when I held it up directly in front of his glasses. "Yes. That's my daughter there, Lois."

Lois had lost her looks later in life. She too.

"And who is this man?"

"That's my son, Irving. And who is this?" he asked me, picking up a photograph that was lying flat on the sideboard. They were old, faded photographs, water-stained around the edges and some sticky to the touch. "That's me," he asked, "or what?"

"I don't know. Who is this? This woman. Beautiful woman. Dark hair."

"Maybe it's my wife."

Yes. The potato then probably no more than a bud. I can't remember any of those women approaching the beauty of this one. And she's the one who died.

"And is this you? With a girlfriend?"

"Yeah. My girlfriend. I had her then. She passed away already."

"You outlive everybody, even your girlfriends."

"Yeah. I had a few girlfriends. I had a few, in my younger years, after my wife passed away. Yeah."

"Did you enjoy that?"

The words have no meaning for him at first. In this question he seems to have met his match. We wait, my crippled hands on my mother's sideboard, which is thick with grease and dirt. The tablecloth on the dining room table bears every stain imaginable. Nothing else here is quite so fetid and foul. And I'll bet it's one of the cloths we never got to use ourselves.

"I asked if you enjoyed the girls."

"Well, yes," he suddenly replied. "Yes. It was all right. I tried a few."

"But not recently."

"What reason?"

"Not *recently*."

"What do you mean what reason?"

"Not *lately*."

"Lately? No, too old for that. Finished with that." He waves a hand almost angrily. "That's *done*. That's *out*. Good-bye, girl-friends!"

"Any more photos? You have a lot of nice old photographs. Maybe there are more inside."

"Here? Inside here? Nothing."

"You never know."

The top drawer, where once one would have found a bag of tefillin, a tallis, a sex manual, the tablecloths, reveals itself, when opened, to be indeed empty. Her whole life was devoted to keeping things in drawers. Things to call ours. Debby's drawers, too, things to call hers. Michelle's drawers. All the existence, born and unborn, possible and impossible, in drawers. But empty drawers looked at long enough can probably drive you mad.

I kneel to open the door to the tall middle drawer. There is a box. A cardboard carton is there. *Not* nothing. On top of the box is marked "Morty's Things." My mother's writing. On the side, again in her writing, "Morty's Flag & things."

"No, you're right. Nothing here," and shut the sideboard's lower door.

"Oh, what a life, what a life," muttered Fish as he led me back to the living room sofa.

"Yeah, was it good, life? Was it good to live, Fish?"

"Sure. Better than being dead."

"So people say."

But what I was thinking really was that it all began with my mother's coming to watch over my shoulder what I did with Drenka up at the Grotto, that it was her staying to watch, however disgusting it was to her, it was her seeing me through all those ejaculations leading nowhere, that led me to here! The goofiness you must get yourself into to get where you have to go, the extent of the mistakes you are required to make! If they told you beforehand about all the mistakes, you'd say no, I can't do it, you'll have to get somebody else, I'm too smart to make all those mistakes. And they would tell you, we have faith, don't worry, and you would say no, no way, you need a much bigger schmuck than me, but they repeat they have faith that you are the one, that you will evolve into a colossal schmuck more conscientiously than you can possibly begin to imagine, you will make mistakes on a scale you can't even dream of now—*because there is no other way to reach the end.*

The coffin came home in a flag. His burned-up body buried first on Leyte, in an Army cemetery in the Philippines. When I was away at sea the coffin came back; they sent it back. My father wrote me, in his immigrant handwriting, that there was a flag on the coffin and after the funeral "the Army guy folded it up for mother in the offishul way." It's in that carton in the sideboard. It's fifteen feet away.

They were back together on the sofa holding hands. And he has no idea who I am. No problem stealing the carton. Just have to find the moment. It'll be best if Fish doesn't have to die in the process.

"I think, when I think of dying," Fish happened to be saying, "I think I wish I was never born. I wish I was never born. That's right."

"Why?"

"'Cause death, death is a terrible thing. You know. Death, it's no good. So I wish I was never born." Angrily he states this. *I* want to die because I don't have to, *he* doesn't want to die because he does have to. "That's my philosophy," he says.

"But you had a wonderful wife. A beautiful woman."

"Oh, yeah, that I did."

"Two good children."

"Yeah. Yeah. Yes." The anger subsides, but only slowly, by degrees. He's not to be easily convinced that death can be redeemed by anything.

"You had friends."

"No. I didn't have too many friends. I didn't have time for friends. But my wife, she was a very nice woman. She passed away forty or fifty years ago already. Nice woman. As I say, I met her through my . . . wait a minute . . . her name is Yetta."

"You met her through Yetta. That's right. You met her through my mother."

"Her name was Yetta. Yes. I was introduced to her from the Bronx. I still can remember that. They were walking across the park. I took a walk. And I met them on the way. And they introduced me to her. And that's the girl I fell in love with."

"You have a good memory for a man your age."

"Oh, yeah. Thank God. Yes. What time is it now?"

"Almost one o'clock."

"Is it? It's late. It's time to put up my lamb chop. I make a lamb chop. And I have applesauce for dessert. It's almost one, you say?"

"Yeah. Just a few minutes to one."

"Oh, yeah? So I'm gonna put up, I call it my dinner."

"You cook the lamb chop yourself?"

"Oh, yeah. I put it in the oven. Takes about ten, fifteen minutes and it's done. Sure. I got Delicious apples. I put in an apple to bake. So that's my dessert. And then I have an orange. And that's what I call a good meal."

"Good. You take good care of yourself. Can you bathe yourself?" Get him in the bath, then walk off with the carton.

"No. I take a shower."

"And it's safe for you? You hold on?"

"Yeah. It's a closed shower, you know, with a curtain. I got a shower there. So that's where I shower. No problem at all. Once a week, yeah. I take a shower."

"And nobody ever drives you down to look at the ocean?"

"No. I used to love the ocean. I used to go bathing in the ocean. Many years ago already. I was a pretty good swimmer. I learned in this country."

"I remember. You were a member of the Polar Bear Club."

"What?"

"The Polar Bear Club."

"I don't remember that."

"Sure. A group of men who went swimming on the beach in the cold weather. They were called the Polar Bear Club. You would go out in the cold water in a bathing suit, go in the water, come right out. In the twenties. In the thirties."

"The Polar Bear Club, you say?"

"Yes."

"Yes. Yes. I do. I think I do remember that."

"Did you enjoy that, Fish?"

"The Polar Bear Club? I hated it."

"Why did you do it then?"

"I swear to God, I don't remember why I did it."

"You taught me, Fish. You taught me to swim."

"I did? I taught Irving. My son was born in Asbury Park. And Lois was born right here, upstairs in this house. In the bedroom. In the bedroom where I sleep now, she was born. Lois. The baby. She passed away."

In the corner of the living room that is back of Fish's head, there is an American flag rolled around a short pole. Fresh from reading the words "Morty's Flag & things," Sabbath only now sees it for the first time. Is that it? Is there just the carton there empty, in it none of Morty's things any longer, and the flag from his coffin tacked to this pole? The flag looks as washed out as the beach chair in the yard. If this cleaning lady were interested in cleaning, she would have torn it up for rags long ago.

"How come you have an American flag?" Sabbath asked.

"I got it quite a few years already. I don't know how I got it, but I got it. Oh, wait a minute. I think it was from the Belmar bank. When I piled up money, they gave me this flag. This American flag. In Belmar I used to be a depositor. Now, good-bye, deposits."

"Do you want to have your dinner, Fish? Do you want to go in and make your lamb chop? I'll sit right here if you want me to."

"It's all right. I got time. It wouldn't run away."

Fish's laughing getting more and more like a laugh.

"And you still have a sense of humor," said Sabbath.

"Not much."

So, even if nothing is left in the carton, I will come away having learned two things today: the fear of death is with you forever and a shred of irony lives on and on, even in the simplest Jew.

"Did you ever think that you would live to be a man a hundred years old?"

"No, I really didn't. I heard about it in the Bible, but I really didn't. Thank God, I made it. But how long I'm going to last, God knows."

"How about your dinner, Fish? How about your lamb chop?"

"What is this here? Can you see this?" In his lap again are the two pieces of mail he was fiddling with when I came in. "Will you read it to me? It's a bill, or what?"

"'Fischel Shabas, 311 Hammond Avenue.' Let me open it up. Comes from Dr. Kaplan, the optometrist."

"Who?"

"Dr. Kaplan, the optometrist. In Neptune. Inside is a card. I'll read it. 'Happy Birthday.'"

"Oh!" The recognition pleases him inordinately. "What's his name here?"

"Dr. Benjamin Kaplan, the optometrist."

"The optometrist?"

"Yeah. 'Happy Birthday to a Wonderful Patient.'"

"Never heard of him."

"'Hope your birthdays are as special as you are.' Did you have a birthday recently?"

"Yeah, sure."

"When was your birthday?"

"The first of April."

Right. April Fool's Day. My mother always thought this appropriate for Fish. Yes, that distaste of hers was for his pecker. Unfathomable otherwise.

"So this is a birthday card."

"A birthday card? The name is what?"

"Kaplan. A doctor."

"That's a doctor I never heard of. Maybe he heard about my birthday. And the other one?"

"Shall I open it up?"

"Yeah, sure, go ahead."

"From the Guaranty Reserve Life Insurance Company. I don't think it's anything."

"What does he say there?"

"They want to sell you a life insurance policy. It says, 'Life insurance policy available to ages forty to eighty-five.'"

"You can throw it out."

"So that's the only mail there is."

"The heck with that."

"No, you don't need that. You don't need a life insurance policy."

"No, no. I got one. I think about five thousand dollars or something. My neighbor, he pays for it all the time. That's the policy. I never carry big insurance. For who? For what? Five thousand dollars is enough. So he takes care of that. After my death it'll bury me, and he gets the rest." He pronounces "death" like "debt."

"Who knows," Fish says, "how much longer have I got to live? The time is running out. Sure. How much more can I live after a hundred years? Very little. If I have a year or two I'll be lucky. If I have an hour or two I'll be lucky."

"How about your lamb chop?"

"A guy is supposed to come from the Asbury Park *Press* to interview me. At noon."

"Yes?"

"I left the door open. He didn't show up. I don't know why."

"To interview you about being a hundred?"

"Yeah. For my birthday. At noon. Maybe he got cold feet or something. What is your name, Mister?"

"My first name is Morris. Mickey is what they've called me since I was a boy."

"Wait a minute. I knew a Morris. From Belmar. Morris. It'll come to me."

"And my last name is Sabbath."

"Like my cousin."

"That's exactly right. On McCabe Avenue."

"And the other guy, the name is also Morris. Oh, gee. Morris. Huh. It'll come to me."

"It'll come to you after you eat your lamb chop. Come on, Fish," I said, and here I lifted him onto his feet. "You are going to eat now."

Sabbath never got to see him make the lamb chop. He would have liked to. He would very much have liked to see the lamb chop itself. It would have been fun, thought the puppeteer, to watch him make the lamb chop and then, when he turned around, take the lamb chop quickly and eat it. But as soon as he got Fish into the kitchen, he excused himself to go upstairs to use the bathroom and returned to the dining room, where he lifted the carton out of the sideboard—it was not empty—and carried it out of the house.

The black woman was still on the top step of the porch, sitting there now and watching the rain come down as she listened to the music on the radio. Awfully happy. Another one on Prozac? Features that could be part Indian. Young. Ron and I were taken by the other sailors to a district on the outskirts of Veracruz. A kind of nightclub that's half outside, sleazy and shabby, in a honky-tonk district with strings of lights and dozens and dozens of young women and sailors at crude tables. As they made their bargains and finished their drinking, they retired to a low-slung row of houses where there were the rooms. All the girls were a mixture. We're on the Yucatán peninsula—the Mayan past is not far away. Admixture of races, always mystifying. Takes a person to the depths of living. This girl was a sweetheart with a lovely personality. Very dark. Decent, smiling, engaging, warm in every way. Probably twenty or under. She was lovely, there was no hurry, there was no rush. I remember her using some kind of ointment on me afterward that stung. Maybe this astringent stuff was supposed to forestall any disease. Very nice girl. Just like her.

"How's the old man?"

"Eatin' his lamb chop."

"Yipp*ee*," she cried.

Christ, I'd like to meet her! Don't stop bangin'. No. Too old. Finished with that. That's *done*. That's *out*. Good-bye, girlfriends.

"You from Texas? Where'd you get that yippee? Yippee-ki-yo-ki-yay."

"That's only when cattle's involved," she said, laughing with her mouth open wide. "Whoopee ti-yi-yo, git along, little dogies!"

"What is a dogie, anyway?"

"A little stunted calf whose mother's left it. A dogie's a calf that's lost its mom."

"You're a real cowpuncher. I took you first for an Asbury girl. I like you, ma'am. I hear your spurs ajinglin'. What do they call you?"

"Hopalong Cassidy," she told him. "What do they call you?"

"Rabbi Israel, the Baal Shem Tov—the Master of God's Good Name. The boys at the shul here call me Boardwalk."

"Nice to meet ya."

"Let me tell you a tale," he said, brushing his beard with a raised shoulder while, by the side of his car, cradling in his two arms the box of Morty's things. "Rabbi Mendel once boasted to his teacher, Rabbi Elimelekh, that evenings he saw the angel who rolls away the light before the darkness, and mornings the angel who rolls away the darkness before the light. 'Yes,' said Rabbi Elimelekh, 'in my youth I saw that, too. Later on you don't see those things anymore.'"

"I don't get Jewish jokes, Mr. Boardwalk." She was laughing again.

"What kind of jokes *do* you get?"

But from within the carton, Morty's American flag—which I know is folded there, at the very bottom, in the official way—tells me, "It's against some Jewish law," and so, on into the car he went with the carton, and then he drove it down to the beach, to the boardwalk, which was no longer there. The boardwalk was gone. Good-bye, boardwalk. The ocean had finally carried it away. The Atlantic is a powerful ocean. Death is a terrible thing. That's a doctor I never heard of. Remarkable. Yes, that's the word for it. It was all remarkable. Good-bye, remarkable. Egypt and Greece good-bye, and good-bye, Rome!

◆ ◆ ◆

Here's what Sabbath found in the carton on that rainy, misty afternoon, Morty's birthday, Wednesday, April 13, 1994, his car, with the out-of-state plates, the only car on Ocean Avenue by the McCabe Avenue beach, parked diagonally, all by itself, looking toward the sloshing-unimpressively-about sea god as it grayly swept southward in the tail end of the storm. There was nothing before in Sabbath's life like this carton, nothing approached it, even going through all of Nikki's gypsy clothes after there was no more Nikki. Awful as that closet was, by comparison with this box it was nothing. The pure, monstrous purity of the suffering was new to him, made any and all suffering he'd known previously seem like an imitation of suffering. This was the passionate, the violent stuff, the worst, invented to torment one species alone, the remembering animal, the animal with the long memory. And prompted merely by lifting out of the carton and holding in his hand what Yetta Sabbath had stored there of her older son's. This was what it felt like to be a venerable boardwalk jerked from its moorings by the Atlantic, a worn, well-made, old-fashioned boardwalk running the length of a small oceanside town, immovably bolted onto creosoted piles as thick around as a strong man's chest and, when the familiar old waves turn on the coast, jiggled up and out like a child's loose tooth.

Just things. Just these few things, and for him they were the hurricane of the century.

Morty's track letter. Dark blue with the black trim. A winged sneaker on the crossbar of the *A*. On the back a tiny tag: "The Standard Pennant Co. Big Run, Pa." Wore it on the light blue letter sweater. The Asbury Bishops.

Photo. Twin-engine B-25—not the J he went down in but the D he trained in. Morty in undershirt, fatigue pants, dog tags, officer's cap, parachute straps. His strong arms. A good kid. His crew, five altogether, all of them on the airstrip, mechanics servicing one engine behind them. "Fort Story, Virginia" stamped on back. Looking happy, sweet as hell. The watch. My Benrus. This watch.

Portrait photo taken by La Grotta of Long Branch. A boy in cap and uniform.

Photo. Throwing the discus at the stadium. Getting ready to make his circle, arm back behind him.

Photo. Action shot. The discus released, five feet out in front of him. His mouth open. The dark undershirt with the *A* emblem, the skimpy blue shorts. Pale color photo. Runny like watercolor. His open mouth. The muscles.

Two little recordings. No memory of these at all. One addressed from him at 324 C.T.D. (Air Crew), State Teachers College, Oswego, New York. "This living record was recorded at a USO Club operated by the YMCA." His voice is on this record. Addressed to "Mr. and Mrs. S. Sabbath and Mickey."

A metal backing on the second record. "This 'letter-on-record' is one of the many services enjoyed by the men of the armed forces as they use the USO 'A HOME AWAY FROM HOME.'" VOICE-O-GRAPH. Automatic Voice Recorder. To Mr. and Mrs. S. Sabbath and Mickey. He always included me.

Isosceles triangles of red, white, and blue satin, stitched together to make a yarmulke. White triangle at the front shows a *V*, below the *V* dot-dot-dot-dash—the Morse code for *V*. "God Bless America" beneath that. A patriot's yarmulke.

A miniature Bible. *Jewish Holy Scriptures*. Inside, in light-blue ink, "May the Lord bless you and keep you, Arnold R. Fix, Chaplain." Opening page headed "The White House." "As Commander-in-Chief I take pleasure in commending the reading of the Bible to all who serve . . ." Franklin Delano Roosevelt commends "the reading of the Bible" to my brother. The way they got these kids to die. Commends.

Abridged Prayer Book for Jews in the Armed Forces of the United States. A brown palm-size book. In Hebrew and English.

Between two middle pages, sepia snapshot of the family. We're in the yard. His hand on my father's shoulder. My father in his suit, vest, even a pocket hankie. What's up? Rosh Hashanah? I'm dressed to kill in a "loafer" jacket and slacks. My mother in a coat and a hat. Morty in a sports jacket but no tie. Year he went in. Took it along with him. Look at what a good kid he is. Look at Dad—like Fish, a camera and he's frozen stiff. My little mother under her veiled hat. Carried our picture in his prayer book for Jews in the armed forces of the United States. But he didn't die because he was a Jew. Died because he was an American. They killed him because he was born in America.

His toilet case. Brown leather engraved "MS" in gold. About six by seven by three. Two packets of capsules inside. Sustained-release capsules. Dexamyl. To relieve both anxiety and depression. Dexedrine 15 mg. and amobarbital 1½ gr. (Amobarbital? Morty's or Mom's? Did she use his case for her own stuff when she went nuts?) Half a tube of Mennen brushless shave. Little green and white cardboard pepper shaker of Mennen talcum for men. Shasta Beauty Shampoo, a gift from Procter & Gamble. Nail scissors. Tan comb. Mennen Hair Creme for Men. Still smells. Still creamy! One unlabeled bottle, contents dried up. Imitation enamel box, bar of Ivory soap inside, unopened. A black Majestic Dry Shaver in a small red box. With cord. Hairs in the head of it. The microscopic hairs of my brother's beard. That is what they are.

A black leather money belt, supple from being worn next to his skin.

Black plastic tube containing: Bronze medal inscribed "Championship 1941 3rd Senior Discus." Dog tag. "A" for blood type, "H" for Hebrew. Morton S Sabbath 12204591 T 42. Mother's name beneath his. Yetta Sabbath 227 McCabe Ave Bradley Beach, NJ. A round yellow pin that says "Time for Saraka." Two bullets. A red cross on a white button and the words "I Serve" at the top. Second lieutenant bars, two sets. Bronze wings.

A red and gold tea chest the size of a small brick. Swee-Touch-Nee Tea. (From the house, wasn't it, to put doodads in, wire, keys, nails, picture hangers? Morty take it with him or did she just put his things there when they came back?) Patches. The Air Apaches. The 498th Squadron. The 345 Bomb Group. I can still tell which is which. Ribbons. The wings from his cap.

Clarinet. In five pieces. The mouthpiece.

A diary. The Ideal Midget Diary Year 1939. Only two entries. For August 26: "Mickey's birthday." For December 14: "Shel and Bea got married." Our cousin Bea. My tenth birthday.

A GI sewing kit. Mildewed. Pins, needles, scissors, buttons. Some khaki-colored thread still left.

Document. American eagle. *E pluribus unum.* In grateful memory of Second Lieutenant Morton S. Sabbath, who died in the service of his country in the southwest Pacific area December 15, 1944. He stands in the unbroken line of patriots who have dared to die that freedom might live, and grow, and increase its blessings. Freedom lives, and through it, he lives—in a way that humbles the undertakings of most men. Franklin Delano Roosevelt, President of the United States of America.

Document. Purple Heart. The United States of America, to all who shall see these presents, Greetings: This is to certify that the President of the United States of America pursuant to authority vested in him by Congress has awarded the Purple Heart established by General George Washington at Newburgh, N.Y., August 7, 1782, to Second Lieutenant Morton Sabbath AS#0-827746, for military merit and for wounds received in action resulting in his death December 15, 1944, given under my hand in the city of Washington the sixteenth day of June 1945, Secretary of War Henry Stimson.

Certificates. Trees planted in Palestine. In Memory of Morton Sabbath, Planted by Jack and Berdie Hochberg. Planted by Sam and Yetta Sabbath. For the Reforestation of Eretz Yisrael. Planted by the Jewish National Fund for Palestine.

Two small ceramic figures. A fish. The other an outhouse with a kid sitting on the seat and another kid waiting his turn around the corner. *We* were kids. We won it one night at the Pokerino on the boards. Our joke. The Crapper. Morty took it with him to the war. With the ceramic bluefish.

At the bottom, the American flag. How heavy a flag is! All folded up in the official way.

He took the flag down with him onto the beach. There he unfurled it, a flag with forty-eight stars, wrapped himself in it, and, in the mist there, wept and wept. The fun I had just watching him and Bobby and Lenny, watching him with his friends, watching them just fool around, kid, laugh, tell jokes. That he included me in the address. That he always included me!

Not until two hours later, when he returned from tramping the beach wrapped in that flag—up through the sand to the Shark River drawbridge and back, crying all the way, rapidly talking, then wildly mute, then chanting aloud words and sentences inexplicable even to himself—not until after two solid hours of this raving about Morty, about the brother, about the one loss he would never bull his way through, did he return to find in the car, on the floor beside the brake pedal, the packet of envelopes addressed in Morty's easy-to-read hand. They had dropped out of the carton while he was unpacking it, but he'd been too emotional to pick them up, let alone to read them.

And he'd come back because after two hours of staring into the sea and up at the sky and seeing nothing and everything and nothing, he'd thought that the frenzy was over and that he had regained possession of 1994. He figured the only thing that could ever swallow him up like that again would have to be the ocean. And all from only a single carton. Imagine, then, the history of the world. We are immoderate because grief is immoderate, all the hundreds and thousands of kinds of grief.

The return address was Lieutenant Morton Sabbath's APO number in San Francisco. Six cents via airmail. Postmarked November and December 1944. In a brittle rubber band that broke into bits the moment Sabbath slipped his finger beneath it, five letters from the Pacific.

To get a letter from him was always powerful. Nothing mattered more. The insignia of the U.S. Army at the top of the page and Morty's handwriting underneath, like a glimpse of Morty himself. Everybody read them ten times, twenty times, even after his mother had read them aloud at the dinner table. "There's a letter from Morty!" To the neighbors. Over the phone. "A letter from Morty!" And these were the last five.

Dec. 3, 1944

Dearest Mom, Dad & Mickey,

Hello everyone, how is every little thing at home. Some mail came in today & I thought sure that I had some however I was wrong. I think someone screwed up somewhere and I think I will try to locate it. If I can I am going to fly to New Guinea and check up.

I awoke at 9:20 this morning and shaved and then made some breakfast. It began raining again so I went down to my navigator tent and painted our Group insignia on my B.4 bag. It is an indian head and I am going to print the name Air Apaches. If you ever read about the Air Apaches you will know that it is our Group. I spent most of the afternoon painting and then we brewed up some tea and cookies for a "nosh."

Mom has anything ever been cut of my letters that I have been writing. I ate supper and then checked to see whether I was flying for tomorrow.

We played cards tonight and listened to the radio. We got some jazz. Incidently we won the game.

I got a bread from the mess hall and we have grape jelly so we made hot chocolate & ate bread & jelly this evening.

Well folks I guess thats about all for now so I will sign off with all my love. Don't work too hard & take good care of yourselves. Give everyone my love & Be Good.

May God Bless & keep you well.

Your loving son,
Mort

Dec. 7, 1944

Dearest Mom, Dad & Mickey,

Hi folks well another day is almost over and I am operations officer tonight. We have been flying pretty often around here as you probably have been reading in the newspaper.

There isn't much new around here that I haven't already told you. By the way if you read about the "Air Apaches" thats our Group so you will know that it was us on the mission. The war began three years ago today.

We put up our tent today and tomorrow I am going to try and put a wooden floor in. Wood is scarce around here but if you know where to go you can usually get some. We are fixing up a shower and a lot of odds and ends to make it homelike. The natives are eager to help us. They haven't much clothes for the Japs took most of it so we give them a few articles of clothes & they will do almost anything for us.

We have air raids quite often but they don't amount to much.

How are things going at home? The food here has gotten better & we had turkey for dinner & get plenty of vegetables.

Well folks since there isn't much more to write about so I will sign off for tonight. Take good care of yourselves & May God Bless you. I love you very much & think of home always.

Heres a big hug a kiss folks.

Good night.

Your loving son,
Mort

Dec. 9, 1944

Dearest Mom, Dad & Mickey,

Hi folks I received your v-mail the other day dated the 17th of Nov. and it sure was grand hearing from you. Mom don't use v-mail for it takes longer to get here then air-mail letters and you can write more in a letter. Your mail comes through now in a little over 14 days so things have straightened out. Let me know where Sid L. is as soon as you find out for if he comes over here I would like to look him up. As yet I haven't received your packages but they should arrive soon.

A few days ago I flew back to our old field to bring back a new plane. I have been here two days waiting and I again looked up Gene Hochberg and we had a good time seeing each other. I bought a new pair of GI shoes and mattress covers that I needed. I found my clothes here and picked up the laundry that I left when I went. Everything was intact and I bought more articles while here. I also purchased a case of grapefruit juice for they are good on a mission when you are thirsty. Last night I saw "When Irish Eyes are smiling" and it was very enjoyable. It rained last night and I was lazy and didn't get up until 10:30 AM.

I am glad to hear that everyone at home is feeling fine. I think I will see how Eugene is doing today. I gave him a wooden floor for his tent yesterday.

Well folks thats about all the bull for now. Be good & May God Bless you. I think of you always.

Your loving son,
Mort

Dec. 10, 1944

Dearest Mom, Dad, & Mickey,

Hello folks well we are still waiting for a new airplane. Yesterday I went to see Gene but I didn't stay long for I had to bring the jeep back to the squadron. I read Bob Hopes book "I never left home" and it was very good. It began to rain about then and kept up until chow time. I went to a friends tent and we played bridge for a few hours. Then we cooked up a little "nosh" of ham & eggs & onions & bread & hot chocolate.

I went to sleep quite late and got up for breakfast at 7:10 AM. Most of the morning I spent cleaning my moccasins with oil and then my co-pilot and I took our pistols and practiced firing at bottles and cans. When I returned I took my gun apart and oiled it. I finished reading my book and then ate dinner. I practised my clarinet.

In the evening I went to see one of our boys who is in the hospital and he should be getting out in a few days.

Right now I am listening to the radio and writing to you.

How are things going at home? I sent home about $222 about a month ago and you haven't said anything about receiving the money-orders. If you received them let me know. And also if you are getting my bonds and $125 allotment every month.

Well folks be good and take good care of yourselves. I miss you a lot & sure hope the war ends soon.

Good night and May God Bless you.

Your loving son,
Mort

Dec. 12, 1944

Dearest Mom, Dad & Mickey,

Well I finally returned today and I ferried a new ship here. I saw a good movie last night and when I returned to my tent we shot the bull for a few hours and hit the sack. I packed our ship in the morning and took off. We flew formation up and the new ships are a lot faster than the others.

The food here is very good and we are still working on our tent. We should have a wooden floor in soon.

We had fresh lamb for supper and good coffee. I picked up a lot of equipment for our tent while at our old field. Things are going quite well around here and I guess you read about the invasion up here. Naturally we participated in it.

How are things going at home? I haven't received mail for the last few days but there should be some tomorrow.

I'm sure glad to hear that Mickey is doing so well with the discus and the shot. Just keep after him and make him practice and who knows he might be in the Olympics.

Let me know whether you have received my money-order of $222 and war bond.

I guess we will be going on leave in a few months.

Well folks that's about all for now. I will keep on writing as often as I can when I have something to write.

Well Good night and May God Bless you. I think of you all often and hope to see you soon.

Your loving son,
Mort

The Japs shot him down the next day. He would be seventy. We would be celebrating his birthday. Only for a while was all this his, a very little while.

THE B-25D had a maximum speed at 15,000 feet of 4848 miles per hour. It had a range of 1,500 miles. Empty it weighed 20,300 pounds. Wingspan of those flat gull wings 67 feet 7 inches. Length 52 feet 11 inches. Height 15 feet 10 inches. Two .5-inch nose guns and twin .5-inch guns in both the dorsal and the retractable ventral turrets. The normal bomb load was 2,000 pounds. Maximum permissible overload 3,600 pounds.

There was nothing Sabbath hadn't known about the North American Mitchell B-25 medium bomber and little that he couldn't remember, and remember precisely, while driving north in the dark with Morty's things beside him on the passenger seat. He remained wrapped in the American flag. Never take it off— why should he? On his head, the red, white, and blue V for Victory, God Bless America yarmulke. Dressing like this made not a scrap of difference to anything, transformed nothing, abated nothing, neither merged him with what was gone nor separated him from what was here, and yet he was determined never again to dress otherwise. A man of mirth must always dress in the priestly garb of his sect. Clothes are a masquerade anyway. When you go outside and see everyone in clothes, then you know for sure that nobody has a clue as to why he was born and that, aware of it or not, people are perpetually performing in a dream. It's putting corpses into clothes that really betrays what great thinkers we are. I liked that Linc was wearing a tie. And a Paul

Stuart suit. And a silk handkerchief in his breast pocket. Now you can take him anywhere.

Jimmy Doolittle's raid. Sixteen B-25s, land-based planes, taking off from a carrier to drop their bombs 670 miles away. From the USS *Hornet*, April 18, 1942, fifty-two years ago next week. Six minutes over Tokyo, followed by hours of pandemonium in our house, two glasses of schnapps for Sam, the annual intake in a single night. Flew right over the palace of the God Emperor (who could have stopped his nutty admirals before it even began if God had given God Emperor just an ordinary commoner's pair of balls). Only four months after Pearl Harbor, first raid on Japan of the war—ten, eleven tons of a medium-range bomber lifting off the deck sixteen times. Then in February and March '45, the B-29s, the Superfortresses, out of the Marianas, burning them to a crisp at night: Tokyo, Nagoya, Osaka, Kobe—but the biggest and best of the B-29s, which did in Hiroshima and Nagasaki, were eight months too late for us. The date to end the fucking thing was Thanksgiving 1944—*that* would have been something to be thankful for. We played cards tonight and listened to the radio. We got some jazz. Incidentally we won the game.

The Jap bomber was the Mitsubishi G4M1. Their fighter was the Mitsubishi Zero-Sen. Sabbath worried every night in bed about the Zero. A math teacher at school who'd flown in World War I said the Zero was "formidable." In the movies they called it "deadly," and when he lay alone in the dark beside Morty's empty bed, he couldn't do anything to get "deadly" out of his head. The word made him want to scream. The Jap carrier plane at Pearl Harbor had been the Nakajima B5N1. Their high-altitude fighter was the Kawasaki Hien, the "Tony" that gave the B-29s a hard time until LeMay moved from Europe to XXI Bomber Command and switched from day to nighttime fire raids. Our carrier planes: Grumman F6F, Vought 54U, Curtiss P-40E, Grumman TBF-1— the Hellcat, the Corsair, the Warhawk, the Avenger. The Hellcat, at 2,000 horsepower, *twice* as powerful as the Zero. Sabbath and Ron could identify from cutout models the silhouettes of every plane the Japs put up against Morty and his crew. The P-40

Warhawk, Ron's favorite American fighter, had a shark's mouth painted under its nose when they used them as Flying Tigers in Burma and China. Sabbath's favorite was Colonel Doolittle's plane and Lieutenant Sabbath's, the B-25: two 1,700-horsepower Wright R-2600-9 fourteen-cylinder radial engines, each driving a Hamilton-Standard propeller.

How could he kill himself now that he had Morty's things? Something always came along to make you keep living, goddamnit! He was driving north because he didn't know what else to do but take the carton home, put it in his studio, and lock it up there for safekeeping. Because of Morty's things he was headed back to a wife who had nothing but admiration for a woman in Virginia who had cut off her husband's dick in his sleep. But was the alternative to return the carton to Fish and then go back down to the beach and charge out into the rising tide? The blade head of the electric shaver contained particles of Morty's beard. In the case with the clarinet pieces was the reed. The reed from Morty's lips. Only inches from Sabbath, in the toilet case stamped "MS," was the comb with which Morty had combed his hair and the scissors with which Morty had clipped his nails. And there were recordings, two of them. On each, Morty's voice. And in his Ideal Midget Diary Year 1939, under August 26, "Mickey's birthday" written in Morty's hand. I cannot walk into the waves and leave this stuff behind.

Drenka. *Her* death. No idea that would be her last night. Every night saw pretty much the same picture. Got used to it. Visiting hours over at eight-thirty. Get there a little after nine. Wave to the night nurse, a good-natured buxom blond named Jinx, and just keep going down the hall to Drenka's darkened room. It's not allowed, but it is allowed if the nurse allows it. The first time Drenka asked, and after that nothing more had to be said. "I'm leaving now." Always mouthed this to the nurse on the way out: meaning, *There's no one with her now.* Sometimes when I left, she'd already be asleep from the morphine drip, her dried-out lips open and her eyelids not completely closed. Could see the whites of her eyes. Either leaving or coming I was sure that she was dead when I saw that. But the chest was moving. It was just the drugged-out state. The cancer everywhere. But her heart and her lungs were still okay, and I never dreamed she would go that night. Got used to the oxygen prong in her nose. Got used to the drainage bag pinned to the bed. Her kidneys were failing, yet there was always urine there when I checked the bag. Got used to that. Got used to the IV pole and the morphine drip hooked to the pump. Got used to the upper part of her no longer looking like it belonged to the bottom part. Emaciated from a little above the waist, and from the waist down—boy, oh boy—bloated, edemic. The tumor pressing on the aorta, decreasing the blood flow—Jinx explained it all, and he got used to the explanations. Under the blanket, out of sight, a bag so that the shit could come out some-where—ovarian cancer hits the colon and bowel fast. If they'd operated she'd have bled to death. Cancer too widespread for surgery. I'd got used to that, too. Widespread. Okay. We can live with widespread. I'd show up, we'd talk, I'd sit and watch her breathing through that open mouth, asleep. Breathing. Yes, oh yes, how I had got used to Drenka breathing! I'd come in, and if she was awake she'd say, "My American boyfriend is here." Eyes and cheekbones beneath a gray turban appeared to be what was speaking to him. Patches of hair all that was left. "I failed chemo-therapy," she told him one night. But he'd got used to that. "No-body passes everything," he told her. She'd just go on sleeping a lot with her mouth open and her eyelids not completely closed, or she'd be waiting, propped up on her pillow, comfortable on the morphine drip—until she suddenly wasn't and she needed a booster. But he'd got used to the booster. It was always there. "She needs a little morphine booster," and Jinx was always there to say, "I have your morphine, honey," and so that was taken care of, and we could go on like this forever, couldn't we? When she had to be turned and moved, Jinx was always there to move her, and he was there to help, cupping the tiny cup of cheekbones and eyes, kissing her forehead, holding her shoulders to help move her; and when Jinx lifted the blankets to turn her, he saw that the sheets and the pads were all yellow and wet, the fluid just seeping out of her. When Jinx turned her, to move her onto her back, onto her side, the indentations of her fingers showed on Drenka's flesh. He'd even got used to that, to that's being Drenka's flesh. "Something happened today." Drenka always told them a story while they were repositioning her. "I thought I saw a blue teddy bear playing with the flowers." "Well," laughed Jinx, "it's just the morphine, honey." After the first time, Jinx whispered to Sabbath in the hallway, to calm him down. "Hallucinating. A lot of them do." The flowers where the blue teddy bears played were from clients of the inn. There were so many bouquets the head nurse wouldn't allow them all in the room. There were often flowers without cards. From the men. From everybody who had ever fucked her. The flowers never stopped coming. He'd got used to *that*.

Her last night. Jinx calling the next morning, after Rosie had left for work. "She threw a clot—a pulmonary embolus. She's dead." "How? How can that happen!" "Her blood work was all out of kilter, the bed rest—look, it's a nice way to go. A very merciful killing." "Thanks, thanks. You're a good scout. Thanks for calling me. What time did she die?" "After you left. About two hours after." "Okay. Thanks." "I didn't want you to not know and to show up tonight." "Did she say anything?" "In the end she said something, but it was in that Croatian." "Okay. Thanks."

Driving Morty's things north for safekeeping, wrapped in his flag and wearing his yarmulke, driving in the dark with Morty's things and Drenka and Drenka's last night.

"My American boyfriend."

"Shalom."

"My secret American boyfriend." Her voice wasn't that weak, but he pulled the chair close to the bed, beside the irrigation bag, and held her hand in his. This was the way they did it now, night after night. "To have a lover of the country . . . I was thinking this all day, to tell you, Mickey. To have a lover of the country which one . . . it gave me the feeling of having the opening of the door. I was trying to remember this all day."

"The opening of the door."

"The morphine is bad for my English."

"We should have put your English on morphine long ago. It's better than ever."

"To have the lover, Mickey, to be very close that way, to be accepted by you, the American boyfriend . . . it made me less fearful about not understanding, not going to school here. . . . But having the American boyfriend and seeing the love from your eyes, it's all all right."

"It's all all right."

"So I don't get so fearful with an American boyfriend. That's what I was thinking all day."

"I never thought of you as fearful at all. I thought of you as bold."

She laughed at him, though with her eyes alone. "Oh my," she said. "So fearful."

"Why, Drenka?"

"Because. Because of everything. Because I don't have the intuition, the intuitive feeling about it. I've been working in this society so long and I had a child who grew up here and in the school system here . . . but in my own country I could have sorted it out with my fingertips. It was all a lot of work for me here, overcoming my inferiority complex at being the outsider. But all the small things I could understand, because of you."

"What small things?"

"'I pledge a legion to the flag.' It had no meaning. And the dancing. Remember? At the motel."

"Yes. Yes. The Bo-Peep-Lysol."

"And it isn't 'nuts and bulbs,' Mickey."

"What isn't?"

"The expression in English. Jinx said today, 'nuts and bolts,' and I thought, 'Oh God, it isn't "nuts and bulbs."' Matthew was right—it is 'nuts and *bolts*.'"

"It is? It can't be."

"You are a wicked boy."

"Call me practical."

"I was thinking today that I was pregnant again."

"Yes?"

"I was thinking I was back in Split. I was pregnant. Other people from the past were present."

"Who? Who was present?"

"In Yugoslavia I had fun, too, you know. In my city I had fun when I was young. A Roman palace is there, you know. An old palace that's in the central part of the place."

"In Split, yes, I do know. You told me years ago. Years and years ago, Drenka dear."

"Yes. The Roman guy. The emperor. Dioklecijan."

"It's an old Roman town on the sea," said Sabbath. "We both grew up by the sea. We both grew up loving the sea. *Aqua femina*."

"Next to Split is a smaller place, a sea resort."

"Makarska," said Sabbath. "Makarska and Madamaska."

"Yes," said Drenka. "What a coincidence. The two places where I had the most fun. It *was* fun. We swim there. We spend all day on the beach. Dance in the evening. My first fuck was there. We sometimes have dinner. They would be serving this soup in these little bowls, and they would go and they would spill over you because they are not experienced, the waiters. They would come with a whole tray and they would carry it; they would come and they would serve it and they would spill it. America was so far away. I couldn't even dream of it. Then to be able to dance with you and hear you sing the music. I suddenly step that close to it. To America. I was dancing with America."

"Sweetheart, you were dancing with an unemployed adulterer. A guy with time on his hands."

"You *are* America. Yes, you are, my wicked boy. When we flew to New York and drove in on the highway, whatever the highway is, and those graveyards that are surrounded by cars and the traffic, and that was very confusing and frightening to me. I said to Matija, 'I don't like this.' I was crying. Motorized America with all the endless cars that never stop, and then, suddenly, the place of rest is between *that*. And they are thrown a little here and a little there. It's so very scary to me, so extremely opposite and different that I couldn't understand it. Through you it is all different now. Do you know? Through you I can think of those stones with understanding now. I only wish now I went places with you. I was wishing today, all day, thinking of the places."

"Which places?"

"To where you were born. I would have liked to go to the Jersey shore."

"We should have gone. I should have taken you."

Shoulda, Woulda, Coulda. The three blind mice.

"Even to New York City. To show it to me through your eyes. I would have liked that. Wherever we went, we always went to hide. I hate hiding. I wouldn't mind to go to New Mexico with you. To California with you. But mainly to New Jersey, to see the sea where *you* grew up."

"I understand." Too late, but I understand. That we don't perish of understanding everything too late, that is a miracle. But we *do* perish of that—of *just* that.

"If only," said Drenka, "we could have gone for a weekend to see the Jersey shore."

"You wouldn't need a weekend. From Long Branch to Spring Lake and Sea Girt, it's about eleven miles. You're driving in Neptune, down Main Street, and before you know it you're in Bradley Beach. You drive eight blocks in Bradley and you're in Avon. It was all pretty small."

"Tell me. Tell me." At the Bo-Peep too, she had always begged him to tell her, to tell her, to tell her. But to come up with something he hadn't told her, he'd have to think pretty hard. And suppose he should repeat himself? Did that matter to a dying person? To a dying person you can repeat yourself forever. They don't care. Just so they can still hear you talking.

"Well, it was small-town stuff. Drenka, you know that."

"Tell me. Please."

"Nothing very exciting ever happened to me. I was never quite in with the right kids, you know. Uncouth little runt, family didn't even belong to a 'beach club'—the rich broads from Deal weren't falling over one another pursuing me. I did manage somehow to get a couple hand-jobs in high school, but that was a fluke, didn't really count for much. Mostly we sat around and talked about what we would give if we could get laid. Ron, Ron Metzner, who nobody looked at back then because of his skin, used to try to console himself by saying to me, 'It has to happen sooner or later, doesn't it?' We didn't care who it was or even what it was, we just wanted to get laid. Then I got to be sixteen and all I wanted was to bust out."

"You went to sea."

"No, the year before that. The summer I was a lifeguard during the day. Had to be—on the beach were the dramatically endowed Jewish girls from North Jersey. And so I worked nights to supplement my shitty lifeguard pay. Had all kinds of after-school jobs, summer jobs, Saturday jobs. Ron's uncle had an ice cream franchise business. They'd come along like Good Humor, ding-a-ling. Blanketed the shore. I worked for him once, hawking Dixie cups from a bicycle truck. I had two, three jobs going in a single summer. Ron's father had a job with a cigar company. Salesman for Dutch Masters cigars. Colorful character to a hick kid. Grew up in South Belmar, the son of the cantor and mohel there, who in those days had a horse, a cow, and an outhouse, and a well in the backyard. Mr. Metzner was the size of a city block. Enormous man. Loved dirty jokes. Salesman for Dutch Masters cigars and he had opera on the radio on Saturday afternoons. Carried off by a heart attack as big as the Ritz when we were in our last year of high school. Why Ron went to sea with me—fleeing selling Popsicles for the rest of his life. Dutch Masters had their place up in Newark then. Mr. Metzner used to go up there twice a week to pick up cigars. During the winter, on Saturdays, when gas was rationed during the war, Ron and I made deliveries all over the county for him on our bikes. One winter I worked in ladies' shoes at Levin's Department Store in Asbury. Pretty good-size store. Asbury was a busy town. On Cookman Avenue alone, five or six shoe stores. I. Miller and so on. Tepper's. Steinbach's. Yep, Cookman was a great street before the riots carried it away. Ran from the beach right to Main Street. But did I never tell you that I was a ladies' shoes specialist as young as fourteen? The wonderful world of perversity, discovered it right there at Levin's in Asbury Park. The old salesguy used to lift the ladies' legs when he tried the shoes on them so I could see up their dresses. He used to take their shoes, when a customer came in, and put 'em far away where they couldn't reach 'em. Then the fun began. 'Now this shoe,' he'd tell them, 'is a genuine *shmatte*,' and all the time raising their leg up just a little higher. In the stockroom I'd smell the inner soles after they'd tried them on. A friend of my father's used to peddle socks and work pants to the farmers around Freehold. He'd go into the wholesalers in New York and then come back and I'd go out with him on a Saturday in his truck—when the truck started—and I'd sell and get to keep five dollars for myself at the end of the day. Yeah, a variety of jobs. A lot of the people I worked for would be quite surprised to know that I grew up to be a rocket scientist. That didn't look to be in the cards back then. The job where I could really pick up bucks was parking cars for Eddie Schneer. At night, down by the amusement area in Asbury, Ron and me, that summer I was a lifeguard. We'd park one car for Eddie and put a buck in his pocket, the other car for us and put a dollar in this pocket. Eddie knew, but my brother used to work for him, and Eddie loved Morty because he was a Jewish athlete and didn't hang around with the nutty, bummy-type hotshot stars but came right home after practice to help his father. Besides, Eddie was in politics and real estate and a thief bastard himself, and he was making so much money he didn't even care. But he liked to scare me. His brother-in-law used to sit across the street and spot."

"What's 'spot'?"

"Bernie, the brother-in-law, would spot a hundred cars in your area and you were supposed to have a hundred bucks in your pocket. Eddie had a big Packard and he would drive down to the area where I was working. He'd pull up, and out the car window he'd say to me, 'Bernie's been spotting you. He doesn't think you've been giving me my fair share. He thinks you're screwing me too much.' 'No, no, Mr. Schneer. None of us is screwing you too much.' 'How much do you take, Sabbath?' 'Me? I'm down to only half.'"

He'd done it—a laugh came from back in her throat, and her eyes were Drenka's! Drenka a-laughing. "You are the easiest shiksa to make laugh that ever was. Mr. Mark Twain said that. Yep, the summer before my brother got killed. Everybody was worried that because of Morty's being away I was getting in with the wrong crowd. Then he got killed in December, and the *next* year I went to sea. And *that's* when I got in with the wrong crowd."

"My American boyfriend." Now she was in tears.

"Why do you cry?"

"Because I couldn't be on that beach when you were a lifeguard. In the beginning here, before I met you, I was always crying about Split and Brač and Makarska. I was crying about my city with the narrow streets, the medieval streets, and all the old women all in black. I was crying for the islands and the inlets of the coastline. I was crying for the hotel on Brač, when I was a bookkeeper still with the railway and Matija was the handsome waiter dreaming of his inn. But then we began to make all the money. Then Matthew came. Then we began to make all the money. . . ." She was lost and took refuge behind her closed eyes.

"Is it pain? Are you in pain?"

Her eyes fluttered open. "I'm all right." It had been not pain but terror. But he had got used to that, too. If only she could. "They said about Americans that they are naive and not good lovers." Bravely Drenka went on. "This nonsense. Americans are more puritanistic. They don't like to show themselves naked. American men, they weren't able to talk about fucking. All this European cliché. I certainly learned that 'ain't' the case."

"Ain't. Very good. Excellent."

"See, American boyfriend? Eventually I am not so stupid a Croatian Catholic shiksa woman. I even learn to say 'ain't.'"

She'd also learned to say "morphine," a word it had never occurred to him to teach her. But without the morphine she felt as though she were being torn apart alive, as though a flock of black birds, huge birds, she said, were walking all over her bed and her body, tugging violently with their beaks inside her belly. And the sensation, she used to tell him . . . yes, she, too, loved the telling . . . the sensation of your coming inside me. I don't really feel the squirting, I can't, but the pulsation of the cock, and my contractions at the same time, and the whole thing so totally wet, I never know if it is my juice or your juice, and I am dripping from the cunt and I am dripping from the ass and I feel the drops coming down my legs, oh Mickey, so much juice, Mickey, all over, all so juicy, such an enormous wet sauce. . . . But lost now was the wet sauce, the pulsation, the contractions; lost to her now were the trips we never took, lost to her was *all of it,* her excesses, her willfulness, her wiliness, her recklessness, her amorousness, her impulsiveness, her self-division, her self-abandon—the sardonic and satiric cancer turning to carrion the female body that for Sabbath had been the most intoxicating of them all. The yearning to go endlessly on being Drenka, to go on and on and on being hot and healthy and herself, everything trivial and everything stupendous consumed now, organ by organ, cell by cell, devoured by the hungry black birds. Just the shard of the story now and the shards of her English, just bits of the core of the apple that was Drenka—only that was left. The juice flowing out of her was yellow now, oozing out of her yellow onto the pads, and yellow-yellow, concentrated yellow, into the irrigation bag.

There was a smile on her face after the morphine boost. Why, this little bit left of her looked almost sexy! Amazing. And she had a question to ask.

"Go ahead."

"Because I am almost blocked out about it. I could not remember today. Maybe you said, 'Yes, I want to piss on you, Drenka,' and whether I really wanted it, I don't think I really pondered so much upon that, how would it be, but I would say that to you, yes, you could, to make you hot and to make you happy, to do things that work for you, or something . . ."

Immediately after the morphine it was never easy to follow her. "And the question is what?"

"Who started? Was it that you took your dick out and said, 'I want to piss on you, Drenka. May I? I want to piss on you, Drenka'? Is that how it started?"

"Sounds like me."

"And then I thought, 'Oh well, this transgression, why not? Life is so crazy anyway.'"

"And why were you thinking about that today?"

"I don't know. They were changing my bed. The idea of tasting somebody else's piss."

"It was harrowing?"

"The idea? It was both harrowing and the idea was exciting. So then I remember you stood there, Mickey. In the stream. In the woods. And I was in the stream on the rocks. And you stood there, over me, and it was very hard for you to start getting it out, and finally there came a drop. Ohhh," she said, recalling that drop.

"Ohhh," he muttered, his grip tightening on her hand.

"It came down, and as it came upon me, I realized that it was warm. Do I dare to taste it? And I started with my tongue to lick around my lips. And there was this piss. And the whole idea that you were standing above me, and at first you strained to get it out, and then suddenly came this enormous piss, and it just came into my face and it was warm and it was just fantastic; it was exciting and everywhere and it was like a whirlwind, what I was feeling, the emotions. I don't know how to describe it more than that. I tasted it, and it tasted sweet, like beer. It had that kind of taste to it, and just something forbidden that made it so wonderful. That I could be allowed to do this that was so forbidden. And I could drink it and I wanted more as I was lying there and I wanted more, and I wanted it on my eyes and I wanted it in my face, I wanted lots of it in my face, I wanted to be showered by it in my face, and I wanted to drink it, and then, I wanted it all the way then, once I allowed myself to let go. And so I wanted everything of it, I wanted it on my tits. I remember you were standing over me, and you did it on my cunt also. And I started playing with myself as you were doing it, and you made me come, you know; I was coming while you were just squirting it over my cunt. It was very warm, it was so warm, I just felt totally . . . I don't know—taken by it. Then I come home afterward and I was sitting in the kitchen, remembering it, because I had to sort it through—did I like it or not—and I realized that, yes, it was like we had a pact; we had a secret pact that tied us together. I'd never done that before. I didn't expect to do it with anyone else, and today I was thinking I never will. But it really made me have a pact with you. It was like we were forever united in that."

"We were. We are."

Both crying now.

"And pissing on me?" he asked her.

"It was funny. I was unsure. Not so much that I wouldn't want to do it. But to let go of my own, you know—would you like my piss, the idea of abandoning myself in that way to you, because I was sort of, not that I wouldn't like it, but how would you react to it, my own piss in your face? You wouldn't like the way it tasted, or that I would offend you. So I was shy about it at first. But once I started doing it, and I realized that it was okay, that I didn't have to be frightened, and seeing your reaction—you took some of it, you even drank some of it . . . and . . . and . . . I like it. And I had to stand above you, and so it made me feel that I can do anything, anything with you, and anything is all right. We're in this together, and we can do anything together, everything together, and, Mickey, it was just wonderful."

"I have a confession to make."

"Oh? Tonight? Yes? What?"

"I was not so delighted to drink it."

A laugh came out of that tiny face, a laugh a lot bigger than the face.

"I wanted to do it," Sabbath told her. "And when it first began to come out of you, it came out in a little trickle. That was okay. But then when it came the full stuff—"

"'But then when it came the full stuff'? You are talking like me! I have made you speak translated Croatian! I taught you, too!"

"You sure did."

"So tell me, tell me," she said excitedly. "So what happened when it began to come out the full stuff?"

"The warmth. I was astonished by it."

"Exactly. But it's very pleasant that it's warm."

"And there I was, between your legs, and I had to take it in my mouth. And Drenka, I wasn't sure I wanted to."

She nodded. "Uh-huh."

"You could tell?"

"Yes. Yes, darling."

"It thrilled me mostly because I could see it was thrilling you."

"And it really was. It was."

"I could see that. And that was enough for me. But I couldn't abandon myself to drinking it quite the way you could."

"You. How strange," she said. "Tell me about that."

"I guess I have idiosyncrasies, too."

"How did it taste to you? Was it sweet? Because yours was very sweet. Beer and sweet together."

"Do you know what you said, Drenka? When you finished the first time?"

"No."

"You don't remember? When you finished pissing on me?"

"Do you remember?" she asked.

"Could I forget? You were radiant. You were glowing. You said, triumphantly, 'I did it! I did it!' It made me think, 'Yes, Roseanna drank all the wrong stuff.'"

"Yes," she laughed, "yes, I think maybe I did. Yes, you see, that fits what I told you, that I was so shy. Exactly. It was like I passed a test. No, not to pass a test. As though . . ."

"As though what?"

"Maybe what I was worried about was that I would regret it. There are many times when one has ideas to do things or maybe you get led in to do something, and afterward there's a sense of shame. And I wasn't sure—would I have shame for it? That was what was so incredible about it. And now I even love to talk about it with you. It was a lustful feeling . . . and a feeling of giving, also. In a way that I could not do to anyone else."

"By pissing on me?"

"Yes. And allowing you to piss on me. I feel that, I felt that—you were totally with me then. In all senses, as I was lying there afterward in the stream with you, holding you in the stream, in all senses, not just as my lover, as my friend, as someone, you know, when you are sick I can help you, and as my total blood brother. You know, it was a rite, a passage of a rite or something."

"Rite of passage."

"Yes. Rite of passage. Very definitely. That's true. It's so forbidden and yet it has the most innocent meaning of anything."

"Yes," he said, looking at her dying, "how innocent it is."

"You were my teacher. My American boyfriend. You taught me everything. The songs. Shit from Shinola. To be free to fuck. To have a good time with my body. To not hate having such big tits. You did that."

"About fucking you knew before you met me, Drenka dear, at least a little something."

"But in my life, married, I didn't have many outlets in this regard."

"You did all right, kid."

"Oh, Mickey, it was wonderful, it was fun—the whole kitten and kaboozle. It was like *living*. And to be denied that whole part would be a great loss. You gave it to me. You gave me a double life. I couldn't have endured with just one."

"I'm proud of you and your double life."

"All I regret," she said, crying again, crying with him, the two of them in tears (but he had got used to that—we can live with widespread and we can live with tears; night after night, we can live with *all* of it, as long as it doesn't stop), "is that we couldn't sleep together too many nights. To commingle with you. Commingle?"

"Why not."

"I wish tonight you could spend the night."

"I do, too. But I'll be here tomorrow night."

"I meant it up at the Grotto. I didn't want to fuck any more men, even without the cancer. I wouldn't do that even if I was alive."

"You are alive. It is here and now. It's tonight. You're alive."

"I wouldn't do it. You're the one I always loved fucking. But I don't regret that I have fucked many. It would have been a great loss to have had otherwise. Some of them, they were sort of wasted times. You must have that, too. Haven't you? With women you didn't enjoy?"

"Yes."

"Yes, I had experiences where the men would just want to fuck you whether they cared about you or not. That was always harder for me. I give my heart, I give my self, in my fucking."

"You do indeed."

And then, after just a little drifting, she fell asleep and so he went home—"I'm leaving now"—and within two hours she threw a clot and was dead.

So those were her last words, in English anyway. I give my heart, I give my self, in my fucking. Hard to top that.

To commingle with you, Drenka, to commingle with you now.

◆   ◆   ◆

Amid the dark fields, halfway up the hill, the living room lights were softly burning. From the bottom of the steep drive, where he paused to reconsider what he was doing—what he had already half-thinkingly done—the lights made the house look cozy enough for him to call the place home. But from outside, at night, they all look cozy. Once you're no longer outside looking in but inside looking out . . . Still, the closest he had to a home was this one, and because he couldn't leave what was left of Morty nowhere, here was where he'd come with Morty's things. Had to. He was not a beggar any longer, not a mischievous intruder, nor was he washing in toward shore somewhere south of Point Pleasant, nor at dawn would someone out for a jog along the beach with the Lab find his remains among the night's debris. Nor was he boxed in beside Schloss. He was custodian of Morty's things.

And Rosie? I'll bet I can keep her from cutting off my dick. Start there. Set modest goals. See if you can get through the rest of April without her cutting it off. After that, you can raise your sights a little. But begin with just that and see if it's doable. If it's not, if she does cut it off, well, then you'll have to rethink your position. Then you and Morty's things will have to find a home elsewhere. In the meantime, display to her not the least apprehension about being mutilated in your sleep.

And don't forget the benefits of her stupidity. One of the first rules of any marriage. (1) Don't forget the benefits of her (his) stupidity. (2) She (he) cannot be taught anything by you, so don't try. There were ten of these he'd worked up for Drenka to help her through a stretch with Matija when just the meticulous way Matija double-tied his shoelaces made her see life as nothing but blackness. (3) Take a vacation from your grievances. (4) The regularity of it isn't totally worthless. Et cetera.

You could even fuck her.

Now, this was an odd thought to have. He could not, on reflection, remember thinking anything more aberrant in his entire life. When they'd moved up north, of course, he used to fuck Rosie all the time, into her up to the hilt all the time. But when they'd come up here, she was twenty-seven. No, first thing was to keep her from cutting off his dick. Trying to fuck her could even work against him. Modest goals. You're just looking for a home for you and Mort.

In the living room she would be reading, in there with a fire going, stretched out on the sofa, reading something somebody at the meeting had given her. That's all she read now—the Big Book, the Twelve-Step Book, meditation books, pamphlets, booklets, an endless supply of them; not since leaving Usher had she stopped reading a new one that was just like the old one that she could not live without. First the meeting, then the booklets by the fire, then in bed with Ovaltine and the "Personal Story Section" of the Big Book, alcoholics' anecdotes with which she put herself to sleep. He believed that when the lights were out she prayed some AA prayer in bed. At least she had the decency, in his presence, never to mutter the thing aloud. Though sometimes he gave it to her anyway—who could resist? "You know what my Higher Power is, Roseanna? I've figured out what my Higher Power is. It's *Esquire* magazine." "Couldn't you be more respectful? You don't understand. This is a very serious business for me. I'm in recovery." "And how long is that going to last again?" "Well, it's a day at a time, but it will be forever. It isn't something that you can just put aside. You have to keep going." "I guess I won't see the end of it, will I?" "You can't. Because it's a constant process." "All your art books on those shelves. You never look at one. You never look at a picture in any of them." "I don't feel guilty, Mickey. I don't need art. I need this. This is my medicine." "*Came to Believe. Twenty-four Hours. The Little Red Book*. It's an awfully tiny aperture onto life, my dear." "I'm trying to get some peace. Some inner peace. Serenity. I'm getting in touch with my inner self." "Tell me, whatever happened to the Roseanna Cavanaugh who could think for herself?" "Oh, her? She married Mickey Sabbath. That took care of that."

In her robe, reading that shit. He imagines her, robe undone, holding her book with her right hand while diddling herself idly with the left. Ambidextrous, but happens to feel more comfortable playing around with the left. Reading and not even aware for a while that she is starting up. A bit distracted by the reading. Tends to like to have some cloth between her hand and her pussy. Nightgown, robe—tonight, panties. The material turns her on; why that is she doesn't quite know. Uses three fingers: outer fingers on the lips, middle finger pressing the button. Circular movement of the fingers, and soon the pelvis in a circular movement, too. Middle finger on the button—not the tip of the finger, the ball of the finger. First a very light pressure. Knows automatically where the button is, of course. Then a little pause, because she's still reading. But it's getting more difficult to concentrate on what she is reading. Not sure she wants to do it yet. The pressure of the ball of the two fingers surrounding the button. As she gets more excited, the ball of one finger is right on the button yet the feeling is somehow spread by the other fingers. Finally she puts the book down. Intermittently now, her fingers are still while her pelvis does the moving. Then back on the button, round and round, the other hand on her breast, on her nipples, squeezing. She has now decided that she is not going to be reading for a while. Takes her right hand down from her breast and rubs the whole thing forcefully with both hands, still outside the material. Three fingers next, over where the button is. Always knows exactly where it is, which is better than I can say for myself. Nearly fifty years on the job, and still the damn thing is there and then it's here and then it's gone and you can spend half a minute looking everywhere before kindly her hands reposition you. "There! No, *there!* Right there! Yes! Yes!" And now she stretches her legs straight out, a long cat stretch, her hands pressed tight between her thighs. Squeezing. Manages a pre-come that way, a *forshpeis,* squeezing the whole cunt hard as she can, and now she has decided: she doesn't want to stop. Sometimes she does it through the cloth the whole way; tonight she wants her fingers on the inside of the lips and she pushes the panties aside. Going up and down now, straight up and down, and not in a circular motion. And faster, going much faster. Then, using the other hand, she slips her middle finger (elegant long finger it is, too) into her cunt. Very fast with it, until she feels the first premonitory convulsions. Moves her legs back up now, spreading the legs apart while bending the knees and bringing the feet together so that, almost beneath her buttocks, the toes are touching. Opens herself up all the way. Wide open now. And constant contact with two fingers on the clit, the middle finger and the ring finger. Up and down. Tensing herself. Buttocks up now, raising herself up on her bent legs. Now she slows down a little. Stretches her legs out to slow it down, bringing it all almost to a stop. Almost. And now she bends her legs up again. This is the position in which she wants to come. Here begins the muttering. "Can I? Can I?" All the while she is making the decision *when,* she is muttering aloud, "Can I? Can I? Can I come?" Whom does she ask? The imaginary man. Men. The whole lot of them, one of them, the leader, the masked one, the boy, the black one, asking herself maybe or her father, or asking no one at all. The words alone are enough, the begging. "Can I? Can I come? Please, can I?" And now she is keeping the pressure even, now a little harder, increasing the pressure, constant pressure, *just right there,* and now she feels it, she feels it, now she's got to keep going—"Can I? Can I? Please?"—and here are the noises, ladies and gentlemen, in combinations peculiar to each woman alone, the noises that could serve as well as fingerprints to individualize the whole sex for the FBI—ohh, ummmm, ahhh—because now she's started, she's coming, and the pressure is harder but not extremely hard, not so hard that it hurts, two fingers up and down, wide pressure, she wants *wide pressure* because she wants to come again, and now the feeling is moving down toward the cunt, and she puts her finger in, and now she thinks she could enjoy having a dildo there, but she's got her finger there, and that's, that's IT! And so she goes up and down with her finger as though somebody were fucking her, and voluntarily now she tightens her cunt to increase the feeling, squeezes tight to give herself more feeling, up and down, while still working the clit. It changes what she feels when she introduces her finger into her cunt—on the button it's very precise, but with the finger in her cunt the feeling is distributed, and that's what she wants: *the distribution of the feeling.* Though it's physically not easy to coordinate the two hands, with supreme concentration she works to overcome the difficulty. And does. Ohhhh. Ohhhh. Ohhhh. And then she lies there and she pants for a while, and then she picks up the book and goes back to her reading, and, in all, there is much here to be compared with Bernstein conducting Mahler's Eighth.

Sabbath felt like offering a standing ovation. But seated in the car at the foot of the long dirt drive leading up nearly a hundred yards to the house, he could only stamp his feet and cry, "Brava, Rosie! Brava!" and lift his God Bless America yarmulke in admiration of the crescendos and the diminuendos, of the floating and the madness, of the controlled uncontrollableness, of the sustained finale's driving force. Better than Bernstein. His wife. He'd forgotten all about her. Twelve, fifteen years since she let me watch. What *would* it be like to fuck Roseanna? A percentage of guys still do it to their wives, or so the pollsters would have us believe. Wouldn't be totally freakish. Wonder what the smell is like. If she even. The swampy scent Roseanna exuded in her twenties, most unique, not at all fishy but vegetative, rooty, in the

muck with the rot. Loved it. Took you right to the edge of gagging, and then, in its depths something so sinister that, boom-o,
beyond repugnance into the promised land, to where all one's
being resides in one's nose, where existence amounts to nothing
more or less than the feral, foaming cunt, where the thing that
matters most in the world—*is* the world—is the frenzy that's in
your face. "There! No—*there!* Right . . . *there!* There! There!
There! Yes! There!" Their ecstatic machinery would have dazzled
Aquinas had his senses experienced its economy. If anything
served Sabbath as an argument for the existence of God, if anything marked creation with God's essence, it was the thousands
upon thousands of orgasms dancing on the head of that pin. The
mother of the microchip, the triumph of evolution, right up with
the retina and the tympanic membrane. I wouldn't mind growing
one myself, in the middle of my forehead like Cyclops's eye. Why
do they need jewelry, when they have that? What's a ruby next to
that? There for no reason other than the reason that it's there for.
Not to run water through, not to spread seed, but included in the
package like the toy at the bottom of the old Cracker Jack box, a
gift to each and every little girl from God. All hail the Maker, a
generous, wonderful, fun-loving guy with a real soft spot for
women. Much like Sabbath himself.

There was a home, inside it a wife; in the car were things to
revere and protect, replacing Drenka's grave as the meaning and
the purpose of his life. He need never lie down weeping on her
grave again, and, thinking that, he was seized by the miracle of
having survived all these years in the hands of a person like himself, astonished at having discovered amid Fish's squalor a reason
to go on at the mercy of the inexplicable experience that he was,
and astonished by the nonsensical thought that he wasn't, that he
hadn't survived himself, that he had perished down there in Jersey, very likely by his own hand, and that he was at the foot of the
drive of the afterlife, entering that fairy tale freed at last from the
urge that was the hallmark of his living: the overwhelming desire
to be elsewhere. He *was* elsewhere. He had achieved the goal.
Now it was clear to him. If that little house halfway up that hill on

the outskirts of this little village where I am the biggest scandal around, if that isn't elsewhere, nothing is. Elsewhere is wherever you are; elsewhere, Sabbath, is your home and no one is your mate, and if ever anyone was no one it's Rosie. Search the planet and you will not find at any latitude a setup more suitable than this one. This is your niche: the solitary hillside, the cozy cottage, the Twelve-Step wife. *This* is Sabbath's Indecent Theater. Remarkable. As remarkable as the women coming out of their houses and onto the street to buy their stringbeans from Fish's truck. Hello, remarkable.

◆ ◆ ◆

But nearly an hour after the lights had gone out at the front of the house and come on again in their bedroom around to the side by the carport, Sabbath was still a hundred yards away, down at the bottom of the drive. Was the afterlife really for him? He was having serious second thoughts about having killed himself. All he'd had to struggle through before was the prospect of oblivion. Alongside fellow mariner Schloss, across from the esteemed Weizmans, a stone's throw from all the family, but oblivion is oblivion nonetheless, and getting himself ready for it had not been simple. What he could never have imagined was that, after being left there to rot overseen by those dogs, he would find himself not in oblivion, oblivious, but in Madamaska Falls; that instead of facing the eternal nothing he would be back in that bed with Rosie beside him, forever seeking inner peace. But then, he had never figured on Morty's things.

He took the driveway curves just as slowly as the car could negotiate them. If he was years in reaching the house it would make no difference now. He was dead, death was changeless, and there was no longer the illusion of ever escaping. Time was endless or it had stopped. Amounted to the same thing. All the fluctuation's gone—that's the difference. No flux, and flux was human life all over.

To be dead and to know it is a bit like dreaming and knowing it, but, oddly, everything was *more* firmly established dead. Sabbath didn't feel spectral in any way: his sense couldn't have been *sharper* that nothing was growing, nothing altering, nothing aging; that nothing was imaginary and nothing was real, no longer was there objectivity or subjectivity, no longer any question as to what things are or are not, everything simply held together by death. No way around his knowing that he was no longer on a day-to-day basis. No worry about suddenly dying. Suddenness was over. Here for good in the nonworld of no choice.

Yet if this was death, whose pickup truck was parked in the carport beside Rosie's old Jeep? A rippling American flag was resplendently painted across the width of its tailgate. Local plates. If all flux was gone, what the fuck was this? Somebody with local plates. There was more to death than people realized—and more to Roseanna.

In bed, they were watching television. That's why nobody heard him drive up. Though he got the feeling—looking at the two of them nestled together, taking turns biting into a plump green pear, whose juice they licked from each other's taut bellies whenever it dribbled from their mouths—he got the feeling that nothing might have pleased Rosie more than knowing that her husband was back and couldn't miss finding out what had been happening while he was gone. In a corner of the bedroom all his clothes had been dumped on the floor, everything of his removed from the closet and the bureau drawers and piled in the corner, waiting to be bagged or cartoned or, when the weekend came, dragged up the hill to the ravine and pushed by the bedmates over the side.

Dispossessed. Ida had usurped his plot at the cemetery, and Christa from the gourmet shop—whose tongue Drenka had held in such high esteem and whom Rosie had waved hello to in town, just someone she knew from AA—had taken his place in the house.

If this was death, then death was just life incognito. All the blessings that make this world the entertaining place that it is exist no less laughably in the nonworld, too.

They watched television while, from the dark beyond the window, Sabbath watched them.

Christa would by now be twenty-five, but the only change that he could see was that the close-clipped blond hair had grown in black and that it was her cunt that had been shaved. Not the model child—never that, far from that—but the child model most provocatively. The hair fell elfinly in ragged little points about her head, as though an eight-year-old had scissored Christa an up-side-down crown. The mouth was still no gaping thing, but the cold opening of a German slot machine, and yet the violet sur-prise of her eyes and the glazed Teutonic snowdrift of her ass, the sweet lure of those uncorroded curves, made her no less pleas-ant to ogle than when he'd faithfully stood by as assistant tool handler and she worked her lesbian magic on Drenka. And Rose-anna, though nearly a foot taller than Christa—even Sabbath was taller than Christa—could hardly have been taken for more than twice Christa's age: even more slender than Christa, small-breasted like her, the breasts probably shaped much the same as when she moved to her mother at thirteen. . . . Four years of no booze, followed by forty-eight hours without him, and his child-less wife, in her sixth decade of life, miraculously looked to be still in bud.

The program they had on was about gorillas. Occasionally Sabbath got a glimpse of the gorillas knuckle-walking around in the tall grass or sitting about, scratching their heads and their asses. He discovered that gorillas do a lot of scratching.

When the program was over, Rosie switched off the set and, without a word, began to pretend that she was a mother gorilla grooming her little one, who was Christa. Watching from the window while they passed themselves off as gorilla mom and child, he began to remember how extensive a talent Rosie once displayed for following his lead when he was trying out stage voices at the dinner table or amusing her along these lines in bed, lipsticking a beard and cap onto the head of his prick and using his hard-on for a puppet. After the show she got to play with the puppet, every child's dream. The real ring of openness in her laugh-ter then—spunky, heedless, a little wicked, nothing to hide (except everything), nothing to fear (except everything) . . . yes, distantly he could remember her enjoying his foolishness very much.

Nothing could have been more serious than the attention Rosie gave to Christa's gorilla coat. It was as though she were not only cleansing her of insects and lice but purifying both of them through this studious contact. All the emotions were invisible, and yet not a lifeless second passed between them. Rosie's gestures were of such delicacy and precision that they appeared to be in the conscientious service of some pure religious idea. Nothing was going on other than what was going on, but to Sabbath it seemed tremendous. Tremendous. He had arrived at the loneliest moment of his life.

Under his eyes, Christa and Rosie developed complete gorilla personalities—the two of them living in the gorilla dimension, embodying the height of gorilla soulfulness, enacting the highest act of gorilla rationality and love. The whole world was the other one. The great importance of the other body. Their unity: giver the taker, taker the giver, Christa perfectly confident of Rosie's hands grazing her, a map on which Rosie's fingers trace a journey of sensual tact. And between them that liquid, intensely wordless gorilla look, the only noises rising from the bed Christa's chicken-like baby-gorilla clucks of comfort and contentment.

Roseanna Gorilla. I am nature's tool. I am the fulfiller of every need. If only the two of *them*, husband and wife, had pretended to be gorillas, nothing but gorillas all the time! Instead they had pretended, only too well, to be being human beings.

When the two had had enough, they fell into a laughing embrace, each gave the other a juicy, demonstrably human kiss, and the lights were flicked off at either side of the bed. But before Sabbath could size up the situation and decide what to do next—move on or move in—he heard Rosie and Christa reciting together. A prayer? Of course! "Dear God . . ." Rosie's nightly AA prayer—he was finally to hear it spoken aloud. "Dear God . . ."

The duet was faultlessly rendered, neither of them groping for either the words or the feeling, two voices, two females, harmoniously interlaced. Young Christa was the ardent one, whereas Roseanna's recitation was marked by the careful thought that she had clearly given every word. There was in her voice both gravity and mellowness. She had battled her way to that inner peace so long unattainable; the agony of that childhood—deprivation, humiliation, injustice, abuse—was behind her, and the tribulation of the—for her—inescapable adulthood with a stand-in savage for her father was behind her, and the relief from the pain was audible. Her utterance was quieter and calmer than Christa's, but the effect was of a communion profoundly absorbed. New beginning, new being, new beloved . . . although, as Sabbath could virtually guarantee her, formed from more or less the same mold as the old beloved. He could envision the letter posted to Hell the day after Christa took off with Roseanna's mother's antique silver. *If Mother hadn't had to run for her life, if I hadn't had to attend that girls' school until she returned, if you hadn't forced me to wear that loden jacket, if you didn't scream at the housekeepers, if you didn't* fuck *the housekeepers, if you hadn't married that monstrous Irene, if you hadn't written me those crazy letters, if you hadn't had those disgusting lips and hands that gripped me like a vise . . . Father, you've done it* again! *You rob me of a normal relationship with a normal man, you rob me of a normal relationship with a normal woman! You rob me of everything!*

"Dear God, I have no idea where I am going. I do not see the road ahead of me. I cannot know for certain where it will end. Nor do I really know myself, and the fact that I think I am following Your will does not mean that I am actually doing so. But I believe this. I believe . . ."

In Sabbath their prayer encountered no resistance. If only he could get everything else he detested to leave not so much as a pinhole in his brain. He himself prayed that God was omniscient. Otherwise He wasn't going to know what the fuck these two were talking about.

"I believe that the desire to please You does in fact please You. I hope I have that desire in everything I do. I hope I never do anything apart from that desire. And I know that if I do this You will lead me by the right road though I may know nothing about it at the time. Therefore I will trust You always though I may seem to be lost, and in the shadow of death, I will not be afraid because I know You will never leave me to face my troubles alone."

And here began the bliss. Stirring each other up took no time at all. These weren't the cluckings of two contented gorillas Sabbath was overhearing now. The two of them were no longer playing at anything; there was nothing nonsensical any longer about a single sound they made. No need for dear God now. They had taken unto themselves the task of divinity and were laying bare the rapture with their tongues. Amazing organ, the human tongue. Take a good look at it someday. He himself well remembered Christa's—the muscular, vibrating tongue of the snake—and the awe it inspired in him no less than in Drenka. Amazing all a tongue can say.

A digital clock face, aglow, green, was the sole object Sabbath could discern in the room. It was on the unseen table at the side of the unseen bed that previously had been his side. He believed he still had some of his death books piled there, unless they were in among the clothes dumped in the corner. He felt as though he had been expelled from an enormous cunt whose insides he'd been roaming freely all his life. The very house where he had lived had become a cunt into which he could never insert himself again. This observation, arrived at independently of the intellect, only intensified as the odors that exist only within women wafted out of them and through the opening of the window, where they enveloped the flag-draped Sabbath in the violent misery of every-thing lost. If irrationality smelled, it would smell like this; if delir-ium smelled, it would smell like this; if anger, impulse, appetite, antagonism, ego . . . Yes, this sublime stink of spoilage was the smell of everything that converges to become the human soul. What-ever the witches were cooking up for Macbeth must have smelled just like this. No wonder Duncan doesn't make it through the night.

It seemed for a long while as though they would never be finished and that, consequently, on this hillside, at this wind-ow, hidden behind this night, he was to be chained to his ridicu-lousness forever. They could not seem to find what they needed. A piece or a fragment of something was missing, and they were speaking fluently together, purportedly about the missing piece, in a language consisting entirely of gasps and moans and exhala-tions and shrieks, a musical miscellany of explosive shrieks.

First one of them seemed to imagine she had found it and the other seemed to imagine *she* had found it, and then, in the voluminous blackness of their house of cunt, in the same immense instant, they landed on it together, and never before had Sabbath heard in any language anything like the speech pouring out of Rosie and Christa upon discovering the whereabouts of that little piece that made the whole picture complete.

In the end, she had been satisfying herself in a way that, were she Drenka, he might have enjoyed. It wasn't that he felt shut out and tragically abandoned because Roseanna was doing anything that, from another tangent, might not actually have stirred him to fellow feeling. Why should he regard as other than resonant with his own greatest creations her creation of an orgasmic haven apart from him? Roseanna's roundabout journey had, from all appearances, carried her back to where they'd begun as insatiable lovers hiding from Nikki in his puppet studio. In fact, his entire fantasy of her masturbating was precisely what he'd been conning himself with as a part of his getting ready to go back and try to . . . try to what? To reassert what? To recover what? To reach back into the past for what? For the residue of what?

And that's when he erupted. When male gorillas get angry, it's terrifying. The largest and heaviest of the primates, they get angry on a very grand scale. He had not known that he could open his mouth so wide, nor had he ever before realized, even as a puppet performer, what a rich repertoire of frightening noises he was able to produce. The hoots, the barks, the roars—ferocious, deafening—and all the while jumping up and down and pounding his chest and tearing out by the roots the plants growing at the foot of the window, and then dashing to and fro, and at last hammering his crippled fists on the window until the frame gave way and went crashing into the room, where Rosie and Christa were screaming hysterically.

Beating a tattoo on his chest he enjoyed the most. All these years he'd had the chest for it, and all these years he had let it go to waste. The pain in his hands was excruciating but he did not desist. He was the wildest of the wild gorillas. Don't you dare to threaten me! Thumping and thumping his large chest. Breaking apart the house.

In the car, he flipped on the headlights and saw that he had frightened the raccoons off as well. They had been out working the garbage cans back of the kitchen. Rosie must have forgotten to latch shut the slatted wooden cover to the rack where the four cans were stored, and though the raccoons were now gone, there was garbage strewn everywhere. That explained the smell of spoilage that, standing outside the window, he had attributed to the women on the bed. He should have known they didn't have it in 'em.

• • •

He parked at the entrance to the cemetery, not thirty yards from Drenka's grave. On the back of a garage repair bill that he dug out of the glove compartment, he composed his will. He worked by the gleam from the dashboard and the overhead lamp. His flashlight batteries had petered out—juice enough for just a pinprick of light, but then, he'd been going on these batteries since she died.

Outside the car the blackness was immense, shocking, a night as challenging to the mind as any he had ever known at sea.

I leave $7,450 plus change (see envelope in jacket pocket) to establish a prize of $500 to be awarded annually to a female member of the graduating class of any of the colleges in the four-college program—500 bucks to whoever's fucked more male faculty members than any other graduating senior during her undergraduate years. I leave the clothes on my back and in the brown paper bag to my friends at the Astor Place subway station. I leave my tape recorder to Kathy Goolsbee. I leave twenty dirty pictures of Dr. Michelle Cowan to the State of Israel. Mickey Sabbath, April 13, 1944.

Ninety-four. He crossed out 44. 1929–1994.

On the back of another repair bill he wrote, "My brother's things are to be buried with me—the flag, the yarmulke, the letters, everything in the carton. Lay me unclothed in the coffin,

surrounded by his things." He slipped this in with Mr. Crawford's
receipts and marked the envelope "Additional Instructions."

Now, the note. Coherent or incoherent? Angry or forgiving?
Malevolent or loving? High-flown or colloquial? With or without quotations from Shakespeare, Martin Buber, and Montaigne?
Hallmark should sell a card. All the great thoughts he had not
reached were beyond enumeration; there was no bottom to what
he did not have to say about the meaning of his life. And something funny is superfluous—suicide *is* funny. Not enough people
realize that. It's not driven by despair or revenge, it's not born
of madness or bitterness or humiliation, it's not a camouflaged
homicide or a grandiose display of self-loathing—it's the finishing
touch to the running gag. He would count himself an even bigger
washout to be snuffed out any other way. For anybody who loves
a joke, suicide is indispensable. For a puppeteer particularly there
is nothing more natural: disappear behind the screen, insert the
hand, and instead of performing as yourself, take the finale as
the puppet. Think about it. There is no more thoroughly amusing
way to go. A man who wants to die. A living being choosing
death. That's entertainment.

No note. The notes are a sham, whatever you write.

And so now for the last of last things.

He stepped out of the car into the black granite world of the
blind. Unlike suicide, seeing nothing was not amusing, and, pro-
ceeding with his arms before him, he felt as old a wreck as his
Tiresias, Fish. He tried to picture the cemetery, but his five-month-
long familiarity with it did not prevent him from wandering off
almost immediately in among the graves. Soon he was breathless
from stumbling and falling and getting back to his feet, despite
the cautious tiny steps he was taking. The ground was drenched
from the day's heavy rain and her grave was up the hill, and it
would be a shame, having come this far, if a coronary beat him to
the punch. To die of natural causes would be the unsurpassable
insult. But his heart had had enough and would haul the load no
more. His heart was not a horse, and it informed him of this,
malevolently enough, by kicking him in the chest with its hooves.

So Sabbath ascended unassisted. Imagine a stone carrying itself, and that should give you some idea of how he struggled to reach Drenka's grave, where, in what was to be his grand farewell to the farfetched, he proceeded to urinate on it. The stream was painfully slow to start, and he was fearful at first that he was asking of himself the impossible and that there was, in him, nothing left of him. He imagined himself—a man who did not get through a night without three trips to the toilet—standing there into the next century, unable to draw a drop of water with which to anoint this sacred ground. Could what was impeding the urine flow be that wall of conscience that deprives a person of what is most himself? What had happened to his entire conception of life? It had cost him dearly to clear a space where he could exist in the world as antagonistically as he liked. Where was the contempt with which he had overridden their hatred; where were the laws, the code of conduct, by which he had labored to be free from their stupidly harmonious expectations? Yes, the strictures that had inspired his buffoonery were taking their vengeance at last. All the taboos that seek to abate our monstrosity had shut his water down.

Perfect metaphor: empty vessel.

And then the stream began . . . a trickle at first, just some feeble dribbling, as when your knife slices open an onion and the weeping consists of a tear or two sliding down either cheek. But then a spurt followed that, and a second spurt, and then a flow, and then a gush, and then a surge, and then Sabbath was peeing with a power that surprised even him, the way strangers to grief can be astounded by the unstoppable copiousness of their river of tears. He could not remember when he had peed like this last. Maybe fifty years ago. To drill a hole in her grave! To drive through the coffin's lid to Drenka's mouth! But he might as well try, by peeing, to activate a turbine—he could never again reach her in any way. "I did it!" she cried, "I did it!" And never had he adored anyone more.

He did not stop, however. He couldn't. He was to urine what a wet nurse is to milk. Drenchèd Drenka, bubbling spring, mother of moisture and overflow, surging, streaming Drenka, drinker of the juices of the human vine—sweetheart, rise up before you turn to dust, come back and be revived, oozing all your secretions!

But even by watering all spring and summer the plot that all her men had seeded, he could not bring her back, either Drenka or anyone else. And did he think otherwise, the anti-illusionist? Well, it is sometimes hard even for people with the best intentions to remember twenty-four hours a day, seven days a week, three hundred and sixty-five days a year that nobody dead can live again. There is nothing on earth more firmly established, it's all that you can know for sure—and no one wants to know it.

"Excuse me! Sir!"

Someone tapping from behind, someone at Sabbath's shoulder.

"Stop what you are doing, sir! *Stop now!*"

But he was not finished.

"You are pissing on my mother's grave!"

And ferociously, by his beard, Sabbath was swung around, and when the light of a powerful lamp was turned on his eyes, he threw up his hands as though something that could pierce his skull was flying into his face. The light passed down the length of his body and then upward from his feet to his eyes. He was painted like this, coat upon coat, six or seven times, until at last the beam illuminated the prick alone, seemingly keeping an eye out from between the edges of the flag, a spout without menace or significance of any kind, intermittently dripping as though in need of repair. It did not look like anything that would have inspired the mind of mankind, over the millennia, to give it five minutes of thought, let alone to conclude that, were it not for the tyranny of this tube, our species' story here on earth would be altered beyond recognition, beginning, middle, and end.

"Get it out of my sight!"

Sabbath could easily have tucked himself into his trousers and pulled up the zipper. But he wouldn't.

"Stash it!"

But Sabbath did nothing.

"What *are* you?" Sabbath was asked, the light blinding him

once again. "You desecrate my mother's grave. You desecrate the American flag. You desecrate your own people. With your stupid fucking prick out, wearing the skullcap of your own religion!"

"This is a religious act."

"Wrapped in the flag!"

"Proudly, proudly."

"*Pissing!*"

"My guts out."

Matthew now began to wail. "My mother! That was my mother! My mother, you filthy, fucking creep! You depraved my mother!"

"Depraved? Officer Balich, you are too old to idealize your parents."

"She left a diary! My father has read the diary! He read the things you made her do! Even my *cousin*—my little kid *cousin!* 'Drink it, Drenka! Drink it!'"

And so swept away was he by his own tears that he was no longer even lighting up Sabbath's face. The beam pointed, rather, to the ground, illuminating the puddle at the foot of the grave.

Barrett's head had been smashed open. Sabbath was expecting worse. Once he realized by whom he had been apprehended, he did not believe that he was going to walk away alive. Nor did he want to. It was played out, that thing which allowed him to improvise endlessly and which had kept him alive. The nutty tawdriness is over.

Yet once again did he walk away, as he had from hanging himself at the Cowans', as he had from drowning himself at the shore—walked away, leaving Matthew sobbing at the grave, and, propelled still by the thing that allowed him to improvise endlessly, stumbled through the blackness down the hill.

Not that he didn't want to hear more from Matthew about Drenka's diary, not that he wouldn't have greedily read every word. It had never occurred to him that Drenka was writing everything down. In English or in Serbo-Croatian? Out of pride or incredulity? To trace the course of her daring or of her deprav-

ity? Why hadn't she warned him in the hospital that there was this
diary? Too sick by then to think of it? Had leaving it to be found
been inadvertent, an oversight, or the boldest thing she had ever
done? I did it! I did it! This was who was living under all the nice
clothes—and none of you ever knew!

Or had she left it behind because she had not the strength to
throw it out? Yes, such diaries have a privileged place among
one's skeletons; one cannot easily free oneself of words themselves finally freed from their daily duty to justify and to conceal.
It takes more courage than one might imagine to destroy the
secret diaries, the letters, and the Polaroids, the videotapes and
audiotapes, the locks of pubic hair, the unlaundered items of
intimate apparel, to obliterate forever the reliclike force of these
things that, almost alone of our possessions, decisively answer the
question "Can it really be that I am like this?" A record of the self
at Mardi Gras, or of the self in its true and untrammeled existence? Either way, these dangerous treasures—hidden from those
near and dear beneath the lingerie, in the darkest reaches of the
file cabinet, under lock and key at the local bank—constitute a
record of that with which one cannot part.

And yet for Sabbath there was a puzzle, an inconsistency, that
he couldn't fathom, a suspicion that he couldn't elude. What
obligation was she fulfilling, and to whom, by leaving her sex
diary to be discovered? Against which of her men was she protesting? Against Matija? Against Sabbath? Which of us did you in-
tend to slay? Not me! Surely not me! You *loved* me!

"I want to see your hands up in the air!"

The words boomed at him out of nowhere, and then he was
fixed in the spotlight as though he were alone among the tombstones to perform a one-man show, Sabbath star of the cemetery,
vaudevillian to the ghosts, front-line entertainer to the troops of
the dead. Sabbath bowed. There should have been music, behind
him the slyly carnal old swing music, ushering Sabbath onto the
stage there should have been life's most reliable pleasure, the
innocent amusement of the B. G. sextet's "Ain't Misbehavin',"
Slam Stewart playing the bass and the bass playing Slam . . .

Instead there was a disembodied voice politely requesting that he identify himself.

Sweeping up from his bow, Sabbath announced, "It is I, Necrophilio, the nocturnal emission."

"I would not do that dip again, sir. I want to see those hands in the *air*."

The patrol car illuminating Sabbath's theater was manned by a second trooper, who now climbed out with a gun drawn. A trainee. Matthew would be riding alone unless he was breaking somebody in. "When he breaks them in," Drenka would boast, "he always wants them to do all the driving. Fresh from the academy, kids on probation for a whole year—and it's Matthew who they used to break them in. Matthew says, 'There are some good kids who really want to do the job and do it well. There are some assholes, too. Bad guys with a don't-give-a-shit attitude, whatever they can get away with, and so on. But to do a good job, to do what you're supposed to do, to keep your motor vehicle activity up and get your cases in on time, to keep your car the way it's supposed to be kept . . .' That's what Matthew teaches them. He just rode with somebody for three months, and the boy gave Matthew a tie clip. A gold tie clip. He said, 'Matt's my best buddy ever.'"

The trainee had him covered but Sabbath did nothing to resist arrest. He had only to start to run, and a trainee, rightly or wrongly, would more than likely drill him right through the head. But when Matthew made it to the bottom of the hill, all the trainee did was slap the cuffs on Sabbath and assist him into the back of the car. He was a young black man about Matthew's age and he remained absolutely silent, uttered not a syllable of disgust or indignation because of what Sabbath looked like or how he was dressed or what he had done. He helped Sabbath onto the backseat, mindful to see that the flag did not slip from his shoulders, and gently recentered on Sabbath's bald skull the God Bless America yarmulke, which had fallen forward onto his forehead as he ducked into the car. Whether this betokened an excess of kindness or of contempt the prisoner couldn't decide.

The trainee did the driving. Matthew was no longer in tears, but from the backseat Sabbath could see something uncontrollable working the muscles of his broad neck.

"How's my partner?" the trainee asked as they started down the mountain.

Matthew gave no reply.

He is going to kill me. He is going to do it. Rid of life. It's happening at last.

"And where are we going?" asked Sabbath.

"We're taking you in, sir," the trainee replied.

"May I ask what the charges might be?"

"The charges?" Matthew erupted. "The *charges?*"

"Breathe, Matt," the trainee said, "just do the breathing you taught me."

"If I may say so," Sabbath offered overprecisely, in a tone that he knew to have driven at least Roseanna crazy, "his sense of effrontery is lodged in a fundamental misapprehension—"

"Be still," the trainee suggested.

"I only want to say that something was happening that he cannot possibly understand. The serious side of it he has no way of assessing."

"*Serious!*" cried Matthew, and pounded the dashboard with his fist.

"Let's take him in, Matt, and that's it. That's the job—let's just do it."

"I am not using words to confound anyone. I do not exaggerate," said Sabbath. "I do not say correct or savory. I do not say seemly or even natural. I say serious. Sensationally serious. Unspeakably serious. Solemnly, recklessly, blissfully *serious.*"

"It's rash of you, sir, to go on like this."

"I'm a rash guy. It's inexplicable to me, too. It's displaced virtually everything else in my life. It seems to be the whole aim of my being."

"And that's how come we're taking you in, sir."

"I thought you were taking me in so I could tell the judge how I depraved Matthew's mother."

"Look, you've caused my partner a lot of pain," the trainee said, his voice still impressively subdued. "You've caused his family a lot of pain. I have to tell you that you are now saying things that are causing *me* a lot of pain."

"Yes. That's what I hear from people all the time, people continuously telling me that the great thing I was called to do in life was cause pain. The world is just flying along pain-free—happy-go-lucky humanity off on one long fun-filled holiday—and then Sabbath is set down in life, and overnight the place is transformed into a loony bin of tears. Why *is* that? Can someone explain it to me?"

"Stop!" cried Matthew. "Stop the car!"

"Matty, get the bastard *in*."

"Stop the fucking *car,* Billy! We're not *taking* him in!"

Sabbath straightaway leaned forward in the seat—*lurched* forward without his hands to steady him. "Take me in, Billy. Don't listen to Matty, he's not being objective—he's let himself get personally involved. Take me in so I can purge myself publicly of my crimes and accept the punishment that's coming to me."

There were deep woods to either side of the road where the police car crept onto the shoulder. Billy stopped the car and turned off the lights.

The dark domain of that night again. And now, thought Sabbath, the feature attraction, the thing that matters most, the unforeseen culmination for which he had battled all his life. He had not realized how very long he'd been longing to be put to death. He hadn't committed suicide, because he was waiting to be murdered.

Matthew leaped from the car and around to the back, where he opened the door and pulled Sabbath out. Then he undid the handcuffs. That was all. He undid the handcuffs and said, "If you, you sick freak bastard, if ever you mention my mother's name to anyone, or anything *about* my mother to *anyone—to anyone at any time anywhere*—I'm coming after you!" With his eyes just inches from Sabbath's, he began again to cry. "You hear me, old man? *You hear me?*"

"But why wait when you can have your satisfaction now? I start for the woods and you shoot. Attempted escape. Billy here'll back you up. Won't you, Bill? 'We let the old guy take a leak and he tried to run away.'"

"You sick fuck!" screamed Matthew. "You filthy sick son of a bitch!" and, flinging open the front passenger door, he violently pitched himself back into the car.

"But I'm going free! I've reveled in the revolting thing one time too many! And I'm going free! I'm a ghoul! I'm a ghoul! After causing all this pain, the ghoul is running free! *Matthew!*" But the cruiser had driven off, leaving Sabbath ankle-deep in the pudding of the springtime mud, blindly engulfed by the alien, inland woods, by the rainmaking trees and the rainwashed boulders—and with no one to kill him except himself.

And he couldn't do it. He could not fucking die. How could he leave? How could he go? Everything he hated was here.